D0828265

BLOOD LAKE

k.j.a WISHNIA

BLOOD LAKE

ST. MARTIN'S MINOTAUR
NEW YORK

www.minotaurbooks.com

Library of Congress Cataloging-in-Publication Data

Wishmia, K. j. a.
    Blood Lake : a Filomena Buscarsela mystery / K. j. a. Wishnia.—1st ed.
        p. cm.
    ISBN 0-312-28186-2
    1. Buscarsela, Filomena (Fictitious character)—Fiction. 2. Women private investigators—Ecuador—Fiction. 3. Hispanic American women—Fiction. 4. Americans—Ecuador—Fiction. 5. Single mothers—Fiction. 6. Ecuador—Fiction. I. Title.

PS3573.I875 B57 2002
813'.54—dc21
                                                            2002069841

First Edition: December 2002

10 9 8 7 6 5 4 3 2 1

Para las familias Correa, Freire,
Mejia, Mendez y Peña

Caveat
This story takes place in a mythic Ecuador.
But, like all myths, much of it is true.

Perhaps, after all, America has never been discovered; I myself would say that it had merely been detected.

—Oscar Wilde

PROLOGUE

A righteous person knows the soul of the beast.

—Proverb

Someone is taking the stairs three at a time. For a moment my chest turns as brittle as glass, and my pounding heart nearly shatters it. But cops don't move that fast, and there's only one set of feet bounding up to the landing. It's not a knock, it's a pound, the door flies open and Johnny bursts into my room. I leap to my feet, scattering my torturously scribbled notes for the all-important political philosophy exam across the bed and floor.

"Juanito—!" I prepare for the thrill of his embrace.

"Where *is* he?"

"You just got out and *that's* what you want to do first?"

But he looks right through me, with blood in his eye, and I realize that he did not just get out. He broke out. And not too carefully, either.

"Then they'll be here any second."

"Where *is* that bastard?"

"Where he always is," I say. "In class, his office or his house."

"I've been to his house! He's not there!"

"Well, he moved since—" Since he turned you and five other comrades in to the secret police and you spent the last year and a half being tortured in an underground jail cell.

"Take me to him!"

I'm listening for the tromp-tromp-tromp of hobnailed boots up the stairs, taking a last look around at the life that I will have to bail out of *immediately* if he's led them to me.

"*Juanita, mi amor,*" he says, "take me there." He's got a stolen police pistol jammed into his belt. "Now!"

I throw a poncho over his head to cover the prison clothes and the gun, take a quick look out the window to make sure they're not blocking off the street yet, and slam the door on my brief, tranquil life as a transfer student at the University of Cuenca.

We fly through the streets, the echoes of our steps on the cobblestones becoming a dozen phantom Furies sweeping through the city behind us. I won't look back. I know they're there.

I was in another part of the country, with a name they wouldn't know, when Johnny's group was hit a year and a half ago. Five were murdered, six were spared, because Johnny's group knew things, and the cops wanted to know things, too. And soon the living envied the dead.

But word got out. Word always got out. About who had turned them in.

And now we're going to visit him.

No knock, no pound. Johnny kicks open the door, takes a quick look at the empty rooms downstairs, then seemingly sniffs the air and propels himself up the shaky stairs to the study. He swings the door open with a whirlwind force that blows Professor Dos Caras out of his chair as papers and volumes of Marx fall to the floor. Dos Caras backs away as Johnny rushes in, trapping him against the window that dangles over the Tomebamba River, looking south across the Knife Valley towards the mountains.

"*No, no, Juanito—*" says Dos Caras, his hands quivering in front of his pallid face like reeds in a storm.

"Don't call me that!" says Johnny, shoving the man's arms out of his way. "You phony!" Johnny curses him. "You traitor! Do you know what we do to traitors?" Johnny's hand comes out from under the poncho holding the stolen pistol.

"No, no!" Dos Caras protests. Johnny smacks him across the mouth with an open hand. It sounds like a car door slamming.

"Please stop him, Filomena!" squeals Dos Caras.

"Who?" Johnny flashes a look at the open door. Then one look at me and he understands. I'm trying to go straight. And I just heard a second car door slam.

Dos Caras ducks away from Johnny and runs straight at me, towards the door. Johnny raises the pistol, but he hasn't got a shot. I get in Dos Caras's way, slam the door shut as Dos Caras starts screaming for the police to come up and help him. Johnny throws both arms around him and tries to stop his mouth with a free hand. But Dos Caras is slimy, and the poncho gets in Johnny's way.

"It wasn't me!" Dos Caras manages to shout.

"Don't lie to me, you chickenhearted little bastard!" Johnny yells, grabbing for him again, stumbling into the desk, knocking over more books so they fall to the floor with a heavy thud, as boots tromp across the wooden floor one flight below.

"It wasn't me!" Dos Caras struggles to speak through Johnny's grip.

"Then who was it?"

Dos Caras's eyes flit to the door. The boots are circling back from the kitchen and dining room.

I'm jamming his chair under the doorknob. Good for about two seconds.

"Stop wasting my time, you dirty *fulana!*" Johnny spits the words in the professor's face, shoving the gun up into the soft flesh under Dos Caras's jaw.

Dos Caras tries to save himself: "It was Luisa Ramera! She did it! I swear!" Dos Caras is squirming, and Johnny's grip isn't good enough. Boots are stomping up the stairs, and Johnny wants to finish him with one shot.

"Hold still, you fucking coward!" Johnny grabs the short oily hair on the back of Dos Caras's head with his left hand, shoves the pistol into the professor's mouth and blasts a hole through the back of the professor's head, taking the top half of two of his own fingers off as he does it.

The gun hits the floor and rolls. Johnny grabs his bleeding finger stubs with his right fist. The door billows out as the cops ram into it. It splits, but holds. We've got exactly two seconds. The gun's in the middle of the floor. I'm about to grab it and empty it through the paper-thin door when Johnny takes a step towards me. Then he turns and runs at the window. The door splinters open. I spread my arms out like a soaring condor, but they knock me to the floor and open fire as Johnny throws his body through the window, shattering the worm-eaten wood and falling in a hail of bullets and glass, towards the rocks and the icy waters of the Tomebamba, seventy-five feet below.

Seven heavily armed cops run over to the shattered window frame and look down. Then they turn and look at me. They've got blood on them from the broken glass.

CHAPTER
ONE

El que se dedica a redimir injusticias sociales tiene que pensarlo muy bien. Tiene que conven-
cerse de que no va a morir de viejo en una
cama. El General Torrijos sabe que va a morir vi-
olentamente, porque violenta es su vida, señores.
Yo sé, y esto está previsto. . . .

*He who dedicates himself to reforming social injus-
tices must think it through. He must realize that he
is not going to die of old age in a bed. I know that
I am going to die violently, because my life is violent, gentlemen. I know, and am expecting it. . . .*

> —Brigadier General Omar Torrijos Herrera,
> Panamanian leader, who died in a suspicious
> plane crash, August 1, 1981

We're making the steepest banking curves I've ever felt, nearly vertical, tugging my gut in new directions, when the plane slices sideways and free-falls heavily through the ether until it smacks the bottom of the pocket, landing on a cushion of air that is actually willing to hold us up a little while longer and carry us in to Guayaquil airport.

I push away the tray table with the "continental breakfast" that I can't finish and wonder, which continent did they have in mind? Maybe Antarctica. I keep picturing all those baby penguins feeding on regurgitated krill.

We slip below the clouds, and I lean over to Antonia and point out the flat green islands floating in the great salt estuary, clogging the mouth of the Guayas River.

The heat hits us even before the doors open.

Then the doors open, and a sticky blanket of tropical heat embraces me as we step onto the old hand-positioned rolling stairway that passes for a gangway.

We climb down the narrow metal steps, our legs wobbly and unsure after so many hours in those narrow-assed seats, stumbling after the clumsy passengers in front of us who are as overburdened as pack animals with sacks and bags and carry-ons full of video cameras, waffle irons and DVD players from the free-trade mecca up north. Then we trudge camel-like across the hot tarmac to the 1960s-era terminal, its Pacific blue doors and windows open to let in the jet fuel–scented breezes.

Going home to a poor country is like going back in time. A time when people still get yellow fever and typhoid and cholera, when one bad harvest means prices soar and two bad harvests mean people die, and anyone who can steal something back from the government is a local hero.

I feel like a tropical turtle who has been wandering for years, over thousands of miles, but in the end I must return to my home-land, to that beach where I was spawned. Except that I was spawned in a cornfield, in a mud-walled shack high in the Andes.

There's no air-conditioning inside the terminal.

We line up to go through immigration. By now my hands are cold and my fingers are tingling. If Antonia notices, she doesn't mention it. I distract myself with the complimentary copy of *El Mundo* that the airline handed out as we went into a tailspin over the Gulf.

I learn that the former minister of Health and Welfare, Octavio Seboso, a repulsive blimp of a man (and you should know that I don't repulse easy), is being asked to explain why the 350 garbage trucks that he bought for the city of Guayaquil ended up costing 1.4 billion sucres more than projected. Watchdogs suspect that Seboso had his hand in the till. Hand in the till, hell! This guy looks like he *ate* the till.

"Why are you reading that paper?" Antonia asks me.

"I'm trying to find out what's been happening since the last time we visited. Why are you reading that comic book?"

"I've learned a *lot* of good stuff from comic books," she says, defensively.

"Like what?"

"Like, if you're trapped in a mausoleum with nothing to eat but a corpse, don't eat it, 'cause the embalming fluid will poison you. I learned that from *Creepy Tales* number thirty-six."

"I hope I never need to use that information," I tell her, peeling back a few pages of boldly inked action to view the glossy and plentiful gore. Yuck-o.

"Then I suppose you also know that if you're planning to conduct any experiments using molecular teleportation, you should make sure there are no flies in the lab first, right?"

"*Everybody* knows that."

"Oh."

Getting through immigration can be very difficult when you've had to start your life over a couple of times. Right now I'm concentrating on getting through the next fifteen minutes. I look up at the clock on the wall. Seven A.M.

The line moves up. I drag my carry-on bag two feet farther and go back to the paper, flipping past an article detailing the municipality's plans to pave the roads linking the new suburbs with the city center, and scanning today's exchange rates, when ripping red bullet holes stop me in midbreath. The man in front turns around to look at me.

"Hot, isn't it?" I tell him, summoning my best smile.

He nods, smiles back at me, takes a look at Antonia and turns back to what he was doing.

There are so many ways to die, so much blood, in color.

The bodies of a man and a woman are indistinguishable under a couple of bloody sheets, while police stand around looking at the dirt. It's a lonely road in the back country near the town of La Trampa about sixty miles north-northwest of here. Both victims were members of the National Democratic Party, whose candidates are favored to be among the victors in the upcoming elections—that is, if they live that long. Sergeant Roca of the North Guayas Police believes that guerrillas are responsible, because the nature of the damage points to Soviet-style assault rifles.

Assassinations were never our specialty. And I've seen enough damage done with "Soviet-style assault rifles" to know that we're not the only ones who had them.

The hot sweat turns cold on the back of my neck. Welcome to the Third World. Check your rights at the door.

Yeah—the brain of the all-night traveler is not a safe place for kind thoughts.

An authoritative voice startles me up out of the open newspaper: "¡*Pasaporte!*"

I hand over the passports. The corporal stares at us, comparing Antonia with her name and photo, then he opens mine, and spends about three times as long staring at my name and photo.

"This girl is your sister? Your niece? Your cousin?" he asks.

"She's my daughter."

His eyebrows begin to flow together. Her American passport gives her name as Antonia Buscarsela Sánchez. That's my last name followed by her father's, because normally she only uses mine in the U.S. and we just lop his off. But in Ecuadorian culture, the father's name comes first, and my passport clearly indicates that my last name isn't Sánchez. So something's wrong. I don't fit the mold, as always.

"¡*Capitán!*"

The travelers behind me curse. I look at my watch. Seven-fifteen in the morning and already above ninety degrees.

The captain lifts one foot, then the other, drifting towards me with the poise of an ocean liner cruising gently along on a hot tropical breeze. He asks what the problem is.

A drop of sweat falls onto my customs declaration card. I blot it out with my sleeve.

The captain takes hold of my passport. "*Señorita*, what is your name?"

Only a half dozen people left alive know that Filomena Buscarsela was once a hotheaded revolutionary who went by the name of Juanita Calle. We were Juanito and Juanita. That was a very long time ago. But now my name is the same one I was born with, and somebody might remember that. This is a small country. And there are a lot of soldiers standing around holding automatic rifles.

"Mom? What's wrong?"

"Nothing," I assure her, then I explain to the immigration police that I'm not married and that Antonia carries my last name in the U.S., where they don't typically use the second family name.

"You are *ecuatoriana*?" asks the captain.

"*Sí.*"

"So you changed your citizenship?"

"*Sí, señor.*"

"Do you have your *cédula*?"

"Of course." I separate my old national identity card from a grimy pile of documents. They examine it closely.

"It's expired," says the corporal, making my chest muscles tighten the way they do when a stray dog is baring his teeth at me, but hasn't attacked yet.

The captain examines my *cédula* more closely, and eventually declares, "She is covered by the extension law." I rediscover the lost art of breathing. He turns to me to explain: "This class of *cédula* is now valid indefinitely. Corporal, update this *cédula*." The captain jams the card back into the corporal's hands, gives me a slightly rakish salute, turns on his heels and sails off to rescue yet another hapless traveler.

The corporal meticulously whites out the old expiration date on my *cédula* as if the task required the same precision as etching the Ten Commandments on the head of a pin with a diamond-head drill, cranks it into a U.S. Army–surplus manual typewriter, and the sound of belabored typing brings visible relief to the tormented souls behind me. Even a hysterical toddler becomes strangely pacified by the sound. The corporal finishes, yanks out my card, sticks it back inside the frayed plastic lamination, puts it on top of my growing mound of documents, and pushes the mound towards me. The next woman on line eagerly squeezes in and places her passport in the corporal's outstretched hand. He isn't even looking up.

I step away from the table and look at the back of my *cédula*. It doesn't say "Valid Indefinitely." The corporal has typed in "*Valida Hasta la Muerte.*"

Good Until Death.

The clock on the wall *still* says 7:00, but I don't care. We finish with the Bureau of Alcohol, Perfume and Cigarettes, and are released into the expectant mob gathered here to meet their aunts and uncles, cousins, sisters, blood brothers, bird dogs, boosters, button men, mitt greasers, mules, ropers and other connections, their eyes glistening in anticipation of the Boreal riches that they shall come a-bearing. A torrid stream within this hot-blooded human ocean disgorges a cluster of friendly faces, including a swarm of little ones I've never seen before getting caught around my legs. Hands grab my overweight suitcase and I'm caught between greeting a dozen relatives, tipping the porter, and making sure that those hands grabbing my bags belong to people I know.

My uncle Lucho lays his sun-dried hands on my shoulders, smiles, and gives me a powerful hug.

Antonia's been away so long it's all new to her. She soon realizes that riding in the metal cargo bed of my cousin Guillermo's pickup truck is a relative luxury, as she stares at all the other pickup trucks driving along with handmade wooden flatbeds, or no beds at all, just bare axles with bulbous gas tanks whose intake pipes are stuffed with rags, the driveshafts exposed and spinning.

The road takes a dip and we lurch onto an unpaved section of the highway. A battered blue-and-white-striped bus drives by with the morning rush hour crowd and kicks up a faceful of dirt at us. It looks like about seventeen men are hanging off the sides and back of the bus, and the conductor is actually climbing over them, hanging off with one hand to collect their fares. He nearly loses it when the bus bounces back onto the paved road. The name of the bus cooperative is Unidos Venceremos. United We Will Win. Not the same as grabbing the M34 crosstown express.

We stop for gas at a crude cement apron, pulling up in front of a flat island supporting three oil-and-grit-covered American gas pumps from the Reagan years, and I have to look twice to realize that the extra zero on the end means that gas prices have hyperinflated by a factor of ten since the last time I visited. *Shit.* So a gallon costs the same dollar fifty as in the U.S., but in Ecuador that dollar fifty is a day's pay at minimum wage.

I chip in ten freaking bucks, feeling uncomfortably wealthy, a culpable accessory to their misery, with perhaps a dash of survivor's guilt thrown in, too.

"It's been really bad since the earthquake hit a few months ago," says my cousin Azucena, who is called Suzie. "It cracked the trans-Andean oil pipeline. Ninety thousand people were cut off from civilization."

"Lucky them," I say.

We pull back onto the road, cut in front of a few buses, and survive long enough to swing onto the Avenida Quito, heading for the *barrio* Centro Cívico, the proud proletarian stronghold and indestructible pocket of resistance where so many of my family live and breed.

The drab pastel walls of the city are covered with so many faded layers of overlapping posters and paint it all moves like a living skin, melding orange-and-yellow campaign posters hawking candidates with Spanish and Lebanese names for every office in the land, from alderman's dog walker to the supreme office of *el presidente* himself, all tattooed with red-and-black verses expressing the radical opinions of the voiceless hotheads. Then a stretch of whitewash announces a truce between the warring factions to make way for a hand-painted mural of undisputed national martyrs and revolutionary heroes: Jesus, Rumiñahui, Espejo, Alfaro, Che, and a huge painting of Juanito Tres Ojos jumping through a glass window towards me, blood and all.

"Filomenita, what's the matter?" asks Suzie. Heads turns towards me.

"Oh, I'll be all right. It's just that flight must have really turned my stomach."

Antonia excitedly describes the air pocket in her unique hybrid of Anglo-Spanish as we stop at a light with the huge face glaring down at me.

All I can say is, "That's new."

Suzie agrees, then her daughter Charrito asks, "Why is he called Juanito Tres Ojos?"

"I don't know," says Suzie. "That's your generation, Filomena."

So I explain that some say it's because he was so sensitive to peripheral movement it seemed as if he had a third eye in the back of his head that allowed him to see police and soldiers sneaking up on him, and others say that he had the symbolic third eye of the true visionary, who will return one day to lead us to a better future. I don't tell her that some say it's from his preferred method of killing his enemies, by blowing a hole in the back of the unfortunate bastard's head.

Our charted course takes us past an ice cream wagon and nine voices scream out conflicting commands to Guillermo, who pulls a maneuver that would get my driver's license *burned* in New York City, bringing the pickup to a halt in front of the rusty metal wagon.

The kids effervesce over the rim of the pickup and converge on the vendor, euphoria personified, as he rings the rack of thick brass bells for them. Oh, to be that age again, where one hundred sucres buys the flavor of your choice and a brief taste of paradise.

"What flavor do you want?" asks my uncle Lucho, pointing Antonia at the long list of flavors advertised in cracked paint on rotting plywood. She says, "Chocolate."

But the vendor's out of chocolate. He's also out of mint, cherry and yerba buena (now *there's* a flavor you can't get in the U.S.), so Antonia settles for *babaco*. The man opens the top of the cart and starts digging out some off-white icing.

Then a scream tears the moment in half.

I turn in time to see a filthy teenager running up the block towards us clutching what can only be a purse he's just snatched. Before my dull brain can fire up, Guillermo lunges for the kid's legs and brings him down onto the rough concrete sidewalk, where they roll around like a drunken octopus flailing its legs spasmodically. I step in to help, and he kicks me in the face with surprising strength for such a skinny boy, as Uncle Lucho pushes in and gets an iron grip on the kid's neck, and the solidly built woman arrives and starts hitting him with her shopping bag.

I remember when Uncle Lucho was strong enough to single-handedly lift a jeep out of the mud.

"You okay?" my female cousins say, helping me up.

I'm rubbing my face. The ice cream man gives me a chunk of ice to put on it. This street is a central artery, and the efficient Guayaquil cops show up in no time in their dark blue pants and clean white shirts, and want us all to make statements. Only I don't want to. My family explains that I just got here, and that the other woman is the real victim, and she's the one who's going to bring charges, so that's okay with the cops, though they do give me a closer look than I'd like. Everyone's happy, except the skinny kid, who, as my vision clears while they take him away, looks to me like he hasn't eaten in days.

My aunt Yolita hurries out of the Correa family store and wraps her strong arms around me, solid countrywoman's arms that have been lifting crates of vegetables and cases of beer since I was small enough to sleep in a cardboard box under the cash register.

"You look great," she says.

"Yeah, getting kicked in the face does such wonders for my appearance," I tell her. She stops my mouth with a broadside of kisses and hustles me under the iron bars and into the family business, which is an all-hours corner grocery and liquor store in an untamed slice of the *barrio*, with a full-sized floor-model commercial cooler that I would like to crawl inside of right now. You can keep your fax machines and wireless e-mails. Hot showers and cold beer are all I ask of civilization.

I return her compliment. She's still a great beauty, but she was an absolute knockout at sixteen, before she started popping out little Correas at the rate of one model per year like a Ford factory. Most of the fleet are at work already: Lucho Correa Jr. is a dentist at the free hospital, Carmita is a secretary in the offices the Ecuadorian Navy, Manolo and his wife, Patricia, make clothing in a third-floor workshop, Suzie has her own store selling plastic bags of all sizes, and César is watching the family store.

Then, living on the second floor, there's my other set of cousins, Ronaldo, Victor and Bolívar Mendez, who are off mixing cement at a construction site; Luis, who's clawing his way up to a law degree; and Fanny's in the U.S. working for Leona Helmsley.

"We're going to kill the fatted calf for you," says my uncle Lucho, winking at me. "Tonight. After work."

"Sounds great. But listen, I've been traveling for eighteen hours and I'd like to take a shower before I hug anybody else."

"*Ay, que vergüenza,*" says Aunt Yolita. What a shame. "There's no water."

"Are you having trouble paying the water bill?"

"Not just us, the whole city," says Uncle Lucho. "It's been out since last week."

A steaming tropical port with 3 million people, and there's no water? This place just got less civilized.

I ask: "How—?"

"Trucks deliver drinkable water every couple of days," says Suzie.

"If they feel like it," says Uncle Lucho, dipping a chewed-up

Styrofoam cup into a large blue plastic storage drum and filling it with water for me to drink.

"No, thanks," I say. I've been away too long, and have lost my resistance to what passes for "drinkable" water in these neighborhoods.

"We boil it," Suzie explains.

The barrel holds about twenty-five gallons. So a typical person lives for a week on the equivalent of one flush of water in an American toilet.

"Do you have any mineral water? I'm dying of thirst."

"Of course, of course," says Yolita, opening up the cooler and removing a frosty bottle of Güitig.

"Just a minute," says César, who is using the bottle opener to serve the customers.

"Never mind," says Uncle Lucho, putting the bottle cap between his teeth and biting it off with one pull. He hands me the bottle and spits the cap onto the floor. Antonia is impressed.

"Don't be *cochino*," says Yolita. "Offer her a glass."

"This is fine." Aah . . .

Two caramel-colored men in oil-stained T-shirts are sharing a big bottle of Pilsener beer on the sidewalk in front of the store. They are already sweating. I check my watch. It's not even 9:00 A.M. "Come here, Filomenita," calls Guillermo. "I got something for you. Give me your watch," he says, already unstrapping it from my wrist.

"What?"

He shushes me, makes my watch disappear and replaces it with what looks like a shiny, new Rolex.

"There!" he says, excessively triumphant. "Welcome back." Guillermo kisses me on both cheeks.

Now I get a good look at the watch. The name, when observed closely, turns out to be Rolux. The factory where Guillermo and seventy-nine other underpaid Ecuadorians grind out imitations of expensive foreign products, mostly for export.

"I'll wear it with pride," I say, swinging my wrist up with a showy snap to check the time.

"Easy!" shouts Guillermo, grabbing my wrist. He looks at the watch, taps the face with his fingernail, and shakes my wrist. The second hand starts moving again, and Guillermo lets out a puff of air. "Careful with it," he says.

"I will be." I'll also keep my other watch around.

"We've got a barrel of rainwater on the roof," says Uncle Lucho. "You can use a couple of pitchers of it to shower."

"*Thank you.*" Two quarts of germ-free rainwater and I'm ready to get down on my knees and sing God's praises. Funny how your values change when you're away from your safe and constant home.

"Now let's get you gals settled in upstairs."

César says, "Watch out by the stairs. We broke a bottle of soda."

"Yeah, there's all this sticky red crap and broken glass on the floor," I observe, feeling a tingling in my veins, and in an eye blink it's gone. "Careful, Toni. The floor's all sticky."

Antonia says, "Okay, so don't go licking the bottom of your shoes."

"That's a good plan under normal circumstances, but—"

"But? You got a but to go with that?"

"I just don't think we should be ruling anything out at this point."

"Mom?"

"Look, I'm just tired and a little freaked out now, okay? I'll feel better after I shower and change."

"*¿Qué significa* 'freaked out'?" Suzie asks.

"That's what I keep asking her," says Antonia, poking me. "Some expression from the Paleolithic era, I think."

"*Neo*lithic, please," I correct her.

We lug our bags up three flights of cement stairs to the upper floors, which the family built by hand under Uncle Lucho's supervision. Upstairs, we unpack the essentials. Suzie sneaks a friendly peek in my handbag. "You carry a lighter?" she asks.

"Sure. You never know when you might need to set something on fire."

T he rich rhythms of Afro-Colombian *cumbias* float through the air like high-grade opium. A turkey my aunt raised on the terrace is slowly roasting over a homemade barbecue crafted from a fifty-five-gallon steel drum cut down the middle and laid on its side, and the flat rooftop terrace is filled with the hot bodies of bronze and brown-skinned family and friends. Some of my relatives would be considered black in the U.S.

I refuse drinks, have others, dance with cousins I haven't seen since Antonia's first communion, and with one of Luis's classmates, who has obviously seen too many American movies where the actors end up in bed after knowing each other for ten whole minutes of screen time, because he comes right out and says he wants to tickle the taco with me. I tell him I've got stuff in my fridge that's older than he is, and to come back when his voice stops cracking.

Then I ask Luis about his own career plans, and he tells me he's going to law school mainly to keep his brothers out of jail. Ronaldo, Victor and Bolívar are good hard workers, but they don't take any shit in a world that demands that *everyone* has to take a certain amount of shit.

I survive some very physical dancing with them, then remove myself and lean against the low wall, looking out over the corrugated tin rooftops on this hot winter's night. (Now there's a phrase you don't hear in New York.) The warmth, the music, the food, the family. *Why* have I been away so long?

Luis leans over and asks me, "So what's it like to live in a country with a stable economy?"

"I'll let you know as soon as I find out."

Uncle Lucho comes over with an open bottle of raw *aguardiente* and fills a glass for me.

I hold up my hand: "Please, that stuff's only good for killing tapeworms."

"So let's kill some tapeworms," he says.

I knock it back and shiver, which makes the men laugh. Uncle Lucho slaps me on the back and pours one for Luis and then himself. They both shiver, too.

Uncle Lucho advises me, "Never drink unless you're alone or with somebody."

I beg off a few invitations to dance. I need to take a breather, so I entrust myself to a hammock made from an old canvas sack, lean back and watch Antonia chatter and flirt with a swarm of budding teens she hardly ever sees, although they share various recessive strands of DNA and Aunt Yolita's dark velvet eyes. She got the gift of being self-assured from me. Unlike her girlish cousins, my daughter prefers functional faded jeans and cargo pants, and even gets her sandals from the boys' section, although I can't complain, since they are cheaper and more practical: the girls' styles this year are—*shudder*—platform sandals. At least we got over that I-want-to-be-a-boy stuff when she was a preteen. I talked to her about it and discovered that she just wanted to have all the fun that boys seem to be having on the TV ads: running around outside, playing, jumping, building, while the girls sit around indoors and comb Barbie's hair. When I told her she could do all of that and still be a girl her face lit up like the arctic sun rising to warm the world.

Now she's at the age where she thinks that phrases like "frog barf" are *hilarious*.

Another one of the law students takes a look at my legs, all the way up to the hem of my dance skirt, and remarks, "If that's what the provinces are like, I'd like to see the capital!" Apparently he's at the age where he thinks phrases like that are hilarious.

It's been a long day. I flop down happily in bed next to Antonia. Suzie sits on the next bed, kicks off her shoes, and starts unbuttoning her blouse.

"So is Raúl helping you with her?" she asks.

"Yeah, we're splitting the responsibilities. I'm taking care of the kid the first eighteen years of her life and he's doing it for the second eighteen years of her life."

Suzie knows what I mean, having also had experience with men who believe that their paternal duties end at conception. "And what's this I hear about you having some *gringo* boyfriend? When do I get to meet him?"

"Stan's a really nice guy. He promised to come visit us as soon as he can get a week off."

"If he's such a nice guy, why are you down here by yourself?"

"To see you," I say.

"Well, here I am," she says, unhooking her bra and shaking herself out. Then she reaches for a pale blue nightshirt.

I listen to the noise of the traffic flowing by, sharp diamonds of light streaking across the bare cement ceiling, and I begin to explain: "I also need to spend a little time in the mountains. The air is supposed to be good for me."

"Of course the mountain air is good for—" Suzie stops pulling the hair from her comb. "Wait a minute. What do you mean?"

When I don't answer, she reaches across the gap between our beds and puts her hand over mine.

"What is it? Is something wrong? Filomenita, you must tell me."

"It's okay, Suzie. I'm all right."

"*Gracias a Dios.*"

"*Sí, gracias a Dios.*"

She waits.

Then, quietly: "So?"

"Well, everything's fine for now, but they removed some benign precancerous tissue from my lungs a while back, and I need some time to recover."

"Lord have mercy. Then maybe hiking around the timberline isn't such a good idea."

"I was thinking about taking something called a bus."

"You going to head up to Cuenca?"

"Sure. Sometime."

"Solano?"

I have to think about that.

"Maybe."

"So what are your plans?"

"I don't know. I wish I could stay for a couple of months and just relax, but I had to promise my bosses a pint of blood every seven days just to shake a three-week stretch out of them."

"Private investigators don't normally get long vacations, I guess."

"It's a lot better than being a cop, but the work never stops. Twenty-four/seven, as they say. Not like here, where we practically invented the *siesta*."

"We didn't invent it, we just perfected it."

I smile. "And I wish Antonia could go to high school here for a few months and learn more about her other culture. Does *padre* Campos still give mass in La Chala?"

"He's still shaking it, all right. He even made the papers a few weeks ago."

"How did he do that?" I ask innocently enough.

"He helped organize a conference of a dozen priests and bishops who wrote a human rights report accusing the government of illegally funneling support to the paramilitary hit squads up North and in the jungle that are responsible for hundreds of killings and disappearances that had been blamed on the rebels. They said most of the victims were simple Shuar *indígenas* who don't support either side."

"They just had the bad luck to live near the oil fields."

"He got some death threats. They all did."

I feel a sudden twinge of trepidation.

"How'd he take it?"

"Like a priest."

I lie here. Up for twenty-nine hours straight and I can't sleep. Things are always a bit more intense here, but I didn't count on this. Not my first day, anyway.

I no longer live these events, they're only memories. And my memory's been wrong before. All I have left are fleeting images of Johnny. The wondrous glow of our first hot food in days searing in a pan, his arms around me, cuddling up next to a crackling fire on the high, windswept slopes, a *canelaso* warming my teenage belly.

And I remember the day *padre* Samuel Campos saved my life.

We were cut off from the ragged mountain pass to our refuge, on a flat grassy plain with no cover. So we took up defensive positions behind the low walls of a ruined farmhouse. We were low on bullets, but we held out with a fairly steady volley that kept the rural army at a distance.

But they knew we were scratching in the dirt looking for empty casings to refill with pebbles and powder.

Johnny wasn't there, so El Pibe was in charge. We never had the luxury of keeping our women away from the fighting, but El Pibe suddenly ordered all the *compañeras* to fall back inside the farmhouse and shoot from there. It was better protection, but not for long. I got in a few good shots, but they saw what he had done and knew what it meant, and in a moment they charged. Through the broken window I saw five of us go down on the first volley, smearing the stones with our blood.

I will never forget—El Pibe was a good friend and cadre lieutenant who helped keep the others off me. In what seemed like seconds they had him surrounded.

"Drop the weapon now!" they ordered. "Drop the weapon now!" They said it at least five times. *"Now!"*

They made out like they wouldn't shoot him. "Come, come with me," the sergeant gestured to him with an open hand.

So he dropped the gun. And they all opened fire on him.

Helluva time to learn rule number one: *Never* give up your weapon. I resolved to kill as many of them as I could before they got me.

They broke open the door and I was standing right there, shoving my pistol into a young soldier's face.

That stopped everything.

We hung there for a moment. He really was young. A draftee whose eyes could not hide the fear. They didn't even try. We should have been playing jacks together, but now I was going to blow him to pieces. He knew it and I knew it and the other soldiers knew it because they started moving again, slowly, and they were raising their rifles.

Then *padre* Samuel called out to the sergeant, told him to stop the killing right now. He walked right up to both of us, put an arm around me and took my pistol away. And he walked me out of there, hugging my body close to his for protection. Then he spirited me away from prosecuting eyes and into a school a hundred miles away where he gave me sanctuary.

I was still a teenager, a runaway, a kid. *Padre* Samuel helped make me a person.

The Catholicism I knew as a child was brutal. *Padre* Samuel showed me a tolerant, progressive, activist Catholicism. He brought me back to life from the brink of self-destructive nihilism. I returned to Catholicism with *padre* Samuel Campos because, he said, God always kept believing in me, even when I didn't believe in Him.

And now I can't sleep. There's not much rest for the vigilant, and nobody gets any sleep around here once they realize how much there is to be wary of.

And now I've got to see a priest.

CHAPTER
TWO

El hombre es el único animal que puede ser des-
plumado más de una vez.

*Man is the only animal that can be skinned more
than once.*

—Ecuadorian proverb

Guayaquil was founded on a tiny patch of flat swampland about
one-eighth of an inch above sea level in the year 1538. No one
knows why. Finding themselves surrounded by the ever-shifting
boundaries of tidal estuaries, the first colonists built split-cane
shacks on thick cane stilts to protect themselves from the rising
waters of the heavy winter rains. Over the years they filled in the
wetlands and built a city laid out in a grid that runs from the Guayas
River on the east side to the estuaries on the west side.

It's still 1538 on the west side.

Wandering homeless people invade this muck-filled swampland
and build sagging split-cane shacks on thick cane stilts. Then they
gradually fill in the waterways with garbage and earth, settle in, and
after two years you'd need an army supplied with tear gas, tanks
and bulldozers to get people out. Don't laugh. It's been done. But
sometimes the people win. The district of El Guasmo on the south
side of town started out with that kind of illicit invasion, and now
400,000 people are living there in cement-block houses with raised
dirt roads and bus service to the city center. You'd need *two* armies
to get them out. They've got the regular army outnumbered.

The district of La Chala is still in the unpredictable tidewater-
and-stilts stage, which is why *padre* Samuel built his school there
on a piece of prime real estate called El Estero del Muerto. Dead
Man's Swamp. It's as picturesque as it sounds.

I was going to go visit him as soon as I got up this morning, but my bowels had other plans. Homemade cane liquor will do that to you. Burnt toast and weak tea help, but not enough.

And remember, there's no running water.

Antonia looks at the charred crumbs on my plate and my sickly pallor, and asks, "What's the matter? Are you black toast intolerant?"

At least she gets a smile out of me. I explain that the term she wants is *lactose* intolerant. "It means you can't digest milk."

"Oh. I always thought it meant you couldn't eat burnt toast."

I need a strong stomach to face La Chala, the *padre*, my past. Is Father Samuel seriously thinking of taking on the paramilitaries— the shadow warriors also marketed under the brand name of "death squads"? He's too old to tangle with the stomp-and-crunch brigade, although maybe that's the point. Maybe he feels he doesn't have a lot of days ahead of him as it is. Still, I feel that way from time to time and you don't see me signing up for any suicide missions.

I dig out yesterday's paper and look at the article again. The newsprint is smeared from too many sweaty palms handling it, causing the red ink from the photo to bleed outside the box and into the text. The victims were Gustavo Paz, the National Democratic Party's candidate for governor of Guayas, and his assistant, Sonia Segovia. The NDP is an ever-so-slightly-left-of-center party that could probably be bought off or otherwise brought to compromise should they happen to win, so assassinating them doesn't seem to accomplish a whole lot politically that couldn't be finagled after the election. I've got to find out more about Paz and Segovia. Who were they? Roving bands of brigands don't use Soviet-style assault rifles. For one thing, they're *really* hard to conceal under short-sleeved tropical shirts. And Sergeant Roca of the North Guayas Police—he must be a real prize, too.

There's been a sea change in Ecuadorian politics. I can almost feel the instability rolling and bubbling beneath my feet. It's one thing to have a sideline smuggling small arms and drugs, and exacting extortionary taxes. But if these clowns have got government backing . . . My stomach jackknifes and I suppress a wave of nausea. So I sit in the back of the store next to the fan with a damp towel on my head for the rest of the hour.

I certainly haven't heard about a resurgence of paramilitary ac-

tivity, although to be frank, the only time Ecuador makes the news up North is when we get hit by another nasty caprice of nature or another humiliating political implosion at the national level.

And suddenly the sounds around me filter through, and I'm listening to César deal with a band of angry homemakers complaining about how the prices have risen again. A thin old man with an open shirt revealing a wintry tuft of white chest hair clinging stubbornly to his dark brown skin holds up a shaking ten-dollar bill that his son sent him from the U.S. César opens the morning paper to find out today's exchange rate, which is 4,450 sucres to the dollar, and counts out some money for the man, who buys a loaf of bread with a few thousand sucres. I remember when a loaf of bread was forty *centavos*—that is, forty hundredths of a sucre. They don't mint *centavos* anymore.

César tells me they don't even mint *sucres* anymore. The smallest coin is the fifty-sucre piece, worth about one cent. Fifty sucres! When I was a kid you could run away from home on that kind of money. Or at least hop a bus to the next province and stay hidden for a week.

By midmorning I'm strong enough to take Antonia around for a little light tourism. We board a bus with the windows removed, just open metal frames empty of glass, a common adaptation in this hot climate. It takes us downtown and drops us in front of an open-air meat market, where hunks of raw red cow muscle lie ripening on the tile-covered tables. I gag and try to hold my breath as we push our way past the smell of slowly putrefying entrails, suppressing the urge to spatter the pavement with black streaks of partly digested toast. Ninety-eight degrees in the shade and no refrigeration will turn someone's dinner into an escapee from a horror film about flesh-eating zombies in about ninety minutes, but nobody else seems to notice.

I'm bent over, staring at a neutral crater on the moonscape gray pavement, until the tiny hairs in my inner ear stop spinning and I finally get my stabilizers back on-line. We cross the Parque General Vargas, more trapezoid-imprisoned greenery and pitted cement, past an American film crew taking fashion pictures of a skinny model wearing a Soviet army winter overcoat over what looks like underwear. She is draping her emaciated body across the main slab

of a memorial marking the spot where three hundred patriots were butchered during the Spanish persecution of practically everybody. They are telling her to lean a little farther backwards.

We walk along the Avenida 9 de Octubre in the shadow of the winged column marking Ecuador's independence from Spain, towards the *malecón*, a seawall named after Simón Bolívar the Liberator, and the river's edge. Antonia watches all the ships go by, taking our choicest shrimp away to the best American restaurants. My family always says that the little shrimp that are left behind have more flavor, anyway. But I think they just need to tell themselves that.

I'm feeling better now, so we walk back along the wide *avenida* looking at all the shop windows. Uniformed guards with short-barreled shotguns protect ordinary household items like imported German electric juicers and Japanese television sets. There's a crowd of people in front of a display window, listening to five different TV voices at once.

"—I'm really a simple man, I don't need silverware," says a light-skinned face on four screens, with white hair and mustache. It's hard to see clearly over all these shoulders. "I'm happy with a paper plate, a plastic spoon, and some *guatita* with rice." *Guatita* is a tasty dish, considering that it's a poor man's stew made out of cow stomach and peanuts.

"Are you saying you would save the country money by calling off the lavish state dinners?" asks an off-screen interviewer.

"*¿Quién es?*" I ask the man next to me.

He looks at me. He's got polished mahogany skin, straight black hair, bad teeth, a fairly clean shirt open to the navel against this heat. Underfed. "That's *gobernador* Segundo Canino," he says. "He's running for president."

Governor Canino? Sure, I remember him. Ex-police chief of Babahoyo, appointed by his brother-in-law, the mayor, when he was thirty-seven years old and had absolutely no experience in law enforcement—unless you count time spent behind bars as experience in law enforcement. How the hell did he get to be a freaking governor?

"If he's elected—"

"It means four more years of the same shit," says a robust man with a toothbrush mustache. A few others nod.

Another TV, another face, a black man wearing a suit and tie against the TV studio air-conditioning, his dark eyes burning with intensity. A caption labels him as Jorge Hernández of the Popular Workers Alliance. He argues that despite the promises, Governor Canino will only continue the cruel, corrupt and disastrous policies of the current administration run by the Centrist Coalition. A polite way of saying, "Four more years of the same shit."

"—while the industrialized economies of the world export their filth to us, in exchange for our richest products, our finest gold and oil, our best bananas, and our precious blood and labor."

I stand on my tiptoes to get a peek. A big-screen image of Senator Ricardo Faltorra, Neoliberal Party candidate. With his high forehead sporting an imperious crown of wavy black hair and his long straight nose, he looks like the face on a Roman coin.

Three more TVs with Senator Faltorra's face, then five more showing the interview with Segundo Canino.

I turn to go, but the voice, the words, catch my attention:

"—under the Military Triumvirate, when nearly fifty bishops and priests were jailed for speaking out?"

"Absolutely not," says Canino severely. "This new group of priests is getting involved in partisan politics. They were given the chance to retract their statements, and they did not. We must re-affirm that priests are prohibited from intervening in political matters."

A couple of policemen are now standing by, wide legged, watching the crowd.

"Come on, Mom, let's go," Antonia protests.

"Yes. Let's go." But something tugs at my retina from one of the store windows. A color computer monitor wrapping up the TV news with a dizzying collage of dueling logos. It's almost hypnotic.

"Mom?"

"Just a minute . . ."

I could probably dazzle and tease it out of them for free, but that takes time, plus I've got a precocious and extremely observant thirteen-year-old with me. So I take the blunt approach, and twenty dollars buys me twenty minutes on the Net. It's the damn *gringo* price, but that's what I get for acting like a damn *gringo*. Time is money, indeed.

I do a standard search on Gustavo Paz and Sonia Segovia of the National Democratic Party, pulling up their obituaries first. Not the first thing I'd like some stranger to come across when searching for clues to my life, but that's how these searches operate. Reverse chronological order.

Paz was a heavyset career politician in his fifties with thinning hair and a face prematurely wrinkled from too much drinking and too many cigarettes. The photo of Ms. Segovia shows a smiling young woman with light, bouncy hair and her whole life ahead of her. Jesus, this is never easy. I scroll back through some articles covering the campaign, and eyeball a few standard quotes about providing more roads and schools and drinking water, certainly nothing to murder somebody over, but then I've always been a slow burn in that department. I don't really have time to check on all the details, so I print out a few sheets to look at later. The sons of bitches charge me a dollar a page.

O ut in the big, wide world I'm a respected professional investigator. Here, I'm kitchen help, getting roped into spending a good part of my afternoon helping my aunt Yolita cut a fifty-pound sack of dried kidney beans into one-pound bags, then separating the pebbles and twigs from three pounds so that Antonia can wash and soak them for dinner. Aunt Yolita insists that Lucho Jr. take the afternoon off from the free dental clinic to go with us since La Chala is such a jagged neighborhood.

I tell her we can handle it, but she insists, even though there's some trouble at the store and it seems like they could use every hand they can spare. The new delivery has arrived, and the price of a hundred-pound *quintal* of rice has gone up 40 percent since *this morning*. César starts charging 320 sucres a pound, and the fickle women narrow their eyes and accuse him of sucking their blood. He asks us to pick up a head of bananas on our way back; they're almost out again.

Lucho Jr., Antonia and I walk down to the Calle Bolivia and

wait for our bus, keeping to the shadows under the block-long balconies which are supported by irregular pillars, creating an uneven shade the length of the street, another design adaptation necessary for survival in this sunburnt climate. Some of you may recall that Charles Darwin developed his theory of evolution while visiting Ecuador's Galápagos Islands. (There'll be a test on that later.)

The curbs and gutters are also uneven, shaped by the hands of men who will starve if they ever run out of curbs and gutters to make, and it looks like our bus is going to be delayed because a group of men and women in clean *guayaberas* and blouses are marching down the Avenida del Ejercito and blocking off the street. They seem peaceful enough, and their demands are simple: water, rice, oil, cooking gas, government accountability. I didn't even know there was a shortage of cooking gas.

Buildings aren't fitted for gas pipelines, which would be disastrous in this geologically unstable region. You have to get an eighty-pound tank from a distributor and bring back the empties when it's time for a refill. Lucho Jr. says, "You have to wait a couple of hours on line, but it's not really a shortage yet."

Oh, shi—

My heart beats faster when I see the white helmets. Two dozen of them. Then I realize they're stopping traffic so the protesters can get through. It's going to take me a while to get used to the sight of cops, even the traffic cops in their blue-and-white uniforms. It's the helmets. The provincial cops wear the same helmets with their military gray-green uniforms.

I stop squeezing Antonia's hand and explain to her what the protest is about.

"There's our bus!" she says, pointing to a dented blue-and-white-striped bus with a hand-painted sign in the front window saying La Chala in bright red letters.

We climb aboard. It looks like the driver bought the body used and built the rest himself. Hand-soldered metal seats are bolted to a boilerplate metal floor. There's a huge battery under the front seat that is also bolted *and grounded* to the metal floor, which has recently been cleaned with gasoline.

We sit down anyway.

Gutters, signs, bus seats—everything in Ecuador is handmade.

I notice Lucho Jr. isn't wearing his gold wedding ring. He tells me nobody wears gold on the streets anymore.

"So what do you do? Put it on when you go to bed?"

"Just about."

We stop in front of an open market and the bus fills up with women carrying plastic shopping baskets overflowing with fruits and vegetables. No meat.

Two blocks later two men get on carrying enormous watermelons. My gut reaction is, that's a bit odd, the market was two blocks back, but I figure I've lost my sense of what passes for normalcy around here.

I should have listened to my gut.

A minute later four huge watermelon halves splatter to the floor and the two men are yelling at everybody not to make a fucking move while aiming two submachine guns at us that are dripping thick, wet watermelon juice all over their hands and onto the floor.

I'm thinking the guns must be awfully slippery.

And that a spark could cause an explosion.

I put my arm around Antonia, ready to protect her, ready to jump out the open windowframe.

It goes pretty quickly. They collect cash, jewelery, watches. They can have the damn Rolux. I'm unstrapping it when one of them gets to us but the other one stops him, points to Lucho Jr., and says, "Not him. He's a good dentist." The partner nods and moves on without saying a word.

Lucho Jr. shrugs at me. I guess he gets some pretty tough customers down at the free dental clinic.

With such a good memory for faces, too.

Everything goes smoothly until the traffic cops notice that the bus isn't moving and start blowing their whistles. The desperados look up, close the loot bags, and turn to go.

Now the driver panics, starts to pull the bus away to avoid a ticket, and gets caught in traffic.

We're blocking the intersection.

Two sets of whistles pierce the air. Traffic cops are trotting towards the bus down both streets, thinking it's a simple traffic violation that they can handle. I want to shout out a warning, but I'm voiceless for a traumatic split second as the first guy kneels on the top step and aims a burst of machine-gun fire at the cops coming up the cross street, who dive to the ground and roll for cover. Two more cops are jogging up behind us. The guy drops to the street and lets them have it from about fifteen feet away, hitting one and sending him flying off his feet into the gutter. The two bandits run in front of the bus into the tangled knot of honking cars.

"Come on!" I tell Lucho Jr., pushing our way through the panicked crowd and jumping to the sidewalk.

Both cops are down. One's got a hand wound, the other's been hit in the left side of the chest, a couple of inches above his heart. I tell Lucho Jr. to help the guy with the hand wound.

My guy's bleeding all over his crisp white shirt. I tear open the shirt to get a look at the wound. Small caliber, bullet visible. He'll live.

Nothing sterile around here. I wipe my hand on his shirt and probe the wound. Then I reach in and pull out the bullet.

I look up.

Five cops are standing over me. Two of them go off in pursuit of the fleeing criminals. The others help me stop the bleeding, elevate the wounded cop's legs, and stabilize him till the ambulance arrives. His thin face is gray and bloodless, with a timid mustache clinging to the underside of his thin, mousy nose.

"What's your name?" I ask him.

"Carlos." It's a cry of pain.

"Okay, Carlos, you're going to be okay. Are you hit anywhere else?"

"My legs hurt."

"You scraped them when you fell."

"Oh—"

"Don't try to talk."

But he makes the effort: "What's . . . your name?"

I swallow. "Filomena."

He says, "Thanks . . . Filomena."

I let one of Carlos's buddies hold his head for a change. I stand up and hand over the bullet. One of the cops takes it and puts it in his pocket.

"Don't you have a plastic bag?" I ask. "Rubber gloves? Bandages? Jesus—!"

"Ease off, Mom, they're just traffic cops," says the little voice of reason next to me.

"Can you describe the two assailants?" the cop asks.

Sure: The first guy looked like a stalk of burnt sugarcane—thin, dusky complexion with tight skin and a sharp nose, and a good memory for faces. The other guy had thick black eyebrows, round nose, dark eyes. Everything about him was darker, heavier, *harder*. They both looked hungry.

"No," I say.

The bus driver wants to know if we're getting back on, since there are no refunds. I tell him no. I need to sit down, clean up, and make sure my daughter is able to handle all this.

Ah, who the hell am I kidding? *I* can't even handle all this. Antonia's just my excuse, my weather vane, my warning track, my canary in the mine shaft. When she freaks, I'll know I'm next in line.

They've got dozens of witnesses. They don't need me.

The ambulance finally comes to take Carlos to the hospital. Lucho Jr. takes my place in the gathering crowd while I slip away, which I would never be able to pull off in New York, especially after removing a bullet from one of their cops. But this is Guayaquil, and the margins are always a little more bendable here.

Once we are safely out of sight, Antonia and I walk a couple of blocks until the numbness wears off, then find a small café so I can step into a tight, smelly bathroom to wash the blood off my hands with a liter of bottled water. I come back out a little bit cleaner and order my little girl a hot chocolate to help bring the color back to her cheeks. I could use a double shot of firewater myself, but I'm still chasing away the last dog that bit me. I look around. It's a quiet café with comforting photos of blue water, white sand and palm trees swaying in the breeze. I start to tell Antonia that she might suffer some kind of posttraumatic stress, and I end up admitting my own anxieties about her safety and my worries that in a few short years she'll be on her own, an undeniable signal of my own irreversible aging and the fragility of life in general, and she's the one who breaks it off, uninterested, over and done with, next topic please. Maybe she's more resilient than I thought.

Guns inside watermelons. I'm going to have to remember that bit for my next jailbreak.

And my shoes still smell of gasoline.

*　　*　　*

*P*adre Samuel's school was built on top of a garbage landfill, surrounded by rotting cane shacks that barely rise above a sewage-clogged estuary that smells like a gastrointestinal disease. The backwater is best accessible by canoe, but that doesn't stop the women living there from going off to work wearing tight, splashy dresses, with their hair styled and faces made up as if Hollywood talent scouts cruised the area daily from passing speedboats.

A few rooftops away, on drier land, stand the church and the parish house, a worm-eaten cloister made of mud, straw, wattle and daub, plaster, reeds, old bones, and probably anything else that happened to be lying around unguarded when they threw the place together. The people say the structure's still holding up because gravity is weaker on the equator. I figure it's because God Himself wants the building to remain standing, since only such a miracle could be responsible for it.

He's got no phone, and the electricity comes from a community-supported linkage of household extension cords that runs into a network of illegal cables siphoning live juice from the hydroelectric power lines four hundred yards downriver.

Service is unpredictable.

I divide a handful of sucres between the beggars squatting on the bottom steps of the rickety staircase up to the second floor. The stairs bow under our weight as though another ounce or so would send the two of us into the marsh in a shower of splinters. The covered balcony offers a dazzling view of the mountainous ridge of the Andes off to the east, my home territory. If the air were a little clearer, Antonia would be able to see the snow-covered dome of the Chimborazo volcano glinting in the sunlight.

There are no closed doors here. The *padre* is not a great believer in personal security.

A dozen people huddling dangerously near the edge of poverty's bottomless abyss are waiting to see him, but the *padre*'s assistant, Ismaél, a gangly *mulato* kid who must be all of sixteen, sees two relatively well-dressed strangers and sends us in ahead of everyone. I tell him we'll wait our turn, but *padre* Samuel looks up from the piles of municipal paperwork littering his table and sees us, his arms fly wide open, scattering some pages, and he shouts, "*¡Ave María, mi Filomena!*" and he comes around the makeshift desk to give me a bear hug that nearly lifts me off the ground.

"Careful, Father, you're losing your papers," I say.

"Nonsense," he says, dismissively. "That's just some rigamarole the city makes me go through to try to slow me down."

He pats my shoulder several times, as if he can't get over how big I've gotten.

The empty-handed people seeking his advice feel our profound closeness, and not one of them utters a peep of complaint about us going ahead of them.

"How are you, *mi hija*?" he asks.

"Good, good, Father. And you?"

"*Todo bien, gracias a Dios*. And this is the little princess?"

"Well, I don't know about the princess part—"

"*No soy una princesa, soy una reina,*" says Antonia. My God. She just said, I'm not a princess, I'm a queen.

The *padre* laughs, big and loud, shaking the liver-spotted skin that's hanging from his thin, aging cheekbones, a quivering reminder of how old he's getting. He asks Antonia how she likes Ecuador, and she politely answers that she likes it very well, Father, even though I know that the whole showering-in-a-pitcher scene and constant mayhem in the streets are no trip to paradise for an Americanized girl who's used to—well, America.

I dwell for a moment on the uncomfortable fact that *padre* Samuel's kind, open face is showing much of the wear of a life devoted to the needy, but don't think I haven't seen him raise the roof off the church when six hundred peasants are listening.

"You've had a rather busy month," I begin.

He smiles. "Not as busy as you used to keep me."

Padre Samuel lives an ascetic life. He has to. Any frivolous embellishments would have been stripped from his chapel long ago, along with the nails that held them in place. In a place this poor, nothing even remotely useful ever sits around very long. I've seen demonstrators block the roads with burning tires, and afterwards, while the cool gray ashes scatter, *campesinos* come with blackened fingers from gathering up the charred steel strands to sell them, after a bit of work, as homemade barbed wire.

His office has a splintery wooden table, three wobbly chairs, a stack of water-damaged Bibles, a transistor radio that he must carry around with him, and a square window opening cut into the wall overlooking Dead Man's Swamp.

So good food and drink are about his only sensory pleasures.

"Let's go somewhere and talk. Come on, I'll buy you a beer," I say.

"If you're buying, I'd rather have a whole meal."

He doesn't pretend.

"Sure."

"Give us an hour," he tells Ismaél, who relays this information to the waiting souls. They do not move. I feel bad, but nobody seems to mind as we tromp down the creaky stairs.

He takes us to a wood-and-cane place with velvet paintings of tropical scenes and framed poster-sized photos of bare-breasted women that *padre* Samuel ignores so successfully he practically *wills* them out of existence. The *salonero* looks us over, then leads us through a bamboo curtain to a deck out back, where we settle into a couple of dockside seats not quite high enough above the water, so that the smell reaches us if the wind's just right. Or wrong.

"This is a bad neighborhood," I tell him.

"There are no good neighborhoods around here, Filomena," says *padre* Samuel. "You know that."

He orders an appetizer of *ceviche de camarones con canguil* and a plate of *lomo a lo pobre, arroz con menestra, patacones y dos cervezas*. The shrimp are still alive when they're brought past us into the kitchen.

The *padre* tells me that his assistant, Ismaél, is a local boy who got caught stealing food from a nearby grocery store a few months ago. The *padre* convinced the store owners to let him give the kid a chance, and he's been working out fine ever since then. This is the kind of work the *padre* does best. But there are still a lot of old memories, prejudices, vendettas.

"And the law doesn't really touch people's lives most of the time here," I say, observing the estuary's fluid borders.

"We are in a place that is often beyond the law," he says.

I shake my head, disgusted at how little has really changed. "I have such a love/hate relationship with Ecuador."

"That's because you have a love/hate relationship with *everything*," he says, making me chuckle.

"True, but so do you. Because I've heard—"

"You've heard that a dozen socially conscious theologians have been getting death threats ever since they issued a report criticizing the government's collaboration with lawless paramilitary units and death squads."

"Yes. Including you."

"Yes, including me."

I check on Antonia. She's looking over the railing, fascinated, studying the water's surface, hoping to catch a glimpse of a poisonous snake amid the primordial ooze.

"But those aren't the threats I'm worried about," he says.

I look into his cool gray eyes with renewed urgency. "What do you mean?"

"Filomena, when the city first approved my permit to build a school here, I got death threats every day. The people living in this filth had never met a person from the outside who wasn't planning to take something away from them, and they were ready to fight, even for that garbage dump, because it was *their* garbage dump. They were afraid that once someone—anyone—got ahold of one piece of land, pretty soon they would lose everything. *Those* were real death threats."

"The ones you're receiving now aren't?"

"Most of them are practical jokes. An initiation rite for snotty-nosed street kids. I know their voices. The threats they make are terrible enough, but there's no teeth in them," he says.

"Yet all the priests who signed that report have been getting similar threats. That's a pretty elaborate initiation rite for a street gang. Whatever happened to hot-wiring cars?"

The *padre* laughs.

"What about the ones that aren't practical jokes?" I ask.

"Just in time to spoil the meal," he says, as his first course arrives. I follow his lead as we clasp hands, bow our heads, and he prays, "Bless us, O Lord, and let us be thankful for all you have given us, for Thou art the Lord, whose word makes all things possible."

"Amen."

"And bless you, too, my daughter. *Audentes fortuna iuvat*," he says, straightening up. "All right, here, take a look at this."

He takes a yellow paper out of his pocket and tosses it across the table at me. I unfold it. It's printed on rough newsprint paper, but the ink hasn't smeared. It's a pamphlet attacking the squatters on the west side of the estuary, accusing them of bringing "every kind of vice to this place of natural beauty, fashioned by the hand of God for his believers to enjoy in its undeveloped state." On the bottom of the last page his name is set in small caps, "Father Samuel Campos."

"What the hell is this?" I ask.

"Obviously, someone wants the squatters to believe that I'm a hypocritical, backstabbing what-have-you, and turn against me."

A hundred questions press in on my brain at once: What would that accomplish? Who would benefit from it? Who wrote this? Where was it printed? What kind of paper is this? Why hasn't the ink smeared? What about the language? Are there any phrases he recognizes?

"Now, who is up to that level of planning and disinformation?" he asks me. "Certainly not the small-time thugs who rig the rackets along the marsh's edge, am I right?"

"I don't know, they're getting more and more sophisticated these days. Anyone with a scanner and a color printer can copy just about anything if they want to."

"Look around you, Filomena. Do you think anyone who had access to that kind of technology would waste it producing *this* kind of nonsense?"

"No, I suppose not. Can I keep this?"

"Be my guest," he says, waving it towards me as if he wished the gesture would make it disappear from his physical plane of existence. He's got a bit of shrimp shell caught between his bottom front teeth. He removes it with his fingernail and spits it out on the floor.

"So what does this mean?" I ask.

"It means we're in more danger today than we were yesterday."

"We who?"

"Everyone who signed that document. *Padre* Aguirre of La Merced, *padre* León of La Esperanza, Archbishop Duarte of Riobamba—"

"Why? What's happening?"

He waits while the *salonero* removes the empty bowl and ceremoniously places the steaming *plato fuerte* in front of him.

"Please tell me, Father."

He draws in a breath, lets it out slowly.

"You've been gone a long time, Filomena. The end of military authority didn't really change the basic rules of power," *padre* Samuel explains. "When I come to a *pueblo*, agents of this supposedly democratic government are already there waiting for me, to see what I am going to do. They think being a missionary means saying, 'Christ did this, Christ did that, hallelujah, amen, go home.' I bring the *true* Gospel with me, and for a lot of people, the true Gospel is a real pain in the butt. But this never happened before, in spite of everything. It started with this administration, assigning secret police agents to keep constant watch on my movements. Someone is always following me."

Oh, crap. Why didn't he warn me? I should have called first. But the *padre* has no phone.

"So I've been seen?"

"You're probably being seen right now," he says, eyeing the salt shaker as if it might contain a hidden microphone and video transmitter. "They're always waiting to catch me rubbing elbows in solidarity with a bunch of radical extremists."

I'm beginning to feel like I should leave through the back door, which in this case would be a rather slimy swim.

"Don't worry, I won't tell them your name." He smiles. "I've been followed before. I never gave it much thought."

"Well, maybe you should start."

"Don't let this sunny disposition fool you, kid. I know how deep this garbage goes. Every few years some would-be banana dictator comes along saying, 'The country needs a strong leader,' and the first thing he does is start compiling a list of enemies to be eliminated, and the regular politicians are usually happy to keep a bulldog like him on a leash for a while, because he's taking care of all the nasty troublemakers while their hands are kept clean. I've seen your family on such a list."

"Too late. They already got them all."

"Your extended family."

"My aunts and uncles? Are you serious? What did they ever do?"

"Not just aunts and uncles, Filomena. Cousins, nieces and nephews, stepsisters, the paperboy, the neighbor, the neighbor's cats. This isn't about what they did."

"Whose list is that?" I demand.

"Doesn't matter. He's been out of power so long he couldn't raise a flag in a high wind."

"*I want his name.*" I say it so sharply that several diners turn and look at me. Damn. I've got to learn a whole new level of keeping my mouth shut. "Sorry."

"Yes, I can see that. Your hotheadedness is going to get you into trouble. I don't know if I should tell you this or not."

"Tell me what?"

He looks at me.

"Okay, I'll take it easy. I promise."

"See that you do," he says, pouring the rest of his beer into his glass. "Because the city likes to keep things subtle, like tripping you up with paperwork and filing deadlines. But last week I was giving mass near Balzar, and five heavily armed men from the North Guayas Militia stopped me afterwards and told me, 'You better watch what you bloody say here, or we'll cut your effing throat.' "

"It's that damn report you wrote."

"I'm just one of the signatories."

"Yeah, I'll bet. Where can I get a copy of this thing?"

"I'll have Ismaél send you one."

Jesús del gran poder. I force myself to take several deep cleansing breaths, until my blood pressure comes down from the high two hundreds.

"Okay, I'm calm," I say. "And I seriously think you should try to protect yourself, or at least keep a low profile, just until this commotion blows over. Or else I could act as your bodyguard. It's the least I could do—"

"*Señorita* Buscarsela," he says sharply, then his voice softens. "Always trying your best to help," he reassures me. "You would have made a good novice."

I smile.

"But, my daughter, the call to serve is a lifelong sacrifice. There is no 'just until this commotion blows over.' I have an evangelical mission to speak the truth, and I will *never* stop speaking the truth."

We eat in silence for a while. Antonia's dropping bits of food into the water and watching the ripples, waiting for a bite.

The *padre* takes a long swallow of beer and wipes his mouth. "You remember Alberto?"

Of course I remember Alberto. *Padre* Samuel sees that and nods. "He's playing around town with a group called Los Cuervos Rojos."

The Red Crows. That used to be our unit's code name.

"I'll look him up," I say.

"Do you remember Johnny?"

"Same as I'd remember being struck by lightning."

He nods. "Yes, I suppose that God can strike you pretty hard sometimes."

"I didn't know He had a hand in it."

And the love. I remember it vividly—in camps, in fields, on horseback, on the run, warm, fleeting, hard and intimate.

"And I remember that he's dead."

Silence.

I look deep into the *padre*'s eyes.

"Don't get yourself killed," I say.

He doesn't respond.

Then: "Thank you for dinner, Filomena. Why don't you two come by during Holy Week and we'll put you to work in the soup kitchen?"

"Sure."

"Now if you will excuse me, there are people back there who need my help."

"Don't you ever rest?"

Padre Samuel tells me, *"Descansaremos en el cielo."*

We'll rest in heaven.

CHAPTER
THREE

Was there a man dismay'd?
Not tho' the soldier knew
Some one had blunder'd.

—Tennyson

I t's overcast. The sky's that dreary, funereal gray that robs the morning of its color, as if someone has wrapped all the brightly painted walls in a layer of dull film and sucked a couple of pints of blood from all the people walking past. Every cloud wafting east across the vast Pacific gets stopped by the formidable obstacle of the Andes, and then it rains. The winter rains are not especially heavy, but they're steady. Persistent. It can rain every day for weeks. There are three types of weather in Guayaquil: hot and humid, hot and raining, hot and flooding.

I'm sitting among the empty beer crates, my elbows propped on a rustic desk piled high with receipts and ledgers, studying the pamphlet Father Samuel gave me. The words themselves offer little more than an outline of his alleged plans to expand his school and drive all the poor people in La Chala from their homes. It's the object itself that offers the most tantalizing clues about its origins. The rough newsprint is thick with absorbed moisture, and still the ink doesn't smear. So we've got high-quality oil-based ink on the cheapest paper available, which presents a discrepancy. Maybe not a significant one, since so many things in this place are cobbled together from available parts like the bride of Frankenstein. But nobody likes to spend money unnecessarily, so this ink issue sticks in my mind as I assemble my own grisly collage across the desktop, consisting of high-contrast ink-jet printout describing the murders of two center-leftists named Paz and Segovia. This ink doesn't smear, either.

It's too early in the investigation for the police to be publicly theorizing about possible motives, but one of the articles from last week mentions the NDP candidates' accusations that the dominant interests in North Guayas are conspiring to defraud the people by rigging the prices of basic food essentials. I need to catch up with today's news. I'd also like to find out if Los Cuervos Rojos are playing somewhere, which seems likely on a Saturday, but somehow in all the confusion today's news got shredded and used as wrapping paper.

Rumors are walking through the neighborhood on a hundred legs that rice is going up again. Dozens of arms are thrusting through the iron bars, fistfuls of sucres trying to buy at yesterday's prices, and the shelves are emptying fast. They're also running low on sugar and cooking oil, and we ran out of bananas yesterday. No bananas! Our biggest export. Pretty soon we'll have to start chopping up the floor and selling the wood piece by piece. Then we can start on the pillars.

Suzie's folding up one-ounce packets of coarse salt in newspaper and speaking over her shoulder at me. "Lucho Freire's in town. He was asking for you."

Yes, another Lucho. From now on, just assume that every Lucho in Ecuador is a relative of mine unless otherwise stated.

"Do you know where he is?"

"No. Try the car shop."

Lucho and his wife, Marianita, kept me from starving after I ran away from home in a stifling mountain village where the schooling stopped in the sixth grade to go to Cuenca, where they had something called a high school. Lucho stakes his life on the family clunker every week, driving it down to Guayaquil to score bulk quantities of industrial chemicals, which he then hauls up the winding dusty roads to the family store in Cuenca, high in the Andes, and cuts them up into pint bottles and two-ounce bags, and resells them at a tiny profit. He's originally from the coast, but she's from the mountains. Around here that's considered a mixed marriage.

He's also a chemical engineer who just might be able to tell me something useful about printing inks.

His brothers have a car repair shop a few blocks north of here. I let Antonia stay with her cousins, listening to music and practicing basic coquetry in Spanish. No need to drag her into the middle of another shootout, if I can avoid that.

I walk up the Calle Portete past a scrap metal dealer who's got a fifty-foot crankshaft from a chopped-up cargo freighter lying in the street, past besieged grocery stores where panicking people are hoarding whatever can be baked, boiled, swallowed, rubbed on, or rolled up and smoked, past a fix-it shop with five TVs running at once on a bench on the sidewalk for advertising purposes. The TVs are chained together with heavy gauge steel, and there's a knot of willing victims there watching, transfixed, as if expecting to absorb their daily nourishment from the cool glow of the cathode ray.

My eyes skip along the row of TVs. There's a Venezuelan soap opera about a rich guy's love for a poor girl, an American-made action movie dubbed into Spanish featuring Chuck Norris chasing after a departing airplane on what appears to be a motorcycle, and three screens full of men's faces and mouths. Some of them are the same faces from yesterday, and some are new, like economist Julio Verdín of the Conservative Freedom Party, who claims that the country's problems are economic, and that he is the man to solve them; and Remigio Desatino of the Radical Liberal Party, who's on a TV with reception that's too poor to understand what he is saying.

I don't see Jorge Hernández today. The mainstream media is probably doing its best to ignore the six-foot-tall black Communist whose eyes burn like rough diamonds. And suddenly up pops a man named Hector Gatillo, who has just been chosen as the Socialist Unity Party candidate from his own hometown, Guayaquil.

The people on the sidewalk cheer.

"That's my man!" says a guy in a light blue T-shirt.

"*¡Ahora sí!*"

The pretty, young newscaster tells us that *licenciado* Gatillo is a social studies teacher at Rolando Aguilera High School, a clean, cash-poor school named after the beloved president we elected when military rule was finally lifted, and who died in a plane crash before he could keep most of his campaign promises.

Licenciado Gatillo is being slapped on the back, getting hugged by schoolgirls in blue uniforms, and laughing into the camera. He invites us all to his victory mass later today at the Church of the Sisters of Christ in the *ciudadela* Aguilera. He's shorter than some of his students, with a round, jovial face and medium-light skin.

Then the mike gets near his mouth:

"They said they'd create jobs," says Gatillo. "They lied."

"Tell it!" The people on the sidewalk cheer him on.

"They said they'd redistribute the land. They lied!"

"Yeah!"

"Tell those fucking *serranos*!"

"They said they'd build more schools—"

"They lied!" the voices echo his.

"They said they'd control food prices—"

"*They lied!*"

"*¡Eso!*"

"*¡Dilo! ¡Dilo!*"

"Hear that, you snotty *quiteños*? It means don't fuck with Guayaquil!"

Man, the only time a bunch of Americans get this excited around a TV is on Superbowl Sunday or when they're clustered outside the MTV studios in Times Square screaming for the VJs to play the latest video by some vapid boy band. Ooh! We love you, Carson! Woooooooo!

I don't know whether to be proud or frightened.

Suddenly all five TV screens fill with identical red, blue and gold horizontal bars and some canned trumpets blare as the presidential seal takes over the tube.

"Oh, maaaaaan!"

"*¡Chusa!*"

"*¡Hijo de . . . !*"

A brief formal announcement, and all five channels are now carrying the image of President Pajizo posing stiffly with the tricolor sash of office draped across his chest.

"*Ecuatorianos,*" he begins, amid a chorus of grumbles. "Several months ago, the trans-Andean oil pipeline was ruptured by an earthquake, an act of God, that drove up fuel prices, and with it the prices of some other consumer goods. The country is calm, and peaceful. Now is not the time for agitation—"

"Especially when it's directed against *you*," someone in the crowd declares.

President Pajizo ignores the man's comment and goes on to list all the public works his government has undertaken, the roads he has built, the bridges.

"Six million five hundred thousand people enjoy the benefits of modern electricity," says the president. "That's two out of three Ecuadorians."

Boy, there's an accomplishment. One-third of the country still lives in a permanent blackout, and he's *bragging* about how small that number is.

"We can do no more because of insufficient funds—"

"Where'd it all go? Check his pockets!" another man suggests, but the president refuses to listen.

"—And you people have been quick, like little children, to protest an increase in your electric bills."

The spin boys cut in with some prepared footage of a couple of stoop-shouldered Indian women in faded ponchos flicking on switches to fire up the single bare bulb that brings a feeble light to their crumbling adobe dwellings.

Pajizo accuses the people of "protesting against nature," and announces new service cuts, new taxes, new price increases.

You can imagine how well that goes over.

One woman sums it up: *"La misma mierda con distintas moscas."*

Or, as they say in Queens, Same shit, different flies.

C allused hands grab me, rough men jab me, I get squeezes, hugs and pecks on both cheeks as my cousins Lucho, Efraín and Fernando welcome me back to their plain cinder-block storefront piled high with used air filters, tailpipes, drive belts and every other oil-soaked thing that can keep a car going long after the odometer has turned over its last zero. I turn down shots of *aquardiente*, because it's two in the freaking afternoon, for crap's sake.

Lucho's brothers reluctantly get back to work fixing a miscegenated jeep with a Datsun 1200 engine in a top-heavy Suzuki body. The engine's got plenty of punch and the body's solid, but the two were joined together by a couple of guys who wipe their asses with straw, according to Efraín's expert testimony, because every week another part falls out. This time it seems there was a bump in the road the size of a raw pea and the universal joint separated from the driveshaft, and the heap barely made it in here with the joint held together with a thick screwdriver and some half-inch hemp.

Lucho Freire is shorter than me, medium dark, with short black hair and a thick black mustache. Before I can ask what he knows about printing inks, he tells me he's come up with a new way of scraping together the difference between hunger and starvation. It's a homemade gas transfer system, and he proudly walks me through the details of his new operation. He buys tanks of cheap supercooled ammonia gas, straight off the boat, hooks them up to the entrance valve of a refitted fifty-five-gallon drum, clamps down the metal lid and releases the deadly gas into the drum, where it dissolves in water. Then he taps the drain valve and bottles the liquid ammonia-water to sell in Cuenca.

It looks exactly like an illegal moonshine operation, and if the entrance valve ever fails, the whole garage fills with poisonous ammonia gas in about three seconds. But it allows him to undersell his competitors by a few pennies and keep his customers.

"Okay, Lucho, you're used to working with hazardous materials. Take a look at this," I say, holding out the flimsy pamphlet.

"What is it?"

"It's a forgery. Too crude to be effective on the literati, but somebody wants the faithful masses to rise up against *padre* Campos."

"*Padre* Campos?" says Lucho, his light tone vanishing. Carefully he begins unfolding the sticky pages as if three fingers of nitroglycerin might drop from them. He reads part of the first page, flips it over to get to the punch line, and declares, "This is the opposite of everything he believes in."

"Right. But there are some really sheeplike fools out there who just might fall for it. And it doesn't take much to shear some of those sheep."

"Hey, watch what you say about us," says Fernando, wiping gritty oil from the jeep's underside off his face and neck with a rag.

"These docile people have no natural defenses against the printed form of lying," I tell Lucho. "And if someone's trying to strong-arm Father Samuel, I've got a vested interest in finding out who it is and giving them fair warning."

"Fair warning? You mean like smearing the lintels over their doorposts with goat's blood?"

"No, I keep telling you, that's for the people you want to *protect*."

Lucho smiles for a second. "Does *padre* Samuel have any ideas who might be doing this?"

"He thinks it's someone from outside the *barrio*."

"That's a mighty big group of suspects."

"Someone connected on the national level."

Lucho looks at the typeset words as if each period were a pistol shot aimed at the tender places on his body.

"And what do you want from me, exactly?"

"I'd like to know what you can tell me about the ink and paper."

He checks his watch. "Nothing. The industrial labs are closed till Monday."

"Don't you know anybody at the university?"

"Sure. The University of Machala, four hours south of here. Listen, Fil, I've got to pick up a *quintal* of rice before it gets too late or we'll end up paying a hundred sucres a pound more for it by tomorrow."

"Hang on. I'll go with you. Guys, can I borrow the newspaper?"

"Just make sure you leave us the comics and the sports pages, okay?" Fernando shouts over the heavy metal thunder of the pneumatic wrench. I shout back my thanks.

Lucho used to work in a rice-processing plant forty miles upriver, surrounded by the paddies, and he knows more about rice than Uncle Ben and the Minute Rice folks combined. So we get into his pickup and drive a few blocks east towards the waterfront, then take a right and join a stream of like-minded pickups heading south with their cargo beds full of supplies, like an urban cattle drive through the pulsing heart of this marginally modern city. Dozens of these mechanical mules are branded with red-and-white bumper stickers supporting Governor Canino's candidacy for president.

We ride on in rhythm with the herd while I check the papers for the latest on the double murder. But there's nothing more besides a few lines indicating "rebel activity" near the towns of La Trampa, Hacha and—

"*Holy shit.*"

"Really? Who blessed it?" asks Lucho.

"Have you got a map of North Guayas in here?"

"What do I look like, a gas station attendant?" he says, shutting the glove compartment. "But I happen to know the terrain up there pretty well, cousin. Ask away."

"What do you know about the towns of La Trampa, Hacha and Balzar?"

"What about them?"

"Where are they? What are they near? How far apart are they?"

"Balzar is about a hundred kilometers straight up the Río Daule, almost to Manabí. Hacha's just over the Río Pucon, halfway to La Trampa, maybe twenty kilometers west of Balzar."

Close enough to fall within the territory of a single armed group.

"They're connected by a road?"

"If you want to go calling it a road, sure. Why?"

"Because last week *padre* Samuel was in a town near Balzar and some punks with guns told him to stop preaching his message of the liberated Bible."

"Which town?"

"I don't know." And of course *padre* Samuel doesn't have a phone. I'll have to go by later and ask him for more details. "And three days ago, two moderately left-wing politicians were ambushed and machine-gunned on the road to La Trampa. I'm inclined to think there's some serious nastiness coming from that part of the world."

Lucho stops for a red light. "And you want me to analyze the paper that pamphlet was printed on."

"Not so much the paper as the ink."

"Why the ink?"

"Because it's more unusual than the paper."

"Okay, cousin. Leave it to me," he says, patting his shirt pocket, which is holding our only piece of evidence. "But I might not get to it until Monday or Tuesday."

"That'd be great."

He throws the truck into gear and eases forward into traffic. "You see a connection there?"

"I'm beginning to feel it, yes."

"So what's your problem?"

Lucho knows my moods.

"Well, I guess I'm bothered by how easy it is to snuff out a life around here, and I'm worried that someone wants to do the same thing to that wonderful man. It's just plain sad."

"Honey, sad doesn't even begin to cover it," says Lucho, turning right and heading into the sun.

After a few short blocks we stop in front of a fortified compound with a mechanical gate and three parallel rows of barbed wire on top that looks like something out of one of those cheesy yet-another-secret-Allied-mission-behind-enemy-lines-that-will-change-the-outcome-of-World-War-II movies they rerun on TV after midnight. You'd think it was a munitions depot, but it turns out to be the wholesale rice distributor.

Private security guards with nightsticks and short-barreled shotguns are patrolling the warehouse entrance. They have to push open the gate to let us in, because the mechanism's broken, I think.

Workers are loading dozens of *quintales* onto a big German-made transport with a wooden cargo bed that somebody painted bright orange. The license plates say AZUAY province, so this rice is also getting ready for the long, strange trip up to Cuenca.

Lucho spots the truck driver and goes over to shake hands with him. They've seen each other traveling the same hard roads every week.

"*Hola, compadrecito, ¿cómo é la cosa?*"

"*Bien mal, don Luchito.* The price is in the clouds this week." The guy's in his thirties, and already going marshmallowy from the driver's seat blues. His shirt is soaked with sweat and he's red-faced from the heat.

"Filomena, this vagabond calls himself Vicente. *Esta chica tan guapa es mi prima.*"

"*¿Ah? Mucho gusto,*" says Vicente, gripping my palm with a sticky hand and shaking it twice.

"My pleasure."

"You both hail from the frozen plains," says Lucho.

"Really? I'm from Cojitambo," he says, which is too close to some other places, so I mutter something inconsequential about the harsh country around there and follow Lucho inside the cavernous warehouse. I'd like to say it gets cooler inside the place, but it only gets hotter under the big tin roof.

"Let me open a few," says Lucho, waving his finger back and forth over a phalanx of upright sacks plopped in the middle of the cement floor. Three guys in dirty blue T-shirts look over and nod. I guess they know a rice man when they see one.

Lucho loosens the plastic knots and opens the coarse white sack, caresses the surface of the grainy mound and comes up with a few samples in his fingers. He bites into one and grinds it between his teeth. He repeats this taste-and-texture test five times before finding the batch he likes and buying it.

A couple of workers try to impress me by helping Lucho lift the *quintal* onto his wooden flatbed. It's only a hundred pounds, guys.

The big truck pulls out, and we pull out with it.

"They have a sale on orange paint, or did somebody get drunk and buy the wrong color?" I ask, as the bright orange monstrosity in front of us pitches on flaccid suspension like a caravel buffeted by the waves.

"Color? Hell, I'd spend the money on some new shocks. Those highland roads are tough on the ass," says Lucho, and while we're both laughing, four masked men armed with handguns and a street-sweeper stop the orange truck and hijack it.

They get my *paisano* Vicente covered on both sides, then two of them climb in the back with the rice. They tell him to keep driving, and they head down the street and make a left at the sugar refinery.

Plans change.

We wait, then I tell Lucho, "Follow them."

"Follow them?"

"Yes."

It's not hard. They don't try to be elusive. The two men in the back have already taken off their masks and are making themselves comfortable, reclining on the sacks of rice. We're heading south. After we pass the free hospital, Lucho says, "They're heading towards the port."

The port? That doesn't make any sense. Rice is shipped by the mountainload every day in such colossal quantities that it's actually priced *cheaper* for export than for wholesale. They're going to lose money on this deal if they try to resell it at the port. Of course they just stole it, so what do they care about losing a few pennies? But people here care about a few pennies. And those thieves looked mighty well fed.

"They're going to El Guasmo."

Lucho looks at me, then nods.

It sounds crazy at first. But we know.

The bumpy paved road becomes a bumpy dirt road leading into the heart of a slum more crowded than our third-largest city. As the truck approaches a central square, several unsmiling men wearing light-colored suits and carrying bullhorns jump onto the truck. They quickly pin four handkerchief-sized red-and-white flags—the Centrist Coalition party colors—on the back of the truck and start announcing to all within earshot, "Fellow *ecuatorianos*, friends, men and women, children and grandparents, come see how *candidato* Segundo Canino keeps his promises! Free *quintales* of rice for the first fifty families! Only one per family, please! No pushing! Share! As Segundo shares with you!"

The two gunmen stay on the flatbed with the rice. The other two step down from the cab and take up positions on either side of the rice, to ensure order. Nobody bothers with Vicente, who stands there scratching his head, waiting for the gunmen to let him have his truck back.

He hopes.

"Well, what do you know about that?" asks Lucho.

Plenty. We used to do it ourselves. I was quite a problem child. Not your typical teen rebel getting suspended for smoking in the girls' room or shoplifting a six-pack of beer. I was a feral, acrobatic seventeen-year-old panther pouncing fearlessly onto the tops of moving trucks, landing on a day's shipment of bananas to hijack for "free" distribution to the poor. But everyone knew the stuff was stolen.

I've seen enough. Lucho wants to stick around and make sure his friend gets back on the road okay.

I walk back to the main road and take a bus with real windows to the center of town.

I'm sitting there watching the hand-embellished buses and cannibalized autos rattle and smoke past my window, thinking about why President Pajizo's Centrist Coalition would steal rice in the name of their chief candidate, Segundo Canino, since the government controls the state distribution sources and could easily arrange as many free giveaways as it wanted to, one of the many advantages of incumbency.

I know what you're thinking: It's some nasty people who are trying to make Canino *look* like a thief. You know, smear him three weeks before the election. But the flaw in that otherwise brilliant theory is that the only apparent witness is a truck driver who's too scared to come forward.

Maybe they're just some exceptionally motivated campaign contributors.

Unless they've deliberately emptied the state warehouses to drive up prices and profits. But why fake a shortage? We have real ones often enough. You want to raise prices, all you need is to wait for a bad year, with El Niño flooding the roads and wiping out entire villages and rice paddies.

Of course the key word is *wait.* . . .

I've got to ask Lucho Freire to check into this. If it's about rice, he probably knows the answer.

I'm thinking about all this and admiring some of the odd bits of 1920s Art Deco and pre-Columbian motifs churned up by the city's turbulent bricolage of warring architectural epochs, when the bus driver throws on the brakes, opens the door, and barks, "Everybody out."

What now?

My shoes crunch against the gritty pavement as I approach the main avenue and the parade of office workers who have sacrificed their Saturday afternoon for the cause of higher wages and benefits. I join the supporters on the sidelines as legions of sun-washed women proudly place their manifestos into our receiving hands.

I collect a bunch of handbills from smiling young women and stern young men, then I slip into the shade, keeping my back to the wall and trying to blend in, trying not to attract the attention of the police, so I can look over the pamphlets. Most of them are routine calls for the government to roll back the recent price increases. Others are sprinkled with jokes and unflattering caricatures of leading government figures, then—like an annunciation—I feel it before I see it. Same texture paper. I hold it up close to make sure. It's the same typeface as the false pamphlet implicating *padre* Samuel. Who gave it to me? I scan the sea of dark-haired souls. He's gone, of course, indistinguishable among the eddies and crosscurrents of kindred ethnicities and facial features, all the eyebrows, lips, birthmarks and beards.

I look at the slick black letters and the unholy words they form. They call for agitation, for uprising, for indiscriminate destruction.

And suddenly the world's a big picture tube that someone's kicking in. Heavy sheets of glass explode, raining deadly diamonds down upon the scattering chorus of innocents, who suddenly metamorphose into survival-mad beasts, tearing at each other's clothes and the flesh beneath, plunging in the battery smoke, each pressing to be the first to get out through the narrow escape routes.

I can't see it all, but there seem to be at least two groups of six or more men walking towards us on opposite sides of the street, smashing windows with iron bars and going after people in the crowd, too. Some of them are well-fed guys in white *guayaberas*, and some are callow young men with angular faces and bulging eyes, working together, covering each other's backs. This is not a random group of irate counterdemonstrators. They've all got the same haircut, for one thing.

Now I'm part of the human tide rushing away, stumbling, and I'm pulling a few people off a fallen blood relation when a big blue wave of police closes in and I try to flatten myself against a pillar as they slap people facedown on the cement sidewalk, but their nets are too fine and I get swept right up.

So much for not attracting the attention of the police.

*   *   *

It smells like shit in here. Or, more accurately, a mixture of shit, piss, vomit, sweat and some things even fouler than that.

And somehow I'm hungry.

You have to bring your own food to an Ecuadorian jail, because the swill they pass around will cramp you up for six hours of diarrhea and dry heaves. It's an efficiency thing. And my family doesn't know I'm here. The cops don't give me a phone call, so if Lucho told them he left me in the middle of El Guasmo, God knows what they're thinking, what Antonia must be going through.

At least I'm not alone. I get to sit on the cracked cement floor and swap recipes with a few dozen other newly arrested "looters." But soon I withdraw to a neutral corner and lean my head against the wall. The cops confiscated everything I had, including the incendiary flier calling for extreme random violence. I'd almost like to thank them for saving me from being beaten up by *agents provocateurs* and ask them if they have any ideas who those guys might have been, since at this point my list of suspects includes members of the North Guayas Militia, secret agents of the National Police or the ASN, mercenaries who could be working for practically anybody, or even city cops getting in some double overtime.

There's little doubt in my mind that whoever printed those fliers are the same people who've been threatening *padre* Samuel, and nobody's got to assign me the job of watching out for him. I'd do that for free anytime. He's got too much left to do to sacrifice his life for the cause, like so many before him who jumped over the wall and out of my life forever.

Eventually I stretch out on the excretion-encrusted slab of concrete for a couple of hours of parasomnia, so it feels like a few weeks after midnight when they clang open the cell door and lead me to an interrogation room that's so bright it stings my eyes.

A man who is being addressed as Captain Verdugo is standing with his back to me, drying off his hands with a rough towel, under a wall clock that reads 02:37. Without turning to face me, Captain Verdugo starts talking.

"You are aware, are you not, that it is strictly forbidden for foreigners to participate in acts of civil disobedience?"

I don't say a word.

"Answer the captain!" says the corporal, who is probably there only to ensure that the captain doesn't kill any prisoners without dividing the jewelry and gold fillings equally among the subordinates.

"I was not participating in the demonstration," I say.

"No? Then how do you explain *these*?" says Verdugo, spinning around and brandishing a fistful of political handbills at me, but I don't get to look at them closely.

Some water drips onto my head from the ceiling. I hope this isn't a harbinger of things to come.

"I'm just here as a tourist."

"Oh? There doesn't seem to be anything about that here in your passport."

The captain shows me my passport, and I see that the page with my entrance visa is missing, having been rather crudely torn out.

The corporal sniggers. I'm watching the captain closely, but his face doesn't change. He spends the next half hour accusing me of trying to overthrow the government with subversive politics, even mentioning at one point his personal belief that rich American Jews and Argentine-Jewish terrorists are plotting the downfall of Western capitalism sometime around 10:00 A.M., next Tuesday, if I followed his logic correctly.

By the time they lead me out of there, I'm thinking that I will never see my daughter again, and the clock on the wall *still* says 02:37.

B ut I'm released the next morning. And as I'm collecting what effects they returned to me (my necklace and watch are missing), my fingers find a crumpled piece of paper in my right shoe that wasn't there before. I open it up. Two words:

Gracias. Carlos.

I look at the guards milling around me, wondering which one is the friend.

*   *   *

It's early Sunday morning, and the streets are silent and empty. The Correas' store is shuttered, and I have to pound on the iron door to get them to let me in. You'd think I'd just risen from the dead by the way they react to seeing me on their doorstep.

I tell them most of what happened, then I take Antonia aside, over by the ice machine, and reassure her that the police made a mistake. "If they ever take me away from you like that again, don't worry, I'll get word to you."

"It's okay, Mom, I'm kind of used to your disappearances. But they were really starting to upset me with all their—you know—"

"I know, honey, I know," I say, clutching her precious form to mine. "I promise you I'm not going to disappear from your life. I'll always come back for you."

"Sure you will," she says.

We hug each other close. There's a sudden *ka-chunk* inside the ice machine that makes us both jump a little. Relief and laughter masking the echo of a whimper pass between us.

Now we all have to celebrate mass together, but I choose the place. The cops didn't acknowledge the importance of that inflammatory flier, but I know someone who might. *Padre* Moisés Aguirre, a.k.a. Father Moe, just another name on the endangered species list. He works the Sunday gig at the church of La Merced, Our Lady of Mercy, a rising white monument to the straight line, edged in cool light green verticals reaching towards the sky.

We take our places on the hard, narrow pews, and I pray for the health and safety of my family and friends during these troubled times.

"God knows your name," declares Father Moe. "God knows the number of hairs on your head and the number of sins in your heart. When you are standing at the gates of heaven, if you try telling God that you are a bank president or an executive, do you think that will impress Him? No. Because God knows who you *really* are and what you've done." He starts pointing at the Christian bodies cramming the aisles, saying, "God knows *your* name, God knows *your* name, God knows *your* name—"

He points near us. I look over and recognize Jorge Hernández, the fiery black congressman who strikes fear into the hearts of corrupt lawmakers, but who can apparently be found on Sunday mornings kneeling submissively before the altar of the Almighty.

When the time comes, *padre* Aguirre ends his sermon: "*Oremos.* Let us pray for the travelers who are facing danger at this very moment. Let us pray for those who are willing to help others in the face of adversity. Let us pray for the strangers among us, that they should understand our misguided ways. Let us pray for the mothers who are having difficult pregnancies and who lack decent health care. Let us pray for the children who do not have enough to eat. And let us pray for the soul of *padre* Samuel Campos, who was murdered last night in his private chambers at the church in La Chala."

CHAPTER
FOUR

Sometimes rumor is the most reliable truth.
                    —Paco Ignacio Taibo II

Our wheels brake to a stop, churning up dust.

Our car doors slam.

The smell of death is drifting off the murky waters of the estuary.

We walk along the dusty streets, blending in with the mud-spattered cane.

The sky closes in with dark, heavy clouds.

The dirt under our feet grows wet.

We hear a noise, a long animal howl of heavy machinery.

The wet dirt is now mud.

We reach the edge of a cane wall, what passes for a corner around here. Beyond it, the road dips, and slides headlong into the marsh. The noise issues from somewhere deep within the exposed radiator of a blackened bulldozer grating its scab-encrusted gears together.

I tell Guillermo to go back and keep an eye on his pickup truck. He refuses.

A dozen shacks trail off to our left, walking off the land on thick cane stilts, a swaying walkway of mismatched boards connecting them.

A group of maybe twenty people ring the solemn scene, rain darkening their speckled clothes, turning the dirt back to mud.

Between their shoulders and shiny black hair, I see flashes of yellow and tan.

Yellow is the soulless machine; tan, the uniforms of the provincial police.

They are bulldozing Father Samuel's church and parish house to the ground.

They have told the people that it's a "hazard."

The sum of a humble man's life is wiped out in minutes. I stand and mentally record it for posterity—the cracking ribs, the sharp snapping of brittle fingers of cane, the plaster dust rising from the mangled lath reaching up to heaven, the lonely stilts supporting nothing but the sour breeze. A soundless voice calling across the cold vacuum of space.

The hateful black-and-yellow-striped machine heaves forward, pulverizes another wall, nearly slips off the mossy edge, then pulls back from the riverbank leaving three support canes standing, tipping to the left and to the right.

"*¿Qué pasó?*" I ask, elbow to elbow with the witnesses.

"The power went out last night, *hombre.*"

"Motherfucker cut his throat."

"Wait a minute—" Voices all chime in:

"They took away Ismaél."

"The power went out in the whole goddamn street."

"From ear to ear."

"With a kitchen knife."

"A switchblade."

"A freakin' machete."

"They found him lying in a pool of blood."

"Hold it, hold it," I say. "Who found him?"

"Ismaél," says the loudest of them all.

"Ismaél? How do you know?"

"I live right here," she declares, pointing to the second shack from the corner. She's a little older than me, heavy without being well fed, and has been chattering away since I got here as if this whole spectacle were a welcome form of entertainment. "He came running out screaming like the hounds of hell were after him, I tell you, he was red as a shrimp and nervous as a turkey on Christmas

Eve and he couldn't have run any faster if he had a chili pepper up his ass—"

"And they arrested him? They didn't just take him in to make a statement?"

"They don't take you away in irons to make a statement, *chiquitina*," says a man in his midforties with oily reddish brown skin, his face and belly bloated from too much bread and soda, cheap filler he has eaten to fool his stomach, but the stomach knows better.

"They say he did it for the money," says the woman.

"What money?" I ask.

"A collection box full of sucres," she says. "Loaded with sucres, more sucres than you ever saw in your life."

"At least a million sucres," he says.

"Maybe even two million," she says.

That's only about four hundred American dollars, but it's a small fortune around here, and there's no way *padre* Samuel kept that kind of money in this old tinderbox on stilts.

"Wait a minute, who said this?" I ask.

"Who said what?"

"Who said he had all that money on him?"

"The police," she says, shouting over the wailing of the bulldozer, and another motley gathering of cane support beams splinters and flattens in the mud.

The sanctuary is gone.

The site is measured and marked off, and forbidden to all curiosity seekers. I go up to one of the construction workers who's dusting himself off and getting ready to have his noon dinner.

"Who told you to do this *today*?" I ask.

He gives me an answer I could have heard on any corner in Brooklyn, New York: "Who the fuck knows? Orders are orders."

Oh, Filomena, just go home, says a voice inside me. *Go back to the mountains and hike to the source of the Río Tomebamba twelve thousand lofty and frozen feet above the sea, fish for trout at four in the morning knee-deep in the ice-cold water of a running stream, or head for the Santa Elena peninsula and squirt sunscreen all over your naked body and soak up those equatorial rays on the beaches near the sleek and seedy hotels of Salinas. Just stay out of this, for once in your life.*

59

Then I look at the smug faces of the police, their pudgy jowls jiggling like raspberry Jell-O as they defile this site, swaggering back and forth astride the fallen, defenseless flesh of the truth.

And God's rain falls down on me from heaven.

Their names are Gilda and Nelson. The furniture a couple of benches last seen at the bus station and some empty banana crates. We're sitting in her one-room shack eating take-out hamburgers with beer and soda. My treat.

The rain is heavy, the street deserted, as the police watch the bulldozer loading the wreckage of *padre* Samuel's life into a pickup truck while a hundred eyes watch them from the shadows.

"That boy was always trouble, I tell you," says Gilda, the words coming out wet and juicy.

"*Padre* should have known better," says Nelson through a mouthful of pickles, bun, the works.

"He always liked other people's stuff," she says, wiping the ketchup from her lips. "The *padre* tried to help, but you might as well dump seeds in the ocean. That Ismaél, give him a hand and he grabs your elbow."

"You actually said that to the police?" I ask.

"What good would that do? He knows how to act like a dead fly. You could watch him till your eyes turn blue without catching him in the act," says Gilda, snapping her greasy fingers. Nelson nods in agreement.

"Now, I want you to tell me what happened, in your own words—"

"Ha! Ha! Ha!" She thinks this is funny. "Will you listen to her? In my own words?"

Nelson starts nodding like a bobble-headed doll with its neck on a spring.

"Of course they're my own words! What do you think? You're gonna hear *someone else's* words from *my* mouth?"

They both laugh, wide-mouthed food-filled laughs.

I look at Guillermo.

Back to them: "Just tell me what happened."

"Well, all the lights went out. Then Ismaél came out screaming that the *padre* was dead." I'm spared the extra epithets because she's too busy munching on her second burger and washing it down with some Cola Tropical.

"When did the power go out?" I realize it's a pointless question even as I'm saying it.

"At night."

"I mean what time?"

"Late."

"Ten? Eleven? Midnight?"

"Yeah."

"Which one?"

"The last one you said," she says, as if my slowness on the uptake is starting to annoy her.

"Right. How soon after that did Ismaél come running out?"

"Right after."

"Five seconds? A minute? Two minutes?" I ask. I know I'm not supposed to be feeding her answers like this, but what else can I do?

"Two minutes," says Gilda.

"How do you know?"

"Well," she says, taking a break from masticating, "all the lights went out, so I went to the window to see if it was just my house or the whole block or maybe even the whole *barrio*, you know? And I could hear the *padre*'s radio playing the Pancho La Pulga show. The *padre* always listened to that show on Saturday nights, he said it gave him ideas for his sermons the next day, which is such a shame before God, that Pancho is such a *grosero*—"

"Anyway—"

"Anyway?"

"How did you know it was two minutes?"

"Oh, that's easy. It was after the second chorus of '*A veces me siento así*,' Ismaél came running outside shouting, '*¡Socorro! ¡Ayúdame! ¡El padre está muerto!*' " Help! Help me! The *padre* is dead!

"The second chorus of what?"

Gilda looks at me wide-eyed. "The hit song. Don't you know *anything*?"

I let that go unanswered. The two-minute time estimation sounds reliable enough. Maybe I can get a match from the radio station.

"I always knew something bad was going to happen there someday," says Gilda.

"They say he plays for the other team," says Nelson with a nudge and a wink.

"Other team?" I ask.

"He's saying *padre* Campos was gay," Guillermo explains.

"Not the *padre*," says Nelson. "Ismaél."

"But you never know, do you?" says Gilda.

"There's *no way* Father Samuel was a *maricón*," I say, speaking their language.

"How would *you* know?" says Gilda, looking me up and down.

"He was always doing the *padre*'s dishes," Nelson continues, knowingly.

"And washing his clothes, scrubbing the floors, sweeping the stairs," says Gilda. "All that women's work, you know? And doing women's work makes you turn gay."

I'm about to say, Gee, that's nice, now why don't you both crawl back into your caves for a few millennia, I'll call you when we harness fire, but:

"I have my own idea," says Nelson, chomping on his burger.

"And what's that?"

He takes another bite of his ground beef and bun. The pieces of beef and bun go into his mouth, where his jaws mash it and water it with salivary secretions until it becomes a thick, pasty mass, which then slides down his feeding tube to his stomach where it founders in a sea of acidic gastric juices. Then he wipes his mouth, turns to me and says, "It was those punk kids."

Gilda agrees. "Thieves and pickpockets. Bunch of lazy good-for-nothings with long fingernails and the blood of a thousand bedbugs in their veins—"

I interrupt: "If they're a bunch of lazy good-for-nothings, why would they want to kill the *padre*?"

"Just to see if they could get away with it," says Gilda.

I don't believe that, but I should talk to the kids just the same. *Padre* Samuel said they were threatening him, and throat slitting is a junior gangland method, all other weapons being prohibitively expensive.

It's time to go.

I didn't stay to talk to anyone in the church of La Merced, I just came straight to La Chala. But now it's haunting me that my old friend and mentor was murdered the night after he spoke to me, by somebody who may have seen me talking with him. Who the hell could it have been? There are no friendly faces among the provincial police milling about outside.

Guillermo offers to wait for me all afternoon if necessary, and he scurries uphill through the thickening mud to take refuge inside his pickup truck, assuming it's still there. I watch him go. The police take a look, couldn't care less about a solitary figure running through the rain, and go back to their work.

The dip in the road is already filling up with water.

I need to talk to the nuns who run *padre* Samuel's school. But first, I set off in search of someone who knows the lives and miracles behind every doorway on this street. I'm treading lightly, since the raised walkway is made up of nothing but loose lengths of driftwood running from pillar to pillar, with considerable play in the middle. Coarse, splintering wood, pilfered and cast-off, this ain't no pressure-treated thirty-year all-weather two-by-eight from your local Home Depot.

More shacks, same results. Nobody knows what really happened, but everyone has five different theories. Some say they heard a radio playing music, but none of them can confirm that it was the *padre*'s.

One last shack. It's got four fishing lines in the water, and the smell of frying fish wafting out the door. Someone's self-sufficient in here.

I knock.

It's dark inside. I stand there letting myself be seen, my eyes getting used to the darkness surrounding a faint blue glow near the floor.

"*Entra.*" An old woman's voice. Raspy.

She's got a thirty-pound gas tank feeding a single burner perched on a flimsy banana crate that's currently doing its best to keep a frying pan sizzling on top. She leans forward to test the fish with a sharp sliver of cane, and a drawn face with dark, sun-dried skin clinging to old bones advances out of the gloom, glimmering with an eerie blue opalescence around the edges.

I disengage my leg and step forward, gingerly testing the matted cane for solidity before I go through the trouble of falling through the floor and ending up in the marshy tidewaters below. There's a queasy springiness, like walking on soggy rice paper, and a feeling that if I'd had that second muffin for breakfast, I'd be exceeding the floor's weight limit.

I introduce myself as a friend of *padre* Samuel's, and ask what her name is.

"Sit down," she says, as if the solution to that problem were obvious. The dark corners of her hovel reveal nothing to sit on.

I take my time finding the floor with my hands, squatting down with my legs crossed under me to distribute my weight as evenly as possible so as not to put too much stress on the rigging. Gravity is very real to me right now.

"Me llamo Filomena," I say. "What's your name?"

She pokes her dinner again with the piece of bamboo, using the precise, careful movements of a surgeon demonstrating a problem for a dozen eager med students, and after much internal discussion with herself, it seems, finally agrees to answer.

"Alicia," she says.

I tell her that *padre* Samuel was a gift to the people he touched, keeping a lot of mountain folks alive until he came down from his hilltop perch to help this starving community, and I'm trying to find out what happened to him, and since four eyes see better than two, I've been asking people what they saw and heard last night.

She doesn't answer.

We sit in silence while I consider how to put it into words, without revealing too much, that Father Samuel was the author of my days, long after the pages in my book of life should have been bled white, and thereafter remained silent and blank.

Then, as if revealing an eternal human weakness, Alicia says, "Whoever talks a lot is wrong."

I nod in agreement. There's a wavelength out there somewhere that we both seem to be wavering near. Sometimes silence reveals a lot, more than Gilda and Nelson's torrent of useless words, which would have to be boiled in a pot and filtered through cheesecloth to produce a nugget of truth.

I have come at mealtime, so she cuts her fish in half and serves me some on a metal plate. I refuse, but she insists. I'm not hungry, I feel bad taking her food, and I don't particularly feel like eating anything that was swimming in this water, but she will not hear me.

I know when I'm beaten.

"*Buen provecho,*" she says.

I eat part of what she gives me, listening to the patter and splishing of the rain outside, then lay the rest aside.

She eats slowly. I wait until she finishes.

She washes the dishes in a plastic basin full of dirty water and dries them. Then she sits down, and lights a murderously strong hand-rolled cigar. Good thing the place is well ventilated.

"The city wanted the land back," she says, after a few puffs. "He wouldn't give it up."

"How do you know that?"

She puts two fingers up to her left ear, smoke hovering around her, as if she were listening to the walls breathing.

"I see." It would certainly be a valuable slice of waterfront in the burgeoning *ciudadela* La Chala, with a high resale value down the road, if there's any way to corroborate the statement. "And what can you tell me about Ismaél?"

After a pause:

"He'll get into heaven," she says, flicking some ash into the water through a hole in the floor. "Heaven was made for those who've messed up in this life."

Hallelujah! If that's true, then I've got a reserved seat right next to the choir.

"*Los provinciales* took him away," I say.

"Not the city cops?"

"That's what I heard."

"Umm. You want me to tell you what I heard?"

"If you would."

"Shots, little girl. I heard shots."

"Are you sure?"

She looks very disappointed in me.

"I mean, are you sure they came from the parish house around midnight last night?"

"Yes. They came from that way."

"Because the police seem to have told some bystanders that *padre* Samuel's throat was cut. I guess I'll have to wait for the autopsy."

She considers this. She takes a deep puff on her dark, gnarly cigar and blows the smoke out the wide-open door.

"Don't you go counting the tiger's stripes," she warns me.

I stand under the eaves of Alicia's shack and survey the scene. A few cement-and-cinder-block houses rise above the rusty red tin roofs of the humbler dwellings, their split-cane walls lashed together with spit, twine and Hail Marys.

The rain washes away some of the smell of death, but I wonder what these people are going to do when the water starts rising.

Padre Samuel's school is only a few hundred feet downwind, at the water's edge, but it's several blocks away by the overland route. It's time to check in with the nuns.

And when I woke up, the man I had given myself to was gone, and I found myself giving birth at home, alone. I had to cut the cord with a bread knife and tie it off myself," she says. "It was so *tiring.*"

We look out on the gray wetness behind the school, past the chain-link fence, through the trees climbing out of the muck on leglike roots, to the dappled reflections of sad-eyed shacks on the droplet-rippled water.

"The night my little Lisabeta died was a night like any other," she goes on. "It wasn't dark or stormy or anything like that. And Father Samuel wouldn't have meant a thing to me, but I was feeling pretty vulnerable, and if I had gotten ahold of a sharp enough sword I would have cut my stomach open with it. We only met for half an hour, but he stopped me from doing it. He made me feel like a person again. Sounds silly, doesn't it? So even though I only knew him for a few minutes, there was always a special place for him in my heart."

Sister Cecilia and I are standing in her office, looking through the cross-shaped iron bars of the open window. Even in this soupy heat, the yellow floor tiles are cool, and the dampness bleeds through the whitewashed cement walls, saturating the air with the dank odor of a subterranean cavern.

"And when I heard that Father Samuel needed someone to help run the school, I resolved to be the one chosen."

"Yes," I say, clutching the cement sill. "He meant something similar to me."

"How could they do this to him? To that beautiful human being?" she asks, as tears fill our eyes, and without anyone asking why, we both let ourselves cry for him.

Eventually, the sound of sirens in the distance brings me back to the material reality of this place.

"Have the police—" I have to clear my throat and swallow. "Have the police been here yet?"

"Yes, but they said they'd be coming back," Sister Cecilia says.

"Then I don't have much time. What did they ask you?"

"They asked me when was the last time I saw him alive."

"And what did you tell them?"

"Last night, at Saturday evening mass."

"Do you remember what time it was?"

"We left him a little after nine," she says.

"Can you be more specific?"

"Maybe nine-fifteen or nine-thirty, I guess."

I'm not going to get exact minutes out of anyone.

"And when did you hear about what happened?"

"Some of the neighborhood boys starting banging on the gate around half past midnight. I ran all the way there and my habit got filthy, then they wouldn't let me up to see for myself."

"Who wouldn't let you go up?"

"The men from the neighborhood."

"Did *anybody* go up to investigate?"

"Somebody said we'd better wait for the police to get there."

"Now, what adult male from this neighborhood would show that much respect for the police?"

"This was different, Filomena. It was *padre* Samuel."

"All the more reason."

"All I know is they kept saying that we'd better wait for the police."

"So who was this somebody who started it all?"

"I—I'm sorry, Fil. I was too upset to notice."

And none of my interviewees mentioned anything even remotely like this. I'll have to ask around again after the initial shock wears off and see if anyone remembers anything a bit more useful.

"Listen, Sister, I've spent half the afternoon listening to every idiotic theory imaginable about what happened—maybe it was a street gang hungry for retribution, or a city agency hungry for territory, and maybe it was a gay love triangle because that's how 'those people' are—but I believe it was triggered by the human rights report and that means he was killed on somebody's orders, and I'd like to know what you think about that. Why would anyone want him dead?" I ask her. "After all these years, why now?"

"Like you said, that report's the key."

"Do you have a copy?"

Sister Cecilia sags a bit. "I should, but they were all in the parish house."

"Which was conveniently carted off an hour ago. Do you have any of those fake pamphlets supposedly written by Father Samuel calling for the relocation of the squatters?"

Same answer, which leaves me temporarily clueless. Damn. Why did I give Lucho Freire the only copy I had? Because I didn't count on *this*.

I wonder. Between Saturday and Sunday evening *padre* Samuel usually celebrated mass at least three or four times. "What did he say in his sermon?"

"He spoke about the election campaigns," says Sister Cecilia. "All the false words and promises used to demonize the opposition. He told the people to look deeper, and to choose wisely."

"Did he ever say anything to you about the threats against his life?"

"No. Well—not really, but—" begins Sister Cecilia.

"Go on."

"Well, it's just that it's so hard to think about this now."

"Take your time, Sister."

We listen to the muffled pattering of rain on tin rooftops.

"It was about three weeks ago. *Padre* Samuel had just given a homily on the passage in Daniel where they drink wine and praise the gods of gold and silver, of brass and iron, of wood and stone—"

"Yes? And?" I ask.

"And when the sermon was over, I asked him about the challenges God had put before him, and he said to me, 'After you've walked through the fiery furnace, you are not afraid of kids playing with matches.' "

Kids again. Damn.

"That sounds like him all right," I say. I try to block everything else out so I can think for a minute here.

If *padre* Samuel had his radio playing loud enough for the neighbors to hear it, then some kid could have snuck up those rickety stairs without him noticing it. But to stage a blackout and lunge into the darkness? Too many ways of screwing it up. And after seeing those bulldozers at work there is no doubt in my mind that this was a professional hit. I'm betting he knew the killer well enough to meet him alone in his office until an accomplice cut off the power in the whole neighborhood. It takes planning, but you don't have to be the *Mission: Impossible* team to pull it off. All you have to do is pull a three-way plug.

I've got to go talk to those street kids.

"I'll be back in a little while," I say, but too late. Sister Josefina comes in, her round *costeña*'s face wet from the softly drizzling rain, and tells us that blue-and-gray police cars are pulling down this dead-end street. In a moment, bored uniformed cops flop against the doorway like wet sandbags, occupying the entrance, and a provincial police sergeant strides through the door.

I'm sweeping up, trying to pass as the maid.

He clicks his heels and salutes Sister Cecilia as if she were a superior officer. He refuses her offer of coffee.

"We have some questions about the money," he announces. "The suspect was caught with two million sucres. We assume this money was stolen from the church."

"We couldn't have collected more than sixty or seventy thousand sucres last night," Sister Cecilia explains.

"Do you have any idea where *padre* Campos would have gotten so much money?" asks the sergeant.

"No, we don't," she says.

"Then we must investigate the possibility that the suspect was paid to commit the murder."

"Are you sure that Ismaél did it?" asks Sister Cecilia.

He smiles. "We don't believe that the perpetrator could have gotten through three locked doors without forcing them and being heard, so it must have been someone the *padre* knew well enough to invite in."

Three locked doors? Where did *that* come from? The nuns look in my direction. I surreptitiously shake my head no.

"The *padre*'s door was always open to anyone," says Sister Josefina.

The sergeant glances over at me, then turns back to the sisters. "You were saying?"

"He never locked his door," she says. "Except at night, of course, like the rest of us. He was a man of faith, but he wasn't crazy."

"No, but he was a weak old man," says the sergeant. "And this Ismaél was the last person to see the *padre* before he was found with his throat cut from ear to ear like a *carnaval* pig. Oh, I'm sorry, Sisters."

He pretends it's a slip, but it's obvious he's trying to get a reaction out of them, and it's starting to piss me off. *Padre* Samuel was strong enough to fight off an attacker with a knife, in which case there'd be defensive wounds all over his body. If he was taken completely by surprise, then it's possible there'd just be the one major wound. But the man I knew was flat broke, kept his door wide open, and was probably shot because someone didn't like his politics. The way the cops are telling it, he was stabbed behind three locked doors and the thief got away with a small fortune in unmarked bills. That's a pretty serious discrepancy.

The sergeant is looking at me again. He doesn't look away this time.

I decide to speak. "When will his body be ready for a Christian burial?"

"And who are you?" he asks.

I blurt out: "Sister Mary Martha," before either of the nuns can say anything.

The sergeant looks me over, taking in my damp shirt and jeans.

"She's a lay sister," Sister Cecilia explains.

Yeah. And it's casual Sunday at the Vatican.

"And you serve God with a broom?" the sergeant asks.

"They also serve who cook and sweep," says Sister Cecilia.

The sergeant chuckles. "We'll be needing to talk to you all again soon. And once again, I am sorry for your loss." And he leaves without answering my question.

When he's gone, Sister Josefina says, "We've just committed a sin."

I'm thinking, Yeah, I commit a lot of sins, some of them far worse than lying to some asshole police sergeant.

But Sister Cecilia absolves us all, declaring, " *'Honesta turpitudo est pro causa bona.'* Crime is honest for a good cause. Publilius Syrus, circa 42 B.C."

Can't beat a classical education.

Street gang. Sounds like the setup for a lame joke, since half the neighborhood doesn't even have streets. There's no time to go downtown, so I head into the parochial kitchen to borrow a knife— a cheap, dull knife with a cracked handle. Great. But it's big enough to impress the boys.

There are plenty of street punks around, but none of them will give me anything more than a twisted snicker. I'm also getting tired of using diplomacy.

Relief comes in the form of a green-eyed adolescent with muddy bare feet who's fighting with a girl and calling her dirty names, pulling her hair until she cries.

I separate them, drag the boy over to a cracked cement wall and lecture him about how girls are the nicest things on God's earth, and that if he can't be nice to them, then he's obviously a worthless punk who deserves to have his ass kicked. And I'm sure he doesn't want his ass kicked.

"Ah, fuck you, *señora*," he says.

I shove him against the wall hard enough to loosen bits of

stucco, and twist his arm way up behind him, hunger-gnawed tendons stretched to bowstring tautness. This is no test of championship skills. It's not hard to outmuscle an emaciated thirteen-year-old, for crap's sake. It's not hard to make him hurt.

"It's *señor*ita," I say. "And don't talk to me that way."

"Why? What'd you ever do for me, you fuckin—"

I give him another demonstration of my skills.

"*¡Ayy! ¡Mujer challashca!*"

"What did you say?"

"Nothing." That was Quichua, the language of the mountain people. I let him have some of his arm back. Flakes of chipped white plaster cling to his shoulders like cement dandruff. He shakes them out.

"And I could call you *chipa huahua*, too," I say, also in Quichua, "but I'd rather use your name. What is it?"

He's about to give his usual answer, so I tighten my grip, and he reconsiders.

"Mishojos," he says.

"Mishojos?" Cat's eyes. "That's a *serrano* name."

"Yeah. My family came to the city to find work. But there's no work, no land, no food. So we ended up here, majorly fucked."

A common story.

"So no *huasipichana*, eh?"

He looks at me. "*¿Eres de mi tierra?*"

"*Claro que sí.*"

"*¿Y qué quieres de mí?*"

Well, we're getting somewhere. I ask him.

"I don't know any kids in gangs," he says.

"Oh, come on. You live around here, right? You've got to know who's in the gangs. That's the reason gangs exist, for God's sake, for everyone to know who you are. Now tell me."

The gang's home base is sinking into the water so badly, one corner is flooded. One of them is pissing out the door right into the estuary.

Hemingway once said that hunger sharpens the senses. But a lifetime of hunger has dulled the swamp boys' senses and drained their sunken eyes of the ability to see anything beyond how to scam their next meal.

But they have the strength to laugh and whistle. The piss-warm rain has picked up, causing my clothes to cling to me most revealingly at this inopportune moment.

"*Ya viene la buena moza.*"

A fifteen-year-old is calling me a hot babe. He must be the leader.

"And what's your name?" I ask, stepping forward. Water comes gushing up through the floor where I put my feet.

"Venenito, sweetie, you want a taste?" he says. More clucks. Time to cut through this.

I pull out the dull kitchen knife.

They laugh at it.

I announce: "I come from *padre* Samuel's past."

Their bodies freeze, as if I were a green ghost risen up out of the scummy swamp seeking vengeance on their flesh. They have a lot to learn about hiding their emotions.

Venenito pulls a knife on me. A cheap stiletto, but dangerous enough at this range. He hesitates, then takes a step towards me. Right. I lunge forward, grab his knife hand, sweep my knife up and whack him across the face with the flat edge as hard as I can. Then I chop at his hand with the dull edge one-two-three times until he loses his knife, and I push him through the cane wall into the water.

One advantage of this tribal subculture: When you beat their leader, the whole army surrenders.

I push the blade back into his stiletto while the other boys give him a hand up out of the water.

"Not bad," I say, handing him back his knife. "Most men would have dropped this on the first whack."

He takes it as a compliment.

"Where'd you learn to fight like that?" he says, looking me up and down as if to verify his initial impression, that I am indeed a woman.

"A long way from here."

They nod as if I have given them a meaningful answer.

"You kids threatened the *padre*," I say.

I let that sink in.

Then: "And I want you to tell me who paid you to do it."

Venenito starts to say "Eat shit" but thinks better of it and changes it to, "Eat cement. We're men of honor."

Glad to see he's got his self-esteem back.

"You were paid to threaten a man's life."

Venenito dismisses that: "If we cared about people's feelings, what would we eat?"

"And what do you think the guys you're protecting would do? Same thing, right? They'd sell you out in a minute. But not *padre* Samuel. Because he was a tough guy. He wasn't scared of anybody. *They* were scared of *him*."

They're thinking about it. Wondering what my payoff's going to be. Okay, here it is. I lean forward.

"And you know something? They're scared of me, too." My eyes burn with the flaming sword of hatred. "So what's it going to be?"

They confer. They want to know what's in it for them. I look around at their shack, currently missing part of a wall.

"Name it," I say.

Their price: A case of beer.

Just add "contributing to the delinquency of minors" to my growing list of crimes.

They think it was city cops. But they're just a bunch of booger-eating street kids living off the refuse excreted by this foul-smelling slum. They know a lot about surviving in this marshy wasteland, but not much about who pulls the strings in the endless corridors of the forbidding labyrinths of power in this country.

"What did these guys look like?"

They all talk at once:

"Just two guys."

"Plain."

"Ordinary."

"T-shirts."

"One of them had a Chicago Bulls hat."

"They had money."

"How much money?" I ask.

"Ten thousand sucres," says Venenito.

"Ten thousand sucres for eight of you?" That's twenty-five cents apiece. The little bastards.

"Each time."

"How many times were there?"

"Just two."

"Three."

"Well, which is it?" I ask.

"Three," a kid says. "You weren't there for that—"

Venenito jumps on him. "Why you little pussy, I'll fucking kill you—!"

"*Knock it off,*" I say, pulling them off each other. "You saw these guys *three times* and you can't tell me what they looked like?"

They describe two guys who could be half the men in Ecuador. They could be working for *anybody*.

I warn them not to cross me.

And I go.

Sure, I can still outmaneuver a bunch of weak, underfed street kids, but I can't go up against the cops and the city and the province, and everybody else in the whole *santo país* who commands a small army of hardened killers, all by myself. I'm going to need help.

Serious help.

CHAPTER
FIVE

¿En qué otro país del mundo hay una provincia
llamada Matanzas?

What other country on earth has a province called
Massacres?

—Guillermo Cabrera Infante
(on Cuba)

o you used to be a cop, huh?"

"Is it that obvious?"

"How else would you be able to talk your way past that pit bull
of a head nurse, on a Sunday?"

"It's a decent hospital," I say. "It's clean, adequately supplied
and staffed. But the military's are better."

"Fuck you, Miss Filomena," says Carlos, smiling.

"Hey, you're the one getting three days of bed rest for a superficial shoulder wound, what the hell are you complaining about?"

"Because if you'd've let me bleed a little longer, they'd be letting
me stay here another week," he bitches.

"You want me to let them shoot you somewhere else next time?"

"I'd appreciate that," he says, closing out this round of cynical
cop humor.

"Anyway, thanks again for helping me out of that jam," I say,
trying not to notice the shifting contours beneath his thin sheets.
"That psycho captain was about to put me away for stealing the
federal gold reserves."

"Too bad somebody already beat you to it. Maybe we should
put out an APB on that Francisco Pizarro guy. Bastard ripped the
whole country off."

"You're a funny guy, Carlos. Not like the other day."

"Wait till I recover, then I'll show you a trick or two, once my blood starts flowing again."

"It looks like your blood is flowing just fine to me."

His eyes brighten, and he strokes his mustache so the bristles stick up.

"Speaking of blood—" he starts to say.

"Not to kill the mood or anything, but a man I know was murdered last night, and I'd like to find out who's handling the autopsy, and where it's being done."

His face darkens. "That's too bad. Where'd it happen?"

"La Chala."

"La Chala? And who took custody of the body?"

"I don't know. The provincial police were mopping up by the time I got there."

"¿Los provinciales? Not the city cops?"

"Is that so unusual?"

His lower lip juts out in the bandaged man's equivalent of a shrug. "I could see it if a floater washed up from their side of the estuary, but they've got enough customers of their own to deal with without having to come trawling for business on our shores, if you know what I mean."

"Yeah, it seemed like a special arrangement of some kind."

"Who's the victim?"

"Father Samuel Campos."

The title clarifies the corpse's significance. Carlos registers that it's not just another nameless loser.

"Doesn't mean anything to me, but I'll try to find out for you."

"Thanks. I really appreciate it."

"Who was he?"

"I heard the city may have wanted the land he developed. Would city cops get involved in that?"

"Sure, and a million other people, too."

"How would I go about confirming that? Who would I ask?"

"I guess you could go to the Department of Urbanization and Land Management. But I've got to warn you—"

"What?"

"You better bring a book."

With glazed eyes and a spiny beard smelling of something plucked from the sea, the street vendor shoves an oily cardboard box in front of me.

"Look, lady. Carriage bolts. A whole box of them. Aren't they beautiful?"

"Thanks, but I'm not interested," I say, making my way towards the tilting spires of Nuestra Señora de la Esperanza, Our Lady of Hope of Balzar. I'm a shorts-and-tank-top-clad tourist with a wide straw hat and sunglasses, although the sun has already set and the sky is glowing with purple magic.

The six o'clock knee drills are just letting out, and *padre* León has a few minutes for me. With his robes on, the priest's thin body looks like a withered sackful of years with white hair and marbled skin.

"What can I do for you?" he asks, eyeing this far-flung tourist curiously.

I take off the sunglasses and tell him who I am.

"Ah, yes. Father Samuel spoke of you many times. We are all very sad to hear about his passing."

"He was murdered, Father. And I think the North Guayas Militia is involved in it."

"You're not going to try to confront them, are you? That's insane."

"No, I'm not going to interrogate them. I just want to look at their faces. And that's one thing I can do that no other investigator can do, especially looking like this."

"Father Samuel said you were always the one looking for trouble."

"I need to see a copy of the report you guys wrote."

Padre León dwells on the wording of my request, then opens the lower desk drawer and fishes out a six-by-eight-inch booklet with a red cardboard cover crudely stapled to it. This is the earth-shaking document that everyone's so afraid of?

The text is more or less what I expected it to be, a measured but spirited condemnation of the misplaced priorities and insults to human dignity inflicted by the Pajizo government, often in rhythmic sequences and word arrangements that I recall from *padre* Samuel's own sermons. I can almost hear his voice echoing through some of the passages, bringing a smile to my lips and salty wetness to my eyes, which I wipe away before it falls. The last page is the most interesting, with its concluding paragraph, and below that an alphabetical list of the twelve authors. *Padre* Campos is near the top, along with *padre* Aguirre of La Merced, Archbishop Carnero of Macas, Archbishop Duarte of Riobamba, Archbishop Lorca of Cuenca, *padre* Malta of Latacunga—it goes on.

"You've practically given them an enemies list," I say.

"Killing off individual enemies is just a distraction from their real goal—taking back the political power they lost many years ago."

"But anybody on this list could be next."

"Their list of so-called enemies includes many targets besides us. Is there anything else you wish to know?"

"Sure. When's the next bus to La Trampa?"

There's a stop in Hacha, then a few hot, wet miles more to La Trampa. Two riverfront towns called Hatchet and The Trap. Kind of makes you wonder what things were like around here back in the old days.

Our bloody history is revealed in the names we have given to the places where the landscape has been scored by a ferocious river of human brutality. The invading Incas named the Cuenca basin *Tumibamba*, Knife Valley, which tells you something about how they dealt with the Cañaris they found living there. Then they headed north to fight the Caranguis in the shadow of Mount Cotocachi, and slaughtered so many in the deep marshes around its base that the place became known as *Yawarcocha*. Blood Lake.

Then the *conquistadores* came along and showed everyone how to *really* get the job done, wading deeper into Blood Lake.

And now we're up to our asses in it.

In the gathering darkness outside my dirty window, the thick, moist foliage begins to dissolve into unknowable and fantastically shifting shades and shapes. The heat draws damp worms of perspiration on my skimpy outfit, but my fingertips are morbidly coolish with trepidation. I'll admit to some fear, since I don't even know the players in the game I'm leaping into.

This is not *Colonel Mostaza* did it in the *biblioteca* with the *cuchillo*. There is not a limited set of suspects, and besides, every Ecuadorian knows that the person who actually may have pulled the trigger was just doing what someone else wanted done. And the Someone Elses in my life experience may be untouchable, but their influence is threaded through the countryside in ways that can be quite visible and also more approachable, if you're wearing the right hat. And the right hat for me is the wide sun-worshipping hat of the horizontal tourist.

I need to prep myself for what's likely to come.

The forest yawns wide, opening up to a relatively well-lit square of single-story cinder-block houses whose owners have clearly opted to put their money into electricity instead of running water. The eerie glow of big screen televisions flickers in and out through the open windows, but all they've got in back is a plastic bucket of filthy water and a hole in the ground.

I am drawn to the bright lights of a general store run by a woman in black who's sitting behind a metal railing designed to keep everything out of reach. She's crocheting what looks like a shroud for a geranium pot. She measures me with a well-trained eye and figures I'm good for one lousy diet soda, so when I start stuffing myself with her homemade bread and cheese she changes her mind and decides to take an interest.

"Not much to do around here after dark," she says, scanning me from the ground up.

"Really? That's not what I heard."

"People hear all kinds of things. Depends on who's doing the talking."

I'm busy licking up cheese crumbs from my cupped hands.

"You want the other side of town, don't you?" she says.

"Maybe."

"Then you're on your own, honey."

"Why? What's to see there?"

"The end of the world, *chica*. No laws, no friends, no future."

"So vote for a new future."

"Don't joke with me. Politicians are all the same. They come and fill their pockets, then they turn their butts around and take off, and nothing ever really changes."

I notice that the top of the metal railing has been stripped of paint by the coins of a thousand customers.

"What do I owe you?"

"Five thousand sucres and an explanation."

I leave her with plenty of cash and the feeling of having been short-changed.

I'm strolling past the barred windows of ordinary people working on minor domestic crises, which seem to ripple out and interfere with the concentric rings of the ever larger crises in which I am entangled, and suddenly I find myself on a dark street where two men in army fatigues are passing broken TVs and plastic serving trays through the window of a gutted house with bullet holes in the cinder blocks.

Crap Crap Crap Cr—

I turn and find a shadow to soak up my silhouette, then I backtrack, pacing evenly and steadily to the corner, and trot up the block to the next dirt street, passing darkened windows and a silence I can feel deep in my reptilian brain. I finally arrive in what was once the center of town, and their territory is plainly marked. The square is glowing with the lights from several bars and whorehouses where I'm sure you can find a few revelers at almost any time. I hope all that bread and cheese helps. I'm going to have to stomach several strong drinks with these maniacs. It's the only way, the latest variation on a very old grift.

I don't know which way this whirligig is going to spin, so I'll have to listen closely and get them to talk and talk, and maybe something will slip out. It usually does. I'm certainly not going to go in there and ask them, "Gee, mister, are you paramilitary guys systematically murdering members of the leftist opposition?" But something a bit more subtle might work. This unit is small enough that a randomly selected corporal or sergeant might actually know something useful, and the right amount of lightnin' oughta get their tongues a-flappin' like a catfish in a tub of bacon grease, yee-ha.

I pick one of the noisier places, so my entrance doesn't exactly stop the beat in its tracks, but within ninety seconds a couple of guys with stripes on their arms have elbowed the grunts away from the barstools on either side of me and have occupied them with such authority you'd think they've been there since the first cornerstone was laid twenty years ago.

"Buy you a drink?" says the sergeant to my right. Not very original, but you've got to start somewhere. His name tag says Musgoso.

"Sure." Order something weak, with lots of ice. "I'll have a mimosa."

"A what?"

"Orange juice and Champagne on the rocks."

The bartender shrugs like he's never heard of either ingredient, and walks away.

"Who's the severe-looking guy on the thousand-sucre note?" I ask, defacing my Spanish with a slightly nasal American accent.

"That's Rumiñahui," answers Sergeant Musgoso, tapping a few liquor-dampened bills.

"Good old Stone-face," says Corporal Polillo, the one to my left.

"He was the last of our Inca warriors. He burned Quito to the ground rather than surrender it to the Spanish invaders," Musgoso tells me proudly.

"Wow, that is so-o-o cool. American money is so boring, you know? You have to look at the numbers to tell the bills apart."

Sergeant Musgoso swigs the last of his beer and wipes his wiry black mustache with the back of his hand.

"The *quiteños* say that Rumiñahui took off and headed into the mountains east of the ruined capital with the last of the empire's gold." He pauses to make sure that I'm listening. "Then the *conquistadores* hunted him down and tortured him like a runaway slave, like a captured animal. They ended up killing him, but he never revealed where the treasure was hidden, and no trace of it has ever been found."

I whistle at the possibilities. "Any gold buried around here?"

"Sure, honey, I know where there's gold," says Corporal Polillo, but the sergeant brushes him back.

The bartender slops a drink in front of me that tastes like bad whiskey and orange soda. I tell him, "I'm going to need more ice."

He looks at me like I've got a hell of a nerve asking him for such a hard-to-find item, but Sergeant Musgoso lays it out for him, "The lady said she needs more ice."

Musgoso continues: "No, they sunk the gold."

"Damn mountain Indians—" says Corporal Polillo.

"And the crazy Spaniards spent years dredging those icy lagoons looking for the gold and silver that the Cañaris sacrificed to the watery depths by the bargeload. Never found a nickel. Pretty screwed-up story, huh?"

"I'll say." And the Cañaris have been wearing black for five centuries in mourning for their lost freedom.

"So what are you doing around here?" asks the corporal. "I mean, there's not a lot of tourist attractions in the area."

"No way. I worship the sun. Can't get enough of it after a winter in New York City."

"New York City? You really live there?" asks the corporal.

"Yeah, sure."

"Which part?"

"Corona."

"No kidding! My cousin Terencio lives in Corona. You know him?"

"Maybe. What's his name?"

"I just said—Terencio."

"She can't tell you without a last name," says Sergeant Musgoso. "Corona's a little bigger than La Trampa, Corporal Polillo."

"Still, there must be *somewhere* worth taking a girl around here," I say.

"How about the steam baths?" suggests the sergeant, and the corporal smiles and nods in agreement.

"What's so special about a bunch of steam baths?" I ask, jaded and unimpressed.

"These are volcanic steam baths," says the sergeant.

"They'll cure your rheumatism right up," says the corporal, using this joke as an excuse to lay his rough hands on my knees. I hope I'm not certifying my own death warrant here.

"I'd love to go, but is it safe?" I say, staying in character.

"What do you mean, safe?" asks the corporal.

"Well, I heard the roads can be dangerous. Wasn't some couple killed around here just last week?" I'm an innocent, wide-eyed tourist.

The sergeant laughs. "Oh, you're safe with us. We control these roads. Nothing happens while we're on watch."

Then who was on watch last Wednesday when Gustavo Paz and Sonia Segovia were ambushed and killed?

"Don't worry, you'll be completely safe with us," the corporal reassures me, and they each toss down some soggy bills and grab a bottle for the road.

A second hapless corporal tries to climb into the idling jeep with us, but Polillo slams the door on him, saying, *"Atrasado, cuy asado,"* which means something like, You're late, you roast guinea pig.

"That guy's one ball short of being a bull," says Musgoso, continuing the farm animal motif.

So now I'm wedged between two unshaven mercenaries taking a long ride through the dark nowhere of night.

"See? Perfectly safe," says Musgoso, taking a swig and recapping his bottle.

"Yes, it's so safe," I say. "Do you have to patrol all the roads at night?"

"It's not that hard."

"Yeah, since there are only three roads," says Polillo, twisting the cap off his bottle. He takes a big wet gulp using lots of tongue on the bottleneck, then he offers me some. I turn it down this time.

"But what if someone ambushed you like they did to that couple. Oh my God, wouldn't you be scared?"

"Scared?" scoffs Musgoso. "We are *men*."

"Nobody ambushes *us*," says Polillo. "We—" He stops himself.

"Well, I just feel so protected," I coo. "What's the role of women in your group?"

"To lie there and be women," says Polillo, clucking at the thought of women having a "role."

Musgoso offers me a hit from his bottle. I guess I have to take a few of these at some point. I take a small sip and hand it back.

"So where are we going?"

"You'll see."

That's not a reassuring answer. We're covering enough distance to be into the next province by now, which means their area of operations could be more extensive than I've read about in the papers. But after a tense stretch of time, we pass a decaying sign reading Baños: 5 km, and I breathe a little easier knowing that there really are volcanic steam baths in the area.

Yes indeed, nothing like a little geological instability to put your mind at ease. It's all relative.

Although you've got to ask yourself what led the Ecuadorians to build the gay little town of Quito on the eastern slope of an active volcano, but there it is. During the early days, the royal capital was hit by a deadly plague of scarlet fever, then the towering Guagua Pichincha volcano began to shake the steep walls of the valley and rattle the rafters of the terrorized city. They thought it was the end of the world. But a tough broad named Santa Mariana de Jesús fasted and tormented her flesh and whipped herself until the crimson glistened on her cat-o'-nine-tails to save the city, and that holy martyr predicted that Ecuador would never collapse as a result of any natural disaster but would self-destruct from bad government.

And a hundred years later, when a European expedition came to survey the equator, they were astounded to see the *quiteños* merrily dancing on top of an active volcano. Sort of an encapsulation of my whole experience. I haven't stood on solid ground since I got here.

We pull in to a dark semicircle of cinder-block huts with shapes so undifferentiated they could still easily transform into a secret place of torture, and it's not until we climb out of the jeep and stagger inside, where we are greeted by a caretaker who gives us towels and fresh branches of eucalyptus, that I begin to allow myself to think that I might actually pull this off and get out of here in one piece.

Let the liquor flow, and the tongues loosen.

Steam rooms are commonly separated by sex, but the commandos dispense with that formality, eagerly stripping down to their boxer shorts and warming fresh-cut boughs of eucalyptus over the wooden grate where the volanic steam billows up, and rubbing themselves with the oily leaves. No one's covering themselves with towels. I peel my top off, keep my bra on, and refuse hard alcohol until they get me a bottle of mineral water to replace the sweat my body's losing.

"*¡Portero, una Güitig! ¡Rápido!*" shouts the sergeant, clearly used to giving orders.

In a moment, the hand of an unseen attendant dangles a bottle in the mist. It's warm, but it's liquid. Still, the tourist in me has to complain, "Don't you guys have a fridge or something?" The battle-hardened veterans scoff at my spoiled feminine American ways, eating me with their eyes as I eagerly swallow the carbonated water. Then I have to take a shot of firewater to placate the boys. Then another. I better watch myself.

"I gotta go pee," I tell them, figuring five minutes away from them is five minutes less time I'll have to spend fending them off.

"Yeah, time to go change the canary's water," says Musgoso, rising unsteadily from the wooden bench.

I let him lead me out into the night air, which is a cool 89 degrees. He stops at the piss-befouled portal of the first hut, and points me two doors down. Giggling, I salute him, my arm as loose as a rag doll's, and wander towards the next hut. I glance inside. A cot and a nightstand made out of hand-cut cane. I look back and confirm that he's out of sight. Then I skip the latrine and feel my way to the next hut, which seems to be full of fishing equipment, then the next one, stumbling into a room stacked with bundles of identical documents, hot off the press, it appears. It's too dark to tell, but they look like the voter petition forms needed to register candidates for elections.

"Can't wipe your ass with those," says Sergeant Musgoso, a dark shape blocking the doorway.

"Oh." I stumble into his arms, pretending to be way more drunk than I am. "S-sorry, I thought you pointed over here."

"No," he says, helping me to the women's privy. "Use this one."

It's a cement slab with a hole chiseled in the middle.

"I can't go with you watching me," I say, cute as a kewpie doll.

He turns his back like a true gentleman, giving me fifteen seconds to plan my next move. Time to turn the amps up to eleven.

I come out of there having lost the ability to walk back to the steam room without the help of a big, strong man.

"Man, by the time you build the birdcage, the bird will be dead," Corporal Polillo complains, seeing us.

"Let's cool off in the pool," Musgoso suggests.

"Yeah, a pool," I say. "Totally."

He issues another harsh command, and the harried caretaker rushes to turn on the lights in a nearby bungalow that's big enough to hold a shallow cement pond. I willingly strip down to my underwear for this one, and slip into the grimy water.

"Eew. When was the last time this was cleaned out?"

"Have another drink and you won't care," says the corporal, dizzily. I oblige. "Take a bigger one," he insists.

"What do you think I am, a two-hundred-pound macho man?" I say. "Women have a much lower body density. The question is, which one of *you* can take the biggest drink?"

Down goes the gauntlet, an irresistible challenge for them to prove their masculinity to me. Or their stupidity.

Same thing.

They smile rakishly and eye each other with the sudden thrill of rivalry. Then they both present the glowing bottles in their hands as if they were saluting the flag, and I stand up, dripping wet, as motivation, and raise my arms, hold them up for a moment just to increase the giddy tension, then drop them, shouting, "Go!"

Both men start chugging down one, two, three-shot swallows, when the last one gurgles back out of the corporal's mouth and he coughs, then puts the bottle back to his booze-drenched lips, but the sergeant stops and declares, "No, no, I win."

"No fair, I started coughing."

And they start arguing like two kids until I tell them the only fair thing is to do it over. Ready. Set. Go!

And they're off, gulping down a full third of a bottle before the corporal's eyeballs start swimming and he spits out his last mouthful into the pool, gasping for breath.

"Ha-ha!" bellows the sergeant, triumphant.

It's a little victory for me, too. Even for guys this big, that ought to be too much liquor for their own good.

"So, doesn't the winner get a prize?" the sergeant says, quoting from the Book of Clichés.

I nod flirtatiously, wade over and snuggle up against him. He's got a bulge in his boxers that would frighten the fish away on a sunny day.

"I'm staying at the Hotel Continental in Guayaquil," I purr. "Do you guys ever get into the city?"

"Oh, yeah, sometimes," he says.

"For business or pleasure?"

"Both," he says, chuckling happily, while the corporal keeps on coughing to clear his throat.

"I can see that you're a real *montuvio*. You must be just as good in a canoe."

"Oh, I am, baby, I am." He gives me that serpentine smile.

"I mean as a fighter."

"Oh, we're good on the water, too, *señorita*. *Somos hombres de esta tierra,* we know our way around every back stream in the gulf."

"I bet you do."

"Swallow too much water, Corporal?" says a fortyish man coming out of nowhere and strutting along the edge of the pool in a pair of knee-length camouflage swimming trunks.

"Yes, sir, Major," says the corporal, still hocking up boogers. The sergeant straightens up and salutes.

"At ease, men," says the major, lowering himself into the water.

"Thank you, sir."

This is both a blessing and a burden. The major's presence should help me extract myself from this tangled web, but I'm probably not to get anything else out of the men now, either.

"Looks like quite a party," he says.

"I was just leaving," I say.

"So soon?" asks the sergeant, crestfallen.

"Yes, I've got tickets for a three-day cruise that sails tomorrow morning, and if I'm not there I don't get my money back. You understand. But give me your name and number, and I'll call you as soon as I get back, or you can look me up the next time you're in Guayaquil," I promise him.

"Okay," says Musgoso, drawing it out into about five syllables. He grabs his pants, rummages through the pockets, and scribbles something on the back of a dog-eared military document. "Because tomorrow, if I've seen you before, I don't remember it."

I climb out of the water, swinging my rear for them, and start toweling the slime off my body.

"Gotta go wring these out," I say, picking up my shorts and top and heading for the safety of the changing room.

I close the partition, remove my bra and try to squeeze as much moisture as I can from it. It's barely worth the effort.

"How are you doing, sir?" I hear the sergeant say.

"I've got blood in my veins and jizz in my balls," answers the major, and the men laugh dutifully.

"More than I can say for that bastard—"

Someone shushes the corporal.

I'm wringing the water from my panties, cursing under my breath. Just when they were ready to open up to me.

"It's those fucking newspaper reporters," says the sergeant.

"Yeah. Someone should cut them open and pull their tongues out," says the corporal.

"Quiet."

"What? Everyone's got their own way of killing fleas," says the corporal, quite drunk.

"Fleas and other animals," says the sergeant.

"Like a great big lion," says the corporal.

"He won't be much of a *león* after we castrate him," says the sergeant.

I'm pulling my shorts on, zipping them up, my ears burning.

"He's still wagging his tail, boys," says the major.

"Sure he is. But one nail knocks out another, eh?" says the sergeant. "*Hay más de una manera de transformar los campos en camposantos.*"

There's more than one way to turn fields into graveyards. But he used the same root word: Campos.

I step out from behind the partition, fully dressed and smiling sweetly for my appreciative audience. The major gallantly orders the caretaker to drive me to Balzar, where I can get a bus to the city. The sergeant tries to convince me to spend some downtime on the cot with him, but I give him an excuse that never fails with his kind.

Why does telling them it's your period always work with these creeps? What's so scary about getting a little woman-blood on their dicks? God knows they've spilled enough of it themselves. But I better get out of here before he realizes I was sitting in the pool the whole time without any pad protection at all.

These are the costliest scraps of information I've gotten, as far as my stomach and liver are concerned, but at least I got a piece of what I was after: They admitted that they control the roads, including partial credit for the ambushes, they claimed familiarity with the system of estuaries down to the city limits, they are very likely involved in printing fake documents, and they made credible threats against newspaper reporters, with oblique references to harming *padre* León. I'd better warn him, first thing tomorrow.

Now I get to slowly sober up during the bleary ride home, staring into the unfathomable darkness and thinking there's worse things than psychos in these woods.

Namely, psychos with power.

But I also come away convinced that they're not the full answer. You'd send your sharpest minds to blot out the name of *padre* Samuel, not the kind of apes who would tap-dance on a man's skull till they heard it crack, like this hard-partying bunch of part-time rapists and full-time assholes. Whoever did this evil thing were skilled assassins, near the upper echelons of this or any of the other organizations that practice killing as a form of crowd control, like the national riot police or the School of the Americas–trained operatives from the Asociación de Seguridad Nacional. I'm going to have to—

A nightmarish vision materializes in the middle of the dark forest, an offensive line of uniformed men signaling for the driver to stop. Five of them board the bus, yank three people out of their seats and accuse them of aiding the leftist rebels who just bombed an electrical tower thirty miles east of here. The three lost souls are taken off the bus and into the waiting arms of the night, while a couple of heavily armed men pace up and down the aisle, scrutinizing our faces. I don't see any official insignias on their arms.

One of them turns towards me, and I become a crumpled scrap of human flesh, clutching the sergeant's note tightly to my pounding chest, hoping that my future doesn't come out of the muzzle of a gun.

Were it left to me to decide whether we should have a government without newspapers, or newspapers without a government, I should not hesitate a moment to prefer the latter.

—Thomas Jefferson

Where are the others?" shouts the man in the green uniform.

Slam! A hard crack on my cheekbone, which must look like a burnt ham by now.

"There are no others," I croak. I plead.

The dragon's teeth sink into my guts, spearing my right kidney like a bolt of lightning.

"Where are the others?"

No. Not the spike.

No more, no more; recoil, cringe. No no no naaa*aaah!*

Slam!

My eyes fly open. I jump awake, ready to get hurt some more.

Uncle Lucho is searching for some lightbulbs in the darkened storeroom, loudly demanding, "Where are the others?"

Holy Mary, mother of God. Phantom pains slowly fade. But they were so real.

Yesterday is catching up with me. It was a very long day and I was so toasted I zonked out on that bus and—and—and for a moment I'm really not sure if it was all real, or if I dreamed a part of what happened. But it happened, didn't it? One thing's for sure, I'm staying off buses for a while.

I soap up, shower off in a pitcher of cold water, then stumble down to breakfast.

And back to reality, where there's still a gas shortage and it's going to take about forty-five minutes to get a fire going, boil a pot of water, grind the beans, and make coffee. Uggh. I cough up some ugly stuff and spit it out in the dry toilet, feeling suddenly old and vile myself.

I lean against some empty banana crates and listen to the soothing patter of the rain, while gently massaging my sides till the needles in my kidneys dull. Aunt Yolita is in command mode, directing the men shlepping the fifty-five-gallon-drum barbecue to a dry spot under the eaves of the terrace so she can cook with wood, a hard commodity to come by in a town where there's no such thing as scrap. At least we've got plenty of packing crates.

"Just like in the country," she says, ever a source of light and hope. "Remember?"

"Yeah, I remember."

Antonia's waiting to use a pot so she and her cousin Priscilla can boil the milk and make some instant pudding in five minutes. Kids today! In my day, instant pudding took *ten* minutes. But we still have to boil the milk.

She tells me they went to the movies last night. Not downtown, with its first-run movies and orderly lines, but in this beat-up neighborhood, where the cashier opens up her iron-barred window, everybody piles up in front of it like wild-eyed refugees trying to withdraw their money from a failing bank before enemy tanks overrun the city, and whoever jumps on top of the others and stuffs his money in the cashier's face first gets the tickets. The picture was so old, Stallone got beaten up by the lead actor.

"You done with the paper yet?" I ask.

"There's no more paper," says Uncle Lucho, wrapping some plantain flour with one of the last scraps of newsprint from what was once a big pile.

"You used up *all* the newspapers?"

"The plastic bags haven't come in yet. Rain delay."

"Even the ones I separated?"

"I don't know. Check the desk."

I go over to the desktop and find it as bare as a bone. *Damn it.* That's what I get for acting as if I were on the job. This amateur detective nonsense is for the birds.

The biggest newsstand is four blocks away, in front of the Civic Center. I trot maybe fifty yards through the rain before the blood starts pounding in my cranium like a squad of marines hammering tent stakes into New Hampshire granite, so I slow to a fast walk and get thoroughly soaked while passing a huge modern apartment building *without* a second-floor balcony for protection from the elements. There's progress for you.

I hand over enough money for the five biggest newspapers in town and walk off with my arms stuffed with soggy misinformation.

Back home to *huevos rancheros* with rice and coffee, coffee, coffee. Filomena's brain shifts towards the rational.

I said "towards."

The two papers from Quito, *Amanecer* and *El Negociante*, don't even report the murder. I guess they have enough crime in the capital not to care about what happens in a swamp four hundred twisted kilometers down the road. And the hometown papers don't do it much justice either. *El Mundo* buries a one-inch item in the police briefs—priest killed in a robbery, a suspect has been arrested. They don't even give his name. *El Despacho* has the only real story, a curious mixture of fact and fantasy:

> The Criminal Unit of the Municipal Police reports finding the body of *padre* Samuel Campos, at approximately 12:30 A.M. Sunday morning on the second floor of his parish house. The cook has been arrested, and is being charged with attempting to remove evidence from the crime scene, including a large kitchen knife believed to be the murder weapon, and with stealing valuable religious artifacts from the victim, which were found in the suspect's possession. Police photographed and videotaped the crime scene in order to preserve evidence that might otherwise be quickly lost, and to quell the speculation about a political motivation for the crime.

Cook? Large kitchen knife? Valuable artifacts? He tried to remove evidence from the scene when he was surrounded by all that swamp? And the first thing he does is run out screaming to attract attention?

I've got to speak to Ismaél before I can believe any of this. But first I have to find out where he is being held.

I have to bang the buttons a few times to get a dial tone, then I call the hospital and find out that my friend Carlos has been sent home from the repair shop. Of course they don't have his home number, so I have to get up the nerve to call his precinct, which feels very much like sticking my arm into a wood chipper. But getting shot in the line of duty puts a shining halo around a guy that dims whatever else is going on around him, and five miraculous minutes later I've got my man Carlos on the line.

"Oh, hey, Miss F. Staying out of trouble?"

"I'm trying. And you?"

"Recovering. Slowly."

"Yeah, it takes a long time. Anything new?"

"Sure. I found what you wanted—that guy Campos's body is in the coroner's lab right where it's supposed to be."

"Good work, Carlito. And—?"

"And I'll let you know anything else as soon as I hear about it, okay?"

"That's great. Thanks for doing me such a big favor."

"Uh-huh. I'm all sweetness."

"So listen, I also want to find out where they're holding the suspect."

"Man, what's up with you? We have a bad connection or something? Or are you going to tell me why you have to know all this stuff?"

Good question, but I'm still in the trust-no-one stage.

"Because I'm worried that nobody else gives a shit."

"That's not an answer."

"I promise I'll give you a better one the next time I see you. Now could you make those calls for me, please?"

"Girl, you know I'm not supposed to be using my arm."

"So don't use your arm. Use some other appendage. Did you see this morning's *El Despacho*?"

"No, my other appendage only reads *El Globo*."

"It would. It's just that I heard that someone blew up an electrical tower last night about thirty miles northeast of here."

"Sounds like pretty big news."

"Yeah, and there's nothing about it in the papers."

We both sit there listening to the flies buzz.

"All right," he says. "I'll see what I can dig up. Check back with me in a day or so."

"Thanks, Carlos."

"And when you do, I'd rather not know anything about it than have you feed me a load of bullshit and try to tell me it's peaches and cream."

"Deal."

My eye falls back to the black words oozing across the rain-soaked newsprint lying face up on the countertop.

Why the hell are the police trying to "quell the speculation about a political motivation" for the murder when that's the most obvious angle? Got an answer for me, Carlos? No, it's never that easy, because that way lies deeper shit than either of us have ever stepped in—shit that I promised I'd warn *padre* León about. I check the directories and there's no listing for him or the church, so I call a grocery store in La Chala and ask them to go get Sister Cecilia for me. I wait, the minutes clicking away, worrying that I'll be disconnected, until she picks up and tells me that *padre* León doesn't have a phone.

"I figured that out. How do you reach him?"

"You can't. You have to call the pharmacy across the street from the church and leave a message. I've got the number right here—"

"Umm, my message is a little sensitive for that mode of communication. Can't he come to the phone himself?"

"He doesn't like phones. I guess it depends who it is, or if it's urgent."

"Well, this is pretty freaking urgent. And he'd come to the phone for you, wouldn't he?"

"I suppose so."

"So why don't you deliver it for me?"

"Hey, Filomena, quit tying up the phone," Uncle Lucho shouts.

"One more call."

I tell Sister Cecilia everything she needs to know. Then I rattle the cradle again, get an interprovincial connection and call my cousin Lucho Freire in Cuenca—you know, the insurance risk who plays around with ammonia gas.

"Filomena! A miracle as always," he says, the line fuzzy with static.

"Same here. How was your trip?"

"I made it back alive. You?"

"Just barely. Have you analyzed the pamphlet yet?"

"Yes. It's a ten percent solution of acidic invective dissolved in a ninety percent concentration of jargon-filled propaganda."

"Very funny. What else can you tell me about it?"

"Sorry, *prima*. All I can tell you is that it's a high-quality oil-based printing ink."

"On cheap-shit paper."

"Yeah, there's that. And the poor offset resolution."

"We knew that already."

"Sorry, but what do you want me to tell you? I don't think there's a lab in the country that can do the kind of work you want done."

Hmm. Maybe I should have just taken it to a print shop.

"Hello?"

"Yes, Lucho, I'm here. Why don't you just send it back to me as soon as possible?"

"Okay, I'll get it in the afternoon mail."

"And it'll arrive next July. You better send it express."

"Express? Do you know how expensive that is?"

"Yes. I'll pay you back when I come to Cuenca, I promise."

Gee, I seem to be making an awful lot of promises this morning, and right now I need to move forward with the biggest one of them all. One of the last things *padre* Samuel told me was that my old comrade Alberto was playing around town with a group called Los Cuervos Rojos. I need to see his wicked smile again, but catching that bird in the act is an after-hours gig, and I've got to knock on a lot of doors today. Besides, there's still one newspaper left on my pile.

El Globo is a scandal-saturated rag that's printed on butcher paper and uses type O-negative blood for ink. Surely they would leap at the chance to run a story about a dead priest lying in a pool of his own blood. But no—no story, no police photos, nothing— though they did have the foresight to print an unlicensed repro-duction of a 1960s *Playboy* centerfold on their front page, no doubt as a public service to those readers who happened to forget during the night that a sexually mature woman generally has two breasts, one on each side, which are best observed if some of her clothes are removed. God bless freedom of the press.

Unsatisfied, I turn back to *El Mundo*, where the story is gradually seeping out that tanks of standing water on the north side of the city are becoming a breeding ground for mosquitoes, and several dozen people have been stricken by a viral fever called dengue. In English it's also known as breakbone fever.

How encouraging.

No cooking gas, no rice, no drinkable water, and now an outbreak of breakbone fever. But I hear the plague of locusts has been put off till next year.

I try to sip my empty coffee cup for the third or fourth time, and I realize I need to push the cup aside and thumb through *El Despacho* again, slowly this time, looking for something that caught my eye before. There it is, a tiny item on page five announcing that presidential candidate Hector Gatillo, the unassuming social studies teacher, will be giving his first major press conference tomorrow morning at the Socialist Unity Party headquarters in the *ciudadela* Aguilera. Could be just the place to talk to some reporters without giving them my life story first.

But first, Alberto the Crow.

I'm scanning the music listings when three shadows fall across my newspaper. I look up. Three men stand at the counter, shoulder to shoulder, dripping with rain and blocking the light. Three dark, unfriendly faces. Well fed, sure of themselves. They're not from the *barrio*.

Suzie asks them what they want.

"We're taking a poll," says the one in the middle.

Nobody is carrying a clipboard.

"What kind of poll?" asks Suzie.

"A neighborhood poll," he answers. "Who are you going to vote for?"

"You mean for president?"

"Yeah."

Suzie shrugs it off as she reaches into the cooler for a big bottle of Pilsener, saying, "My husband tells me who to vote for."

She opens the bottle, serves out three full glasses of beer.

They almost reach for the glasses.

"And who does he want you to vote for?"

"Oh, you know, that guy you men all support."

"You must mean Segundo Canino," says the one in the middle.

"*That's* the one," says Suzie, acting as if the name has just popped into her head, even though he's been governor of the province for the past four years.

The three men smile.

"Then you won't mind putting up this poster of our *candidato*, will you?" he says, as the one on his right peels off a red-and-white campaign poster from a thick stack under his arm with a photo of Canino on it and the words ¡SEGUNDO PRESIDENTE! in eight-inch-high letters.

They pass it through the bars, and Suzie stands it behind the liquor bottles.

No, that's not good enough.

They give her some tape, and Suzie hangs the poster above the counter where the whole neighborhood can see it.

That's better.

The men smile, drain their glasses, and move on to "poll" the auto parts store across the street. Nobody pays for the beer.

"You're going to have to let me borrow that 'husband' of yours sometime," I say.

"You're welcome to him," she promises.

I'm complimenting Suzie on her performance when César returns from his morning mission and we have to help him carry in a *quintal* and a half of rice.

"Seventy-one thousand sucres," he complains. "How are we supposed to buy it at seven hundred and ten sucres a pound and sell it at three hundred and twenty sucres a pound, with government inspectors coming around seizing the inventory and fining storeowners who sell it for more?"

For once, I don't have a snappy comeback.

Suzie and César agree that they will have to keep the price posted at 320 and sell it for 710 only to people they know, and tell everyone else there's no more rice, sorry. They start measuring out the precious white grain into one-pound sacks while I go back to scanning the papers.

A small black square in the middle of the entertainment pages announces that Los Cuervos Rojos are playing at the Peña Condorito. On a Monday night? That's Guayaquil, where the party never stops.

I waste a couple of hours at the ruins in La Chala, trying to interview a bunch of terminally suspicious people who won't volunteer useful information to outsiders.

"What did you hear?"

"Nothing."

"Who told you to keep away from the crime scene?"

"Nobody."

And I can't cut through it all with leading questions like, "How loud were the gunshots?" which would only suck me into a gooey snake pit of hearsay and spurious statements. They all had their radios up too loud, apparently. Maybe I could take a canoe around to the miserable shacks behind the parish house, which are up to their knees in oily water about seventy-five yards out. But not today, I've got too much else to do.

I do an about-face and cover half a mile of gravel roads before I spot a taxi with no meter.

"How much to the *barrio* Centro Cívico?"

"Five dollars."

"Five *dollars*? Don't you take sucres?"

"The sucre ain't worth shit, honey. Take it or leave it."

He knows anyone on foot this far out is not in a position to negotiate. I take it.

It's all quiet at the Correas' store, so I manage to talk César into going to the Municipal Department of Urbanization and Land Management for me, to find out who has an interest in the former site of *padre* Samuel's parish house. He knows his way around those twisted corridors, and I'd offer him my firstborn male child in return, but the kid's already promised to someone else, and besides, I believe there's some kind of commandment against it, too.

While César's swinging the shiny steel hammer against that particular hard place, I take Antonia downtown for a special lunch of traditional Ecuadorian favorites, like *bola de verde*—yummm—that I almost never make at home because they all take forever to prepare properly, since the recipes were invented back when the women were expected to stay in the kitchen all day long cooking for the men—and that's not just a load of feminist bullshit, mister. I grew up watching barefoot women gutting chickens and grinding corn and milking goats while the men went out drinking and whoring. But the price for this extravagance is that Antonia has to sit on a bench with me eating ice cream and providing my cover for an hour while I check out who goes in and out of the offices of the Agencia de Seguridad Nacional.

I watch the faces and bodies as they come and go. There are certainly a lot of big guys with broad shoulders and Coleman lanterns where their jaws should be, but you'd expect that on a Federal police force. Not a lot of scrawny intellectual types on the job. No women either, except for the secretaries in their matching eggplant-colored uniforms. Time to modernize, guys. Someone should go in there and tell them that there is no coffee-making gene on the X chromosome. Although to be frank, I'm not really sure what I expect to see here. Maybe just a familiar-looking body type, like a couple of the bruisers who broke up the demonstration two days ago with iron bars. They couldn't have looked more like a unit if they had been marching in formation. I could get lucky and spot one. It's a city of 3 million people, but there are only so many pigs to go around.

"Yo, Mom. Refill on the ice cream?"

"Sure, honey." I give her some money. "But come right back."

"No, I'm going to wander around aimlessly for a few hours," she says.

"It's just a parental reflex," I'm explaining, when a spot of color catches the corner of my eye and I turn to see a guy in a dark green muscle shirt wearing a Chicago Bulls cap exit the building and head north with no particular urgency. It probably doesn't mean a thing. Chicago's a popular destination around here, and people send stuff home, especially American stuff. But I'm still committing his physique to memory: black hair (of course), reddish brown face with a wispy excuse for a mustache and two days of beard growth, stocky legs and an upper body like a well-oiled jelly donut. I know those terms don't always go together, but I'm trying to freeze an image here, and the guy looks like a well-oiled jelly donut, okay?

The guy's still in sight when Antonia comes back with a scoop of papaya ice cream in a paper cup.

"Come on," I say, grabbing my bag. "We're following that guy up there."

"Oh." She eyes our target skeptically. "Why him?"

"Just curiosity."

Donut Boy is ambling along so leisurely we have no trouble quickly closing the gap to twenty yards, where we hang back.

"What if he's just going to buy a lottery ticket or something?"

"Then we haven't lost anything by trying."

"Hmm." She licks some orange ice off the plastic spoon. "So when are you going to teach me something really cool like how to pick locks?"

"As soon as the law allows it."

"You mean, like, never," she says, bitterly. "You know, all the other kids get to spend their winter vacations playing hockey, building snowmen, going to Disney World, fun stuff like that. I'm learning how to shadow fat losers in Ecuador."

"Okay, but let's do a little profiling here. A guy with that kind of body shape isn't going to be walking very far."

"Somewhere with air-conditioning, I hope."

She has a point there. It is midday at the earth's midpoint, when the unforgiving ultraviolet burns right through the atmosphere and punishes everything in its path.

"Tell you what, if you can bring your grades up to a B plus in algebra, I'll show you how to pop the lock and hot-wire a car."

"*Yes.*"

Great. I should write a parenting book. But under a new law, convicted felons can't profit from the sale of books detailing their crimes.

"Well, what do you know?" I say, more to myself than to her. "Looks like Donut Boy's the civic-minded type."

"Donut Boy—?"

"Never mind. But I guess you got your wish. He just went into the local office of the Board of Elections."

"So what do we do now?"

"We go in after him."

"But he'll see us."

"Toni, I know what I'm doing. The trail ends here for now."

"Thank God," she mutters.

We go inside. My daughter groans like a surly bear. The air-conditioning is out, so they've got the lights off, which only adds to the cryptlike stillness of the place. All it needs is a few torchères and a stray skull or two kicking around under the cobwebs off in the corner to complete the effect. Donut Boy is nowhere to be seen. He must be in the back office somewhere. So either he works here or he's on familiar terms with someone who does. Okay, file this away for future reference.

"So what do we do now?" Antonia asks.

I go up to the burnished slab-of-cement counter and demand the clerk's attention.

"Yes, what do you want?" he says, clearly vexed at having to deal with a live human.

"I'm volunteering for Hector Gatillo's campaign. Could I have one of those petitions to collect signatures for him?"

"Gatillo doesn't need any more signatures. He's already on the ballot."

"What about the other people on his slate?"

The clerk grunts some kind of admission, reaches below the counter and slaps a petition down in front of me. I couldn't swear to it, but it looks very much like the ones in the bundle of documents I saw in the darkened shed in Baños.

"I'll need two forms of identification," he says.

"Wouldn't you know? I left them at the bank. Come on, honey, we'll come back later."

"That's it?" she whispers as we hit the sidewalk.

"That's it for now. Unless you want to hang around across the street until the guy comes back out."

"No freaking way."

"Fine, but just so you know, that's how it's supposed to be done."

"Sounds boring."

"It is. Now we've got one more job to do."

"I hate you. Go die."

Ah, uncensored adolescence.

We take a cab to Our Lady of La Merced.

They're trimming the candles and purifying the fonts, and a man sweeping the aisles tells us that Father Aguirre is in the rectory. We traverse the sepulchral coolness of the cobalt-and-ivory tiles to a small reception area overseen by a Sister of Mercy who instructs us to take a seat and wait our turn. A couple of urgent male voices are filtering through the worm-eaten door, but I only recognize the *padre*'s.

"—and most of them were arrested illegally," says the other voice.

"There's nothing I can do about that," says *padre* Aguirre, openly professing his impotence.

"And the clinic is a joke. The shelves have been emptied by thieves on both sides. Some of the inmates even knocked down the wall between their cells so they could sell the bricks and buy medicine for a sick comrade," says the other man, each word leaving a smoking trail of passion and outrage. "Surely you can help us start a campaign to resupply the clinic?"

"That's possible, yes."

"One young man has spent four years in jail without coming to trial for smoking a single joint."

"Well, there's not a lot of sympathy for drug offenders in this parish—"

"Thanks to pressure from the Americans."

"We have to work within the system, Jorge—"

"Wait a minute, you can't go in there—" the sister protests.

"Father Samuel Campos is dead and you're talking about the prison system?" I accuse Father Aguirre.

"At least five inmates die there every week," says the tall black man, his eyes crackling with static electricity.

"I'm sorry, Father, she just forced her way in—"

"It's all right, Sister," says the *padre*. "We're all a little upset by what has happened."

Padre Aguirre is leaning calmly against his desk. Standing across from him, all six-feet-two inches of Congressman Jorge Hernández are now focusing his intense gaze on me.

"I'm sorry about *padre* Campos," says Hernández, "but he is only one man. I'm talking about hundreds."

"So am I. A lot of lives are going to be ruined if we don't expose whoever's responsible for this."

"And you are—?" the congressman challenges me.

Father Moe steps in to referee this fracas. "This is *señorita* Filomena Buscarsela and her daughter, Antonia. She's a longtime friend of our dear departed *compañero* Father Samuel. They're visiting from the United States."

"The United States?" says Hernández, eyeing me suspiciously.

"You've heard of it?"

Sometimes humor is my best weapon. His grave expression cracks for an instant and he grins in spite of himself, then he puts his game face back on and the grin is history.

"Sure. Isn't that the place where poor kids kill each other over designer shoes and sweaters?" he says, accusingly.

"Yeah, that's the place," I admit.

"Tell me something. The poverty in Ecuador is much worse than in the U.S., yet we hardly ever see equivalent acts of depravity here. Can you explain that to me?"

I feel like a first-year law student being put on the spot by a hard-nosed professor. I muster the best answer I can under the circumstances.

"Well, the thing is, most of the poor kids around here don't really know what they're missing out on. They never see the world outside their miserable slums. But in the U.S., they see it every day—on TV, in magazines, movies—it's the *proximity* to the incredible wealth at the top of our society that makes their poverty seem so unbearable. And it's not just kids. I know people who make a couple of hundred thousand dollars a year who think *they're* poor because they spend their lives looking up the ladder at the people above them who make even *more*."

The sharp-eyed political economist leans against the bookcase and ponders this. "So what you're saying is that even some of the wealthiest Americans by our standards are actually working-class, because they must still sell their labor, however high-priced, to those above them. And so they end up being no different from pork bellies or any other product that is hoarded when the market is up and dumped when the market collapses, if it serves the needs of greater capital. This is truly fascinating."

I'll say. My congressman can't even put two sentences together. But we're talking Queens, here.

"I do have a long list of obligations this afternoon," says *padre* Aguirre. "So please tell us why you have come."

I hesistate.

"You may speak freely," he says reassuringly.

Antonia's oddly quiet. I stand there clutching her hand and tell the two respected public figures how worried I am that the North Guayas Militia may have entered a new phase of operations, launching a campaign to root out and destroy the opposition once and for all. And by opposition I mean everybody they don't like. And that's half of my friends. They listen with half an ear until I tell them about last night, and how I witnessed the seizure of three suspected rebel sympathizers.

"Rebels? There hasn't been any rebel activity in the province in years," says Hernández.

"That's what I figured," I reply.

"Can you substantiate these allegations of the militia's intent to commit mass murder?" asks *padre* Aguirre.

"No, I don't have any solid physical evidence yet, but I still wanted to warn *padre* León to be careful."

"Father León has lived safely among the wolves for years and they haven't bitten him yet," says *padre* Aguirre.

"Yes, but I'm saying there seems to be a new breed of wolf out there."

"They are creatures of habit," he says, dismissively.

"Maybe they have a new leader or something."

"I haven't heard of any major shifts in their organizational structure," says Hernández. "But it's worth looking into."

"Well, someone needs to go further up the pecking order than I did, because I can't show my face around there anymore."

I leave there feeling less than satisfied about having accomplished anything, and head for home base.

César comes back from the city offices looking like he's been to an old-fashioned exorcism, and has gained nothing from the experience.

But I've still got one more play up my sleeve, and it's time to roll those dice.

R ickety roadhouse walls bend around sweltering bodies crammed elbow-to-gut, and the air is filled with blood-warming music that makes my muscles tingle and hum. Polished guitars edged with blazing red-and-yellow neon lift up the bittersweet voices singing of the sad, sad life in the Andes, the rising notes holding me in their plaintive whorls, before uncoiling and leaving me breathless. *Pasillo* music.

A couple of waiters are dashing around, dripping with sweat, trying to deliver bottles of *aguardiente* and Coca-Cola to the tables before the customers lose their tempers and shoot them.

The overheated bodies, the smell of raw cane alcohol, the swaying pier, the smoke—for a moment the swirling waves of shapes and sounds mix in the sensory blender like the hot rushing of foul fluids spiraling down some kind of vertiginous toilet. I have to find a window and breathe some air, while Suzie starts making friends with one of the waiters. Ever since a hired killer left a mass of scar tissue in my lungs, dealing with the smoke in places like this is one of the hardest parts of any investigation.

Two stern-faced men wearing dark gray suits and ties from the original *Dragnet* are twanging away on a set of road-weary acoustic guitars, while two prematurely hardened women sing of betrayal in love in harmonies that make my soul vibrate like a fluted wineglass that's about to shatter.

After a few minutes, Suzie's new friend body-surfs through invisible eddies in the crowd towards us, holding a chair and a tiny round table over his head. He makes some room for us amid the events in an area of space so densely occupied by other masses that Einsteinian physics may be playing an unseen part here. But Suzie and I are mathematically unprepared to solve the perplexing problem of successfully mapping two posterior volumes onto the same closed-plane surface, i.e., trying to fit our butts onto the same chair. I should have paid more attention during freshman calculus.

A half-litre bottle of *aguardiente* is plunked down with an energetic *thud* on the table in front of us.

"I'm not quenching my thirst with this stuff," I tell Suzie. Part of my plan is to live through this evening.

The next act comes onstage, a trio consisting of a box-shaped woman with a veiny stone face and a lung capacity that would scatter her enemies before her like so many ants, a sallow accordianist who looks like they keep him in the beer cooler between sets, and a fat, ugly guitarist with two contrasting sets of knife scars on both sides of his face.

I was there when he got them.

They look like they've been touring lawless rubber plantations with sweaty burlesque shows since the days when the Oldsmobile Hydra-Matic transmission was a curious novelty, but their angelic voices fuse with tremendous majesty. I drink in the woeful *pasillo*, marveling at how a people so drained of blood and scarred by each passing conqueror can make such honey-sweet sounds out of our suffering.

"Man, this music is better than sex," I say.

"How would you know?" Suzie kids me, then she downs a slug of *aguardiente*. "You're not having any?"

"I had enough last night—"

"So? That was last night."

"And I need to stay sharp." I snag a waiter and deposit a ten-dollar-bill in his sweaty shirt pocket, and tell him I want to meet the guitarist.

When their set is over, my stygian guide invites me down a narrow corridor past a seemingly solid wall of liquor and beer cases and a back room where the musicians stand around smoking and chatting. I follow him through the smoky darkness, and step through a door into another world, an unstable place, its edges slippery with moss and mold. The Río Guayas is sweeping south, the far coast lost in unelectrified darkness.

Alberto is adrift in a sea of mist and smoke, his face glowing red as he breathes in the hot gases from his burning cigarette. He turns with a satyric leer that vanishes in a puff of smoke when he recognizes me, leaving a pale afterimage hovering in the air as the mist closes in.

"Hello, Alberto."

"He-e-ey, Jua—" He stops. I give him a hearty hug, and whisper my name in his ear. "Filomena!" he says. "I heard you were around."

I don't like the sound of that, but I want to keep it friendly for now.

"How do you stay in such good shape?" I ask, patting his big, round belly.

"By exercising my arms every night," he says, and illustrates by hefting a two-pound bottle of *aguardiente* to his lips for a long drink. "Ahh!"

He offers it to me.

"No, thanks. I'm staying away from the stuff."

"*¿Cómo? Ah.*" He pinches me lightly under my chin. "*¿Siempre la sacerdotisa, eh? Más católica que el papa.*" Still the Priestess, eh? More Catholic than the pope.

"Prettier, too."

"Depends which pope," he says, his right hand waffling. But under the cover of laughter, Alberto looks a little green.

So I ask him what he knows about *padre* Samuel's murder.

"No more than you do," he admits.

"I haven't told you what I know."

"You know what I mean. Don't mess with me," he says.

"Okay, okay. My big question for you is, Why now? He's been a thorn in their paws for more than thirty years. The human rights report was only the latest tweak."

"But it gave them the opportunity."

"To do what?"

"To demonstrate their current policy. You know, threaten them all, kill one."

"Well, I'm worried that there's been a change of policy. Do we still have any sympathizers among the provincial cops?"

"I'll let you know," he says.

"You don't know?"

"I'll have to ask around."

"What do you mean?"

He leans on the fragile driftwood railing, looks out at the shapeless foggy blackness.

Water flows by.

"Look, Filomena," he says. "Some people think you betrayed the movement."

"You mean, because I left it?"

"In other ways, too."

Silence.

"Well, they would be wrong."

The wet mist thickens around us.

"Some of us are still active, and some are trying to reinsert themselves into society. They even own private property," he says, turning towards me. The rotting boards bend underfoot. "But some of your old friends have found that their mercenary skills are useful. Valuable. And that working for many sides has its advantages."

There are twenty-two official political parties in Ecuador, at last count, and plenty of unofficial ones.

"So you better walk around like a fly with a hundred eyes," he says. Then: "Sorry."

A light drizzle of rain begins to wet my hair.

"In a way, Juanito betrayed us," he says. "He broke out of jail to commit a messy, personal revenge murder instead of rejoining us."

"You think of Johnny as a betrayer?"

"Not me, no. But others do."

"So what's their problem with me? He's been dead for most of my adult lifetime."

"*Has* he?"

"What the hell do you mean?"

"I don't know. I've heard rumors."

"There's *always* rumors. Some people are still waiting for Che to come back."

"Him, no. His spirit, yes."

My heart is pounding.

"And what about Johnny's spirit?" I ask.

"His spirit is out there," he says. "I have felt it."

"Where?"

"Where else? In the mountains, of course. *El altiplano*."

"In Cajas?"

Yes. Among the jagged rocks. I can get there, but I can't do it alone. Even a nutcase like me knows it's too dangerous to scale the western ridge of the Andes by yourself. The place is called Cajas, or Coffins, because so many travelers have died while trying to cross it. And I'm not about to spend a week chasing a dead fantasy around the misty crags of coffin-land, although somebody seems to want me to go looking in that direction, which is reason enough to avoid it. I've got plenty to deal with right here in Guayaquil. But I think about feeling his spirit again. If I ever wanted to conjure his ghost, I'd need someone to go with me. Someone I can trust.

Alberto nods. "We need his spirit recaptured for the movement."

The wind picks up.

"You still carrying the harp for him?"

"It's been twenty fucking years, Alberto."

"And you're being evasive."

Drizzle wets my face.

A square burst of yellow light, clattering, a voice: "Oh, *there* you are!"

It's time to go back in. The heat envelops me in its gummy flaps. People are dancing to a spicy-hot cumbia:

> "*A veces, a veces, a veces me siento así.*
> *A veces, a veces, a veces me siento así.*"

That song. I turn to Alberto. "You know this song?"

"Sure, Pancho plays it all the time on his show."

I give him a vacant look.

"Pancho La Pulga?" he says.

"Oh, him."

"You mean you don't know? You're slipping, comrade. Panchito was the first guy in the province to report the *padre*'s murder."

"He was? When was that?"

"Late Saturday night."

"What time?"

"I said late Saturday—"

"What time *exactly*?"

"Oh." His eyes close with concentration. The lines of his face tighten. You'd think he was passing a kidney stone. "Okay: It was right before our last set—so—about one-thirty."

"What time is his show?"

"Ten P.M. to two A.M. every night except Sunday on Radio Lamar," says Alberto.

"So he's on the air right now? Where is Radio Lamar?"

"Calle Ayacucho and Rumichaca, fifth floor."

"Still memorizing phone books in your spare time?"

"We give live broadcasts from their studio all the time. He's a good *compañero*."

"He's okay?"

"Uh, yeah."

"You're *sure*?"

He's sure.

"The government keeps trying to shut him down," he says.

"Okay. Let me know what you find out about our friends with the tan shirts, will you?"

"What exactly do you want to know?"

"Everything."

It's raining. But it's a relief to be out of that club.

We catch a windowless cab that's got a rusty beach chair with frayed plastic straps for a front seat. Suzie negotiates the fare while I have a coughing fit that leaves my chest burning and raw.

"Jesus, you sound terrible," she says.

I ask the driver if he can get Radio Lamar. The taxi's doors were borrowed from another car and bolted on, but it has a working radio. That's priorities. The driver changes the station for us, and a throbbing Afro-Caribbean beat rattles the tiny speakers.

The reception gets clearer and clearer as we pull up in front of the five-story poured-concrete testament to man's faith that an earthquake is not an imminent geological event but a capricious and unfathomable Act of God.

Suzie has to haggle some more with the driver. Somehow the meter got turned on and there's a discrepancy.

We duck through the rain, start up the stairs, and experience the curious effect of hearing the congas and claves *bip-bop-bam*ming from the taxi as it pulls away from the curb melding into the same stir-fried rhythm coming from the control room five flights above us. Elevator? What is this "elevator" thing you speak of, *señor*?

We're out of breath and starting to sweat by the time we reach the fifth floor. No one's there. I look around. Thousands of CDs and some old records are stacked in shelves wrapping around all four walls, leaving space only for the door we just came through, a bulletin board plastered with broadcast regulations and obscene political cartoons, a broom closet and a cinder-block window opening up near the soundproofed ceiling.

I hear a muffled flush that is not part of the music, and a mustachioed man with faded blue jeans and long graying hair tied into a ponytail under an LA Dodgers baseball cap steps out of what I must revise my description of as being the broom closet, one hand zipping up his fly.

"Do I know you?" are the first words out of his mouth. No embarrassment about the other thing.

"No, but where I come from the Dodgers are considered to be a bunch of bums."

"Excuse me a minute," says the DJ, lunging for the control panel just as the music stops. He must have had that trip to the toilet timed to the millisecond, because he arches sideways over the mixing board, flips a switch and cuts in on the air, effortlessly says his piece, an ad for Cristal, *"el whiskey de los ecuatorianos,"* slips a CD into the laser-eyed machine, then turns back to his two midnight guests.

"So you're Pancho La Pulga," says Suzie, admiringly. He eyes both of us like an ace reliever deciding what we're most likely to swing at, and whether to pitch this down the middle or straight at our heads. "My brothers listen to you all the time. It's nice to meet you."

It's nice to meet us, too.

"Why do they call you Pancho La Pulga?" I say.

"They call me a flea because I make *el presidente* Pajizo and his lapdogs itch where they can't scratch," he brags. "And to a bunch of dogs, anything they can't scratch is a flea."

I make the effort to chuckle. "You must get a lot of surprise visits."

"All the time. Some of them not as friendly as this. Excuse me—"

The phone is ringing. He answers. I hear the faint tinkle of a woman's voice.

"You got it, sister. And keep shaking your butt to Radio Lamar," says Pancho, pulling the disc. Back to us. "You were saying?"

"You take requests?"

He opens his arms to the shelves around us.

"Can you play 'A veces me siento así'?"

"Oh, that. I play that one all the time."

"Did you play it two nights ago?"

"Sure, a couple of times. Everybody wants dance music on Saturday night."

"What time did you play it?"

That gets a raised eyebrow.

"I'm trying to establish a time of death," I say flatly. "What time did you play it?"

"Oh, it was more than an hour into my show. I'd say eleven-thirty or so."

"Are you sure of that?"

" 'Course I am."

"Do you keep a log?"

"Fuck no."

"Then how can you be so sure?"

"Same way a tailor who's been in business for twenty years knows you're a thirty-eight C the minute you walk into his shop, *mi dulcita*," he says, measuring Suzie's ample playing field with an experienced eye. She almost blushes.

"And the second time?" I ask.

"Second time what?"

"When did you play the song for the second time?"

"Oh. Near the end of the show, maybe a quarter to two."

"And when did you get the news?"

"Look, what the fuck is this?" he demands.

"A friend of mine said you were the first radio station in the province to report *padre* Campos's murder, and I want to know how you found out about it. *That's* what the fuck this is."

He takes a moment to stare at me, then he crosses his arms and lets me know that's all I'm going to get out of him for now. Okay. Time for Suzie to work her half of the court.

"*Oye*, Panchito, this is very important to my cousin Filomena. Never mind about how you found out, okay? We don't care."

"Now that's what I'm talking about," he says, unable to keep his incisors from showing as she turns on her wondrous charms.

"Just tell us *when* you got the news about the bastards who killed the *padre*."

"Oh. Well, I suppose that's okay to tell you. We got the news about a quarter to one. I announced it maybe half an hour later. I remember because I stopped everything."

"Why'd you wait half an hour?" I break in.

"Hey—we like to verify stories like that."

"Good point. How'd you verify it?"

"Hey, who are you, anyway?"

"I already told you, she's my cousin Filomena," says Suzie.

"And I'd like to know if you have any idea why someone would want Samuel Campos dead."

"Sure. He was a fag," says Pancho, making a hand gesture that would be recognized in any boys' locker room in the Western hemisphere.

"Somebody killed him because he was gay? There'd be a lot more murders in this town if *that* were the case. Try again."

A lot of people in Ecuador haven't accepted the idea of homosexuality yet. But then, a lot of people in Ecuador haven't accepted the idea of the *lightbulb* yet.

"It was a crime of passion," says Pancho. "He must have heard some fag's confession, then threatened to expose the guy if he didn't come up to his room and—"

Pancho chooses this moment to display another gesture requiring the use of both hands.

"Get serious," I tell him. "If a priest is forcing you to have gay sex, you expose him, you don't kill him."

"Yeah, but not everyone thinks the way you do, honey," advises Pancho. "Maybe they went down to the kitchen to have some fun, or maybe it just got a little too rough and—" Pancho slowly draws his thumb across his throat from ear to ear, pressing deep enough to leave a pale white line before the blood rushes back in. "Fags are pretty unpredictable."

I let that pass. One battle at a time.

"So you think maybe they were playing around at a little culino-erotic stimulation and it got out of hand? That's some turn-on," I say.

"Hey, it takes all kinds."

"I was thinking more along the lines of a political murder in retribution for the report they wrote condemning the government's human rights abuses," I suggest.

"Listen, stop acting like he was such a fucking saint," says Pancho. "Pajizo *gave* Campos that land when he was still mayor of Guayaquil."

"In which case the report would be seen as a double-cross, the penalty for which is—"

"He fucking *blessed* Canino at that asshole's victory mass! That didn't make him too popular with some people, you know."

"*Padre* Campos gave Segundo Canino's victory mass?" I ask, astounded. How come I didn't know this?

"Sure as shit, *muñeca*. Next time count all the freaking beans first, okay? Now, I'd love to keep arguing, but I have a show to do."

CHAPTER
SEVEN

The price of freedom is $1.25 a pound.
—Thomas Jefferson
(no relation)

The palm trees are painted white.

Everything is painted white. Walls, benches, the first six feet up the tree trunks, all white.

The sidewalks are swept. There's almost no filth. It's remarkably hot.

And it's even hotter inside.

Open-shirted reporters set pocket tape recorders on the table, photographers ready their lenses, video crews double-check their connections while the TV reporters fix their hair and have their makeup retouched.

Pale blue-and-white flags, the patriotic colors of Guayaquil, are displayed on posters and T-shirts and plastic ribbons draped around the room like bunting. Otherwise, the walls are bare. It's only been Hector Gatillo's campaign headquarters for about an hour, but it's already swarming with clouds of rapacious press corps drones, humming and eager to begin nipping at his heels, the gluttonous prelude to several weeks of scrounging for every scrap of cartilage and gristle that rolls off the table.

I'm stepping carefully through the buzzing colony, searching for a reporter from *El Despacho*, when suddenly I have to cough. My lungs are still irritated from all that smoke last night.

There's a surge of activity near the side door. Bodies bearing network logos compress around me, and the TV lights flare up. Hector Gatillo bursts through the door encircled by cheering fans like a boxer on his way to the ring, his arms up in the air as if already embracing victory.

The three biggest national TV news crews are here. Suddenly they have to take this guy seriously.

They get the first question.

It's a lame one:

"*Señor* Gatillo, what is your campaign about?" says the reporter from Ecuavisa.

Gatillo nods towards the cameras and says, "It's about teaching the people that *they* have the power to make things better. That a man can be a man without stepping on his neighbor. It's about learning to have confidence in yourselves, and to stop believing that your oppressors are all-powerful, because they're not."

Voices cry out:

"*Señor* Gatillo—"

"What about the education budget—?"

"The rice shortage—?"

"Pesticides in the shrimp—"

"The military—"

"What specific programs—?"

Gatillo's assistant points to another TV reporter. "The *señorita* from TeleAmazonas."

This one's even lamer. "*Señor* Gatillo, what is your campaign slogan going to be?"

Gatillo's crew look around, at each other; they haven't thought of that yet. Then Gatillo does something I'm not sure I've ever seen a politician do before: he tells the truth.

"We have no slogan," he admits. "Perhaps, during the campaign, the people will come up with one. Yes, I will let the people answer that."

"*Señor* Gatillo—!"

"Inflation—"

"The external debt—"

"Threat of terrorist—"

"Oil—"

"Guerrilla activity in the jungle—"

"Exchange rate with the dollar—?"

One of Gatillo's bookends picks a white-haired man with a bit of a potbelly. "The gentleman from *El Despacho*."

I'm straining to get a better look.

"*Licenciado* Gatillo," he begins, using the schoolteacher's formal title. It takes me about five words to place his accent as Argentinian. "What about the accusations that there is a pact between your party and President Pajizo's Centrist Coalition?"

Loud, angry murmurs from his followers, but Gatillo silences them.

"To do what? Draw votes away from his chosen successor, Segundo Canino?" Some snickers. "The people know I stand for change. *Real* change. These rumors are meant to scare the poor uninformed voters away from me. Do you realize how ridiculous this is? The government party is so unpopular that they are trying to weaken my candidacy by suggesting that I am aligned with them!"

Laughter and applause from his followers.

"The *señorita* from Channel Three News."

"*Señor candidato*, how would you describe yourself to our viewers?"

"Short, fat and ugly."

Damn, he's honest.

"What about the narco-dollars that are supporting the rebel movement in the *oriente*?"

"The rebel movement isn't the only thing that's funded by narco-dollars, people. The right-wing paramilitary hit squads supply themselves the same way. Frankly, I'm much more worried about the government's recent decision to allow the United States to use the Manta Air Force Base to launch attacks against Colombian rebels operating in the border region, which I believe is a greater threat to regional stability than our tiny and increasingly irrelevant rebel movement."

There's another burst of shouting from the reporters elbowing each other and pressing forward to get in the next question. I'm pushing against the crowd to get to the Argentine newsman before I lose sight of him.

Then a sudden surge of pressure to my left squeezes me into a pocket of air, close enough to look directly into the elderly reporter's heavy-lidded eyes. They're gray and watery. The press credentials dangling around his neck read:

Ruben Zimmerman
Senior Reporter
El Parecer, Buenos Aires
Special Assignment to *El Despacho*

"You ask tough questions, *señor* Zimmerman. How closely is the Argentine press following the campaign?"

"They couldn't give a *cola de rata* about the campaign. I am following it independently."

"Three thousand miles from home? That's pretty damn independently."

He looks at me suspiciously. "Are you a reporter?"

"No, but I feel a desperate need to talk to one."

My joke falls flat. He stops taking notes and looks at me sharply, making no effort to mask his irritation, sighs at the futility, and snaps his notebook shut.

"There are twenty-four hours in a day, you know. The least you people could do is quit bugging me when I'm in the middle of an assignment. All right, so what is it this time?"

"Sorry. I seem to be getting off on the wrong foot here. Could we talk outside?"

"Yeah, sure, fine, whatever."

We push through the bodies past a spotlit woman telling a TV camera, "—direction remains to be seen, but *señor* Gatillo declared today that the people will answer that question for him. In the *ciudadela* Aguilera, this is Julia Ramírez, TeleAmazonas." Just like up North.

The sun presses down on me like a steamroller on hot tar.

"At least you're prettier than the last one they sent," he says. "Come on, let's get this over with."

My God, someone more paranoid than me.

"Look, I'm not what you think I am. I guess you must be getting harassed by the police a lot," I try to reassure him, without success. "Or is it immigration?" I ask.

He stops in his tracks and glowers at me. "*Señora*, I have been hounded and targeted by the secret armies of six different countries—the National Intelligence Service, the First Army Corps, the CIA, ACHA, DINA, DIPC, SID—"

"Sounds like everyone but the meter maids are after you. Come on, let's go get some coffee and catch up on old times."

I take him across the street to a café with a low-hanging forest of white ceiling fans whirring away. He closes one of his shirt buttons.

"You cold?" I ask.

"At my age? Always. So who on earth are you?" he asks, settling noisily into a cane chair.

"Sometimes I ask myself the same question. I guess you could say that I'm also a South-American-in-exile, only in my case banishment led to the United States." I hand him my passport as proof, but it's not terribly convincing.

"It *looks* real," he says, "especially the holographic strip, but what does that mean these days?"

Too bad my tourist visa is missing.

"Look," I begin, "I just came down here for a few weeks to visit my family."

"Then what do you want from me?"

"Why do they keep hassling you?" I ask.

"Because they can."

"We have a lot in common, *señor* Zimmerman."

"So far I only have your word on that."

"Well, that's the first thing: we're both extremely cautious."

"And why is that?"

"Because the man who baptized me was found murdered three nights ago."

He slowly lowers the menu and regards me with his world-weary eyes.

"Your paper was the only one that reported it," I say.

"The priest? The one who—?"

"The one who used to mediate between the army and the rebels. Yes. His kind are an endangered species."

"You knew him?"

"Knew him? I'd be a pile of bones in a shallow grave if it weren't for him."

Suddenly he's very interested in my life story. I give him the two-minute version, then it's his turn. He tells me all about the shit he's seen as an investigative reporter in a place where the rivers overflow with shit.

His first book was an exposé of the genocidal atrocities committed by the Argentine military during its dirty wars, and his second book is a memoir of his long years of suffering in an Argentine military jail after the first book came out. Don't look for either of these at your local bookseller's. Now he's researching a third book that he's going to call *The Bloody Trail*, a catalogue of evidence that a series of assassinations of prominent Latin Americans was actually a single "operation." His list includes labor organizers, environmentalists, congressmen, an archbishop, and three presidents, including Rolando Aguilera of Ecuador.

"Aguilera's plane smashed into a mountain," I say.

"His plane crashed in the mountains," he says. "But—"

A crustaceous old man shuffles over to us. I order a *café con leche*. Mr. Zimmerman wants his as black as it comes, the coffee equivalent of a neutron star, if possible.

He continues cautiously: "They won't let me examine the evidence."

"What evidence? They cleaned up the wreck the next day, just like they did in La Chala."

Hmm.

"Then we have the same problem," he says. "Governments are all the same. They think that if nobody stirs the pot, the lumps will sink to the bottom quicker, out of sight."

"They might be right. I think somebody's trying to do that with the murder of *padre* Campos. What do you know about that?"

"No more than you," he says.

"Yeah, people keep telling me that, but someone at your paper knows more than I do."

"If you mean the boys on the police beat, then I think it would be rather dangerous to pursue."

"But why—?"

"May I join you?" says a voice behind me. My tailbone gets a thousand-watt jolt, but I manage to stay in my seat and not soil the cushions. Zimmerman barely blinks. A flak-jacketed man smiles down at us, dirty-blond stringy hair down to his collarbone. Time to gather my frizzy hair with an elastic band so it doesn't look quite so much like Elsa Lanchester's fright wig in *The Bride of Franken-stein*. This humidity really microwaves my hair and accentuates its hybridity, the curly-dominant genes mowing down the straight ones like an iron scythe raking through a forest of raw spaghetti.

"Hello, *señor* Connery," says Zimmerman. "You may speak to the *señorita* in English. She's a *paisano* of yours."

"Yeah? You're from the States?" says Connery in honest-to-God American English as he sits down next to me.

I shove over. "Yeah. New York fuckin' City. How about you?"

"Portland fuckin' Oregon, babe."

"But you're originally from Chicago."

"Wha—Is it that obvious?"

"Chicago's a great town," I say. "Lot of Ecuadorians there."

He laughs self-consciously and brushes the hair out of his eyes. Bit of a kid for a man in his midthirties. Not very worldly for a Latin American correspondent. He says he's trying to make the leap from covering Little League games to front-line news.

"Then why are you here? Everyone knows the big stories are in Colombia and Peru," I say.

"Gotta start somewhere," he smiles, big and sincere. "My name's Peter. What's yours?"

"Filomena Buscarsela."

Unrecognized Command.

Does not Compute.

The waiter ambles over to our table and plants himself there as though he's just moved as far as he intends to move in this geological epoch. I remind him that we ordered two coffees. Peter asks what there is to eat. The waiter makes a halfhearted gesture in the direction of a hand-painted placard.

"*Cuero de chancho*. That sounds good," says Peter.

I caution him: "You really want pigskin simmered in rendered fat? Ecuadorians love it, but most Americans think it's like eating a fried football."

"I'll take it," says Peter.

"It's your life," I tell him.

Meanwhile the waiter is engaged in a slowness contest with the lamppost, and the lamppost is losing.

Ruben checks his watch and says, "I have to get back to the paper. Care to come with me?"

"There's some stuff I've got to do first," I say. "Later?"

He checks his watch again. "Sorry, I've got a deadline. Every minute counts."

I smile.

"Did I say something peculiar?" he asks.

"No, it's just that Ecuador was never a place where every minute counted. It's going to take some getting used to."

"A responsible journalist delivers up-to-the-minute information, *señorita* Buscarsela," Ruben replies, tapping his watch for emphasis.

"Fine. Is tomorrow good?"

"Sure, come by around eleven. I'll be on the third floor going blind in front of a computer screen."

"I thought I warned you not to visit those porn sites," Peter jokes.

Ruben shakes hands with us and shuffles out of the café.

"Been down here long?" I ask, looking around for the waiter, and still waiting for my coffee.

"Only a couple weeks. You a reporter too?"

"No." I answer his obvious follow-up: "Just visiting family."

"Ruben Zimmerman's part of your family?"

"Sure. We go way back." Back to Adam and Eve's cousin Rosita, maybe.

No waiter yet, but a barefoot boy comes around to our table holding a sheaf of tattered lottery tickets clipped to a square piece of cardboard.

"Buy a ticket," says the boy.

"I don't play the lottery," I tell him. I gamble enough with my life as it is.

"Bu-u-u-y-y-y a ti-i-i-icket," pleads the kid in a practiced but transparent whine.

"No."

"Bu-u-u-y-y-y a ti-i-i-icket."

"I said no."

"Bu-u-u-y-y-y a ti-i-i-icket."

"Okay, I'll buy a ticket," says Peter, rewarding the little brat for his persistence. "How much?"

"*Ocho mil,*" says the kid. Peter starts reaching for his money.

"The hell it is," I say, grabbing the kid's clipboard. I take a close look at the tickets. "They're supposed to cost thirty-five hundred sucres each."

"I heard the *señor,* he asked for two tickets."

"That still leaves you overcharging by a thousand sucres," I say.

"The *señor* is a North American. He has money."

"All right, gimme two tickets," says Peter. "What's a thousand sucres, Ms.—?"

"Filomena." It used to be enough to raise an army.

"Filomena. I won't forget that again. Here, kid. Keep the change."

"He will," I say.

"Lighten up. What's two bits between rich Americans?"

"I just don't think you should be letting him make it dishonestly."

"Nice sentiment. But you know, one time in India I saw this barefoot girl who got like eighty cents for every thousand bricks she carried."

"This isn't India."

"I know. I mean, put yourself in his shoes—"

"I *was* in his shoes, Mr. Connery. I went barefoot until I finished fourth grade, but I *finished* fourth grade, and high school and college, too, without short-changing people. I may be a rich American to him, but I wasn't always that way, and I didn't get there by cheating people. I've been working since I was that little snotnose's age, and it hasn't made things any easier."

The waiter crawls over with the small black coffee that Ruben ordered before he left, his gaze drifting upward as if the alien vessel that he has been expecting is two hours late already and he is getting impatient.

Ecuadorians are among the most patient people on earth. They have to be. They've been waiting for a decent government since 1533.

*　　*　　*

Carlos, my man. How's that autopsy going?"

"Bad news, F. We can't find the body."

"What do you mean, you can't find it?"

"I mean it's not there. It might've been transferred to the provincial morgue."

"Might have been?"

"Man, stop repeating everything I say. Sounds like the phone's broken."

"It's just that—" I stop myself from saying too much. "Okay. See what you can find out. And if you come up short, you can make it up to me."

"How?"

I give him Donut Boy's description and a promise of reward if he brings back anything useful for me.

I dodge the sun in a sliver of shadow, trying to fool my skin into thinking it's cooler, and wait for the bus that'll take me to the city center.

Yes, I take a bus. In fact, I take *two* buses. Hey: the odds are only 1 in 5 that we'll be assaulted.

Now I've got to trek all the way across the city to La Chala *again* and try to get a few things straight in my mind that the humidity just keeps on curling. And I sure hope it's not a big freaking waste of time like my last visit.

The police reportedly discovered *padre* Samuel's body at around 12:30 A.M., but I've got two separate accounts suggesting the time of death may have been closer to 11:30 P.M. You can dump a lot of evidence in an hour, if you know how. And a lot of people in this town know how.

I try to cut through all the obvious crap first. There's nothing to convince me of the suggestion that the *padre* was gay, because I'd have known about it before now. It's not as if the issue of sex never came up. That selfless, peace-loving man admitted to the scope of his sexual feelings when we discussed the vow of chastity as one of my principal reasons for not joining the sisterhood, so I think we can scratch the deranged-rent-boy-with-a-knife theory.

On the other hand, some of those Chala whores are pretty quick with a straight razor. It could have been a woman. God knows the *padre* was human. But he had plenty of chances to be with women that he did not take. Poor women, grateful that he had helped them, who had nothing to offer in return but their womanhood. He probably knew them all by their first names.

But even a swan's shadow is dark. And enough money will buy you a person's soul in a place that desperate.

What about Canino's victory mass? What would lead my old friend and savior to do such a thing? Or course, so far I've only got Pancho La Pulga's word on that, which is a pretty flimsy foundation for any theorizing. Yeah, he played me like a mixing board, all right. My astonishment couldn't have been more obvious if flashing lights and sirens had come popping out of my head wailing *weee-oooo-eeeee-oooo-eeeeeeeeee.* . . . How pathetic.

We pass the sweeping, epic monument to Alfaro with the vibrant sickle-shaped waves of humanity pushing him forward. He is not isolated on a rearing steed, sword waving emptily towards the luxury hotels across the square; this leader is being propelled skyward by the unstoppable force of the people. Yeah, it's propagandistic, but aren't they all?

We are all links in the chain of action. One lone nut didn't make Samuel Campos disappear from the face of the earth. Someone gave the orders. Someone engineered the blackout. Someone had two political opponents and a rebellious priest killed, with the threat of more to come, and someone sure as hell mopped up afterwards. Why are they killing people? To "destabilize" the economy? Hell, the economy is so unstable already a good breeze would knock it over. No—this is a specific plan to get rid of these major opposition figures *now*, because the ruling party and their secret armies want a lock on their power in the upcoming election, or maybe they are just figuring, Hey, now's our chance, in the middle of all this other mess. Who's gonna notice? And where the hell is Ismaél?

And my biggest problem is that I could cut off three fingers and *still* be able to count how many people I can really trust on one hand.

I simmer with the frustration of the modern warrior, whose battle lines are not clearly drawn, whose enemies do not stand and announce themselves in heroic couplets, and who wears her deepest battle scars on the inside, where they are unseen.

I may not be able to get the big guys who work behind the curtain, but I ought to be able to get the actual killers. I'm good at that sort of thing.

Because the forces of repression aren't as monolithic as you might think, or I wouldn't be here. I've lived through five military takeovers and a couple of overthrows. Too bad my brother wasn't so lucky. Yeah, I don't talk about him much. I hardly remember the smiling teenager whose battered body rolled up to our doorstep covered with bloody morning dew. And I never got revenge on his killers.

It was such a long time ago, we actually had a left-wing president. Then the future right-wing president ordered the army to surround the chambers of Congress and hold them all hostage. And the Ecuadorian Air Force buzzed the capital and bombed their brothers on the ground. The loser was president for eighteen hours.

My brain is starting to hurt, since I stayed up way too late chasing musicians all over town and the caffeine is wearing thin. I need a second wind without an infusion of stimulants, 'cause I need to be awake, but I need to be sane, too.

However, unable to find a branch outlet of the Fountain of Youth in this target area, I just have to paint a smile on and act like I'm ten years younger and stop at a supermarket—yes, we have such things in Ecuador—and stock up on goodies. Candy and potato chips for the kids, cartons of cigarettes, bread and barbecued meat on a stick for the folks who love meat (these people can't get enough of it), lots of cheap *aguardiente* and even the extravagance of bottles of beer. It's all a matter of speaking their language better.

I spend the early afternoon hours sloshing around the muddy potholes of La Chala, making freely with the good cheer, dispensing belly warmers at three and four fingers a shot, and trying to find out if anyone heard anything unusual or can tell me *precisely* what time the blackout occurred. The general outpouring of words is no better than their previous silence. People heard every imaginable sound *except* gunshots, and there's very little agreement about the blackout, although there's a general clustering around 11:15 to

11:30 P.M., until I find one guy who swears his electric clock stopped at exactly 11:17, right in the middle of "*A veces me siento así.*" Others agree.

I reconfirm that Gilda was watching the street as soon as the power went out, and that Ismaél came running out a couple of minutes later. She adds that the police came soon after that. How soon? She's pretty sure it was right before Pancho rang the midnight gong, halfway through his show.

According to the official version of events, the *padre* was still alive then. I'd sure like to see the police report explain *that* one.

Which means the murderer must have been with *padre* Samuel and struck the instant darkness fell. Then what? You either hide the body, or you get the hell out of there. (There was *nothing* to steal in that place—certainly nothing like 2 million sucres.) How did the killer escape? Under cover of darkness? During the confusion after Ismaél ran out? Or out the back window, down a rope to a waiting boat? Who'd go to *that* effort?

Or maybe I've been looking at the wrong side of this whole thing.

But first I go to the school to ask the nuns about *padre* Samuel giving Canino's victory mass.

Y es," Sister Cecilia says, "he did give that mass, even though he felt that it was a shameful manipulation of the believers' faith for political purposes."

"Then why did he do it?"

"Because they asked him to."

"Who asked him?"

"Three men. They said he owed them a favor."

"You recognize any of them?"

"No. I've never seen them before."

"Could you describe them?"

Yes, but her minimal descriptions fit three-fourths of the men on the bus I took over here.

What did Canino's rude boys do? Threaten to take back the land, bulldoze the school? Why force a political enemy to bless you in public? Just to remind him who's boss? Or to set him up? Make the hard-line radicals think the *padre* was a turncoat and put him on their shit list. It's been done.

Pancho went for it.

And so I have to consider the possibility that *padre* Samuel may have been killed by a far-left splinter group. It's a little harder to fit the police cover-up into that explanation, but not much: Alberto warned me that a lot of my old friends weren't so friendly anymore.

Fuck.

Fuck fuck fuck.

My daughter is downtown, safe from all this.

But I'm here.

I find someone who's willing to lend me a canoe for a few sucres so I can go snooping around the estuarial backwash and see what I can dredge up besides higher life insurance premiums. Man, my Allstate rep would have a heart attack if he could see me wobbling unsteadily on this putrescent backwater. But I get my legs soon enough, and paddle around Alicia's shack to the open grave where the church and parish house once stood. There's nothing left of it but some jagged bones, but rebuilding it in my mind, I figure it would have been about a sixteen-foot jump into the water from the *padre*'s window. Not at all hard, but then what do you do? Swim through this muck? At night? A rope would have taken time to secure, assuming you could secure *anything* to that ratty old lumber, but I have to admit that someone *could* have snuck up on him this way. Of course, to do it swiftly and silently would require some serious paramilitary training, and maybe I don't like where this is going, but it could have happened that way.

I wonder if Alberto's getting the word out yet. I'm going to need friends.

I punt around among the miserable shacks that have isolated themselves from the rest of humanity, and which are only accessible by canoe, trying to find out if anyone saw or heard anything on this side of the water. Even with my arms full of peace offerings, they won't let down their guard and I still come up empty.

By the time I paddle back to the landing, I'm starting to smell like one of Porky Pig's less endearing relatives. There's a kid standing there, waiting. Seems like he's waiting for me.

Mishojos.

He jumps into the canoe, shoves off and steers us out into the middle of the wide, flat water. We float with the current for a bit, then he paddles towards a maze of closely knit shacks.

It's starting to cloud over.

"So where are we going?"

"Further down the river," he says. Well, yeah.

We float between the thin splintering stilts, dwellings the Sumerians would have considered a bit primitive. Thick bamboo poles, clusters of reeds tied together with corn fiber, roofs thatched with wide green leaves. Some of them don't even have four complete walls.

Hovel, sweet hovel.

"Miss Filomena?"

"Yes?"

"One of the people you were talking to says he heard gunshots that night. *Bang-bang*, one right after the other."

"Thanks for coming forward with that. What else did he say?"

But instead of answering, he juts his chin towards the bow. I turn.

We're pulling up alongside a long, dark boat, a sleek modern version of the aboriginal dugout canoes. The pilot is wearing a big straw hat that completely covers his face. He does not tip his hat to me. In fact, he keeps his face covered the whole trip. I look back at Mishojos as we pull away, staring back at me impassively from the shadows, the borrowed canoe rocked by darkening waves.

It starts to rain lightly.

We go downriver a couple of miles to a different slum on the edge of the warehouse district, a no-man's-land north of the new port.

Onshore, a second sentinel with an enormous straw hat leads me through an endless tangle of battered cane shacks to an alley behind a warehouse, a dead end of cinder block, brick and cane. Uh-oh.

"Stand there," he says, backing out of the alley.

Rats. End of the line, blocked three ways. I'm wondering if I'd rip my fingernails off trying to claw my way up the bricks when voices start talking to me through the cane wall.

"We have guns trained on you."

"Okay," I answer. "Just don't fire any of them."

"That depends on you."

"Good. I trust myself not to try anything crazy."

"You better not," says one.

"Why are you looking for us?" says another.

I don't even know who I'm talking to, of course.

"If we were the other side, you'd be dead right now," one of them says, as if reading my thoughts. "Talk, woman."

"About—?"

"Don't fuck with us, girl. The Crow said you wanted five minutes of ear time. Well, you got three. Now talk."

"I want to reconnect," I say.

"Why?"

"Because the official story is that a delinquent teenager knifed *padre* Samuel Campos for some quick cash. But it smells to me like the first shot in an all-out war on the progressive forces that have been keeping the jackbooted militia types in check," I say.

"Then maybe you should have figured out that Campos's death is being used to flush out people like you."

"I'm not that important."

"You think they care?"

I have to admit that they could be right.

"Look at you," they say. "Standing all alone in an alley talking to a wall."

Yeah, it feels like I'm talking to a wall, all right.

"Well, somebody's jerking me around, and I want to know who's pulling the strings. And I figured you might know something about it."

"Those are two different things," they reply.

"Okay. You have eyes and ears, and the little blackbird should have told you that I'm trying to find out if there's anyone with the provincial police who's friendly enough to talk to me."

"We're not telling you a damn thing about them."

"No, of course you wouldn't. But I've done a lot of things I used to think I would never do."

"You mean like betraying the movement, *Juanita*?"

Control it, girl.

I answer, "*Ante eso en mi tierra corre sangre.* Anyone who accuses me of betraying a single member of the movement owes me the favor of a duel *hasta la muerte.*"

To the death.

Nobody says anything. Then:

"Let's talk about Juanito."

Throat. Tight.

"*Well?*"

"You know something about him?" I ask.

"There's nothing to know. Tell us about the last time you saw him."

I don't answer.

"*Well?*"

Okay, asshole, if that's how you want it: "The last time I saw him, Johnny was so blinded by rage that he almost broke down my door. He didn't care if he led the cops right to me and they burned me alive."

"Bet that really pissed you off," says one.

"And no one saw you for a long time after that," says another.

"I had to skip out."

"You could have gone underground."

"Sure, and lead the *federales* straight to my unit."

"But you didn't. You left the country."

"Out of sight is out of sight. What's the difference?"

"So you thought hiding out as a New York City cop was the perfect cover?"

"Okay, so you know about that."

"Yeah, we know about that. He left you in a roomful of cops, Juanita. So how'd you get out?"

"*Fuck you.* I got out without taking anyone else with me, and I can still look at myself in the mirror."

"How'd you get out?"

By spending a year and a half in a maximum security prison, you bastards.

"I got out," I say.

They take a moment to discuss that among themselves.

"Then what are you doing here?"

"I'm trying to find out who killed Samuel Campos. It wasn't you guys, was it?"

"And who will benefit from this knowledge?"

"Anybody else on their shit list, *amigo*. Even you."

Pause.

I tell them, "I'm going to keep digging."

Longer pause.

"We'll let you know."

The boat's gone.

I have to find my way back upstream by heading through this muddy maze to the main highway where I flag down a bus heading north, get off in the city center, and take another bus back to La Chala. I want to ask Mishojos what else he saw and heard.

But when I get there, there's a gathering of souls at the water's edge, pointing and speaking excitedly, their white and yellow clothes flapping animatedly, almost luminous. I wedge myself in and see the green-eyed mountain boy floating faceup, the blood long gone. A warning to me, and to all others.

This was a local hit.

For the first time since I've been here I truly feel like someone's eyes are upon me, right now, watching for my reaction. Well, here it is: *You cowardly piece of shit.*

And poor Mishojos, lost in all this, just one more thing floating in the swamp, all his hopes and dreams sinking deeper into the sludge and dreck. His skin's not even waterlogged yet, but his eyes are already cold, silvery fish eyes staring up through the scummy surface, staring up at me saying, You, Filomena, you are the reason this happened to me, and you must find out who, and why, or these eyes will follow you around for as long as you live.

But I have my own child.

And I spend the rest of the day reminding myself of that.

CHAPTER
EIGHT

Don't grieve for the dead: they know what they're doing.

—Clarice Lispector,
A Hora da Estrela

S tan.

Oh, Stan, that's my man.

Did you miss me, honey?

Yes. Oh, yesss.

"Wake up, Filomena! ¡Levantate!"

Ugh.

"What?"

"Phone call!"

Head filled with glue. Brain packed in bubble wrap. The blood's all down in my clit, I think. I stumble to the phone.

"That you, F?"

"Carlos? It's—" Too early to focus on the clock.

"Yeah, listen. Nobody at the ASN fits the description you gave me, and about that other thing? That body's gone totally missing."

Missing. That word. So empty. So full of evil.

"Okay, never mind about the body. When is the coroner going to issue a death certificate?"

"No, I don't think you get it, Miss F. I'm at the end of the road on this one."

"You sure are." *Click.*

Damn. Without proof of death, it's as if he just disappeared. And, to put it in cold police detective terms, his body would have been the best piece of evidence about the killer's method of operation.

By the time the creature wrapped in a human skin named Filomena makes it down the cement stairs for coffee, an express package has arrived from Cuenca. It's the *padre*'s pamphlet.

I slurp up some coffee and toast, then Uncle Lucho helps me find the best print shop for my needs. They take one look at the paper and wave an arm towards reams of the stuff stacked on their shelves, up to the ceiling. The typeface is a standard one, twelve-point Helvetica Light, laser-printed for an offset press. But the ink intrigues them. It's unusually water-resistant. Very expensive. Probably imported, says the master, handing back the pamphlet and wiping his hands on his ink-stained coveralls.

So I'm back to the same jawbreaker as before: high-grade ink on cheap-shit paper. Maybe the militiamen just stole a cache of fancy ink—it would suit their MO to a T. Or maybe somebody's getting paid to look like a regular organization, and they decided to skimp on the paper and pocket the difference. Or else it's a combination, some kind of collaboration between two normally distinct groups—you supply the ink, we'll supply the paper, and that way nobody can trace it back to either of us. Boy, if that's their game, it's working.

Back home, armed with a second cup of coffee, I pick up today's *El Despacho* and turn to the police briefs. Nothing about a young boy's life ending at thirteen, but on the second-to-last page, under the soccer scores, is a two-inch article. No byline. It reads:

Janitor: I Killed Priest

Ismaél García Parra, janitor of the church and parish house in the *barrio* La Chala, confessed to the shocking crime of murdering *padre* Samuel Campos, whose body was found with numerous stab wounds early Sunday morning.

The guilty man admitted that he used a kitchen knife to commit the crime after police detectives noticed scratches and bruises on his face and forearms as a result of the victim's unsuccessful attempts to defend himself.

Jesus, they can't even lie right. It took them *three days* to notice scratches and bruises on the suspect's face and forearms? And the details keep changing like a smooth-talking sex killer who keeps getting caught with his facts down: Sure, we left the bar together, but she went to the burger place on Madison and I went home. You say she was a vegetarian? Well, maybe it wasn't a hamburger place, it must have been the donut shop. The one near the park. Yeah, the park. Then we separated. These scratches? My cat made those.

I'm rushing out the door, electrified with the desire to head straight over to the offices of *El Despacho*, but Antonia stops me.

"Mom, when are we going to do something together? Like go to the beach or see some Inca ruins?"

"The Inca ruins are in the mountains. Maybe we can go next week. Just give me a few more days, okay?"

I'm not sure if she understands. I haven't told anyone about what happened yesterday in La Chala.

But I'd better stay away from there for a few days. Let 'em think I'm spooked, which isn't so damn far from the truth.

As I approach the main avenue, I notice that the walls of the *barrio* are sprouting vast fields of red-and-white Canino posters like poppies swaying in the breeze after the fertile rains, thanks to that last "poll."

And it'll be harvest time soon.

I buy copies of all three dailies, and cast my lot in for another bus ride. Now, the Greek epic heroes used to literally cast their lots into a warrior's helmet, something that would come in handy in case another riot starts. I could also use one of those divine-intervention deals, too, if anyone up there is listening. Hello? Athena? Ishtar? Hello?

I comb through the papers page by page. Each one says that Governor Segundo-the-Chosen-One Canino is planning a rally to-day. I've got an urge to see the man himself. The man *padre* Samuel owed a "favor."

There's nothing about the other murder, not even in *El Globo*. Guess it wasn't sensational enough. After all, kids die of hunger every day without it making the papers.

We head uptown, where whole buildings have been rebaptised with the colors of the various political parties. And unlike the progressive United States, backwards Ecuador doesn't permit any of its political parties to use all three of the colors on the national flag—red, yellow and blue. So there's an awful lot of red and white, some pale blue and white encroaching, a smattering of yellow and white—the Neoliberal Party of Ricardo-of-the-Noble-Opposition Faltorra, which has a much stronger following in the *sierra*—and a dozen smaller parties doing what they can with orange, green and black.

For some reason nobody wants to use purple.

Some impish part of me would vote for the first bastard who had the balls to use purple.

You don't want to know what else my impish parts would like to do.

These civilized city buses actually come to a complete halt to let people off, so I wait behind a covey of female office workers stepping daintily off the bus in high heels sharp enough to puncture the hull of a nuclear submarine, then I hit the ground and race-walk along the Calle Colón towards the river. Pretty soon the street is crawling with white-shirted office workers and cops and firemen and the idle eyes of passersby.

I pick out Ruben talking to another man and glancing up at the offices of *El Despacho* across the street from them. It looks like the whole building has emptied out.

"*Señorita* Buscarsela." He smiles affably, shaking my hand like an old friend. "Just in time for our latest disaster."

"Which is?"

"A bomb threat."

"We get them all the time," says the other man with breezy dismissiveness.

"Uh-huh. Listen, can you tell me who wrote this article?" I show them today's crime report, with Ismaél's so-called "confession" in it.

"It reads like it's printed directly from the police department's press release," says Ruben.

"Well, how can I find out more about how it got in there?"

"You can't go into the building now," says the other man.

And pretty bloody conveniently, too.

Ruben suddenly remembers his manners and introduces me to *señor* Claudio Moscoso.

"Are you an investigative reporter?" I ask.

"No, nothing that exciting. I cover the oil business."

"Oh? And what's new there?"

"Actually, there's been a major disruption in the *oriente*," says Moscoso. "Hundreds of Shuar Indians have seized control of five pumping stations."

Ruben picks up excitedly, "They're threatening to occupy more sites and shut off the flow of two hundred thousand barrels a day in exports."

"What do they want?"

"I'm sorry?" says Moscoso.

"They don't want oil," I say. "Our money doesn't mean shit to them. So what do they want?"

"Oh. They're protesting the damage to their fields and fishing grounds. During the extraction process the oil companies spill about ten thousand gallons of crude every week, and maybe four times that much in toxic waste."

So they want survival.

"Who organized them?"

"I beg your pardon?"

I look at him, trying not to say, Are you *sure* you're a reporter?

"The Shuars aren't afraid of anything," I say. "Except maybe evil spirits. They'll surround an army helicopter with twenty tribesmen armed with nothing but bamboo spears and raw courage. But they're pretty insular. Intertribal communication is not their strong point."

"Uh, that's correct."

"So who helped them organize? Earth First? CONAIE? CONFENIAE?"

"There's no direct evidence of outside involvement," says Moscoso.

"And what about the army?"

"They have mobilized fifteen hundred troops," he says.

"A three-to-one ratio for a bunch of naked Indians."

The Ecuadorian army relies on U.S. support, so they don't usually crush the opposition to a fine powder when *gringo* interests are involved. But when it's just a bunch of landless peasants in the middle of nowhere . . .

"I mean, are they going to try to negotiate, or are they going to call out the gunships?"

"Honestly, I don't know," he says, but after some prodding from both of us, Mr. Moscoso admits that some sources suggest that an elusive guerrilla group may have helped organize the Shuars, but the government and the oil industry want that kept hush-hush.

A disruptive, peasant-based guerrilla action. It almost sounds like—

"*There* you are!"

I spin around, legs apart, weight balanced.

"Where you guys been?" says Peter in that hopeless *gringo*-accented Spanish. "How 'bout this bomb threat, huh?"

Gee, got any beer? What's on TV?

"We have been right here," says Ruben.

"I was looking all over for you, dude," says Peter, brushing the hair out of his eyes. "Wanted to make sure you got out okay."

Ruben pats him on the back. "I'm old, but I'm not *that* old."

"I hear people saying maybe the Black Condors had something to do with this," says Peter, lowering his voice to a conspiratorial stage whisper.

"The Black Condors wouldn't blow up a newspaper," I say.

"Oh? Then what *would* they blow up?"

I don't answer.

Ruben explains to freaking Clark Kent here that the Ecuadorian guerrilla movement is really very small compared to some of the neighboring countries, and that Americans don't realize that the damage they cause is way out of proportion to their numbers. When you see a single set of high-tension wires scalloping up a mountainside like a seventh-grade string art project, you realize how a band of straggly guerrillas can take out the electricity in half a province with *one* well-placed bomb.

Hell, you could do it with one well-placed swing of a sharp ax.

Peter nods understanding.

Prematurely.

A street cop in a dark-blue-and-white uniform struts over and tells us that it's going to take them most of the day to secure the building.

"Come on, *amigos*, we've got work to do," says Moscoso, tipping his thumb up to his mouth in the international sign language for quaffing a few *tragitos*.

Ruben says, "We can work out of my hotel room. It's got a phone, a laptop, a TV, everything but a fax. Come on."

"Has it got a bar?" asks Moscoso.

"You've got to bring your own, my friend. That hotel room booze is too damn expensive."

"Give me your room number and I'll come by after the rally," I say.

"Governor Canino's rally?" asks Peter. "Can I go with you?"

"Sure, let's go."

The two reporters head east towards the river. Peter and I head north up the Calle Escobedo.

"If you really want to make a name for yourself writing about the guerrillas," I advise him, "you should head to the Amazon. Some of the factions might even talk to you."

"Really? They'd talk to me? Why?"

"To get their side of the story out."

"Cool! What do you mean by 'faction'?"

Cabal, combine, gang, clique, offshoot, wing, splinter group.

Maybe I should make him write it one hundred times on the blackboard.

I tell him about the fragmentation among the far-left guerrillas, groups that do not support destructive action—like bombing newspaper offices—who prefer to develop support among the peasants by helping them with such mundane duties as enforcing ineffective land reform laws.

"Yeah, sure. Like kidnapping."

"Bagging an oil company executive may seem like a body slam to the corporate system, but it's a poor substitute for collective action. Anything less is just pissing on the monolith."

"That was Roberto El Rey's specialty, wasn't it?" he says. "Kidnapping and ransoming oil workers?"

We're passing the cathedral.

"Maybe I could interview *him*," he says.

"You better update your material. Robby Rey was ambushed and killed four years ago."

"Are you sure?"

"It was in all the papers. With photos of army officers standing over his body."

"And you believe that?"

"It was him, all right."

"How do you know?"

What is this, the dialogues of Plato?

"Look, you're showing a healthy distrust of the official version of events, but the police and dozens of witnesses identified him, and the movement never denied it."

"What do you mean?"

"By their silence, the rebels were acknowledging that the official report was probably true."

"Okay, if you say so. Bad example. But aren't there other cases where that never happened? No one ever claimed to have found the bodies of Tiradientes, or like that other guy, Juanito Tres Ojos."

"He's dead."

"How do you know?"

I know.

"Because they'd be proudly declaring it if he were still alive."

"Not if they wanted people to think he was dead."

"What would that accomplish?"

"Make his myth grow."

"He believed in action, not myth."

We're coming up on the Avenida 9 de Octubre, which is crammed to the gutters with *guayacos* trying to steal a glimpse of the rally. The air is full of blinding white banners, hard to read in the midday sun, and the echoes of loudspeaker-chewed words bouncing off balconies and cornices before they reach our confused ears. Segundo-the-Chosen-One speaks:

"You see these other candidates! *-ates!-ates!* When they come here they are surrounded by bodyguards! *-ards!-ards!* What's the matter? *-er?-er?* Are they afraid of the people of Guayaquil? *-quil? -quil?* I have no bodyguards! *-ards!-ards!* Because God protects the just! *-ust!-ust!*"

Oh, let's not drag God into this.

"When they killed our *compañero el arzobispo* Oscar Romero! *-ero!-ero!* I saw that he was not afraid! *-aid!-aid!* Because we all know that the best security is Jesus! *-us!-us!*"

Poor Jesus. First the Inquisition, now this.

There's a hooting that heralds the passing of a nine-foot wooden cross through the rank-smelling streets, and a cheer rises from the rowdy *segundistas*. Peter keeps craning his neck and brushing the hair out of his eyes, but he still can't see anything. I make him give me a leg up, grabbing a window shutter for support, and I see Segundo, his arms wrapped around the crucifix, helped by two or three men, stepping down from the stage and carrying the daisy chain and ribbon-draped cross through the swarm of closely pressed bodies.

I've got to hand it to him. You'd never see Old Man Pajizo hauling a nine-foot wooden cross in ninety-five-degree heat under the direct sun, or see Ricardo-of-the-Patrician-Profile Faltorra sweating through his *guayabera* like this.

Of course, if he really wants to emulate the Savior so much, I'd be happy to oblige with some ten-penny nails and a claw hammer.

Peter lets me down, and says, "You wanna go over to Ruben's place?"

I tell him I'll join him later.

I've got a funeral to arrange.

W e can't have a traditional funeral ceremony without his death certificate," says *padre* Aguirre, the sibilant sounds sliding from his lips. "It's very strange to hold such services without his body."

"These are strange times. Look, I'm not asking for a traditional burial service, just *some* kind of memorial. He never got his Last Rites."

I look up at the high, blue vaulted ceiling, expansive and full of light, unlike so many of the dark adobe earthworks in the Andes they have hallowed in the name of *el Cristo pobre*, the Poor Jesus. There's something special about a place like this. No matter how hot it gets outside, it's always cool inside the church. Must be the convection from all those souls on ice.

Salvation in cool blue.

"He never received the final sacrament," says *padre* Aguirre, rubbing his smooth, heavy chin.

"He deserves a service."

Our Lady of Mercy looks silently down on us, praying for our salvation, I hope. Scattered voices murmur penitential prayers among the dark wooden benches, the susurrant syllables slipping by our ears.

"Tomorrow, noon," he says. "Just the family."

"Just the family."

Two blocks west of the church, five guys wearing pro-Canino T-shirts are kicking the crap out of three guys wearing pro-Gatillo T-shirts. They really take politics to the next level here, unlike our comfortably bloated, money-taking, deal-making middle-of-the-roaders up North.

Word is that Congressman Newton Camargo of Canino's Centrist Coalition attacked fellow congressman Felipe Delgado of Gatillo's Socialist Unity Party over a matter of honor on the steps of the Chamber of Deputies in Quito. Camargo's bodyguard drew a gun, and Delgado shot and killed the guy.

They were *both* carrying guns? Who needs guerrilla warfare when *congressmen* shoot at each other!

So apparently the police decided that this was the moment to teargas the Houses of Congress. Naturally, the cops later denied acting out this dearest fantasy of every voter in the country until Ecuavisa TV showed a clip of three white-helmeted policemen lobbing smoking cannisters into the Senate chamber through a side window. Being a cop just isn't the same anymore in the age of video cameras.

Which reminds me of the old South American joke: Why do the police always travel in threes? One can read, one can write, and the other's there to make sure the two intellectuals don't go communist.

Anyway.

The street fight didn't distract me from the fact that I marked three familiar faces when I left the church: a shoeshine boy, a

brown-skinned Rubenesque woman shading herself under a bloom-
ing red bougainvillea, and a shifty-eyed runt with a Cantínflas mustache, wearing a gray zippered jacket and pretending to read a
rolled-up newspaper.

I lose him in the late lunch-hour crowd of a busy department
store and head east to the riverfront.

Ruben's on the fourth floor of the Hotel Cordero, overlooking
the Malecón Simon Bolívar and the river. Pretty nice address for an
investigative reporter-in-exile.

When I walk in, the place is jumping like a TV station on
election night. Ruben, Peter and Claudio Moscoso are watching a
live broadcast from the Amazonian oil fields, where assault troops
are surrounding the Shuar protesters, and simultaneously listening
to President Pajizo on the radio declaring that *el narcotráfico* is now
considered "a crime against humanity," with a five-year minimum
jail term for being caught with so much as a marijuana seed and a
ten-year minumum for the slightest trace of cocaine. They are also
printing out Web pages and fanning through today's editions of
eight newspapers. The clipped and sorted results of Ruben's weeks
of research form a desktop collage twenty layers thick. It's so noisy
nobody hears me come in. I'm standing over Ruben at his desk
before he looks up, startled by my appearance.

"You're late," he says, checking his watch.

"Late for what?"

Moscoso takes the cigarette out of his mouth and waves it at
the TV screen. "A reporter from Channel Three News just accused
our friend Zimmy here of being a communist *and* a CIA spy, a liar
and a charlatan who has sold state secrets to the Peruvian military
at a hundred thousand sucres a pop—"

"Which entitles me to buy five candy bars, I believe, at today's
exchange rate," says Ruben. "It's a bad time to be an old *cagatintas*
like me, digging up twenty-year-old conspiracies no one wants to
hear about. The real money is in gossip columns, celebrity inter-
views, and the in-your-face garbage on the Internet."

"They don't know that you're going through these old morgue
files, do they?" I say, riffling through a yellowing pile of clippings
on the death of President Aguilera.

"It's a small country. Nothing like that ever stays secret for long."

"He's right," Peter chimes in. "Twenty-six journalists were killed last year worldwide, ten of them in Latin America," he says, sounding as if he were quoting directly from *Facts on File*.

"None of them here," I say, coming to Ecuador's defense. Although we do lose a lot of planes in the foggy mountains.

And it's time to use the bathroom.

A minute later I exclaim: "You've got hot water!"

"Man, what part of town do *you* live in?" says Peter.

Oh, fuck off.

I mean: "You are going to have to let me use your shower sometime, *señor* Zimmerman."

That sparks a round of whistling and off-color remarks, the least profane of which is, "Nice to know you've still got some *cojones*, Zimmy."

"There's hot water in my hotel room, too," says Peter.

Then: "Quiet! Turn up the TV!" shouts Moscoso.

"Oh my God—"

The sound: "—pipeline blast killed at least forty-three people instantly, fire injuring hundreds more—"

The sight: grainy black humans run at me, jungle green faded under gray skies behind them, fireballs inside thick rolls of smoke rising from the flat, blackened earth, pots, pans, scorched shapes on the ground, can't tell if they're human or not.

"—leftist rebels are suspected—"

"Man, it looks just like Vietnam," says Peter, slowly.

O jungle, my jungle.

Something has died.

T he censer swings.

The smoke rises.

Voices rise, chanting the requiem in Latin, the words drifting upwards like sparks from a funeral pyre.

I sit in the shadow of St. Anthony, praying for help finding my *padre*'s killers.

The perfumed vapor rises towards heaven, the reminder of a life turned to smoke.

In Ecuador, "to turn to smoke" means to disappear, to vanish without a trace.

They say that when my grandmother lay dying on her musty sickbed, consumed by a mysterious disease the simple country herbalists couldn't cure, when she finally let out her last breath, the room filled with a strange sweet perfume that hung heavily over the wake for three days, and lingered in the folds of their clothes, then followed the procession to the graveyard, and finally faded with the dissipating mist as they tamped down the earth over the plain pine box. The hardbound people of Solano say that no one has ever smelled that exact perfume before or since.

Padre Aguirre is being assisted by an ancient, decrepit priest, the kind who needs help breaking the Host in half, and a couple of Sisters of Mercy.

They spread a dark purple cloth with black fringe across the flat slab of the altar, and he gives a solemn mass for the missing body and anoints the empty space with oil.

I clasp Antonia's hands in mine, and listen to *padre* Aguirre's oration.

"I will say of the Lord, who is my refuge and my fortress: that He will deliver thee from the snare of the fowler, and from the noisome pestilence, and under His wing shalt thou find refuge. His truth shall be thy shield and buckler. Thou shalt not be afraid of the terror by night; nor of the arrow that flies by day—" He turns the page.

In midsermon, almost midword, the *padre*'s voice wavers for an instant, then he proceeds.

"—nor of the pestilence that walks in darkness; nor of the destruction that wastes at noonday. A thousand shall fall at thy side and ten thousand at thy right hand; but it shall not come near thee. Only with thine eyes shalt thou behold and see the recompense of the wicked. Because Thou, O Lord, art my refuge."

After the service I sully the inviolable sanctuary with the mundane particles of dirt on my shoes, and beg to see the Bible. *Padre* Aguirre turns it around, and there, lying on the illuminated pages, is a copy of the last page of the human rights report, with a red line drawn through *padre* Campos's name, and a red arrow pointing to *padre* Aguirre's name—a watery red ink that drips down the page and bleeds through the paper.

CHAPTER
NINE

A buena hambre, no hay mal pan.

When you're really hungry, there's no such thing as bad bread.

—Ecuadorian proverb

ierda!
Where is that shifty-eyed little runt? Where is that cloven-hoofed motherfucker? I'd like to rip out his trachea with my fingernails and show it to him before he drops to the ground and bleeds to death.

I go on like this, profaning this holy place with my desire to kill that yellow rat bastard, until my prefrontal cortex kicks in with the abstract rationality that I didn't actually see him today, and that it could easily have been a hundred other guys.

And what really pisses me off is that back in NYC this written threat would be a fantastic piece of evidence, covered with fingerprints, ink types, and all manner of forensic traces, but I can't do a damn thing with it here. I can't take it to the cops. It probably came from them.

I urge *padre* Aguirre to call the Servicio de Investigaciones Criminales and have them take it to a lab for analysis, but even as I'm saying the words I know it's probably not going to happen.

It's pouring when we step out of church. The gutters swell with swirling rainwater, sloshing up onto the sidewalks, leaving faintly greenish semicircles in their wake.

Now I remember why I left Ecuador. And suddenly it seems like such a long way back to my aunt and uncle's hearth in the *barrio* Centro Cívico, a long way back through the murky whirlpool of time. The pull of the past is too strong here, an irresistible undertow that increases the weight of my sins. I'm already up to my knees in blood, and the level is rising. How high will it rise before this is over, I ask myself, since I left my wet suit at home, along with my Sanforized Wonder Woman costume.

I also have a life in the present, and it is undoubtedly not in this place. At least, that's how I feel until we get back to the Correas' house and the smoke from Aunt Yolita's open-flame *parrillada* seeps under my skin and subverts my thought processes, settling into that place within the primitive nerve centers of my brain where food smells live, fogging them with the aromas of memory and other diffuse sensations whose parting wisps reveal the core of a twenty-year-long hunger.

I'm halfway into my second plateful before I stop myself.

"You're eating like you just got out of jail," Uncle Lucho noodges me.

"Is there something you're not telling us?" says Suzie. "Filomita's always been good at smelling trouble before it happens."

Yes, the beast within me remembers, and the smell of flame-seared soul food transports me to the faraway barren mountainsides where we always survived on the run with the dense, compact fuel of rice and beans. But in the briefest moments of rapture, we would feed the fires of victory and toast each other with meat and maté, and prepare to strike out once again at the savage heart of capitalist imperialism.

Like the time we robbed a bank in broad daylight—Johnny could be pretty outrageous—and we were chased high into the mountains by the rural police, first in jeeps, and then on horseback. We galloped ahead, halfway up the south face of Runa Shayana, then holed up behind the high rocky outcropping we had supplied for a shootout with the *rurales*. They had the law on their side. We had vastly superior positioning, and brushed them back repeatedly, driving them away.

That was in Cajas.

Coffins.

Again with the coffins.

My reverie is broken when my cousin Carmita comes home

looking pale and greenish. She's got muscle pain and fever, too. They send for the doctor, a shriveled man with thick glasses and a $900 toupee that wouldn't fool a nearsighted badger, who announces that she has dengue.

"It's spreading south through the city," he says, writing out a prescription. "It's hard to get the medicine. The Health Department won't classify it as an epidemic even though there are over two hundred thousand cases of it."

Two hundred thousand cases is not an epidemic?

"Maybe they're waiting for it to turn into yellow fever," says Uncle Lucho.

The doctor nods. "It's certainly true that dengue can lead to outbreaks of yellow fever. The same thing happened in Cuba twelve years ago, and again in Venezuela four years ago."

"Sounds like it's making it's way down the coast."

"It's a sign all right," says Uncle Lucho.

"Anyway, the government's trying to prevent price-gouging by fixing the selling price of this medicine, but the shelves are still empty," he says, raising his wrinkled hands in a futile gesture to the God of beggars.

Meaning the pharmacists who stocked up on the medicine two weeks ago at a higher price would rather keep it in the back room than dispense it at a loss or be closed down for selling it above the official price. We should sell this idea to Parker Brothers.

Sounds like another job for the almighty dollar.

"I'll get the medicine," I say, grabbing the prescription before Uncle Lucho can beat me to it.

But it's not that easy. The local pharmacies are closed down or mobbed with people who are desperately scrambling for the same thing while their loved ones are lying on a bed of nails because they can't find the medicine.

Hard to carry off a nice, discreet bribe under these circumstances. So I head uptown towards the fancier stores, and find myself planted in the middle of a sidewalk standoff between a barefoot guy in ragged cutoffs and a backwards baseball cap, his white shirt open and flapping, in a tug-of-war with a supermarket employee and a guard who's keeping one step back wondering who he should shoot first.

The barefoot man is fighting for a ten-pound sack of rice, yelling that the only thing his family has eaten for days is a watery soup of boiled green plantains that he managed to grow in a garbage-filled strip of dirt behind his shack. No breakfast or dinner.

He yells at them: "What are you gonna do? Shoot me over a bag of rice?"

Somebody should know you're on the brink of serious chaos when people are willing to die for food. And I can't get involved. If I'm arrested again, they'll deport me.

But I sure feel like kicking off this civilized veneer and raiding this food conglomerate's warehouse and scattering brightly colored bags through the air into the joyfully upraised hands of needy men and suffering women and hungry children.

But no.

If they arrest me again, they'll do a lot more than just deport me. And there are worse places than jail they can take you to. Hell, yeah.

So the conglomerate gets to keep on profiting from people's desperation while I slink away in shame. *Cada uno sabe donde le aprieta el zapato*, we say here. Everyone knows where their own shoes pinch them. And right now my own personal pinch is getting anti-dengue medicine for my cousin Carmita.

It costs me a couple of hours and thirty dollars, an absolute fortune down here, half a month's wages for a working man, but I get it, after verifying that the label is clearly printed, the expiration date legible, and the seal unbroken. Yes, I've done this before.

I get back to the Correas' flat and my Aunt Yolita makes me a nice restorative cup of *paraguay*, the only wake-up herb named after a country, although in Paraguay they call it yerba maté. It's bitter.

"Any sugar left?" I ask.

"Not even enough to help the medicine go down."

It takes several tries to get a dial tone. I'm three blocks away from my current home base, using a public phone, which in this part of town means someone who can afford to buy a phone and get it connected sets it up on a crate outside their door and sits there charging people 500 sucres a minute to make a call.

But it shouldn't be tapped.

I finally get through to Ruben and arrange to meet him in the hotel bar.

It's still raining when I get there.

Ruben is sitting at the dimly lit bar with his back to me, watching the end of a soap opera on a wall-mounted TV and waiting for the news to come on. He doesn't hear me come up behind him.

"You ought to watch your back more carefully," I say.

He gets to his feet and lightly kisses my cheek, our custom in these parts, and gestures to the empty stool in front of him. I sit there facing the door.

He orders another whiskey and soda and offers me whatever it is I'm having. I stick to the "and soda" part. Sheep can't afford to get buzzed when they're passing through wolf country.

After the usual barfly small talk about the history of oil exploitation in Ecuador's Amazon, he returns to his second favorite subject, his theory that President Aguilera was assassinated.

"Why?" I ask. "He was the most popular president we've had since—"

"Yes?"

"Since Alfaro."

"Who was also assassinated."

Hmm.

"He had the broadest backing among the indigenous groups of any president since *el viejo luchador* himself," he says. "And he was carrying a sealed draft of the most radical land reform legislation in the history of the republic on the plane with him when it went down."

"How do you know what was in a sealed piece of legislation?"

"There is another copy of the draft in the presidential archives—yes, it's a wonder it hasn't been destroyed yet. And a careful reading of the legislative records clearly shows that he was working on it at the time of his death, and that he intended to submit it to Congress within two to three weeks. Then his plane crashed."

I have to think about this for a while. There's an ad on TV for an Ecuadorian credit card asking me, "What are you thinking of buying?"

A rocket launcher, actually.

"Aguilera's plane was a twenty-seat propeller-driven craft operated by the military," I say.

"Precisely. The military."

"The ink may still have been wet, but the new Constitution was already in force. What were they planning to do? Whack Vice President Andrade also? What for? Another takeover?"

"I believe that they were acting on orders from a higher authority." But there's no one higher than *los militares* in this country.

"Outside the country," he says, following my unspoken thoughts.

The rain falls heavily outside the windows. Cars hiss by, sudden cones of light transforming the raindrops into a thousand luminous daggers plunging into darkness.

"It was a long time ago," I say. "But the word might still be around in the military."

"Yes," he agrees. "But so far all I've got to show for it is a nice set of brick marks on my forehead from smacking it against the big green wall of military culture," he says, bringing the tumbler to his lips.

"Well, don't look at me."

The news comes on. Tonight's top story is the food riots, and it's all on film. Nothing I don't know already, until *licenciado* Hector Gatillo's face pops up and he's asked to comment:

"The people are handcuffed to old ideas," he says, tapping both index fingers on his forehead. "The policeman can smack them over the head, the speculator can make them crawl on their knees and beg for a bowl of rice, but they will not rise up against them. No, they pull out their machetes and turn on each other, just as their fathers did before them, as their children do in the schoolyard, and as they have seen in so many *gringo* movies on TV, which is exactly what our oppressors want."

A man in the street, a scarf tied around his face to mask his features, has another opinion: "They tell us our demonstration is illegal! That we have to get a permit first! Well, let me tell you, Fernando Pajizo, there are going to be *a lot more* illegal demonstrations, and your attack dogs won't have time to crack down on them all!"

Store owners complain about the damage, and women cry for their sons who have been arrested.

And, oh yes, an American fighter pilot was shot down by guerrillas in the *oriente*. The U.S. government says that they never saw the guy before.

"Listen, *compañero* Zimmerman," I begin. Ruben turns away from the TV. "When are you going to get me the name of the reporter who filed the stories on *padre* Samuel Campos's murder? What's happening with that?"

"I'm sorry," he says, "but I haven't had the time to find out anything yet."

"What's the big deal? I mean, he does work at the same paper as you, doesn't he?"

"I'm just a stringer at *El Despacho*. But don't worry, I wouldn't be much of an investigative reporter if I couldn't track down one lousy crime columnist for you."

"Be careful."

He lets out a *humph*, kind of a strangled chuckle. "You think that nasty little mess is more dangerous than trying to expose an international conspiracy to assassinate three presidents?"

When you put it that way—

"I guess not."

The phone in the bar doesn't work.

They tell me I can use the one at the front desk, but I'd rather not.

Outside, the rain is coming down in heavy sheets of gray lead. I ask Ruben if I can use the phone in his room. But when I pick up the receiver, I get nothing but dead air.

I press the button several times, get plenty of clicks and static, but no line out. I hang up and try again. And again. And again.

Finally, a dial tone. It's a rotary phone with a loose dialing wheel, so I have to hold on to the cylinder with one hand and dial slowly with the other, the old-fashioned way. At least I don't have to crank up the battery first.

Alberto's voice.

"Is that *la familia Miranda*?" I ask. It's code for "Someone might be listening."

"No. But I'll take a message."

"I want to know if there's been any progress."

"No. Nothing so far."

Nothing so far. Well, at least nobody's turned up dead.

Today.

I actually get up early enough to see my second-floor cousins Ron, Vic and Bolí Mendez before they head off to work at their construction gig, which pretty much starts at sunrise and ends at sunset, six days a week.

Then I spend the morning with Antonia, teaching her how to make *humitas*. It's a simple dish. All you have to do is carefully strip the corncobs and set aside the leaves; cook the corn whole in boiling water; scrape the hot kernels into a bowl; mash them and mix them with eggs, butter, cheese, baking powder, sugar, salt; spoon out some scoopfuls; wrap the scoopfuls in the leaves you stripped from the corn, and steam them. It only takes a couple of hours. They're a little like tamales, and making them is no more trouble than baking your own bread, starting with threshing the wheat and hand grinding it under a millstone until it turns to flour, all by yourself.

They're good with hot cocoa on a cold day.

Guayaquil has no cold days. It's a mountain dish.

I put three on a plate and bring them downstairs to Suzie in the store, and see that we're running low on rice again.

There's nothing more in the papers about *padre* Samuel's murder. A little news, quickly forgotten.

But on page four, it says that a speeding truck overturned on the Panamerican Highway while carrying six thousand pounds of unregistered rice in hundred-pound sacks. According to the driver, who was arrested for reckless endangerment, the truck had no point of departure and no destination. He was just taking the rice for a nice drive in the country.

Suzie turns the radio to some dance music (note: *all* our music is dance music) and I help her take inventory of the half-empty shelves. It's a quick job but a hot one, what with the dancing, and soon all that butt-thumping leaves me lying flat on the beer cooler, catching my breath.

I don't even budge when the radio starts playing "*A veces me siento así.*" I just need a break from being Ms. Goddamn Superhero all the time. Who needs that kind of pressure? But don't worry, I've got my afternoon all planned out, starting with going down to the newspaper office to get some answers.

Oh, I've been getting plenty of answers. It's just that none of them are any good.

From the corner of my eye I see a dark-skinned, sweaty casualty of President Pajizo's economic policies approaching the store, trying to maintain his gyroscopic equilibrium but staggering as if he just might slip and fall off the planet. His ribs are sticking out like a bony xylophone with a thin layer of leathery skin stretched over it. He asks for a bottle of Coco Loco, one of the many available cheap, hard, machine-made alcohols. Suzie makes the sale, and this insignificant statistic five figures to the right of the decimal point on the gross domestic scale wanders away with it, heading for that sixth column, the millionths.

"How is that stuff?" I ask, nodding towards the diminishing row of Coco Loco bottles on the shelf.

"Dreadful," she says. "It's all chemicals. You can catch the same buzz from drinking mimeograph machine fluid."

"Yum yum," I say. "So you realize you're part of the problem."

"I didn't see you stopping me."

Girlish laughter bursts from the storeroom and spills over to where I'm lying. Antonia and her cousins Priscilla and Marjorie have captured a member of the illustrious race of giant Guayaquil waterfront cockroaches and put it in a jar. It's nearly two inches long. I ask them, "Are you going to study it or use it for breeding?"

"But Mom, it's only one cockroach."

"There is no such thing as 'only one' cockroach," I say, as the oily creature scampers around the glass walls searching for an exit. "And if those suckers ever get organized, we're all in big trouble."

The music is interrupted by a paid political ad for Governor Segundo Canino promising free breakfasts for elementary school children, cheaper medicines, and a sound monetary policy. The voice trumpets: "His decision not to build the Gulf of Guayaquil oil platform saved the country *one hundred billion sucres!*"

"Right. And his decision not to build a rocket to Neptune probably saved the country one hundred *trillion* sucres."

"Better be careful what you say in this neighborhood," says a familiar voice in American-accented Spanish.

I sit up. Peter's standing at the iron-barred window, watching me cross my legs on the beer cooler.

How the hell did he find me here?

"Ruben told me where you live," he says, anticipating my question. "I hope that's okay with you."

"Sure, I guess. What's on your mind?"

Suzie's giving him the eye.

"You wanna go to the bullfights this afternoon?" he asks. "I've never seen one, and I'm dying to go. How 'bout it?"

Bullfights? They're not really my idea of fun. "They do them differently here, you know. Bulls are expensive, and they can't afford to kill one every day."

"No kidding? So what do they do?"

"Chase it around until it gets tired," I say.

"Well, I'd still like to go. Interested?"

Suzie's giving *me* the eye.

Wouldn't you know that a needlelike itch chooses this exact moment to sting my upper thigh? Heat and sticky shorts, dammit. I can't scratch now with my crotch forming a flying V in front of this man's gaze, so I stand up and give my hem a discreet tug. That's better.

What the hell. I need to spend *some* time with my daughter, and I'll still have time to run over to the newspaper office afterwards.

"Give me five minutes to change into some long pants," I say.

And some good running shoes.

Three inches of last night's downpour still lie stagnant in the gutters. The storm drains are full, and the sky is heavy with dark, portentous clouds. We tiptoe between the puddles like a trio of ballerinas on our way to the coliseum.

"I didn't realize you were so, like, Ecuadorian," says Peter.

"What do you mean?" I ask.

"Well, I thought you were an American like me—"

"I am an American citizen."

"I don't mean that. I mean, uh, I didn't realize your family lived in such a—oh, crap. I'm sorry. You must think I'm a jerk."

I'll give him points for that.

"No," I say, making the effort to flood my voice with warmth and understanding, "just typical. You've grown up with only one side of the story."

"Story . . . ?"

Hoo-boy.

"Okay. Like when a big U.S. corporation builds a factory down here, Americans are all told it's such a risky proposition that it's practically an act of charity, so the Department of Commerce waives all duties and taxes and even rent sometimes. And when the workers get four dollars a day, you're told that's more than most other jobs pay in Ecuador."

"But it's still a sucky wage," he says, shaking his head.

It is indeed.

"I mean, like Americans are so fat and complacent, you know? But when you see what really goes on down here, how poor people are and stuff? You just feel so fuckin' powerless. Know what I mean?"

"Yeah. I know what you mean."

"But hey, listen," he goes on, "I've been looking for a way to like impress you, okay?"

"You've been looking for a way to impress me."

"Yeah. Well, Ruben told me you were trying to find out about this, you know," his voice drops, "this murder case?"

Sounds like Ruben's been telling him an awful lot.

"Well, I had to flash the cash, but I finally got this provincial cop to say that he heard that your friend's body was snuck out of the police morgue to the morgue at that Social Security Hospital."

The free hospital. But—

Sure. It makes sense. Hide it among all those nameless bodies.

He stands and faces me. "I bet I can get inside the place."

Chalk one up to the big, dumb American. He may come in handy after all.

"Are you any good with a camera?" I ask.

He smiles.

We spend an hour watching them irritate a bull. (Hey: in Peru they use dynamite.) Antonia recoils at one heart-fluttering moment when the bull dodges the matador and gores one of the horses and spatters its gray-white rump with blood. But it's only a flesh wound, apparently, and the show goes on. I buy my starving adolescent some homemade coconut candy from a chipped enamelware tray carried on the head of a roving salesman, a shirtless young *esmeraldeño* with steady eyes and quick hands, doing some of the only work a poor Afro-Ecuadorian male can get in this big, indifferent city.

When it's over, and we're snaking our way through the crush of people, Antonia announces her retirement from blood sports. She gets no argument from me.

As we're crossing the street, the out-of-place sound of a car accelerating catches my ear, people and buses divide and a tan Mercedes splits from the herd, heading right at us. I seize Antonia with a flying tackle and shoulder roll between the stopped cars, legs splaying into the wet gutter. I hear a thump and look up to see Peter lunging headfirst over the hood of the car, face smashing into the windshield and body rolling up onto the roof before falling off into the street.

Four cars and a taxi skid to a halt. Antonia and I rush out into the street as an excited crowd gathers. I kneel down beside Peter. His face is torn and covered with blood, soaking his shirt, but he's conscious. The taxi driver steps out of his car. People are offering useless contradictory advice and I hear myself saying, "Never mind that, just get him to the nearest hospital," and some of the men standing by help me load Peter into the back of the cab so we can turn around and speed off towards the free hospital. Bullets of sweat are streaming down the taxi driver's neck as he outruns red lights and cuts off vehicles as if they weren't there.

I look at Antonia and find myself counting her arms and legs, her fingers—my God, I'm panting for breath. She looks at me, breathing hard, her eyes wet with tears that won't fall.

A man's hand closes around mine. I look down at the bloody wrists, mashed watch, bloodstains on my clothes. Blood everywhere. I let him hold on to me.

I lean close to Peter's ear and whisper, "You picked a helluva way to get to the hospital."

"But I wasn't . . . trying for the morgue," he answers.

I sit in the gray, featureless hallway. The nauseating smell of rotting organs, filth and urine sticks to me like a chemical weapon in this dreadful heat. I wash my hands in cold water, scrubbing up to my elbows, but I can't change out of my blood-caked clothes.

And I can't seem to stay away from hospitals.

Cousin Lucho Jr. came and took Antonia home, but first I had to watch them clean and bandage several abrasions on my one-and-only daughter's precious skin, leaving me agonizingly aware of what a mistake it was to try to bring her with me and "teach her the ropes" or some such idiocy. When I think that she could have been taken from me, or . . . When I think that . . .

This is getting deeper than I ever feared.

We're both going to have a few bruises on our elbows and knees tomorrow. But Christ.

Peter's lucky, they say. No major internal damage. But his fender's pretty banged up and he's certainly not going anywhere for a while. His face is heavily bandaged. He strains, his voice muffled, and manages to tell me that he is still willing to try to get into the morgue.

I tell him I'd rather have him lie still and recover.

"You took one hell of a hit."

He says he'll be okay.

"I'll come back tomorrow," I say, patting the cast on his arm. "Call me if you need anything."

I ask the nurse if there's anywhere I can change out of these gory clothes. I'm willing to ride home wrapped in a towel at this point, if it's clean enough. Since my cousin Lucho works his second job here, I get a special favor: a cold shower and some mismatched lost-and-founds. I'm so grateful you'd think she's just donated me one of her kidneys.

I step out into the street, grab an uptown bus, fall into a blank-faced trance and somehow manage to space out, miss my stop, get off and find myself in the Parque del Centenario. The Independence monument is a dull black shaft pointing at the dark gray sky. Rain is due any minute.

The military are giving a show of strength, parading down the Avenida 9 de Octubre.

I'm dressed like a junkie, carrying a bag of bloodstained clothes, still recovering from shock, and uneasy about being in this crowd, so I wander over to the Parque Victoria where I can sit on a bench, gather my thoughts and watch the iguanas beg for food, just like New York City pigeons.

The man next to me gets up and leaves his paper. I open it, staring, not seeing.

Then I come across a death notice: Ecuador's first woman police officer. Martha Consuela Gallegos was a detective, thirty-three years old, mother of three small children, and was shot in the filthy streets of a slum town just a few miles south of the Colombian border. Thirty-three. I bet we would have liked each other.

Throats clear. I look up from my paper. Two military officers are standing over me.

One of them is a man I should have killed a long time ago.

One must forgive one's enemies—but not before they have been hanged.

—Heinrich Heine

He's Captain Ponce now, as thin and colorless as ever, with a light straw mustache, sharp cheekbones, and nerves spun from some lightweight tungsten alloy. His tightly drawn face crinkles slightly around his eyes and mouth, the only sign of age.

"May we join you?" asks the other green shadow, whose name is Lieutenant Lasio, according to his polished bars and machine-sewed name tag. Unlike Ponce, he's got a round boyish face with playful eyes, straight dark hair, and a thick black mustache.

"Sure," I say, folding up the paper, my mind regretfully releasing the fading image of Detective Martha Consuela.

Lasio sits, uses the paper as an icebreaker.

"Lot going on these days, huh?"

"I guess."

"You following the election campaign?"

"I'm staying away from it," I say. "How about you?"

"It's bad," says Captain Ponce, his trademark clipped speech slicing the air like a razor. "Very bad for the country. If that socialist teacher Gatillo wins, all the foreign investors will pull out."

"And it's not like they're throwing buckets of money at us right now," says Lieutenant Lasio. "Only way to get rich is to marry an American, *¿no cierto?*"

"We're not all rich."

"With a dollar worth *six thousand sucres*? Come on!"

"Problem is those *gringa* babes don't speak Spanish," says Captain Ponce, tearing into each word like a hunting dog on a rabbit's neck.

"Maybe you can help me with my English?" says Lasio. "Let's see—how the heck do they say it? Oh, yeah: *Hell-o. How are you miss señorita?*"

"Fine, thanks. And you?" I say, playing along.

"*Do you like*—uh—*Guayaquil?*"

"Actually, it's getting kind of scary."

"*What is 'scary'?*"

I look at them both. "It means I'm afraid."

"*What is 'afraid'?*"

"Frightened. Fearful. Do you know the word 'fear'?"

"No."

"That's really something," I tell them in Spanish. "When I get back to the United States I'm going to tell everybody there that the officers in the Ecuadorian Army do not know the meaning of the word 'fear.'"

That gets some laughs.

"Join us for dinner," says Captain Ponce.

I look at what I'm wearing.

"I have much nicer clothes at home."

"I bet you do," Lieutenant Lasio leers.

"Besides, I'd better be getting back to my family."

"No, I think you better come with us," says Captain Ponce.

He eats quickly, his fork darting between his dish and mouth like an agitated lizard, as if at any moment the piercing clarion call of the bugle will be summoning him into battle.

"You're going to drop dead of a heart attack someday, *hermano*," says Lieutenant Lasio.

"I'm not afraid of death," says Captain Ponce, barely chewing before he swallows. "Well, I wouldn't want to have my guts ripped out in an alley in this filthy town. But dying high up in the mountains, now that's sweet. It's just like going to sleep. It's delicious. *Delicious*."

"You go out laughing," Lieutenant Lasio assures me.

"Bleeding to death, too. It's easy. I took a bullet in the chest near Paquisha in the *oriente* and I didn't feel a thing. Until the doctors started to patch me up. *¡Salonero! ¡Ají!*"

"*Sí, señor,*" says the waiter, rushing over with a dish of hot chili pepper sauce.

"Still, I'd rather come back from battle alive," I say.

"Of course, but not incapacitated," says Captain Ponce. "I'd rather die than be incapacitated."

"Or disappear," says Lieutenant Lasio.

"Yes," says Ponce, looking at me. "Many great warriors disappear."

"Great warriors become legends when they disappear," says Lasio. "I mean that we'd rather die cleanly than be declared missing in action because your decomposing body is washing up somewhere downriver—"

"We know what you mean, Lieutenant," says Ponce.

"With no one there to mourn for you or to see you properly buried—"

"All right, Lasio. Now I need to discuss something privately with *señorita* Buscarsela."

Lieutenant Lasio rises abruptly, smiling at me, and asks, "May I see you again?"

"Uh, sure."

That satisfies him more than it should.

He's gone.

"*¡Salonero! ¡Otra cerveza!*"

"*Sí, señor.*"

"Never fails. Rebels acting up because of the elections," he says. "Three months ago, north of La Sofía. Near the Colombian border. They took six infantry units by surprise. Had to call in air support. We chased them all the way to the river, but they got away. Took down a few choppers and tore us up the middle with ground fire and booby traps."

He lets that sink in.

"That's pretty damn impressive," he says. "We both know there aren't a half dozen rebel leaders in the whole country with that kind of training, and Juanito was the only one who worked the *sierra* and the *oriente* with equal skill."

"He trained a lot of people. It could have been anybody."

"You didn't answer my question."

"What question?"

"Is Juanito alive?"

A spasm jolts a weak spot in my chest, then flutters away unseen. *Damn it.* But I can't help it. Involuntary flashbacks to the interrogation room.

"I would have heard from him." My voice sounds like cold air flooding a cracked vacuum tube.

"But you're not sure."

I was sure a week ago. I don't answer.

"Okay, okay," he says. "They've also been attacking police and military bases in the province of Morona Santiago. Eating away at U.S.–backed efforts to protect the oil supply."

"I don't think I'm supposed to know that."

"So you didn't hear it from me. Little closer to his home turf, eh?"

"Hmm." Why should I believe him?

"They spent three days warning people to stay away from the army base outside of Macas. Everything from spray-painted wall grafitti to laser-printed statements hand delivered by masked courier to Radio Sangay. They're setting up their own Web site, too. Then last week they took out the power, stormed the installation and burned all the files, without killing a single civilian. When it was over, the rebels helped carry wounded soldiers and officers to the hospital, reprimanding them for putting up a fight."

That sounds like someone I once knew.

Johnny was always a quick thinker. Irreverent. Shameless. Like the time we were holed up in a bank during a botched "redistribution" effort and he distracted everyone by setting fire to the money so we could get out alive.

That time.

I shake my head. "Johnny's idea of kindness was to shoot a person in the heart instead of the head and leave them with a good-looking corpse."

"Can I ask you something?"

Well, his interrogation methods have improved. I give him an open look.

"What did you see in him?"

I'm sorry to say this, sad as it is: "There were only a handful of people in this world who I could truly count on. He was one of them."

Captain Ponce nods. "Loyalty is a noble emotion," he says. He wipes his mouth, pushes his plate away.

He asks point-blank, "Do you hate me?"

"I don't hate anybody. I just remember things."

We sit silently as the waiter clears the table.

"Why are you back here?" he asks.

"I just came to visit for a few weeks. Really. Then *padre* Samuel Campos was murdered."

"Hmm. I saw about that."

"I'd give anything to examine his body, speak to the suspect in person."

"Nothing I can do. The police have him."

"Where?"

"That's police business."

"*Padre* Samuel saved *both* our lives," I remind him.

"Yes. But I owe *you*. You were supposed to kill me."

"And you me."

"Yes."

I finally ask him, "Why are you only a captain? I thought you'd be at least a major by now."

"Don't you know? That's right, you weren't here. I tried to kill the president."

I call my family to let them know I'm fine, and to make sure that Antonia's okay.

We find a waterfront bar. Noisy. Dark. Anonymous. I'm certainly dressed for it.

Eyes gleam sideways in the shadows, looking at me, at him, at the uniform, memorizing the details.

Keep looking. You'll never see me in these rags again.

Ponce finds a remote corner, offers me the darkest spot. Quite chivalrous, really.

A minute later the barman comes over. A record for this place, I think.

"Two *canelasos*," Ponce orders.

One eye narrows to a slit. This crusty old suds merchant clearly knows that only some crazy *serranos* would order a warm drink in the middle of the hottest season.

Normally the idea would be never to attract attention, but it's a little late for that. With his stiffly brushed parade uniform and tight-assed commanding style, Ponce might as well order a flaming zombie.

We toast each other.

He orders more. Some men do not know how to sip alcohol. And soon the thin blade of his tongue softens and the words start to bubble up and percolate out of him.

"You probably didn't even hear about it up in the *Yunay*, but it was big. Big scandal. The armed forces wanted to buy twenty-five German fighter planes. The best. Better than the overpriced crap the Americans sell us, anyway. Total cost, five billion dollars. That's right, dollars. Think the Germans want to fuck around with sucres?"

"I guess not."

"Anyway, getting congressional approval for them was a bitch. But our luck held out and the rebels struck. They ambushed and killed three *consejeros*. Then they kidnapped a couple of oil company workers and a desk sergeant from Quito who later turned up in a ditch with the initals of the movement carved in his forehead."

"That doesn't sound like—"

Right.

"So thanks to all that rebel activity, the government declares a security crisis and the deal goes through. Then the shipment arrives. *Five planes.* So where's the rest of the shipment? The finance ministers are going nuts, threatening to go to war against Germany. Can you imagine? War with Germany?" Ponce laughs. "Where's the rest of the shipment? Where's *the four billion dollars*? Two hours later we receive sealed orders to report to the Ariel Air Force Base, where President Pajizo's socksucker, General Duarte, makes us spend the night burning documents as if we were abandoning the city to the enemy or something. Lots of big German words, but I can read the numbers. And it sure looks like a contract for five planes at two hundred million dollars apiece. Then around two in the morning we were told that a mistake had been made, and that some of the documents had to be 're-created.' So they start retyping the documents and re-signing General Vélez's signature. The German's the same, I guess, but the numbers aren't. It looks a lot like a contract for twenty-five planes at a total cost of five billion.

"Now, we fought in the Peruvian jungle with General Vélez and—well, you know what the conditions were like—and we're loyal to him. So one of us cracked open the oyster and when General Vélez heard that Pajizo's *compadre*, General Duarte, was ordering us to forge incriminating documents with his signature on them, he dug in at the Manta Air Force Base with hundreds of his men.

"That night a dozen of our most experienced fighter pilots received orders from the president himself to arm their jets and bomb Manta. They responded that they'd rather join Vélez and bomb the presidential palace, if that was how he wanted to play it. When Pajizo figured out that ninety percent of the military stood behind General Vélez, he backed down. But the next day all the press releases and all the TV reports said that *we* had tried to overthrow the president. I felt sick. Was this my Ecuador? The Ecuador I fought for on three fronts and would die for at a moment's notice?"

He looks me in the eye. In spite of everything, there's a bond there.

He goes on. "Within hours, General Vélez was charged with treason, found guilty and sentenced to ninety-nine years in the stockade, when you and I know damn well that the maximum sentence allowed under the Constitution is sixteen years. It's as if the law is nothing but dead letters to those guys.

"Now every true soldier's blood was boiling as soon as we found out about it. We're discussing what sort of action we should be taking, when I get word that General Duarte wants to see me. They escort me up to his office, and he orders me to select fifteen commandos for a special job. So I assemble a team of the most trustworthy men you'd ever want to meet, and the next morning we're standing on the tarmac awaiting further orders. But General

Duarte's nowhere in sight. It's starting to get weird. The next thing we know the president's plane is landing, and the commanding officer's missing. We went on parade to meet him, and there's Lieutenant Colonel Abismo ordering us to disarm. Then that dickhead Pajizo gets off the plane surrounded by nineteen or twenty bodyguards. Suddenly there's a shot from I don't know where and his bodyguards form a circle around their man and start shooting *at us*, for fuck's sake. They killed *seven* loyal officers."

Another order of drinks has appeared. I leave mine alone. Ponce gulps his down and continues: "But we're fighters. We spend our lives training for this kind of shit, and within seconds we were taking cover and shooting to kill every one of Pajizo's mother-raping bodyguards. It was completely insane. Nobody was giving orders. Somebody shouted, 'Kill Pajizo!' And I hear Pajizo yelling, 'Get your hands off me, I'm the president!' Then the TV crews arrived—I don't know who the hell sent for *them*—and I got thrust up in front of the cameras to explain that *el presidente* had tried to change our republic into a dictatorship, and that we would release him as soon as he set General Vélez free. They actually asked for proof that the president was still alive! So we brought him out. And that piece of dog waste, Fernando Pajizo, got on TV and said that he was ordering General Vélez's release, and that he would not seek action against the 'commandos' of the Ariel Air Force Base. He told us off-camera that if he ever went back on his word, we could spit in his face. But somebody sure busted me down to captain. And I'm still waiting to get within spitting distance of his face."

"You're lucky that's all they did." If that story's even half-true. I ask him, "How come you're free?"

"I've only lost three lives. I still have four left."

And he smiles.

Must be the light. I'd swear he has eyes like a cat.

W e stand under the white arches on the perimeter of a deserted square and watch the rain pummel the streets.

Captain Ponce tells me he has to report to Shushuqui in three days, deep in the northeast jungle. Oil country. But first he wants to do me a favor.

"There is one person who might know something about why anyone would want your precious *padre* wiped off the map."

He pauses for effect, the manipulative SOB.

"Herrera."

My bag is starting to smell like a slop bucket full of rotting sheep parts.

"Herrera?"

"An old comrade of yours, yes? He's in the military prison."

I listen to the sound of the rain stippling the expansive puddles.

"How is he?"

"We're keeping him alive."

My eyes question him.

"If he were in the police prison, he'd be dead by now."

There's a standard to measure yourself by.

But some rules can be bent. He thinks he can get me in to see my old *compañero*.

He says, "You see? General Duarte's not such a bad guy."

"Yeah: If we had trains, he'd make them run on time."

Take you home on my motorcycle?"

"No, thanks."

"Don't want me to know where you live, eh?" he says, smiling like he already knows it.

Too bad. It would have been quicker. And taxi drivers remember. Oh, well.

I'm damp enough to grow moss on my back but past the point of caring by the time I climb aboard a windowless bus with no interior lights, except for a ring of blinking colored bulbs around a glowing picture of Jesus.

Someday we're going to put our own rocket ship into space and the command module is going to have a strip of orange shag with tufted pom-poms on the instrument panel, rows of gaudy Christmas lights around the portholes, and one of those postcards of Jesus that winks at you hanging from the rearview mirror.

No one looks at me too hard. But they can smell me.

When I get home, I take the bag of clothes up to the rooftop sink and try to wash them by hand. But the blood is stiff and set by now, and parts of it are as hard as paint. None of the traditional household remedies will get it all out.

I walk five blocks west and toss the bag into a communal dump.

Clouds pass, swirling and gray and threatening, but the rain holds off while the whimsical sky delights in toying with us.

It's not making my unhappy task any easier, peeling back the gummy cloth to see my sweet Antonia's uncorrupted knees looking like someone took a cheese grater to them. And the passing night has revealed further blue-black badges of cruelty, which have emerged and spread like gruesome sunspots across her celestial skin. I wash off some of the phagocyte residue with warm water, pat her dry, dab the wound with disinfectant and stick on some fresh gauze bandages.

"Does that feel any better?" I ask.

"It still hurts when I bend it."

"So don't bend it," I say, stroking the smooth skin near her boo-boo. "I got kind of banged up myself, but I rolled with it a little better. Your knee's going to hurt for a couple of days. Are you okay?"

"Yes."

"Are you sure?"

"Yes," she assures me.

"Good. That's good. Do you think you can make it to the hospital?"

"I have to go back to the hospital?"

"No, I mean, do you want to come to the hospital with me to visit Peter?"

"Not really."

"Oh." Serves me right for asking. "Tell you what, we'll go and spend twenty minutes there, then we'll do a museum and some shopping, if you're up to it."

"Yay!" How sweet it is to hear that sound, just the way she used to say it when she was four years old. Of course I don't tell her that.

I'm also hoping that seeing Peter recover might help ease any remaining trauma she might have.

So this is our little family outing on a Saturday morning. A trip to the free hospital, a place where pregnant women are crammed two to a bed and you have to bring your own sheets.

But they have sprung for the handsome young *gringo* and have scrounged up a couple of mismatched sheets that are more gray than white. In fact, Peter looks very well taken care of. He's feeling better, and Antonia tells him about the three-foot-long iguanas she has seen lurking in the city parks.

I spend the rest of the morning sifting through a few precious grains of the dwindling sands of time with my daughter, visiting the spotlit galleries attended by gaunt, chain-smoking avant-gardists with dark circles under their eyes, then passing between the vigilant, unsmiling ones who guard the austere chambers that house thousand-year-old earthenware pots and painted clay jaguar figurines and flat masks of beaten gold representing the sun god, and the modern Latin American soul-stirring paintings of Guayasamín and his sibling artisans reflecting our torturous condition. Then it's out for a special lunch at a typical eatery where nothing is canned, and someone else has to wash, peel, and chop up the fruit, then put it into a blender just to make a couple of glasses of juice for the two of us. And of course it's also special because it's just she and I being the mother and daughter we're supposed to be. Maybe we're like this all the time in a parallel universe somewhere out beyond the visible horizon of my life. A place like that would be heaven.

There is a haze surrounding the people and events involved in this," says Ruben, looking out his hotel window towards the white wave crests forming on the river. "It's almost like a halo of darkness. The deeper you look, the less you see, until seeing so much nothing starts to mean something."

I nod with sincerest empathy.

"Listen to me," he says, quickly dispelling his words and sentiments with a backhanded wave. "I don't know what I'm saying."

"Oh, yes, you do," I reassure him. "You know that somebody planted the phony details of Ismaél's arrest and confession in your paper on two separate occasions, and that this fairy tale is likely to become the official version of the events. And we both know that you've got to have some serious kind of power to pull off a scam like that. The *padre* was a hard man to make disappear."

"So, unfortunately, the circle widens," he says.

"Only in terms of the invisible puppet masters," I say. "The skunks who actually pulled the trigger are out there, and I'm going to sniff them out. Eventually the circle closes in. You just find me that reporter."

"I'll have his name by this evening. Come by afterwards, no matter how late. My midnight lamp will definitely be burning."

"I admire that in a man."

"Admire what?"

"Endurance."

He smiles.

There is a rough knock at the door and a bellhop comes in bearing today's stack of newspapers.

"I called down for these three hours ago," Ruben complains.

"*Mañana* comes all the way from Quito," says the bellhop.

"Always excuses! How do you expect the country to progress when all they ever do is make excuses?"

The bellhop fixes his eyes on a spot somewhere between Nairobi and Easter Island as his way of answering that one.

After he leaves, Ruben says, "I did find out one thing that would interest you."

"Yes?"

"My contacts were able to confirm that the North Guayas Militia has a new leader, a man named Colonel Alboroto. He came up through the ranks and seized the chance to take power as soon as he could."

"So aside from being opportunistic, what's he like?"

"Murderous, apparently."

The blue shadows are edging into the night, car traffic on the avenue picking up that eerie glow of a procession of sleek dragons with fiery nostrils, when a couple of particularly bright headlights stab my nighttime-adjusted eyes. It's a drab green jeep, driven by a harried-looking corporal in combat fatigues.

"Miss Filomena Buscarsela?"

"Yes."

"I got a message from Captain Ponce."

Alone, without even a pencil to take notes, I am led underground through the narrow, wet-walled corridors into a cold concrete room.

They sit me at one end of a long table under a low brick ceiling with instructions not to move, and give me plenty of time to soak up the icy indifference of this windowless room and the stale smell of embalming fluid.

Herrera is brought in, hands cuffed behind his back, dark hollows in his skin testifying to his lack of hot meals. Here and there purplish welts slither out from under his dusty prison clothes, tracing the endless trail of binding and beating he has been forced to walk. Some of the marks are months old. Some of them are quite fresh.

The guard sits Herrera down at the other end of the table, unlocks a cuff so Herrera can set his hands on the table in front of him, then ratchets it up again, tightly. Then he stations himself in the middle of the room between the two of us.

"Ten minutes," says the guard.

I check my watch.

They're probably recording this, too. I look up. The grimy lightbulb above us carelessly squanders most of its energy illuminating the water-stained ceiling, where an intricate network of cracks and canals runs wild with the insane patterns of pain.

Flaws in the surface. Where do they lead?

"Why are you here?" asks Herrera.

"A friend of mine has been charged with a murder he didn't commit and I'm trying to clear him."

"Too bad for him."

"The murder of *padre* Samuel Campos."

He takes a moment, then the hard shell is back. "Yeah? So?"

"You knew the *padre*, even before I did."

"And?"

"So tell me about him."

"Why?"

I check my watch again.

"Why should I tell you anything?" he says.

It's a legitimate question.

"Who else have you got to tell it to?"

Seconds tick away.

"I'm sorry, Freddy—"

He shushes me. Movement exposes skin.

A hideous network of scarlet and pus-filled electrode burns shrinks from the light beneath his collar and cuffs. I suppress the sudden evil urge to break the guard's head open against the concrete walls.

"How've you been?" he asks, out of the blue. "I hear you've got a daughter."

Gulp.

"She as pretty as you?"

"Prettier."

"Uh-huh. As smart?"

"Smarter. She's got the benefit of learning from all my screw-ups."

"Then she must know how to be careful."

"Yes."

"Good," he says. We spend a few fleeting moments listening to the silence between us, then his words take on a subtle gravity. "One must watch what one says."

"Yes. One must always watch what one says."

"Campos did pastoral service in Loja for a while, remember?"

"Yeah."

"Same year Aguilera's plane crashed."

Right. Of course.

"There was a power blackout. It blocked radio transmissions in the whole province."

I'm thinking back, trying to piece it together from memory. There was another blackout . . . ?

"Some *campesinos* came running, told us a plane had crashed in the valley. You know the place."

"Yes."

"All those mountains around and the plane crashed *in a valley*?"

It's coming together now.

"We had a lot of combat experience between us," he says. "We knew the difference between a complete airplane wreck and a partial one. It sure looked like it had blown up in the air."

The guard doesn't move.

"A couple of unmarked trucks drove up, and they cleared the debris away in a few hours, before most of the country had even heard the news. The official explanation was that it would 'facilitate tourism.' Tourism!" He pounds the table. "At the site of a plane crash? Couldn't they even bother coming up with a decent lie?"

His voice reverberates off the slate gray stones.

A paint chip falls from the cracked ceiling.

The guard blinks.

"Farmers live way up in those hills. Tending sheep. Surefooted folks, they are. One of them climbed down the rock face and told a few of us he saw the plane going down *already in flames*. So maybe it didn't explode on contact like they said in all the news and TV reports. The *padre* told him he had to go down the road and describe what he saw to the authorities. But the next morning, before he could tell his story, he was found at the bottom of a gorge. Slipped, they said."

Why didn't *padre* Samuel ever tell me this?

"Time's up," says the guard.

As he leads me back upstairs, the guard says to me, "Don't worry about him. He's always babbling some commie nonsense."

I ask Lieutenant Lasio to let me out a few blocks from Ruben's hotel.

He pulls over, bars the door with his arm and says that he won't let me out unless I answer his proposition with one of the standard synonyms for "yes." I tell him I didn't bring my thesaurus with me.

"I happen to know that you're married and that your wife lives in Quito," I say, pulling away.

"She understands." Lieutenant Lasio laughs. Now there's an original line. "Tell me something," he says.

"About what?"

"The enlisted men all grumble about Captain Ponce 'cause he's such a hard-ass. How come you get along with him?"

"I once pulled a thorn out of his paw."

"Hmm. I think I've done that a few times myself," he says with a bright, toothy smile.

I take a cautious roundabout route to the hotel, which is not easy, since it's dark and the collected rainwater is flowing three feet out from the clogged gutters into the middle of the street. But I'm really anxious to talk to Ruben and find out what he's learned.

We're getting close.

I can almost touch it.

A cantankerous-sounding truck with a creaky flatbed turns the corner and lurches along the street in my direction. I keep walking, keeping a wary eye on the truck. The way it slows and rattles to the curb just ahead of me has a dreamlike I-knew-this-was-coming quality to it, helped along by the sticky gobs of streetlight dancing on the rippling water and the close, still heat of the night.

The driver stops the truck, and his partner climbs out and starts walking calmly over towards me. He is fat enough for me to outrun him if I have to. He swaggers up to me as if he's going to ask me the time but instead he says, "What are you doing here? Got a name? Got a *cédula*?"

"Sure, now I've got a question: Who the hell are you?" I answer.

By now the driver is standing on my other side, triangulating me between two unfriendly bodies and a cement retaining wall with the rushing river behind it.

"Show her," says the driver.

The first guy pulls a plastic ID card out of his pocket and holds it up for me to see. It's his picture all right, on a card that identifies him as a member of the National Police. And?

"We're police, *señorita*," says the driver.

"All right, I'm getting out my *cédula*," I say, slowly reaching into my pocket for my national identity card. It's still "Good Until Death."

They look at it. I haven't lived at the address on the card for nineteen years.

"Where do you live?" asks the driver.

"In the *barrio* Centro Cívico."

"Then what are you doing here?" asks the partner, as if there were some crime in being found outside my neighborhood.

"I thought the curfew was repealed."

"And if we wanted to search you, see if you're carrying any drugs? *¿Acaso un pito?* Some marijuana?"

Oh, terrific. One uncorroborated report and I get ten years in the local hellhole.

On paper, Ecuador's law books protect me against this kind of warrantless search and seizure. But there are no law books on this street corner. The law begins and ends with the cops who are standing in front of me right now, guns in their belts, blocking my way. And I don't have any reason to believe that they're on duty, either. Or if they're really cops at all.

So I turn out my pockets and stand there with the empty fabric dangling from my hands and nothing but lint on my fingers.

"Where's your passport?" asks the driver in a flash of flat-footed inspiration.

"I don't need to carry it around with me when I've got a valid *cédula*," I explain.

"You have to carry your passport with you at all times."

"Oh." That clause must have been amended to the immigration laws late this afternoon, because I was legal this morning.

"We're going to have to take you in for questioning," says the driver. They open the way for me. The path between them leads straight to the open door of the truck.

I glance at their belts.

I could probably shoot my way out of this.

If I had a gun.

They put me between them—leaving my hands and feet free so I can claw their tender places and kick my way through the windshield if I have to—and, somewhat to my relief, take me on a bumpy ride straight to the nearest police station.

No passport, eh?" says a sworn member of that dreaded gang, Hell's Bureaucrats, astride the leather throne behind his desk, chain-smoking Full Speeds, the cheapest and smelliest brand on the market. Filterless. "You'll have to pay a fifty-dollar fine."

"*Fifty dollars?* I haven't got that with me."

"You haven't got fifty dollars with you?"

"If I did, your boys would have found it."

They let that one pass.

"Then you must fill out the alternate form, which authorizes payment in sucres, at today's exchange rate, which is—" He flips languidly through a thumb-smeared copy of *El Mundo*. "—Six thousand seven hundred and seventy. So that makes—" He works it out on a calculator. Twice. "—Three hundred and thirty-eight thousand five hundred sucres."

"I don't have that on me, either," I say.

"You don't? Are you sure?"

"Who the hell walks around Guayaquil at night with that kind of money in their pockets?"

The pricks behind me whisper comments about the kind of women who do, then the fat-assed cop who collared me says something about how Buscarsela sounds a lot like *buscona*.

It means whore.

They laugh about it.

Yeah, I haven't heard that one since eighth grade.

At least this is playing out as farce instead of tragedy. Maybe a routine shakedown after all, to fulfill their quota. Completely arbitrary.

"Then you will also have to fill out this promissory note," says the Devil's auditor, and he shoves both documents across the desk towards me.

"Got a pen?" I say.

The bureaucrat shoves a pen at me. I start to walk away.

"Hold it!" says the bureaucrat. "Two hundred and forty sucres."

"What?"

"The charge for those forms is two hundred and forty sucres."

I take a close look at the forms and see that they are both embossed with the municipal seal and cost a hundred twenty sucres each. So I dig into my cash and hand the bureaucrat the grungiest bills I can find. And the bills around here can get pretty grungy.

But my luck is still holding. He could have told me that the official forms are only available from city hall starting at 8:00 A.M. Monday morning.

I sit in a wobbly plastic chair and fill out the forms, then hand them back to the bureaucrat, who seizes them with his cloven hooves.

"Profession?" he blurts out, one more unfilled space staring up at him from the standardized form.

Stormer of gates? Chaser of dreams? Tireless enemy of evil? Working mother?

All of the above.

"Private investigator."

He groans slightly while lifting a massive binder, and starts flipping through sheet after sheet of computer printout.

"That's not in the profession book," he announces forbiddingly.

He slides the fateful tome around and shows it to me. Apparently there's no feminine entry for *investigator*. Guess I'll have to change professions.

Or change genders.

I'm leaning close when he blows the smoke in my face so it goes straight down inside me and scorches my tender air sacs in half a hundred places with lye-tipped needles.

"Just put down homemaker," I say, coughing viciously. This farce is wearing thin.

"*Cédula,*" he says.

I produce my *cédula* again.

"Voting card."

"I'm not allowed to vote. I'm not a citizen."

"*Cédula tributaria.*"

Jesus, somebody should teach these guys how to use *verbs*.

"I don't file taxes. I don't live here. I'm not a citizen."

The bureaucrat compares the data on one form with the data on the other form, then when everything seems to be just about ready and in order, he clips them together.

"*Una foto.*" Oh, God, no.

"I don't carry photos of myself around with me—"

"I can't process the papers without a photo," he says, tossing them aside and turning his back on me so he can start shuffling through a pile of papers like he's got a thousand other things to do. I don't believe this.

On second thought, I do.

It's nearly midnight.

"Where can I get a photo taken at this hour?"

Ah, it just so happens that the bureaucrat has a Polaroid in the back. The fee? Only ten dollars.

I don't have it, but he'll take my watch.

'm looking forward to a few minutes under Ruben's shower and washing the stale *eau de police station* off me in a steady stream of warm water.

I rap lightly on his door.

I would have called ahead but someone ripped the receiver off the pay phone at the police station.

I give another rap, pass a few seconds watching the wallpaper age, then try the knob. It turns and opens in.

Blood-flecked pages of notes are being scattered by the breeze and blowing out the open window like the last fading fragments of a shredded human life.

He's slumped at his desk, facedown in a soggy mass of clotted newspaper clippings, black blood and newsprint all smeared together.

There are also three gaping exit wounds in his back that speak of a skilled assassin firing in rapid succession from about five feet away.

It wasn't the throat cutter.

I touch his neck. Cold enough.

The blood's still wet in spots. Couldn't be more than an hour old, which means this happened while I was being held up by the police. If that's a coincidence, then I'm Queen Elizabeth's long-lost love child, Princess Filomena of Corona.

Do I just get out now before the cops show up? Or should I call the bastards? They're probably watching me. I'd better call.

It takes five tries to get a dial tone. I tell them when and where.

I don't have much time.

I go around the room gathering up Ruben's notes. I have to pick the loose, blood-spattered sheets out of the potted plants, from under the couch, even pull them off the iron grillwork on the balcony. They make quite a bundle. I can see a few sheets drifting along El Malecón and into the Río Guayas where they float out to sea.

I leave the sodden newspaper articles where they are, under Ruben's body.

I'm sweating.

I look around, trying to memorize everything. There doesn't seem to be any evidence of a struggle. No ejected shells anywhere nearby.

Three closely spaced shots. Small, maybe .22 caliber. This killer knew what he was doing.

Yeah, I said "he." There are traces of some mighty big footprints on the rug in front of the desk. I stand and try to gauge the approximate angle of the wounds.

Then I notice something. Ruben is not wearing his watch. I check his pockets, under the desk, in the drawers. I shuffle through the remaining newspaper articles still piled neatly on his desk, and there is his watch, under a few undisturbed clips, wrapped in newspaper.

I unfold it.

It's a crime article from *El Despacho*. Byline: Javier Putamayo. Our man.

It's hard to think straight right now, but I try. Ruben was expecting me. He was going to show me this article, but he hid it instead, which means he had some time to think before he died. So the killer was probably someone he knew, not the ham-handed North Guayas boys, who wouldn't have given him the chance to leave me this, and whatever it means, I'm not leaving it for the cops. I could use a new watch, too.

I grab the rest of the articles, put them together with the note pages.

Fuck waiting for the cops. Fuck being watched. I'm out of here.

Down the back stairs, past the old steel cans overflowing with sulfurous heaps of rotting garbage and out through the alley into the loathsome and endless night.

I've got to go underground.

Tonight.

CHAPTER
ELEVEN

El pobres rispetao único cuando puede matar.

The poor man is respected only when he can kill.
                                    —Ciro Alegría,
                                    La serpiente de oro

In a crowded marketplace four men emerge from the shadows, their barrel chests bathed in light and their faces lost in darkness. They surround me and say, We have something for you, hold out your hand. I slowly turn my palms up, and they place a large black-and-yellow-striped beetle in the hollow of my left palm. I can feel the bug's chitinous legs twitching as it tries to crawl under my skin. Then my flesh becomes like melting wax, sucking the huge insect in and closing back over it, leaving a walnut-sized black-and-blue lump with a thick ridged seam down the middle sewn up with coarse black stitches. My eyes are coated with a veil of film that I can't wipe away. I wander around the blurry place holding out my hand to the wise-eyed Indian women asking, What is this? One woman recoils from it as if it were evil, but another woman says, No, it means you have a child somewhere who is far from your love, who does not feel its warmth. Oh my God. How do I find this child and offer her my warmth? What gray, lonely limbo does she inhabit?

But there is no way to find her in this hazy place, where the walls are always melding with the shadows, and suddenly the shapes melt away, leaving me in a strange, dark place, filled with the smell of fresh earth and chalk dust. Dark skeletal outlines form above me and a hard cement floor materializes beneath my spine. Somehow I fell asleep.

I check my hand. It's smooth and flat. No violet-colored lumps. Lord have mercy.

The child that never was. A work-related miscarriage. Brought on, they said, by my spending a fourteen-hour ride on rough roads hidden in a truck bed. In Spanish, a miscarriage is called *un aborto*. Yeah, it's the same word.

She would have been ours. Mine and Johnny's.

I'm stiff and sore. There's a knot between my neck and right shoulder blade that feels like a malignant goblin is stabbing me with a bayonet whenever I turn my head to the right. The bare cement floor of a building under construction is not the ideal place to get a good night's rest.

So I lie there and think.

Three people dead and one in the hospital, red-inked threats and some well-orchestrated police harassment. Somebody's in an awful hurry to get things done. Where's the fabled Ecuadorian inefficiency? Because I'm seeing precision at every turn, like an expert knife thrower, just missing me every time.

Maybe that explains the stabbing pain in my back. I reach around and massage the base of my neck with my hand and ponder the sensation of being impelled to move in a particular direction to avoid being pinned to the wall by their blades.

They're trying to drive me to act. To run. To betray, like Johnny did. Ah, Johnny . . . Do they really think you're still alive? And that I'll lead them to you? Do they expect me to go scampering blindly over the Andes like a bitch in heat to find you, without looking back at the hot and skanky trail I'm leaving? Or do they just want me to believe that you're alive, figuring I'll beat a path straight to one of your lairs like some avenging angel out of a Gothic folktale hacking her way through the hundred-year-old overgrowth of prickly vines to awaken you with a kiss? Okay, I'll admit that the impulse is there, but I'll be damned if I'm going to disregard everything I've worked to cover up for the last twenty years.

And I'm not alone in that.

I pick up my bundle of notes and articles, which still have some flecks of blood on them, dried to a dark burgundy brown, and reread the article that was wrapped around Ruben's watch. He must have cut it from yesterday's *El Despacho*. It's about an active wing

of the Black Condor Brigade that has blown up key petroleum fa-
cilities and organized community takeovers of oil wells and pumping stations, and sabotaged airstrips as far south as the Río Santiago
near the Peruvian border and as far west as the Amazonian towns
of Arapicos, Chiguaza and Macas—Macas being mighty close to the
Andean foothills and the long arm of the law.

And the byline: Javier Putamayo. Unusual spelling. Most Ecuadorians spell Xavier with an *X*.

X is the unknown. *X* means nothing. But sometimes if you look
at nothing long enough, you begin to see something.

I'm trying to reconstruct something I wasn't there to see. The
only story that fits the grisly tableau I walked into is that Ruben
didn't realize that he was in deep trouble until sometime *after* the
killer showed up. So it was someone who did not alarm him at first.
A friend—or someone he thought was a friend, like his contacts to
Colonel Alboroto, the new paramilitary leader. Because if those
mercenaries had shown up with their high-caliber side arms a-
blazing, Ruben would have been puréed all over the room. No, this
was a quiet killer's precision weapon. Very precise indeed. And the
only way to leave a clue like this, if it is indeed a clue, would be if
they chatted for several minutes while Ruben pretended to be working, unconcernedly shuffling through his papers, when in fact he
was searching for this article and flagging it with his wristwatch,
hoping I would recognize it for what it was. Resigned to his own
death. One last struggle for the old warhorse.

But of course we'll never know his version of the story.

It was someone who entered without resistance. They talked a
bit, then—quick death from a small gun. It matches the MO for
padre Samuel's murder. I'm looking for the same person. And whoever wrote this article is part of the puzzle. I look at it again.

The Black Condor Brigade. The Río Santiago. Macas. I wonder.

Swat! Damn mosquitoes! Breeding like hell in all this stagnant
water. Hope they don't give me dengue. The last thing I need right
now.

Insects. Buzzing around my briny flesh, perceiving me as nothing but a heap of inanimate smells, something with no mind, diffuse, dissipating, drifting among the sea of odors surrounding these
murders, like the seaborne air currents wafting me towards the

mountains where a special kind of clay is found, the clay from which I was made, to a place where the streams run as cold as death's touch, and the few remaining Cañaris who inhabit the jagged hills are so miserably poor that they swear it's a happy occasion when a child dies because that means she doesn't have to suffer through the agony of life in this world.

But there's no such convenient fatalistic option for me. Just the foot-tingling vertigo of forging ahead into the cold, clear emptiness, making it up as I go along, plotting deadly expeditions into the blank white spaces where the chart ends and there are no guidelines.

I'll just have to draw in my own.

R usty nails snag my clothes. Rough-ridged tin scrapes my skin. I prop myself up on my elbows, take a breath and hold it—which I know I shouldn't do, I need to remember to keep breathing as I peer over the rooftop. There are cops in the street, on the sidewalk, on every floor, buzzing from room to room, throwing my stuff out the windows, running up and down the stairs, hassling my family. I lie there listening to my cousins answering and arguing and pleading, but their ignorance of my whereabouts is real and frankly that's better for them. My aunt is in the store loudly accusing them, What have you done with her?

And they laugh.

But they are convinced.

I can't even risk a phone call. Not yet. I'll have to wait till the Mendez brothers go to the construction site tomorrow morning. I hope nobody's watching them too closely.

But as I watch my sweet Antonia struggle to keep her jaw set resolutely while her lips are quivering with doubt, a thousand crystalline shards slice through my once untamable heart.

Child rearing has really slowed down my killer instincts. I've been chaining my wild, unbroken spirit to the plow horse of parenthood every sunrise, an act that requires supreme effort and self-denial, and I can't just turn all that nurturing off.

I find a boy hanging out in front of a candy store who's willing to deliver a three-word message for me: Mom's fine, kid.

Now I need to sharpen my claws for the next step.

And I'm going to need some real weapons.

*S*eñor Putamayo has no office. He files from the field," says the receptionist.

"Aha."

I've made it to the fourth floor of *El Despacho* without being accosted, but it's starting to smell like another dead end. Does she have a contact number for him? No. A home address? No.

"Can you tell me what he looks like?"

"No, I've never seen him. Maybe one of the regular weekday girls."

"Right, that makes sense. Just one more thing. Do you have this typeface on your computers?" I'm holding up the anti–*padre* Campos pamphlet.

"Sure we do." She calls it up on her screen for me. Twelve-point Helvetica Light. A perfect match. "Everybody's got that one."

Then I scramble out of there before the police dogs catch my scent.

The sun's piercing rays prick my eyes, which somehow tickles my nose, leading to an explosive incongruous sneeze on this oven-baked concrete pier. I cross my arms and look around, still feeling a dull twinge between my shoulder blades. I take a few steps wind-ward and perch my knee on the empty packing crate for a micro-sized Japanese washing machine and stare out at the river's swelling fury, swirling and churning within inches of overflowing its banks and flooding the city. I watch and wonder at all the sailors and fishermen who keep destitution at bay by trawling the black and formless face of the deep from sun to sun, gleaning a fistful of its jealously guarded fertility and bringing it safely into port.

A shirtless man offers me a handful of pirate videos of the latest Hollywood action movies. I turn them down.

I watch two dockhands have way too much fun tossing preg-nant sacks of corn flour onto a pallet, then settling onto the forklift for a leisurely ride back to the loading dock, one kidding the other the whole time about his paunch, lightly patting his big stomach.

Bells jingle as the ice cream man scrapes the bottom of a five-gallon carton to slap together a vanilla cone for a brown-skinned six-year-old boy.

Things seem quiet enough. Normal. I walk around, taking stock of the merchandise, the Swiss-Colombian watches, the Taiwanese wind-up toys, the Aiwas, Sonys and Osterizers and their Peruvian counterfeits, keeping an eye on the glass eyes staring back at me in neat little rows, then I slip inside the old iron-and-glass-roofed warehouse, with its high-flying Palladian pillars and ornate painted metal fan tracery, and those nice dark windows that haven't been washed since 1928.

Inside, enterprising merchants are selling over-the-counter thorazine, "contraband" Colombian coffee and, spread out on a low table, black market pacemakers cut from the chests of recently departed donors.

It is shockingly easy to purchase a gun here, and it doesn't take long to spot the man I want.

"So what do you need, *mamacita*?" he asks.

"I need someone who can keep quiet."

"And what does this quiet person have to offer?" he asks, directing me towards his all-American products.

"Not guns."

"What, then?"

"Knives."

"Any particular kind?"

Sure.

"Thick-bladed front-opening lock-back stilettos with good balance and throw weight. Preferably." A shiv, the kiss of death, as they say.

He takes a moment.

"They come twelve to a box. How many boxes do you want?"

He thinks he's going to sell me a gross of pocketknives with pretty-colored handles. Right. But I need the real thing.

We find a discreet storeroom, and he brings plenty of samples. I reject a few paint scrapers immediately as obvious crap without even touching them.

"Come *on.* . . ."

I spring the McDonald's Happy Meal blade out of one and chuckle, toss it on the table. "I wouldn't open letters with that."

He begins to open his eyes to the light of reason. Several heavier knives clunk down on the table. I test them for solidity, sharpness, heft, set aside my top four picks, choose one, sheath it in my pocket, and face him.

"Come at me," I say.

"What—?"

"Come at me."

I hand him a yard-long piece of splintery packing crate lumber and order him to run at me while swinging the jagged club at my head.

"Uh . . ."

"*Do it.*"

He does it. I block his upraised arm, twist it behind his back and bring the open blade to his throat.

"Too slow," I say. I leave the knife quivering in the tabletop and pick another. "Come at me."

The guy gulps.

"Come at me."

We go through it again. A little better this time. I flip the knife around, seek out its true center, wind up and lodge the thing in the far wall. I try another. Too heavy. The last one's sprightly and sharp. I painstakingly eliminate the finalists, sifting them down from three to two to one, and test that one again and again to make sure. It's probably one of the tougher sales this guy's had to make this week.

I give him some money the cops didn't find, and tactfully remind him of a simple truth: "You don't know me."

A lonely dinner in a greasy hole, a few quick prayers in the last row of a sleepy church, and I slink back to the construction site under cover of darkness, only to spend a rough night full of whacked-out parasomniac visions and wake up to find a debauched tribe of flies doing the conga dance around my gamy flesh. Two days without a shower and it's as hot as the branch office of hell.

Hell itself is *much* hotter.

My punishment perhaps for letting a couple of killers drop three victims in my pathway. Now I've got to reach across the mortal divide and make it up to them the hard way. Which shouldn't surprise me, I guess, because in Ecuador, *everything* has to be done the hard way. It's taken this country a hundred and fifty years of constant struggle, but we've finally reached a state of perpetual crisis, jerked around like a manic skeleton on *el Día de los Muertos*, All Souls Day.

Actually, a skeleton would be an improvement over the current state of this enigma. All I see is a few bone fragments, and there's a lot of connective tissue missing. Putamayo filed some carefully scripted police reports for the same newspaper, and Ruben didn't know him. But Ruben did know his killer. That was practically the first thing he said to me, "Not *you* people again." Which sounds like it must have been a branch of the National Police, the same guys who waltzed me around the floor while somebody was doing the dance of death with poor old Zimmerman, because those two slime bags could have tossed me in the river and instead I was left standing. And the only reason I can think of for that surprising condition is that they think Johnny's still alive, and they want me to flush him out for them, even if it means quitting the oily, piss-warm waters of the Río Daule for the wind-whipped ice lakes of the far Andean provinces. Because in Ecuador, the power is concentrated in such a small segment of society that one person could significantly shift the balance of that power with a handful of explosives and a penchant for deviant behavior.

First I have to find a better place to hide. I have to get out of here before the mosquitoes penetrate my protective layers of filth, find out I'm vulnerable and send for reinforcements.

Because there are places that I *can* get answers, places that lie nearer to my natal terrain in the lichen-filled niches high above Cuenca, where all my kinfolk hail from, up near the timberline where I am still known as the wandering child, and of course our refuge. The deep hideout that no one *ever* found. I wonder. The police will be controlling all the major interprovincial roads, and I'd be spotted in an instant if I tried to enter my old hunting grounds from the Cuenca basin. But they probably wouldn't be expecting me to come at them from the *other* side, hiking ten thousand feet up from the coast, hugging the banks of the Río Norcay all the way up to Cajas, since that's so fucking crazy.

Ha ha ha.

The cloudy sky lightens with the approaching dawn, but stays heavy with rain and impending bleakness. I look around the site. There's not much to work with here besides rusty wheelbarrows full of stagnant water, piles of sand and big round stones for laying foundations and stretching the cement, which is very expensive.

Big round stones.

Old as the mountains.

So primal. So quiet. Not to mention a cheap, plentiful resource around here.

The morning activities slowly unfurl, spilling out onto the pavement, but I've got to stay still, lurking among the thick cane pillars propping up the moist, primordial ooze of the third floor, which is taking days to dry in this weather. The cement is watery, spread a little thin. They're trying to keep costs down on this humble project, a narrow house for a working family who have put aside every cent until they could throw something together that's better than a cane shack on the water. But it's unreinforced cement with no superstructure. This is how they stretch the sucre. One crack and it all comes down, which is why all those Third World earthquakes do so much damage.

My cousins finally arrive, dressed for dirty work but still cleaner than me. I whisper their names and suddenly no one cares about dirt as I am swept up with an ecstatic devotion usually reserved for visions of the Virgin Mary appearing in the clouds. They exalt me as a cousin by blood and for spitting in the face of authority. No higher praise is available from them.

Bolívar wants to go tell the family right away but I say, "No. Go home at lunchtime like you always do. And bring back Patricia."

Ronaldo and Victor nod.

W hat's the most durable fabric?" I ask my cousin's wife.

"Leather or canvas," says Patricia. "But you need a special needle and thread."

"If I buy the materials, can you make it for me?"

"Claro que sí." Of course I can.

"Oh, Filomena," says Bolívar, enticingly, "look what else we brought you."

"Mommy!"

Time to work on my skills. I hand Victor an apple and tell him to throw it at me from ten paces off. He flings it underhanded. It arcs towards me, transformed into a swelling red hand grenade, then I chop it in half in midair.

"So?" says Vic. "That's pretty friggin' easy."

I pick up one of the halves, brush some of the gravel off, and toss it back to him. He throws it back at me and I chop it in half. We do it three more times before I miss.

Not good enough.

I practice all afternoon with Antonia helping me until I run out of fruit.

Then I ask the boys to take a break so they can take up scattered positions around the site, Bolí perched on the third floor, Ronny behind the rock piles, Vic roaming wherever he chooses, me standing in the muddy arena between them while they take turns pitching a mixture of objects at me. I spear the wood chips, duck the pebbles and stones and flinch at the handfuls of flying sand. At least there's no roofing tar involved. I tell them to mix it up more, and instantly regret it as a big chunk of cement slams into my shoulder blade.

"Ow!"

"Sorry," Ronny apologizes.

"My fault," I say, rubbing my sore spot.

I train through mist and drizzle until the sky starts paying off in big wet quarters like a high-rolling slot machine, then I huddle with Antonia under the rough cement pillars while the men go foraging for food. Yes, I've regressed to the social roles of the Paleolithic era.

Again.

I ask Antonia if she remembers the time we got caught in a cloudburst on a rocky bluff high above Solano, and the only shelter we could find was the tiny hilltop shrine with about six square feet of roof protecting the dull green wooden cross, and we crouched under it together sharing our warmth for nearly an hour watching the half-inch hailstones roll to a stop at our feet before it was safe to leave.

"No," she says.

"Oh?" And I remember it so vividly, hugging her for so long. I thought that would be one of the memories that we shared.

"Aunt Yolita says it always rains on Good Friday," she says.

"It usually does."

"But it's been raining all through Lent."

"Well, God is very religious," I say.

Slick velvet leaves flutter to life. Flush purple lips split by a trickle of water, thick concentric rings of wetness gathering towards a slippery reddish brown bump that gurgles and swallows as I approach the black canal that puckers and slurps as if it were trying to speak to me, filling me with wondrous premonitions and obscure sensations and dreadful nightmares that my mind resists, my hands push away, and then—

My hand's on the knife.

Three brothers stand over me, shaking me and telling me I have to clear out for a while because the contractor is coming by to inspect the site and check on their progress. Is it me, or am I having more than my share of ultraweird dreams lately?

I need to keep away from the site for a couple of hours, so I strengthen my blood with a sinus-clearing cup of seafood-and-onion *ceviche* from a sidewalk cart and a few ounces of muddy coffee.

The streets are turning into canals. The only fashionable way to get by is with rubber sandals, knee-length pants, and not thinking about what you're stepping in or sloshing through. I buy a clean copy of *El Despacho* and seek higher ground, climbing the steps of a public building belonging to the Ministry of Culture so I can drop anchor and dry out.

And there it is in big, bold letters: **WANTED BY THE SIC-G**
Me.

My eyes bounce along the columns grabbing clumps of information:

> allegedly found the body of Sr. Ruben Zimmerman
> witholding information about the murder police are
> seeking Srta. Filomena   disappeared from last-known
> address without informing the National Immigration
> Police   in violation of   anyone with information re-
> garding Srta. Buscarsela   1 million sucres reward.

It's me all right, and they just happen to have a photo of me taken in police custody the very same night that the body was found.

Aw, crap. All I need is for Sergeant Musgoso and Corporal Polillo to recognize me and those paramilitary creeps will be after me, too, if they aren't already. Maybe they don't read the papers. Maybe they don't read. Or at least make it so they get the papers a few days late, please.

I've got to get away from all this and slip out of the province. Not an easy task, with so few navigable roads out of here. After all the rain, this burg is practically an island connected to the mainland by half a dozen bridges, all easily patrolled and easily sealed.

I spend an anxious hour telling myself that the one-million-sucre reward for turning me in is only about $200 at today's exchange rate, so I can still offer any would-be tipster twice that amount, and there are maybe fifty thousand women in Guayaquil with dark frizzy hair, dark brown eyes and olive skin who might pass for the tired face in the coarsely screened reproduction of a blurry Polaroid original.

Not that that's any reason to celebrate.

I take a few minutes to trade up to a bigger pair of sunglasses, a nondescript dark blue baseball cap, and a thin black band to tie my wiry hair back into a ponytail. Then I head back to the construction site, my pace steady, keeping an eye out front and back to convince myself it's safe to approach. When I show Bolívar the bad news, he tells me not to worry, nobody's going to turn me in. I'm getting a rep.

Yeah, but a few more weeks of this rice shortage and people will be hungry enough to chew each other's tits off.

But he's got something for me from Patricia, wrapped in a dirty rag. A stiff black leather sling.

It's time to break it in.

I used to hunt birds and rabbits with a slingshot, like a lot of mountain kids, since there was never enough food at home. And later, it came in handy when someone's gun jammed or when we just ran out of bullets completely and had to send people crawling along the ground looking for unexploded casings, then we'd lay down a cover of sling stones.

I select from the pile of smooth, round stones.

Then I scratch the chalky outline of a head and shoulders at eye level on a cement wall and practice, ignoring tired muscles, until I can hit it between the eyes three times out of five from thirty feet away. It should be nine times out of ten from fifty feet away, but I haven't got the time to retrain myself to that level of refinement right now.

The Mendezes watch me while they work mixing cement and laying bricks, fascinated. As the shadows lengthen, at that miraculous fleeting moment when the rooftops shimmer with illusory gold, they climb down the ladders, dusting themselves off.

I ask them to attack me.

"Yo, give it a rest, girl," Ronny says.

"Sheee-it," Bolívar editorializes.

"Okay, okay."

We'll try again tomorrow when everybody's fresh.

It rains all night. The ground is so saturated, the puddles quickly spread until the rough piles of dirt and sand and rock stand isolated like a primeval mountain chain above the featureless, flooded world below. Soon the muddy water streaks across the sidewalk into the street and merges with the raging current, gathering momentum for its inexorable march to the sea.

It's time to gather up some supplies for my long trek to the *sierra*. But first, one more hour with my child.

*   *   *

I watch the trio of rubber-booted inspectors extract some money from a fruit tomato vendor because the prices on his rain-soaked cardboard sign are no longer legible, but they walk right past a sharp-toothed man selling a few soggy *quintales* of rice for three times the official price as if he were invisible.

At one edge of the muddy bazaar, a group of highland women wearing bright orange-and-magenta *polleras* are selling *mote* corn and ground *machica* to the quiet men from Cañar who have come looking for work in the vast, alien city. I hang out near these un-assuming people, watching and waiting for the warm, kindly woman taking her grandniece shopping. Eventually they appear, and Aunt Yolita brings my beloved Antonia to me so I can explain to my worldly eighth-grader that I have to go to the mountains.

"Is it cold in the mountains?" she asks.

"The way I'm going? Yes. Very."

"Are you taking your earmuffs?" she says.

I smile and tell her when she was little she used to call them "earmuffins."

"I don't want you to die," she says, unexpectedly meeting my gaze and sounding very mature.

"Well that's good because I don't want to die, either," I say, trying to keep it light. But I can't hold back the bodily surge of emotion, and pretty soon there's nothing left to do but hug her, tightly.

"You pray for me," I say, suddenly having a hard time swallow-ing. "God listens to you."

I turn to Aunt Yolita, who makes me lean forward so she can bless me, pressing her quietly suffering fingers to my head and heart.

Angry shouts pierce the air. There's a scuffle over by the grape-fruit stands, sending a few oranges flying upwards. Apparently thiev-ery is involved. I stay out of it this time. And when the police inspectors show up to investigate, I'm a distant memory.

I struggle to keep my balance on the wobbly wooden boards, grab hold of the slippery, wet ladder and climb up to the relative safety of my hideaway, looking forward to a night's rest on my cement-sack bed before I make the journey.

A sigh of relief.

Then I—*ick*! A mess of those two-inch roaches scatter as I lift my backpack. I better empty it out and make sure none of those nasty creatures are in there laying eggs. The bundle of Ruben's notes has a thin layer of cement dust clinging to it, which I brush off. I'll have to slip it to the boys tomorrow morning, and tell them to keep it in a safe place till I get back.

Clunk.

Out falls a watch.

It's not Ruben's watch.

It's the broken "Rolux" watch Guillermo gave me, which I haven't seen since I was arrested.

There's a note taped to it:

Juanita:
Lomas de Mapasingue. Calle Cuatro y Zapatero.
22:30.

Under the bloodred glow of the gel-covered lights in the back room of a *cantina* where the only other women are a pair of sagging, dead-eyed professionals, I call up the offices of *El Despacho* and ask if I can speak to their ace crime reporter, Javier Putamayo. *Buzz. Click. Buzz. Beeeep.*

"Hello?" Click. "Hello?"

I finally get connected to a petulant twenty-three-year-old who tells me with lazy authority that *señor* Putamayo is on assignment in Cuenca for the next two weeks covering the political violence there.

In Cuenca?

"Didn't you hear? Governor Segundo Canino was speaking at a rally for the *Trabajo, Familia, Patria* Society when someone in the crowd shot at him. Canino's brother was hit in the leg. He's in the hospital now."

A flesh wound. And the wrong guy. My, my.

The killers in this country don't seem to have any trouble missing when they're going after my friends.

* * *

Mapasingue. A spattering of glowing pinpricks in the night trace a sparkling trail of human habitation on the inky black hills that separate the fashionable suburbs from the industrial zones and the highway west to the oil fields of the Santa Elena peninsula. Finding the intersection of Fourth Street and Zapatero is going to be quite a challenge among the nameless mud slides that pass for streets on these Hooverville-laden slopes. Of course it's only a matter of time before some real estate magnate realizes what he can get for hilltop property this close to downtown.

"*Hágame el favor*, which way is Calle Cuatro?"

"*Por allá.*"

That way.

Well, that narrows it down to one of the four cardinal directions.

People don't give out much information, and even when I try to buy some, there is little agreement as to the actual location of things.

"Keep going—"

"Over there—"

"Further on—"

"Up that way—"

At this rate, I'll never find the place in time. But somebody is out looking for me, and news of a strange woman wandering around the squatters' shacks alone at night asking for directions travels as fast as the news of a governmental collapse. Possibly faster. After all, governments collapse with some frequency down here. Unfamiliar women handing out five thousand *sucres* at a touch are not quite as common.

I'm tramping slowly up a steep incline, trying not to lose my footing and slide down the mud-lined trail to the bottom of the hill, when a hand reaches out and a woman's voice offers to help me up. I seize the hand, lodge a foot against a welcome hard place— I think it's a buried log—and lift myself up to the next level of steep, muddy ground.

"Nice one, Juanita," she says.

I let it go by.

"I wish you hadn't alerted the entire neighborhood with your generosity," she says. "Word moves fast."

"Then you should have given me better instructions. Cigarette?" I ask, as a pretext for shoving one in my mouth and flicking open my trusty metal lighter so I can have a look at my surroundings, but she knocks the flame out of my hand quite abruptly.

"Don't do that again," she says nastily.

"And don't talk to me like that, *hermanita*," I say, feeling around for my fallen lighter. "I'm wanted in four provinces. If anything, I'm the one who shouldn't want anyone to see my face."

There is a pause in the darkness. I wipe the mud off, spin the Zippo's wheel and hold it up again. My guide is a pixieish light-skinned woman with short straight black hair. She looks closely at my features, watching for suspicious signs of stress. I see enough of her to feel confident that she isn't carrying a concealed harpoon launcher, anyway, and get enough of a glimpse of the street receding behind her to convince myself that nobody is going to try to lead me off a cliff or something cute like that.

I smile at her. She could be me at nineteen. I snap the lighter shut, drop my cigarette in the mud and let her do whatever her face muscles want to do while we're both seeing blue-flame afterimages in the darkness.

"You're not from this neighborhood, either," I tell her.

Pause.

"I'm from Ambato," she says, taking hold of my elbow and leading me away down the street.

"How'd you get me that message?"

No answer.

"I'm just trying to find out if it's legitimate or not," I say.

"It's legitimate."

We turn down a lane doing double duty as a drainage ditch, and I sink up to my ankles in mud and filth. We slough through this for a while, then come to a clearing with a darkened shack in the middle of it, isolated from the others by at least forty feet and perched on the edge of an incline that slopes off into unseen depths. If ever a spot was tailor-made for trouble, this is it.

My guide gives a few sharp syncopated raps on the door, pushes me against it, and disappears. A swish of air and a military-issue semiautomatic presses against the side of my head.

A flashlight stings my eyes.

Nothing else moves.

My heart waits for the next beat.

Apparently, I pass the test.

The door swings open and a masked man motions me in with a sudden deflection of his gun away from my frontal lobes towards the darker recesses of the shack. I step inside willingly enough, thus demonstrating my mental incompetence and establishing a case for absolving me of any illegal actions that I may happen to take within the next few minutes.

The interior wouldn't get much of a write-up in *House and Garden*, but it might rate a sidebar in *Soldier of Fortune*. There's a propane lantern and single-burner camping stove, furniture made from cardboard boxes, and a small but worthy arsenal that might cut this group a few respectably sized blocks of territory in Brooklyn, but I wouldn't try to overthrow any governments with it. And there's two more people with old-fashioned outlaws' kerchiefs covering their faces from the eyes down pointing deadly weapons at me. The one who's working the door pulls my shoulder bag away from me and throws it into a corner.

"Thanks," I say. "It was getting heavy. Mind if I sit?"

The three masks look at each other. I wait a few more seconds and decide that it's okay with them if I pull out a cardboard box and sit down.

They've been eating. There's a plate of *haba* beans on the table with some cheese and a bowl of *ají*.

"Why have you been trying to see us?" asks a woman's voice from behind the mask directly opposite me.

At least the presence of women confirms that they're leftists.

Leftists I can deal with.

"That watch you sent me—it shows you still have some friendly ties to the police. And I need to know what secrets the cops are keeping from us about who killed *padre* Samuel Campos and Ruben Zimmerman."

"Zimmerman was an apologist for the bourgeois media," she says. "And Campos was a pawn for the *pajizocistas* who deserved to—"

"Campos saved my life, damn it."

Guns leap closer on three sides, violating my personal space. We stay like this for a while.

"Look," I say. "My nerves are stretched pretty tight as it is without you folks pointing those things at me, so could we please stop wasting time like this? Sure, you've got a right to be nervous. So frisk me already and get it over with, but *stop* pointing guns at my head."

Well, I've said my piece. If I'm not dead within the next two minutes, I might make it into tomorrow. Hey—maybe I'll get lucky and see the middle of next week. I cross my hands between my knees and while I'm in that position some bizarre impulse compels me to take my pulse. It's relatively normal, which will make it easier to count off two minutes, if nothing else.

Opinions are divided. The woman seems to soften, but the men are hard as igneous rock. The guns stay trained.

"I'm also interested in finding out who killed Mishojos," I say.

"Who?" says the woman.

"Enough of this! What are you *really* after?" says the man behind me.

What am I *really* after?

"Mind if I have a bean?"

"Sure, go ahead," says the woman. What a country: even the *guerrilleros* know how to feed a guest.

I reach for a steamed *haba* and dip it into the *ají*. *Very* spicy.

"That's good *ají*," I tell my hostess.

"We heard you were looking for Juanito," says the man in front of me.

"So why should we help you find him?" says the one behind me, leaning close enough for his hot breath to stir his mask and raise the hair on my neck. "Maybe you want revenge."

My knife's in my pocket, but I'd be dead before I got it out. I have a second bean, and my casual munching allows them to relax their grips on their guns for a moment. I slide my feet a little closer under me, knees bending, and start slowly shifting my weight forward.

"I don't think he can be found," I say. "I think he's been dead for nearly twenty years. But I've got to know."

"What kind of mother abandons her daughter to answer a twenty-year-old question?" says the woman.

"A rotten one," I admit.

"Oh, boo-hoo," says the man in front of me.

I reach for another bean, dip it into the *ají*, seize the rim of the bowl between my thumb and forefinger and toss it into the man's eyes. Almost as good as pepper spray.

The woman's gun flies up as I spring up and ram my head into the guy behind me, butting his jaw like an Argentine soccer player and quickly spinning around and getting him between me and the guns. This guy has spent more time arguing over petty changes in the wording of some subversive pamphlet than learning how to kick some bastard in the balls and take his gun away from him, which works out to my advantage in this instance.

Before his two *compañeros* have time to steady their weapons on the two of us, I've got the guy pinned in front of me with his gun pressed to *his* head for a change.

"Now *listen* to me, you stupid assholes!" I instruct them. "I am about to give you the only proof I can give you that you ought to be able to trust me."

Before they can react to that, I raise their comrade's handgun up into the air, let it dangle freely from one finger, and fling it onto the floor at the masked woman's feet. Then I shove the guy away from me, leaving myself completely open to their fire.

"There," I say. "I could have killed the three of you and gotten myself a medal for it if I wanted to. Do you believe me now? Sorry about your eyes, *amigo*."

I think the woman smiles behind her mask. She lowers her gun to go wet a rag and wipe the *ají* out of her *compañero's* eyes.

"What should we do with her?" he asks.

The woman turns to answer him. She never gets the chance. The air crackles with a bunch of nearby bursts and a row of enormous holes tear through the cardboard wall looking like they come from a .45-caliber machine gun. *Shit.* My first reflex is to dive onto the floor behind some cardboard boxes—like they're *really* going to protect me against a hail of spinning .45 slugs, but there you have it, instinct in its purest form.

"*¡Maldita!*" The guy I disarmed curses me. "Fuck! She led them to us! Kill her!"

But the other two are already down. Maybe hit. The guy reaches for the pistol I just forfeited, but a cascade of bullets rips up the cardboard between his outstretched fingers and the silent gun.

The bloody woman lifts herself up like a vampire rising from the grave, her shell-shocked eyes already a dead weight. She flops her gun heavily on the table and starts shooting at me, through me, past me to the invisible targets outside.

Whoever's out there responds by directing a discharge of throat-level fire so dense that it cuts completely through what remains of the walls, and the roof falls in on us as we both dive for his handgun. I reach it first and when he grabs the gun with both hands I get a forearm around his throat and roll out through the collapsing wall and into the mud outside, hitting the night air on bent knees with a gun pointed at this guy's head for the second time tonight.

Then something strange happens. A well-equipped team of provincial cops stands perfectly still in the hot night air, lit up by the chilling ice blue aura of a couple of portable tungsten arc lamps, ready to shoot anyone who comes out of the shack, but some phantasmal quality about the two of us spotlit like this, one held prisoner by the other one's gun, momentarily spares us the indignity of reddening the mud with our entrails. Orders can come from too many sources to be fully reliable, and something about our perverse dumb-show tableau has the officer in command wondering if perhaps something he should have known about has gone very wrong, slapping his ass down on the line right next to mine. Am I one of them? I can't very well be the enemy if I'm holding a gun to the other guy's head.

I don't give the commander time to double-check with headquarters. I pull the poor bastard to his feet and walk him in front of me, keeping the gun pressed to his temple.

But there's no opportunity for negotiations. The police grab him from me, seize the gun, immobilize the two of us and poke gun nozzles into the impressionable flesh of my neck and ram one just under my left breast. There are too many people with guns in this town. My inner spiritualist automatically forms a prayer, and sometime between "forever" and "amen" a voice steps out of the clouds and says:

"Fine work, Sergeant. But we'll take it from here."

The hot bodies pushing close to me stop pushing. There's some debating in lowered voices, some paper rattling under a flashlight. Then all of a sudden I cease to be a pincushion for loose gun barrels and the bodies withdraw, shrinking away as if in awe of the unearthly powers of the man in the blue camouflage fatigues.

He steps into the light and the glowing face of Captain Ponce looms above me.

In a second I'm walking again with Captain Ponce's support. He takes me down the muddy slope and away from there.

"Relax. It's not your turn to die yet," he says, with that curious twinkle highlighting his feline smile. "But we're even now."

CHAPTER TWELVE

La muerte a mí me escribió
Yo la carta aquí la tengo,
Lo malo no sé leer
Y la letra no la entiendo.

Death wrote me a letter,
I've got it right here in my hand.
Too bad I can't read his writing,
All those words that I don't understand.

— Traditional Afro-Ecuadorian *décima*
(Province of Esmeraldas)

Muddy, bruised and shaken, I crawl up to the second floor to gather my things and make myself missing before anyone else shows up to spoil the party. I'm about to grab my backpack when I stop myself. The radicals knew where to find me, and one of them seems to have tipped the cops to make it look like I betrayed them.

I rummage around for a stick of scrap wood, then, crouching behind the rough-edged wall, I risk my left arm to carefully poke my backpack. Nothing happens. I gently lift the flap and ease the stick inside. I poke around enough to satisfy myself that it's not going to blow up in my face, anyway, then I get up and take a quick inventory of the contents. Leather slingshot, money, notes. Everything's still here. Great. I'm out of here.

But first, I take a minute to cross the bare cement floor to the half-finished bathroom to relieve myself. The toilet isn't hooked up yet, but what can you do? There isn't a door, either, just a few staggered boards hastily nailed up, the cheap kind that are cut from laurel with the bark still on them. I piss without paper, and my underwear has to absorb the remaining wetness. A minor discomfort, considering.

As I'm lowering the seat cover out of habit, through the gaps between the boards, I hear someone creeping around down there, in the dark.

Fight? Flight. Fight? Flight. *Fight.*

I've got a knife in my pocket, but this calls for something heavier. My eyes flit around, settling on the two-foot slab of porcelain covering the toilet's reservoir. Naah, too bulky. Not when there's a pile of copper pipes lying at my feet, tailor-made for the occasion. I carefully lift up a four-foot length of it, trying not to make the telltale clanking sound of hollow metal tubing, and position myself behind a flimsy barrier of laurel, figuring that if he's armed with anything like what everyone else who's after me is armed with, half an inch of dead wood won't make a difference.

The ladder creaks.

Someone who knows me would have whispered my name by now.

Come on, you worthless bastard, I'm ready for you.

Creak. Why is he taking so goddamned long? What, does he have to stop for breath on every rung?

Creak. I have to blink several times to clear a milky film that's clouding my vision, then I force my eyes to stay wide open and prepare to strike.

Don't get me wrong, there are nice parts of Guayaquil. I just never visit them.

Here he comes. A few more inches. And . . . a flash of pale white skin and dirty blond hair.

"Jesus!" I cry out, verbally releasing all that coiled-up energy.

Peter reels backwards and recovers. "Filomena! What are you doing?"

"Nearly breaking your skull," I say, dropping the pipe and pulling him up. One of his arms is in a cast and his face is still deeply scarred and bandaged.

"Oh my God, look at you," I say, my fingertips grazing his face.

He recoils. "Don't touch it!" he says, with some harshness.

"Sorry, I—it was just a reflex. What are you doing here? How did you know where to find me?"

"I was discharged a few hours ago. You've got to get out of here. There isn't much time."

"I know. Did you find out anything about *padre* Campos—?"

"He wasn't there. It was a false lead."

"Damn it."

"Yeah." He checks his watch. "Every minute counts here."

There's that *gringo* idea again.

"You've gotta see this," he says, holding up the early edition of today's *El Despacho.*

I angle it towards the streetlights, and read that *padre* Malta of Latacunga was wounded by an unknown gunman late yesterday, in the shadow of the snowcapped volcano of Cotopaxi, as he spoke with the paper's roving investigative reporter, Javier Putamayo. There's a photo of the reporter, a stern-faced intellectual type with a thick beard and glasses.

"I've seen this guy," I say. "At one of the rallies." Which one was it? I recall dimly that he was observing the mayhem, so it must have been the one that was disrupted by counterdemonstrators. Yes, I'm sure of it. "And now he's in the sierra."

"Never mind that, Filomena. The cops are saying that they found a weapon and traced it to you. I heard it over the police band and hopped a cab to your family's store. They're saying it was a stolen .45-caliber military-issue semiautomatic, the same gun that killed two bank guards a week ago, taken from a group of terrorists ambushed this evening. Report said three of them were killed and one got away."

Sirens are approaching out in the night.

Three of them were killed. And I handed one of them over.

Shit.

And they've got my fingerprints all over the gun.

"They'll be watching the airports, the bus station, for all I know they'll be stopping cars on the street," says Peter.

The sirens are getting louder. I keep waiting for the Doppler shift that will reassure me that the trouble is in some other part of town. It never comes.

I grab my backpack and stuff the notes into his hands. "Peter, this is what Ruben was working on when he was killed. I need you to investigate a man named Colonel Alboroto of the North Guayas Militia. I'm going after Putamayo."

"Okay, get your stuff together and let's go," says Peter.

"No. I'm going alone."

"You can't go alone!" he yells after me. "They're controlling the provincial borders!"

"I know a way to get through."

I drop to the ground. He tries to follow me. "How will I find you?"

"I'll find you," I call back, running out into the street without looking back at the glare of red-and-orange lights bursting on the horizon ahead of the coming dawn.

I only have to bang on a few doors before one of them opens and the good people of Guayaquil see to it that I get food, a shower and a change of clothes. Praise God.

Sometimes femininity has advantages. I doubt that a strange man pounding desperately on doors in the middle of the night in this distrustful neighborhood would get much of a hearing.

I leave the kind Samaritans under a rosy early morning sky and seek out one of those thirty-seat low-riding motorized canoes that takes us across the river to Durán, the first major checkpoint for buses leaving the city. I can probably get a bus that will take me twenty miles inland to Boliche, the next place I might have to worry about being stopped and questioned. If I can slip off just before we get to town, there's a turnoff that'll take me south-southeast through the lush overgrowth to the fertile green slopes of the majestic and immovable mountains.

I've exchanged my all-terrain bad-grrrl jeans and running shoes for a short, shiny aqua dress with a matching bandana and low black heels that make me look like every other housewife along the riverbank within a fifty-mile radius. I hope. I also took the time to put on makeup and curl-and-gel my steel-wool hair into strands of springy curls.

A pair of agile crewmen lend me a hand getting off the ferry, and I demurely accept, trying not to stand out. Demureness is easy. Walking is hard in the stiff, unsupportive shoes along these muddy streets and cracked sidewalks. I don't know how these women manage it while carrying a thirty-pound basketful of groceries. No wonder the men think we need help climbing three wooden steps.

I step over a pile of muddy lettuces and skirt purposefully along the market's edge until I come to a group of reasonably clean-shirted men loosely gathered in the receding shadows alongside the IETEL telephone building. I make an instant judgment and entrust one of these shady street bankers with my grimiest ten-dollar bill, telling him that my cousin Byron just sent it from the U.S., and about how my cousin Byron is the manager of a Footlocker in the Mill Creek Mall in Secaucus, New Jersey, and other meaningless gossip that the guy tunes right out like he's supposed to. Then he hands me more than ninety thousand sucres. I tell him he's made a mistake.

"Please, *hermana*, I don't make mistakes with money," he says, and shows me today's *El Mundo*. In the two days since I've bought a newspaper, the sucre has lost nearly half of its value against the dollar.

I take my empty basket and reenter the marketplace to do some ordinary grocery shopping, hoping to board a bus and pass for a local woman who is only traveling a few miles from home. I get some onions, dried beans, *plátanos*, *achiote*, green peppers and other sundries at nearly twice what they cost yesterday morning, but rice cannot be had at any price. It has vanished from the shelves, leaving nothing but dry maggot remains. Well, almost: one tin-hearted gouger holds up a three-pound bag of rice and tells me I can have it for twenty dollars or, if I prefer, he can take it out "in trade."

I almost tell him, Sure, just give me a minute to sharpen my gelding shears. But no, we want to fit in. Play along. Survive.

I walk away.

Because I can. But if my children were starving?

The carnival-colored buses move slowly through the crowded market street, young boys serving as figureheads come to life, trumpeting their destinations with sirenlike voices for the benefit of those who cannot read the distinctly painted signs over the high windshields. Baroque red lettering on a yellow background spells out Cañar; the green-and-yellow *busetas* of the Cooperativa Sucre are bound for Cuenca. And I'm the luckiest woman in the world when I spy a dusty new bus rolling along with an orange-on-white sign spelling out Naranjal in plain, thin brushstrokes. That's southeast of here and right on my route.

The bus is already full, but the driver is a rambling man who always has room for one more grateful woman in a slinky dress. I squeeze between several other grateful women who have come to do their shopping. I see onions, parsley, *platano*, tomatoes, peppers. No rice. No milk. No meat. I wonder what it would cost them.

The teenage girl on my left is recently married, because her virile, black-haired husband has got her wrapped in the crook of one muscular arm and there's no sign of kids yet. The woman on my right is only a few years older, but the baby-a-year system has already started to wear her out. She's got a roundish face with a sharp nose, a true child of the coast and the *sierra*. It must have been hell growing up with her mixed origins written on her face like that for all the narrow-minded world to see.

The nicer interprovincial buses have big, clean windows, opened wide to let in the hot coastal breezes. A deliciously sweet aroma from the chocolate refinery fills the air as we pull up to the toll-booths that mark the entrance to the big two-lane highway east. The police check for overcrowding and other blatant disregard of safety standards, and we're on our way.

I look the part pretty well, and I can keep it up as long as no one looks past my grocery basket and asks to see what I've got in my other bag, which is basic mountaineering survival equipment: jeans, hiking shoes, extra socks, high-energy food, thin woolen blanket, toilet paper. Pretty suspicious stuff for a swamp angel to be carrying.

Not nearly as suspicious as the two weapons stashed underneath.

But no gun. If they catch me with a gun, I'm finished. Of course, I might be finished no matter what they catch me with.

We pick up some more stragglers and leave the industrial zones behind, and the gray roadside opens up like a flower into lush green vistas that reach from one horizon to the other. Wide blanketing groves of palm and banana trees sweep across the rich, volcanic soil, promising to feed us and replenish our depleted souls. Providing we live to see the next harvest.

Shacks on cane stilts line the edges of the fields. I stare out the window at them, then my eye flits over to the young husband, who curls up the corners of his mouth and blows a kiss at me. His wife jerks her head at me with hawklike precision, but I'm already averting my gaze, looking out the other window, contemplating the words of the famous explorer Alexander von Humboldt, who had already climbed Chimborazo and surveyed the equator before Lewis and Clark stumbled across Montana. When he saw the vast deposits of unrealized wealth on this "new continent," he remarked that Ecuador was like a beggar seated on a bench of solid gold.

Things haven't changed much.

The driver keeps stopping to pick up more paying passengers— a couple of old men with caged chickens, a young worker with two sacks of cement, a pair of real *montuvias* carrying a head of mature, yellow *plátanos* between them, kids selling candy and chewing gum and soda in plastic bags, because the reusable bottles are worth more than the soda inside them, until the bus is overcrowded with animals and people exuding the strong smell of the country and clucking, laughing, talking while they rest their tired bones. The woman to my left is broadcasting amplitude waves of hostility because her young husband won't stop looking at me, and the whole idea of this disguise thing is not to be looked at, so I turn away and start talking to my weary-eyed seatmate.

"Would you believe this shopkeeper wanted me to lift my skirt up for three pounds of rice?"

"Oh, y'mean Magrato. He's alwayspullingthat," she says in that unbelievably fast littoral dialect. "Somewomendoit, y'know."

I try to show mild shock, surprise.

"You're notfromroundhere, are ya?"

"What do you mean?" I say, my heart pounding.

"Justsomething 'bout ya."

"We just moved from Milagro."

"Longwaytogotodoyershopping, eh?"

"Well—"

"I know. With prices th'waytheyarenow, it's cheaper t'ride allth'waytotheport and buy what ya need there. Paininth'butt, though," she jokes.

I smile. "It sure is."

"Howmanykids ya got?"

"Two. But one died."

"Ay ay ay," she says, nodding. "That's hard."

She tells me her name is Ernestina, and she has four of her own plus her husband's parents, an aunt and three little cousins to take care of. I wonder how she does it, what she gives up to feed eleven mouths. I mean besides her sanity.

A thick, sweet smoke is rising from the fields and depositing bits of black ash on my tomatoes and my eyelids. It's burning time for the sugarcane harvest. I rub the filthy particles from my eyelashes as we pass truckloads of soot-covered *zafreros*, sinewy sugarcane workers standing shoulder to shoulder in the cargo beds of carbon-coated industrial transports, with white eyes and streaked, dark faces looking hopeless, hungry and glum. An army of machete-wielding day laborers envying the poor women one notch above them. If only someone would organize them . . .

Then we get stuck behind some heavy equipment, and thick, black clouds of truck exhaust billow in through the windows tasting of underrefined, lead-based diesel fuel, which is good, 'cause I haven't had a carcinogen all week.

As we pass the entrance to the Ariel Air Force Base, the road starts getting slick with water. After a few kilometers, it's several inches deep. People coming the other way are saying that the Río Bulubulu has overflowed. Just short of Boliche we come to a complete halt. The water is two feet deep, and soldiers are politely telling us to get off the freaking bus.

They say the roads are washed out and all vehicles must turn back, but if any of the passengers want to, they can walk about five kilometers south and cross the Río Culebras by rope bridge.

It means River of Snakes. Oh, joy.

We wade through thigh-deep muddy water till the shopping basket in my arm begins to drag, so I switch arms on and off until a dumb fatigue slowly sets in, sinking its iron hooks into my irritated muscles. By now I'm ready to toss the damn basket, but I need to carry it with me at least until I get near the foothills.

We finally reach the Río Culebras. From where I'm standing it looks like the fourth day of creation, and God hasn't had His coffee yet.

Soldiers and local men are waist-high in muddy water, helping women clinging to a thin rope across the turbulent river.

This is it?

"Where's the bridge?" I ask.

"Washed out yesterday," comes the answer. "All we've got is this rope."

I wait while being slowly sautéed out here under the pitiless noonday sun, worried that pretty soon I'll be bright red. And I don't know which is worse, getting a nasty sunburn or giving myself away as a *serrana*.

When it's my turn, two smiling teenagers in mud-soaked T-shirts help me off the bank and into the water. The river's current is brutally powerful, and I'm trying to keep all my gear dry. Shit. Even the old women are crossing the river better than I am. They're used to this. I'm not. The water's nearly up to my chest, and I'm wearing the wrong clothes. My dress is tight and clingy, and these stiff shoes are now agony, causing me to clumsily misjudge the underlying surface. I slip into a hole that everyone else managed to avoid, and lose the grocery basket while failing to keep my survival bag from dropping into the water.

"*¡Ay, caracho!*" I can't help cursing my bad luck.

The waterlogged bag seems to triple in weight as I pull myself up and get the rope under my left arm, creating a wake that batters my face with astonishing force, rough hemp fibers cutting into me. I throw my right arm over and hang there with the rope sawing away at my armpits. But I'm breathing. I wait for another surge of strength, and keep going to the other side.

Strong arms wet with greenish brown camouflage drag me up the muddy riverbank, where men with heavy boots ask me too many questions.

"Who are you?"

"What's your name?"

"Are you all right?"

"What's in the bag?"

"Where are you from?"

"When did you—?"

"Why—?"

"How—?"

Ernestina appears at my side and tells them to leave me alone already. I'm totally drained.

My knees sink into the wet mud and my head sags. There's no clothes dryer for fifty miles, and it's insanity to go climbing mountains in wet clothes. Even I'm not *that* crazy.

They think I'm upset about my lost groceries.

When I raise my head, a girl about Antonia's age is walking

barefoot up the muddy road, holding a heavy toddler nearly half her size. Refugees from somewhere. They both look at me. The toddler still has a baby-fat belly and cheeks, but his wide, sad eyes show that he already understands all about the shitty hand fate has just dealt him. The girl has straight black *mestiza* hair parted in the middle, and her eyes bore into me, asking for something I cannot give, yet also showing pity for me. And the horizon of mud stretches far and wide behind her.

I stare at an abandoned pickup truck wallowing in wet silt, disgorging mud from every orifice like some postmodern allegorical sculpture of the sin of gluttony, and I ask myself what the hell I was thinking, trying to save the whole damn country by myself. *Todo el santo país.* Then Ernestina bends over, holds out her hand and says, "You'll have plenty of time to rest later. Let's go."

Half a mile onward the road reemerges from the gray glop and we get a ride south to Churete, pop. 12-1/2. Then we climb aboard a banana truck, a real modified clunker that sits eight in a plywood piano box with holes cut in it for the steering column and the pedals, which discharges a cubic mile of black hydrocarbons at every turn of this twisty road. Our kindly driver takes us past Puerto Inca and leaves us with a nod and a wink just outside of Jesús María, near the feet of the sleeping giants where my new companion dwells.

When we get there, Ernestina starts a fire so I can dry my things off. She looks them over in great detail but doesn't say a word. By late afternoon I'm changing into my fire-stiffened jeans and she's feeding me much-needed sustenance and offering me a tempting place to stay for the night. But no.

I've got to keep moving.

I stamp the caked mud from my hiking boots and with rough, rope-burned hands push open the splintery pine door that has weathered a thousand tempests and put my weight onto the sagging boards of this dark, dingy *cantina* a couple of leagues in country, up in the lush, wet hills of the western ridge.

Agua Caliente. You gotta wonder what else they've got to offer in a town called Hot Water.

The sun settles swiftly into darkness.

Darkness breeds mystery.

I am the mystery.

Eyes glassy with drink and candlelight watch the rugged female stranger approach the bar, order a *canelaso,* and sip half of it. Ears buzz straining to catch slithering sibilants in guarded tones.

She needs a man who knows the mountains.

They find such a man. Wiry and strong, with a drooping gray mustache. He is called Fredo.

I tell him I need someone to go with me as far as Cuchichaspana, a place called Burnt Pigs, right in the middle of Cajas. I can take it from there. And I expect him to provide cooking pots, provisions, rope and a tent. Yes, I can pay.

Then it's settled, he says, he'll see me before sunrise and I say, No, I need a place to stay. I'm going with you. (Where I can keep an eye on you all night long.)

He knows what this means, so I lay down the green leaf until he accepts. You don't fuck around with something like this.

A man who knows what to expect is as good as two men.

I don't let him out of my sight, don't let him speak to anyone else until he gets the gear ready, until he says, "Well, then, it's time to sleep."

We depart in darkness.

The Andes is the youngest major mountain chain in the world. Unlike the broad high plains of Bolivia to the south, here they're a narrow, snakelike backbone jutting up from the flat coastland, studded with smoldering snowcapped volcanic peaks reaching as high as twenty thousand feet on the eastern and western ridges, with a string of fifty-mile-wide basins running between them, where the mountain people built their sun-dried cities of clay.

And so the thick-skinned *serranos* huddle together in the snug, sleepy valleys, leaving the high wilderness with its jagged, wind-scarred peaks and deep, murky lagoons to the crows and the outlaws.

On a flat map, it's only about twenty miles in a straight line from Agua Caliente to our old hideout in Cajas. But the Andes aren't flat, are they? It's more like sixty miles stretched out, and the trail rises more than fourteen thousand feet in some places. That's why I need someone who knows the western slope. I know the east slope of the intermontane *cordillera*, but it will take a couple of days to get there, and I'm not spending the night alone at twelve thousand feet. For some reason.

Right now we've got a long way to go, zigzagging up slippery muddy paths bordered by thick wet foliage.

Hours stretch by without words.

We've been climbing all forenoon in silence when Fredo asks me, "You want to go there by the Yanacocha?"

"No. It's too cold there." The rocks around the Yanacocha are so high the water looks dark even during the day. Hence the name: Black Lagoon.

"*Bueno*. We'll go by the Tukyacocha."

"There are some dangerous bogs around that lagoon."

He stops, turns around and faces me.

"All right, all right, the whole trip's dangerous," I say. "Lead on."

Cajas has such cheery place names: Tukyacocha, Ataucocha, Ayapampa. Trap Lagoon, Coffin Lake, Cadaver Valley. And of course farther north there's good old Blood Lake.

But once you haul yourself up there, you've got some solid rock under your feet. Right now, we're still in landslide country.

We stop for lunch and survey our progress. The coast stretches out like a great, green blanket a couple of thousand feet below. But a solid sheet of gray, rain-bearing clouds is rolling in from over the Pacific, right above us.

We continue climbing.

There is a place where the hot, wet air from the coast meets the cool, crisp air of the mountains, forming an impenetrable white mist that obscures the world for miles at a time, a place where the sun never shines. There are probably some species right here in this narrow strip of earth that have never seen the sun, and which don't exist anywhere else. By sundown we reach this magical place.

Fredo warms up some *canelasos*, advising me that sugar and alcohol are good for keeping your blood pressure up while you climb. He gets no argument from me.

We sit around the campfire warming our food, and actually speak some words.

"Got your face a bit red down in the valley," Fredo observes.

"Yeah." My skin feels stiff and leathery, and one drink makes me so loopy I crawl into the tent to pass out before I try to do something hilarious like float off the mountain.

I shiver and draw my blanket in closer around me.

Don't be fooled by the thick clouds. At this latitude, the sun's ultraviolet rays fly right through them. And so the Ecuadorian Andes is one of the few places on earth where you can get a sunburn *and* freeze to death at the same time.

I awake to blackness.

The nights are twelve hours long here. A long time to stare into darkness.

Eventually the clouds thin out, revealing fragmented pieces of sky. Strange stars circle in unremembered orbits, except for a few old friends like the Southern Cross that start to take shape above me.

We set off before sunrise, as the mountains start to emerge, cutting sharply into the sky. I had forgotten how the Andes look by the first early morning light. So distinct. They look like they were made yesterday.

The wet, green grass gives way to brown scrub and saw grass. The mud changes to packed, wet earth. The air grows thin and cool, bone-penetratingly dank, and the moss-covered cliffs lose their tops in the white, misty clouds. We inhabit a thin region of color and shape, sandwiched between thick layers of impenetrable mist. A narrow band indeed.

Welcome home.

My heart is pounding at about two hundred beats a minute and I'm filling my industrially scarred lungs to full capacity at every breath with the sharp, icy air, but it's not enough.

Dizziness.

I need to stop. To sit. To stare at a clump of quinoa trees that dredges up memories of the dark forests of my childhood, when my mind was so full of phantasmagoric visions I saw strange, threatening shapes in the dirty smears on a window, in the splattering of mud against a thinly whitewashed wall, in the rotted base of a dead tree, which all seemed like portals for the multitudes of evil creatures coming to seize me with their sharp claws and take me back to their world, a hostile and ever-changing world without friends or family. Monsters from the deepest trenches of the unconscious invading the conscious. Nowhere to run when the enemy is your own mind.

Fredo nudges me back to reality, offers to make me a *canelaso*.

"I'm all right, thanks. Let's keep going."

But I'm clearly not as strong as I should be. It's taking longer than I was prepared to endure to get to the pass, and we just keep going higher and higher. Low, flat-leaved cactuses rip at my ankles. I'm not stepping around them like I should.

Purple heather. Nice color.

We enter a grove full of towering green columns of spiny San Pedro cactus, so deceptively innocent with its brassy fanfare of white flowers, but behind its many Spanish names lurks its original name, in Quichua. I just can't remember what it is. Or the Cañari word before that.

"Hey, Fredo, what's the Quichua word for *el gigantón*?"

He looks at the ground and says he doesn't know. After all, he's just a *costeño*.

I take out my water bottle and drink. The wind blows a low, hollow wail across the plastic bottle's open mouth.

The sun is low. Another half hour of light.

We reach a high ridge surrounded by still higher ridges spearing up through the ground like escapees from the center of the earth, and finally look down on the long-awaited lagoons of Cajas in the rocky valley below.

There are hundreds of dark lagoons, stretching in every direction. But we've made it.

I can barely move.

Fredo pitches the tent, makes the fire, warms the *canelaso*.

Achachay! It's as cold as a warm day on Neptune. And the air feels thinner than it should be.

And I think about all those New Yorkers whose idea of a challenge is trying to catch a cab going up Third Avenue in the rain. I can barely orient myself. The North Star lies invisible below the horizon, behind a leaden curtain of clouds and mist.

Sheesh!

Must be the exertion and the altitude. This *canelaso* really knocks me

CHAPTER THIRTEEN.

Cold.

I was a cold and penniless eighty-year-old peasant, my feet frigid and useless, clinging to a torn, filthy old poncho and dying of cold on the floor of some muddy drinking shack in the bone-cold mountains, and all these younger peasants full of warmth and life were standing around drinking and laughing at what I was saying, which is that I had a lighter to make a fire up on the hill, and that something is happening to me, I don't know what. And when I kept saying that I really did have a life somewhere else they laughed, because everyone knew I was a penniless old beggar who had been saying the same crazy nonsense for at least forty years. Nobody knew me. I was alone.

And so cold.

I had been lured to that place by people who kept swearing they were helping me. That Don Lucho was coming, that they were going to take me to a *curandera*, and didn't I want something to drink? But the place felt like a graveyard and they were doing nothing to stop the warmth from slowly seeping out of me until I was stiff and rigid and chilled.

No puede ser. No puede ser. Morir aquí. De frío. No puede ser. It can't be. To die here. Of cold. It can't be. And I kept repeating this, lying on the floor of that muddy mountain tavern, when I finally realized that I had left everything behind, that no one would ever speak my name again, except in a cautionary folktale about cold. About crossing the mountains alone and letting yourself get too cold.

Ñucaca Miguelmi cani.

A voice.

As I stumble through the rain, the spongy bright green moss and the squishy wet ground might as well be the jungle, snagging me, leaking cold water through my shoes, icing my feet.

I smell humans.

And I keep coughing up stringy, slippery crap that sticks to me and to everything I touch, creating a viscous, gooey webbing that clings like resin, which I can't wipe off my hands. My stomach's pretty empty and I'm coughing so hard that it's coming out of my lungs. A ton of crap from the city. Black tar.

Sticky black tar everywhere.

YOU ARE IN MY LAND NOW

No. I know I'm not dead because I can still see and feel things. I'm still at the border between mortality and the neighboring country, I still have a ways to go before I am in the final place of Death, the central square of his kingdom.

Flutes and drums. Funeral drums.

Lights.

And they kept saying, Don't you want a drink? It'll warm you up. But I knew it was all lies. They had taken me to a lonely marsh near a lagoon or a river and they were waiting for me to die so they could rob me and dump the body. And he was still offering me a drink, as if he were my friend—*as if he didn't know the drink would make me even weaker and they wouldn't have to work so hard to do it*. This was the end.

Cold. Biting into my bones.

Ñucaca Miguelmi cani.

And I was totally curled in upon myself, trying to ward off the icy vacuum of deep space, of coldest darkness, trying to fend off the toothy, gaping jaws of a legion of fiery-eyed fiends from hell trying to devour me. And there were just a few droplets of warmth left in me, and the forces that thrived in this dark realm were talking to me, trying to convince me to give up that last bit of warmth and go with them and be theirs from now on, and it was a struggle between a part of me that began to say, Well, hey, what's life anyway, just one form of energy becoming another, so I'll go on as something else, and another part that kept saying *¡No! ¡Hasta el último!* Until the end.

GIVE UP

> I was a weak, cold, disoriented animal, and these killers knew it.
> And I was never going to be warm again.
> I called out to family, friends, all creation.
> That last switch was still working.

Ñucaca Miguelmi cani.
My name is Miguel.
Tiaca, ima shutitac canqui?
What's your name, *señorita.*
Fi . . . lo . . . me . . . na . . .
Canta imata nanan?
Where does it hurt?
Mana nanachina. Me no hurt.
Bad Quichua.
Chiri. Cold. *Chirina.* Me cold.
Mai uncushca. Very sick.
Ari. Yes.
Spanish.
Un soroche tremendo . . . un frío . . . como me voy a morir.

Terrible mountain sickness . . . cold . . . as if I'm going to die. I felt strange saying it, but I had to say it. And then he felt my wrist and said *No hay pulso* as he shook his hand in the local gesture of being empty-handed, of having nothing.

No pulse.

No no no . . .

And I go mad trying to withdraw from the evil place. It's squeezing the blood from my veins.

GIVE UP NOW

Got to keep the blood contained. Inside. Where it's warm. Warm . . .

When will I see my daughter again? Will she recognize me? Or will I be two hundred years old and withered from the eternal cold?

I remember him helping me, and that I could barely walk. I told him, even then, that he had saved my life, that he was a friend, repeating it as I held on to him for support, my arms stiffening.

I wake up cold. Wearing pants and a shirt, a sweater, a thin, dirty blanket wrapped around me. No tent. No Fredo. No fire. Nothing but what I've got on. I get up. I walk around. Trying to get warm. So cold. Have to make a fire. Can barely hold the lighter. And then this ridiculous paranoid feeling that I had started a wildfire. I tell myself, Come on, you're not losing it that much, you know you didn't set the underbrush on fire. But then I'm not sure. And I realize—I'm not sure if the mountain is on fire or not? Man, that's outrageous. Get back in bed.

And at some point I was curled up on the ground, energy dripping out of my body, slipping into a very colorful but somewhat disturbing otherworld complete with particolored flappers in sheer tube dresses eating creamy hot dogs, whores with gaily painted faces sprouting eyelashes whose tips end in wet black dots, bearded transvestites dressed in mod-influenced negligees and bowler hats, smiling sideways at me in front of the striped wallpaper, and me saying, Okay, I'm another energy form in another dimension, but there's got to be a way back to my body and my life, and if it takes me forever, I'll find it. My only concern was how much time would pass back on earth before I could get there . . . but then I found myself curled up in darkest, coldest space, my hands aged, arthritic, the skin burst and bleeding, yet holding on to some impalpable life-warmth, holding it within my chest. And voices were telling me to give up, already, that this was it. That I was part dead anyway, and that it wasn't so bad. My legs did feel lifeless, and no, it wasn't so bad.

But it was just so empty, it was nothing to head into willingly. No long, glowing corridor of warm, white light with a friendly figure at the end beckoning to me.

You know, if I had seen that, I just might have gone.

But it was just such cold, dark nothingness, and I was holding on. I was saying, No, not yet.

Not *never*, just not yet.

This is what I will see at my end, and I know it, but this is not the end for me, not yet.

And I think that is when I got up and said to myself I am sick, and went to find help.

They wanted me to give them the lighter and I wouldn't because the lighter was the only "proof" that I was still sane, that there was still a physical reality out there and that I was connected to it. The fact that they wanted me to give them the lighter proved that it, at least, was *real*.

The last shred of sanity I had left was *knowing* that I was going insane.

The still-warm fires of my heart were retreating to my innermost core, but the periphery had dissolved. I was not in my body, or on the hilltop, or anywhere. I had permanently lost my way in Death's lonely land.

And yet I knew that they'd find my body, all right, but that my mind would be somewhere else, madly lost twenty-three universes away. But the madness meant nothing next to the nearness of death.

Death was bodiless in the blackness, just a voice, coming from all around.

And then there was the unwelcome impression that various parts of my body were splitting open. Fingertips hopelessly crevassed and oozing sticky-thick blood into the canyons of my palms.

No stars.

Just blackness.

But now the sleep is just as cold, so I keep going, keep fighting, keep resisting, because as long as Miguelito wanted the lighter from me, that meant it was real, and they were just waiting, wearing me down, just letting me get weaker and weaker, knowing that I was on the way out, on the frozen road to death.

I was outside on a rainy night, hugging the cold, wet metal fence in front of her house. They said her name was Norma. I remember asking rather loudly what was taking so long, and turning away from her house to shout her name to the distant mountaintops lost in the thick, wet blackness. And Miguelito said, Relax, and one time it helped, I did relax, but another time it didn't, he said, Relax, you're among friends, and I stepped away from him, saying, *Ningún amigo*, you're no friend of mine.

Norma arrived and asked many things I can't remember, except, What hurt me? I managed to say the cold more than anything, and she said my blood pressure must be very low, and I trusted her. But then her face changed in front of me. She was someone else who had shown up tonight because Miguelito had alerted the entire underworld that he had gotten ahold of an out-of-her-mind *gringa* who was soon going to be easy pickings.

So I've got to keep going. But how? They're so much stronger than I am. They keep telling me everything's okay, the liars! They keep trying to get me to take a drink for God's sakes. If I could just get warm I'd be okay, but they just won't let me they they they

Blackness.

And she left me with Miguelito in a cold wet place, saying she was going to go get some medicine or something, and smiling an evil, knowing smile, then she left me alone with this evil man, her partner in this conspiracy, and I realized that there was no way out of it now, I was definitely never going to find my way back and I was going to die of cold, far from my loved ones, with people to whom I meant nothing, and everything was slipping away into darkness. I don't remember fainting, but I did wake up with bruises on my cold, gray fingers.

I was lying on the floor saying *No puede ser*, and someone was above me, repeating what I said to somebody else.

Ñucaca Miguelmi cani.

And then it was a voice, *Soy Miguel*, in the darkness, and then there wasn't darkness. Strange wobbly shadowy figures hovering over me, and someone wearing a very real Miguelito mask was trying to get my lighter, but the flesh was peeling off his face and falling to the ground. Blood on my hands. Raving. More blackness.

I woke up and kicked the blankets off.

Darkness.

I woke up and kicked the blankets off.

We were in a dark place, but light was coming from behind the big man, making him only a dark silhouette. Other dark figures were shoving blankets on top of me, perhaps telling me to get warm, but I was convinced that they wanted me to give in to the *soroche*, to embrace the warm sleep of death, and I preferred being awake and freezing, so I pushed them away. I wasn't going to give in to death that easily. The corona of light glowing behind them gave a convincingly otherwordly air, but I couldn't tell if they were servants of heaven or hell. They were angels and devils fighting over my soul, and I said I will only talk to God.

I would be happy to go off with Him, but not these unknown dark figures.

And there was more darkness.

And then a voice coming from a dark figure in a darker room was asking *¿Antonia es el nombre de su hija?* which only made it worse, an appalling attempt to get my confidence, trying to say my daughter's name to me, when I was convinced that the three figures dressed in black weren't real but part of the bottomless psychic ocean I had entered way back on top of the ridge. And the one near me smelled of death. . . .

Some people say that the unconscious is structured like a language, but it's not. The unconscious is structured like an ocean. I know. I've been there. And I was drowning in it.

I did not trust the men groping around in shadow. They were sucking the blood out of my legs, and I kicked away their rubber bottles, and I pushed him away telling him *No te conosco*. I don't know you.

And I kept passing out.

A dark room. A dark figure that smells of death is asking me, as if we've been talking for quite some time, *¿Antonia es el nombre de su hija?* Where am I? I refuse to talk.

Blackness.

Warmth. Praise God for warmth. I never want to be cold again. I was willing to bargain, thinking about giving them all my money to let me live, but another voice kept telling me to be quiet, to keep it all to myself.

I kept waking up and another one would be there. Two men,

one woman. The first guy, trying to talk to me and get me to take a drink. The others just waiting until I was somehow ready for whatever they were going to do to me. Something kinky. I couldn't even imagine. But they knew. They were smiling about it.

I woke up and stared at a massive orange blur near me. It was warm, glowing bright orange, but I did not recognize it. There were small reptiles crawling in the darkness beyond the fringes of the glow. They asked me how I felt. I was getting warmer finally, so I said I felt good about getting warm but bad as well because I still didn't trust them. It was something pretty direct. They had lizards crawling all over them.

More darkness.

Somewhere in here I had dreams about more psychedelic goings-on involving twiggy ladies with British accents sitting on odd contraptions in their nighties, corpulent black folks working in a fish restaurant on the Mississippi River, huge serpentine arms of flesh slapping the muddy water, a living catalogue featuring a dark-skinned smiling woman named Terry Traynor (according to the voiceover) with a slightly bulging middle modeling skintight park ranger pants with a loose green shirt, and ultra-high-tech weirdness where executives made phone calls from the roofs of computer-generated buildings while triple laser beam beacon light sources played on them for their amusement, and the number of people on those roofs and the myriad light sources made it look like something from a high-tech twenty-first-century depression-era musical. Got that?

The roosters crowed. *That* brought me back. For the first time all night I was sure that I was *not* in another dimension, that I was in—or had made it back to—this one. That night was becoming morning, that I was still in Cajas, and that this probably was Doña Norma's house, like the guy kept telling me. They still wouldn't let me see the roosters, to verify. But after a while I accepted it. I was so grateful for the realization that I was alive, that I had succeeded in finding my way back, as I swore I would back on the hilltop while I fought against what I have fairly good reason to believe was Death. And I was so happy. I accepted the drink. Talked to the man in black. Told him I had a life to get back to and that with his help, I was going to get back to it. Not for my sake, because I was a worthless skank who had brought this all on myself, but for my special girl, who still needed me, who still deserves a mother. For her sake, I need to get back, still talking as if I had "gone" somewhere. Which, as I say, maybe I did.

I just opened right up. It all flooded out, as if my brain were unfreezing. Maybe that's what happens when you get your life back, or at least when congealed hypothermic blood starts to pulsate and run again. I talked in my still-somewhat-strained Quichua, but I know I switched into Spanish for a long while, and I have no idea what he made of *la loca* from the valley who was calmly, quietly cursing and gently slapping the hard adobe wall with her palm and fist to help her "concretize" things. I was even able to converse calmly despite the fact that the man in black had a three-foot lizard draped over his shoulders, hanging down next to the crucifix around his neck, trying to blend in. I even switched back into Quichua and I was able to be quite coherent in Quichua and I knew I was fine at that point. But it just felt so good to be just plain warm. I didn't want to move from that nice warm bed, ever.

By the time Doña Norma came in to see me the next morning, I was fine. I could tell them a lot, but there were many gaps. They filled some of it in for me so now it flows like this. But in some sense, this is a lie, this is not what happened, because now it almost makes sense. But at the time, it only made the most twisted "sense" of paranoid delusion, and that was the scariest part of all.

Coming back from the dead is a little like being reborn.

And I never want to feel that cold again.

CHAPTER
FOURTEEN

The meek shall inherit the earth but not the mineral rights.

—J. Paul Getty

Allillachu canqui?
  Ari, allillami cani. Canca?
Ñucapish.
Better now you are?
Yes.

Norma pours the simmering herb tea into a glass. It's a bright, rosy pink.

It's warm.

I cradle it in my hands, put my face to the rising steam, drink in the warmth.

The warmth.

Thawing brain trying to think. Fredo. He knew I had money. Must have figured I had more. Did he...? No. Money... doesn't seem to matter... now....

And I drift off to sleep murmuring something.

Warm hands on my forehead.

The sun is nearly directly overhead when I wake up and finally see my surroundings clearly, a one-room mud-walled shack with bedrolls for four. Two brothers with rugged Incan features stare down at me. Francisco and Hernando. They've got me wrapped in every cloth, blanket and poncho they could lay their hands on, and I am lying in the one real bed in the place, too. Even at high noon under the equatorial sun, it is cool indoors at this altitude.

What name you are?

I Filomena am.

What you are?

I traveler am.

You pretty woman are.

I smile.

*y*ou hungry are?

"Yes."

"You need more *mote*," says Francisco, pinching my bony arms, and laughing.

The middle knuckles on my right hand are bruised and sore. I don't know how that happened.

They bring me a steaming bowl of soup with a side of rice and *mote*. I refuse the rice, feeling bad about what a tremendous sacrifice it is for them to feed me, but they will not hear of it, and I'm too weak to insist.

"There was no blood in your hands, your feet," says Francisco. "You go crazy."

"Yeah. I sure did."

"You tried to hit me."

"I'm sorry."

"That's okay. You swung at me and then you stopped yourself one inch from my face."

Oh. Then who did I hit?

Norma says they tried to get me to come into her house, but at the door I said that they were going to rob me, and I refused to go in.

I don't remember that.

From what they tell me, my limbs were stiff and shrunken and they squeezed and squeezed my fingers but couldn't get any blood into them. Then they placed hot water bottles on my legs to help get the circulation going, but to me it felt like they were draining the blood out of me like vampires.

234

I always knew that hypothermia means your body starts shutting down the blood flow to the extremities. I just never knew my body considers my head an "extremity." So my brain wasn't getting enough oxygen, causing me to have wildly paranoid hallucinations. Not the best defense mechanism under the circumstances.

"Your heart was beating very strongly," says Francisco. "That's why you're still alive."

So I wasn't exactly at Death's door, but I was definitely walking up his driveway. And I had just enough sense left to know I was losing my mind.

"You came through the Chiripungo," says Hernando.

The Gate of Cold.

"Not many travelers come through there," he says.

"*Huachacmama*, leave her alone," says Norma. "Let her rest."

The boys obey their mother.

The sun is just starting to stitch its golden threads along the tops of the green-gray hills when I wrap myself in a borrowed blanket and step outside. The two brothers are digging a grave for somebody under the bright cloudy sky. Not for me, I hope.

And of course their country shack has no big iron gate.

The distant rumbling of an airplane on its way to the big city in the valley beyond the hills rapidly crescendos until, with a roar that actually hurts my eardrums, the big jetliner tops the nearest ridge and thunders out of the sky above us almost close enough to touch it.

The two men stop digging, standing in the pit they've dug, to watch the jet fly over. When they see me, they leap out of the grave and invite me to share their breakfast.

Coffee with fresh cow's milk, *machica* with thick brown sugarcane syrup, *mote*. Bright orange country eggs straight from the chicken.

It goes right to my muscles.

When it gets to my brain an hour or two later, I ask them who the grave is for.

"Our father."

"Miguelito."

A piece of air gets caught in my throat. No way to hide it.

"I—I'm sorry. . . ."

"It's time to bury him."

"Where was he last night?" I ask.

"He's been lying in the barn for three days."

Three days.

"What day is it?" I ask.

The brothers eye me, each other. Hernando gets up and leaves.

"Monday."

Monday? It sure feels like I lost a day in there somewhere. But no, we definitely reached Cajas late Saturday, then my endless night of madness dragged on till Sunday morning. So it couldn't have been the same Miguelito, could it?

I start feeling around in my clothes for money. Cleaned out, except for a few soggy thousand-sucre notes in my shoes and a heel-worn credit card that's going to be pretty useless around these parts. My ring and silver necklace are still there.

"We also found these on you," says Hernando, standing in the doorway, dangling the lighter, knife and sling from his outstretched hands.

He plunks my gear on the table, his eyes probing for a reaction.

"How long have you been away, sister?" asks Francisco.

"A great long while."

$\int$ parks float up into the inky blackness as a soul climbs the smoky ladder rising to the sky from the funeral fire.

All of their white clothing has been put away. The family will wear black for a year of mourning.

Doña Norma fans the embers to a bright red heat, then she stirs a quart-sized kettle of boiling herbs, while Francisco strums the guitar that I think is issued to every third male on the continent at birth. All the men seem to know how to pluck a few tunes on the curvaceous ol' wood nymph.

She removes the kettle from the heat, pours the rejuvenating liquid into glass jars with three fingers of cane alcohol already in them and passes them around.

Eulogistic words are spoken, tongues loosen, then begin to

stiffen again as blood-warmed skin chills in the night air. I stare into the orange reflections of flame in my glass jar, spinning through space on the razor tip of this faraway mountain chain, fingers of frost feeling their way up my ribs, with only a tiny kernel of heat in front of me keeping them at bay.

The line between the two is so thin.

Doña Norma serves me a steaming plate of rice and beans with fried *yuca*, excusing herself for how poorly she is feeding me.

"Don't say that, *mamá*. It's delicious."

"*Tía Filomena, maimanta canqui?*" asks Hernando.

"I'm from Solano."

I can almost see their brains working on it. That may have been a mistake. But it's hard to lie to the people who just saved your life.

I stare at the full plates and the huge pot of rice, wondering how they can afford to eat so well. Norma looks at me through the flames, and says, "There are some kind rebels who steal grain and fertilizer and give it to the poor."

"Ah," I nod.

"Bullets cannot harm them."

Hernando disagrees: "Mother, the police kill rebels all the time."

"Not when they are doing the work of God. Then they cannot be harmed."

"Even the police know that," says Francisco.

They talk about the local rebels, some of whom have become living legends, known only in the highlands of Ecuador, mostly for snagging a few head of cattle from the biggest ranchers, or a truck-load of grain from the big *haciendas*, and occasionally smashing the windows of some chickenshit bank in a small town and tossing fistfuls of grubby money to the people outside. But a little rebellion goes a long way in a nearly medieval system that a revolution should have wiped away centuries ago.

It's probably too late now, since we're all working for a bunch of multinational King Midases whose power would have been the envy of any of the absolute monarchs of old.

"There is one that I have not seen in a long time," says Norma. "*El carihuahua.*"

Babyface.

His Indian name, before he became known as Juan Tres Ojos.

"His spirit walks these hills," she says.

The brothers become animated.

"He could steal the saddle off a galloping horse," claims Francisco.

"He could steal the spots off a leopard."

"He could skin the Devil and sell it back to the old goat by the square yard!"

"And there was one who was with him," says Norma. "She had a good heart, and a proud heart. In Llacao they tell how she arrived before the soldiers came and warned the villagers, and every one of them saw how the rain did not touch her. They could see the thick, wet drops spreading across her captain's cloak, but her head remained dry."

Silence.

"But I see you have a long way to travel, daughter," she says. "You need your rest."

The morning comes gray and rainy, which is actually good for me. The police are generally undermotivated enough about combing the back woods for uncooperative undesirables like me, and the lousy weather ought to just tip the balance to my side.

My hosts outfit me with a poncho and an oversized woolen hat that makes me look like somebody's grandfather. I'm okay as long as no one checks too closely for a cheekful of gray beard stubble.

I'm about ready to leave when Francisco tells me not to go yet, that he has a *carabina* he can lend me. I say good, I might need it. He rummages around behind his bedroll, and brings out what he has been calling his *carabina*. But the language variation between our two sides of the mountain is enough to cause a bit of a misunderstanding. Where I come from, a *carabina* is a rifle. What Francisco calls a *carabina* is clearly a duck hunter's scatter gun, which is going to be about as useful over mountain-range distances as a fistful of sand.

But it'll have to do. *Mamá* Norma wraps up a midday meal for me, and it takes me nearly twenty minutes to convince them to accept the money I am offering. They finally give in when I explain that this is not a charitable donation: I am taking their gun, and I may not come back with it.

Hernando says, "It's almost eight-thirty, you'd better be going."

I've noticed that nobody has so much as a wall calendar around here. I ask him how he knows it's almost 8:30, and he just grins at me.

Francisco runs back inside and gets some more ammunition. He says ammunition, but what he's talking about is wadding, black powder and hollow lead pellets, the kind of antiques you see under glass in museums in the U.S. I don't believe I'm taking this stuff, but I stow it all under my poncho anyway. All I need now is a chewed-up cigar and someone playing a bamboo flute on the soundtrack and I'm ready to take on any varmint who crosses my path.

"*Chulla vida,*" says Francisco.

We only get one life.

But I'm beginning to feel like I've had more than that.

Distant drums echo down through the valley, and my feet start falling in a proud rhythm across the *pampa,* squishing along towards the Filo de Ladrones. Thieves' Ridge. I'm getting my stamina back, and my lungs are handling the thin air much better this time. I wonder if it's all that stuff I coughed up. If indeed that really happened . . .

The ground starts to harden as I head up the ridge. I stand and breathe awhile, sucking in the brisk mountain air, my brain clearing with each passing gasp like a dirty window being wiped clean with a squeegee. Once I'm up there, I'll slip down the slopes to the Río Yanuncay, the back way into Cuenca.

We held this ridge for months.

Inside the cave, I find evidence of visitors within the past year. There are traces of a campfire and a garbage pit which I dig up to see how recent it is. I sift and sift, looking for a special clue, but come up with nothing. Of course. There's a big black cross on one wall, drawn with a crumbly piece of charcoal, but anybody could have done that.

What did I expect? A certified letter with a return receipt for my RSVP?

Yet I feel let down.

No time for that. Keep moving.

I inch along the sheer rock face until I can drop down to the brush and climb down like a human rather than a mountain goat.

The clouds have held off for a while, but the condensation is so suffusive that water is dripping from the jutting rocks and the terrain gets squishy again. I follow the flowing water down to a narrow valley between the ridges, divided by a small stream that feeds into the Yanuncay. I squat for a moment, watching the clear mountain water flow, the tiniest capillary in a continent-wide network that eventually converges into the largest river system on earth.

My brief moment of reflection is shattered by the heart-stopping bark of the great beast. I'm assuming attack posture as a hairy black body comes crashing through the wet, overgrown weeds and springs through the air at me.

I've already got the gun out and I fire. I had forgotten how a shotgun blast fills up the space in a high valley like this from mountaintop to mountaintop, proceeding in two successive wave fronts of sound and shock, followed by a dying cry, echoing away. They must have heard that one in the city.

The diffuse spray of blood-speckled pellets is not enough to stop the huge dog from flying into me with enough force to uproot a small tree and knocking me to the ground under his repulsive weight. But the little pellets have done their job. The dog is quite dead.

The ground beneath my back begins to vibrate. A horse's hooves. I push the bloody dog off me. No time to reload this moldy musket. I zing out my stiletto and saw through one of the broad radiating branches of a blue *penco* cactus and crouch down into spear-chucker position, one hand on the ground, both ears open.

As the rumbling hooves close in on me I spring up and launch the needle-tipped *penco* at the sergeant's uniform like a harpooner in a twelve-foot rowboat aiming for a sperm whale's eye.

He starts to say, "You are going to fight me with *plants*?" but the sharp tip of the yard-long *penco* shaft pierces his skin as he blocks it to keep from losing an eye. I whack him above the ear with my breech-loading flintlock, yank him from the saddle and knock the pistol out of his hands. There's an electrical moment of fumbling before I am able to grab the gun properly and point it at him. I smash his radio against a rock, then I leap onto the horse and turn it around, firing a few keep-away-from-me shots past the horse's butt that set the noble brute tearing off at a gallop across the narrow valley as if the Devil himself were chewing on her tail.

Nice switch, but I'll never get into Cuenca looking like a stage-coach bandit.

My best chance is to make for Soldados. If I had more time I could trade in this blue steel semiautomatic for some hard currency. But I've got no time, no takers, a damn big horse, and the rural police will be on full alert within an hour, as soon as that guy makes it back to his command post. Otherwise, everything's going smoothly.

An eight-mile ride.

I tie the horse up behind a brake of scrubby trees and prickly bushes with bright red and yellow flowers, near some grass and water, turn my wretched poncho inside out to hide the dog's blood-stains, and slip into town.

I have no choice.

I sell my silver and gold.

I buy a used *pollera*, a stiffened-straw Azuayan hat and some cheap black shoes one cut above going barefoot. I find a dirty, dank place to strip off my muddy clothes and wrap them up in a bundle. Amid fecal smells and dripping water, I begin my transformation. The last step is braiding my frizzy hair on both sides, then I step out into the bright sunlight and join a collection of *cholas* piling onto a decrepit bus riding on a set of tires that look like they were retreaded the same year that Goodyear invented vulcanizing. It's heading for Cuenca.

I've only got a few sucres left, just enough to reach the city. So I freeze with disbelief when I hear the driver telling the women in front of me that the fare has gone up four thousand sucres and I'm way short. And way fucked. I can't wait for the next bus. Even if I went back and hocked the saddle, this town would be swarming with *rurales* by then and I'd be standing there with hot bridles dangling from my sweaty hands. Fifty cents short and it could be the end of the road for me.

I turn to a pair of round-faced *cholas* dressed in stiff orange *polleras* and red sweaters and beg them to help me.

"*Maiman rinqui?*" says the taller one, looking up at me.

"*Cuencamanmi rini.* I need four thousand sucres. I'll pay you back as soon as we get to the city."

"*Mana imata charinchicchu,*" says the other one, turning me down.

"It's only a few thousand sucres."

"Oh, is that all? Try dragging a bucket full of cow's milk all the way into town if you want to make a few thousand sucres."

"I'll give you back five thousand. What am I saying? I'll give you back *ten thousand*—"

"*La plata se apega a la plata,*" says the shorter one. My money's just sticking together. Or, a bit more generously, it takes money to make money.

But the other one takes my hands and turns them over, feeling their smoothness, studies the color of my pupils, and decides to lend me the bus fare.

"*Diussulpagui,*" I say, thanking them with genuine gratitude for their kindheartedness. God will repay you.

We climb aboard and grab three seats together. They figure they've bought the rights to my story, and I'm somewhat ashamed to say that I invent something. They tell me their names are María Natividad and María Esperanza, and they're heading to the sheep market to buy some wool to knit into ponchos.

We rattle along just fine until we round a bend in the river outside Sustag and run into a roadblock. It's the army, not the *rurales.* It could mean anything. Two brown-skinned conscripts in green fatigues carrying bulky wooden-stocked rifles step up inside the bus. One stations himself at the front, the other walks slowly down the aisle, looking directly at our faces.

María Esperanza giggles and covers her blushing cheeks with her poncho. I don't want to draw attention with any suspicious behavior, forgetting for a moment that such excessive humility is "normal" behavior for a *chola.* The kid with the rifle stares at me. My features aren't quite as Indian as my companions, and he's coming closer, gazing down at me. But I have walked through rivers of mud, I haven't bathed in days, and the overpowering smell of manure and earth convinces him that I spend most of my time among farm animals. What a victory for our side.

Fifteen harrowing kilometers later we pull into the animal market and the relative safety of anonymity. I tell my newfound sisters to come with me to the center of town so I can pay them back, but María Natividad dismisses me with a wave of her hand and an aphorism:

"Cuando mucho, mucho. Cuando nada, nada."

A sentiment so simple it's hard to render into English, but basically, When you've got it, you've got it. When you don't, you don't.

I tell her once again God will pay them back. His credit's better than mine, anyway.

I need to find a phone. I need to call Antonia and talk to her and tell her I'm all right, and remind her to keep praying for me, and tell her that I miss her and I'll see her soon. But there's a good chance some unseen ears will trace the call back to me in Cuenca, and it can be hard to make a quick exit from a town like this, all snug in a basin eight thousand feet above sea level, rimmed by mountains that climb several thousand feet higher still. Cuenca didn't even have a paved road connecting it with the outside world until the 1970s. The city's first automobiles were taken apart on the coast, carried up the mountain on the Indians' backs and reassembled here so they could putter around the bumpy streets of the old center with no particular place to go.

Now the paving stones and spun-sugar colonial stylings and the unfinished cathedral are awash in the orange-tile-and-white-cement sea of the new neighborhoods. But there are still only two real roads out of here, and they're both guarded by military checkpoints.

It can get cold enough to grow frost on your bones when it rains this high up. But right now the sun is out and the center is hot, close and bustling like something out of a Dantean fever dream. Although in some ways it's more like Sherlock Holmes's London. Social stratification is so ingrained here, you can deduce a person's rank, profession, and personality from three blocks away. See that guy? Light skin, confident walk, European-style business suit? He's a well-made banker with connections, married, with two children and a maid. That woman? Company-issued uniform, harried look, rushing to attend to urgent tasks? Office underling, single, lives at home with her mom and her five sisters. That guy who's been wearing the same set of grimy clothes for half a lifetime and doesn't particularly feel like rushing anywhere? He's a day laborer, and he'll never be anything *but* a day laborer. And the ones on the bottom rung are indentifiable by their tribal clothing, which may be decorative and colorful or soiled by thirty harvests, their faces dark and angular as the mountains that nurtured them, many of them walking with a stoop that has been shaped by five centuries of fire and fraud, also known as "civilization."

I'm trying to get the stoop just right, to take a few inches off my height and not stick out in any way.

I have a lot of family around here, but I haven't warned them I'm coming—that is, they might be expecting *me*, not a *chola cuencana* who smells like a she-goat. My best bet is my cousin Lucho Freire, the guy with the poison gas operation, who works a second job in a hardware store near the Diez de Agosto marketplace. There's a man sitting in the shade under the arches near the open square with a manual typewriter set up on a low table, typing out the words spilling from the mouths of the unschooled parents of emigrés for whom the letters of the alphabet might as well be the arcane and sinister symbols of some deranged medieval alchemist. The professional letter-writer. How lucky I am that I don't need *his* help.

I cross the Calle Mariscal Lamar, named after a hero of the War of Independence who later attacked Ecuador from the south with an army raised in Peru, which comes about as close to encapsulating Ecuador's blighted history as any single example I can think of. I mean, the guy's a traitor *and* a national hero at the same time.

Lengths of hanging chain of various weights dangle over the doorway like strings of beads in a Moroccan bazaar. I spread them apart, and they clickety-clack together behind me as I step inside. The store has not altered its muted rustic interior in decades. Worn wooden compartments keep the fax machine and the ultraviolet counterfeit banknote detector out of plain sight. Varnished shelves rise to the ceiling crammed with such must-have items as chunks of sulfur by the pound, pitch and nitre for homemade gunpowder, vegetal and aniline dyes for hand-loomed cloth, square-headed horseshoe nails, spools of hatband ribbon for the local straw hat trade, brittle slabs of tar to be melted over a fire and brushed on for waterproofing wood, and lumps of black bees' wax from the Amazon jungle for strengthening cheap twine, all weighed out on brass balances so venerable and true they just might be the ones St. Peter uses when it comes time to weigh our souls against that feather. Even the pope looks down approvingly from his vantage point high up among the carefully stacked packets of antimony and multicolored layers of tissue paper.

The crowd of *campesinos* jostles me with market day urgency. Eight members of the Mejia clan attend to them, weighing an ounce of cloves, breaking off chunks of solid tar with pick hammers, measuring out combustible powder for fireworks, and occasionally knocking a few sucres off the price of bulk orders.

"*¿Sí, señora?*" Lucho Freire asks me.

"It's *señorita*."

Eyes widen.

Opening a wooden gate worn as smooth as a saint's nose by ten generations of passing pilgrims, he invites me to step under the yards of hanging hatband ribbon to the rear of the store while the customers watch the tallying pencils closely. I once gave them a calculator as a gift. They said they couldn't use it because the country folk don't trust them.

Safe from prying eyes, I slide the rural patrolman's 1911 semi-automatic out of the folds of my *pollera* and ask Lucho if he can sell it for me.

It's shiny and blue-black against his sturdy palm. He flips it over and looks at the serial number etched above the grip. This ain't no duck hunter's gun.

He looks at me.

"It's worth a couple of hundred dollars," I say. "I'll take fifty."

"I don't have that kind of money, Filomena."

He smells the barrel.

It's been fired, and he knows it. He checks the clip. Three live bullets, one in the chamber. I guess I should have dumped those.

He waits for an explanation.

And waits.

"You got a place to stay?" he asks, then answers himself: "No, of course not. Why don't you come by tonight and eat with us and we'll sort this all out. Okay?"

"Thanks, Luchito."

"You'd do the same for me."

"Yes, I would."

He looks around to see if anyone is listening and asks what's going on with me. I tell him it's something that I can't explain right now.

"You're not acting like your usual self," he says, understating things a bit.

"I know. I really stepped into a whole bunch of shit that I wasn't expecting. A bunch of shit I thought was over and done with."

"Sounds like you should have packed some hip waders, cousin."

"Yeah, and a nose plug."

He nods. I'm turning to go, back into the sweat and stink.

"Oh, and Lucho?"

"Yes?"

"You got running water?"

"The hills are full of it."

I cross the central square of the Parque Calderón, where a spiritless statue holding a wilted flag depicts another moment of defeat from one of our many wars. At one edge of the park stands a small pink marble pillar with a bronze flame on top, a relatively recent monument to Abdón Calderón (no relation), a believer in democracy who thought that winning a majority of popular votes would be enough to force the general-in-command to relinquish the power he wielded over a lost generation of *ecuatorianos*. The general had other ideas. Someone shot Calderón, and he took five weeks to die.

Cuenca is not as saturated with political propaganda as Guayaquil is, but there are still plenty of posters elbowing each other in the eye in roughly equal amounts of left-liberal yellow-and-white and reactionary red-and-white, with a few blue-and-white posters sprinkled about, covering up the cracks in the walls. Populist hero

Hector-the-School-Teacher Gatillo hasn't got much of a following in the *sierra*. Yet.

Someone is pasting up the red-and-black posters of the left-wing Popular Workers Alliance party. Yellow letters scream: DARWIN HERNÁNDEZ FOR NATIONAL DEPUTY. VIOLETA ESPOLAZO FOR PROVINCIAL DEPUTY. There's only a photo of Hernández. I guess they don't have the money to print two photos.

I could use a quick cash loan myself, but everyone I know is nearly as broke as I am, and the International Monetary Fund stopped taking my calls after that whole Argentine meltdown thing. I'm a little hesitant about using my credit card in a cash machine, wondering if it's worth the risk of sending up that electronic flare. But Ecuador's still a little behind the U.S. in credit card surveillance techniques, so I figure maybe it's worth a shot.

Outside the bank a beggar in tattered rags looks around guiltily to see if anyone is watching, then starts pushing the bright blue buttons on the ATM to see if any crisp new bills come out. At least *someone* still values the sucre.

I take up a spot next to him like we've known each other for decades. How's it going, old man? How are the old bones treating you? Are you getting enough to eat? Good. I look around, slip my card in and punch in the numbers. Nothing. Rejected. I try again, and enter the digital void. *Crap.* The machine swallows my card and nearly chokes on it, as far as I can tell from the audible grinding of wheels inside its satanic body. Then it gulps it all down and the transaction screen appears like a blessing from the gods of gold and silver and brass and iron. I punch in a polite request for a hundred dollars. The gods of gold think about it for a moment, then cancel the transaction and eject my card. Great. I may have just told them where I am and I'm *still* five cents short of a nickel.

I take my card out of the machine. The beggar holds out his hat to me, and I have nothing to offer him.

I walk a few blocks east and try to lose myself in the crowd at the 9 de Octubre market, circulating among the upland Indians in their mud-caked boots and the animal market smells, stepping over rotting oranges and unidentifiable vegetable matter in the gutters. It works for a while, though I almost give myself away when I nearly crack up in front of a hundred witnesses after coming across the cultural incongruity of a quiet old woman sitting there in a black sweater selling gaudily packaged bootleg American tape cassettes, calmly oblivious to the incomprehensible English lyrics booming out of the box next to her:

> Bang bang bang
> Grab ahold of my thang
> So you can put it in your place
> Don't want to shoot it in your face
> Oh no!
> Bang bang bang
> Gonna slam you with my thang
> So you can do me all right, baby
> You can do me real tight, baby
> Oh yeah!

Globalization marches on.

I take my time wandering through the masses of people piling onto the buses leaving the market, meekly making my way past the mud-spattered whitewash and political grafitti towards Lucho and Marianita's store, when all of a sudden this overwhelming sensation creeps over me that someone's following me, close enough for me to feel them. I measure off the steps to the corner, gripping the handle of my knife as I walk slowly towards a store window, where on the pretext of examining some imported Chinese claw hammers, I check out what's going on behind me.

Nobody. Nothing.

That doesn't mean they aren't there.

I shower off a few festering days of grit and slip into a clean, dry pair of pants, telling myself that I ought to be able to walk around safely inside the city without being recognized and dragged off to a cell in leg irons.

"Pull up a chair," says Lucho as I squoosh in between their sprightly brood of children aged eight, twelve and sixteen—Fabiola,

María Auxiliadora and Juan Carlos. "Where five can eat, six can eat." It's a local saying.

The portions are small. A little vegetable soup with *mote*, extra bread and milk for the growing teens. Marianita asks me to forgive her for offering so little.

"Nonsense," I say. "This is everything I could possibly ask for." Though I notice the larder is emptier than usual. "What happened to that *quintal* of rice you got?"

"Gone," says Lucho.

"The whole family needed it," says Marianita, who has nine brothers and sisters, including one in the U.S.

"This is the only thing left on the shelves," says Lucho, opening a bottle of *aguardiente* and pouring out a couple of shots. He slugs it back and shudders (this is a chemical engineer who makes his own ammonia, mind you), then gestures for me to do the same. I beg off. I've done enough messing with my blood sugar for one week.

We try to call Guayaquil, but the interprovincial phone lines are damaged due to flooding.

"Maybe tomorrow," says Lucho, relaxing by the window and opening up the newspaper.

Marianita tells me they found a trunkful of my grandfather's things in an old toolshed in Solano, and it's still there if I want to go through it. I tell her I don't have time right now. Someday, maybe.

We're talking about the bygone days in that dusty old town halfway up a cliff-hugging drive into southern Cañar when a truck lurches to a halt in front of a shuttered building across the street and a cop gets out and stands guard in the feeble circle of light from a streetlamp while four workers dressed in dark blue coveralls prepare to unload a shipment of sacks marked Potassium Nitrate.

"They're working late," says Lucho.

"What's that stuff?" I ask the chemistry expert.

"Fertilizer."

"They need a cop to guard some fertilizer?"

"People will steal anything these days."

Sacks fall. *Whompsh! Whompsh!*

Lucho stops talking. His fist tightens around the newspaper.

"You hear that?" he says.

Whompsh!

"Yeah. What about it?"

"That's not fertilizer. Those are sacks of rice."

I know better than to ask, "Are you sure?" This is a man who can judge the freshness of a *quintal* of rice by grinding a single grain of it between his teeth.

"Who owns that building?"

"The Central Bank," he answers, his throat constricting.

It takes them nearly forty-five minutes to carry it all inside and shut and lock the big double doors. When they're gone, we go downstairs and have a close look at the street in front of the empty doorway. The cracks between the cobblestones catch a bit of light, revealing a few scattered grains of bleached white rice.

"There must be room for thirty or forty thousand *quintales* in there," he says, looking up at the darkened windows.

In one warehouse, on one street, in one sleepy neighborhood in an isolated mountain town two hundred kilometers from the nearest rice paddy.

Normally, I'd say the big rice producers are hiding the stuff to drive the price up. Simple, right? But Lucho says this is a government-owned building. What's *their* angle? Besides taking their cut, I mean.

To drive up desperation.

The easiest way to turn decent folks into killers is not to feed them for a couple of weeks.

Lucho is shaking his head. All that rice.

We have a saying in Spanish: What good is a gold chamberpot when you're pissing blood?

f ilomena, wake up!"

Jesus Christ, won't anyone let me finish a dream in this country?

"I looked into selling that gun for you," says Lucho. "We'd have to file off the numbers, engrave new ones, and match them with a registered owner's permit. It could take a couple of weeks."

Legally, yes.

Unless you have the money to bribe some civil servant to forge the documents, which of course we don't. That's the whole problem in the first place. Or else you sell it directly to the scum of the earth, but I don't feel like placing a weapon of this quality into their undifferentiating hands.

Lucho's got the early shift across town, so I help Marianita push up the big steel shutters. Light floods the family chemical supply store, revealing a yellow-and-white poster proclaiming FALTORRA: THE PEOPLE'S CHOICE FOR PRESIDENT!

"You really support this guy?" I ask her.

"Well, he's a good man, in his way," she says deferentially. "But some of the people around him are not. And one day three men came by carrying those posters and said they were taking a poll—"

I finish the sentence for her, but probably not with the words she would have chosen.

I sit down and go through the top third of the stack of newspapers they use for wrapping powdered chemicals, checking the headlines in *El Mundo* and catching up on the local gossip in Cuenca's *El Mensajero*. There's nothing about a rural sergeant being assaulted on the pampa near the Río Soldados.

I observe all the early morning activity in the street, and when a swarm of eight-year-old newsboys comes through, their faces sculpted by streaks of dirt, I get Marianita to buy me a copy of Guayaquil's *El Despacho* and right there on top of page three is an article with Putamayo's byline saying that in his capacity as governor of Guayas, Segundo Canino is launching an investigation into a series of extremist threats against priests who won't "collaborate" with the government.

Dateline: Cuenca.

I've got to find this guy.

Cuenca's not that big.

I call a few of the major downtown hotels and get nothing. So I call a few more. The same as nothing.

It takes me twenty minutes to get through to the offices of *El Despacho* one province away and ask if they know where in Cuenca Javier Putamayo is staying. I get nothing squared with a fucking cherry on top. Ever since he was attacked, they have to think of his security.

Of course.

I dig down to last Wednesday's paper, throw it on the table and sweep the pages aside until I find Javier Putamayo's picture. It's a little blurry, as if their file photo were taken at the paper's Christmas party or something. He's holding a drink, and wearing a striped polo shirt that emphasizes the expanding gut of a guy who's starting to go soft around the middle years. His thick beard and glasses add to the general impression of bodily roundness. I cut the photo out, slitting the paper with a razor blade.

I tell Marianita I'm going to have to send her a check to pay for all these calls. My tab is off and running.

I fold up the photo, put it in my bag and head to the center, where I spend a good part of the morning canvassing the high-end hotels, showing them the photo and trying to grease my way past their unresponsive security chiefs, but you can only bluff your way so far with an empty hand.

I widen the circle to the midrange hotels, and an hour and five hotels later something finally goes my way as I find myself in the lobby of the Hotel Gran Colombia staring at a fresh-faced desk clerk who just opens up and says,

"Oh yes, *señor* Pena. He's staying in room five-oh-eight."

"Is he in now?"

"No, he went out about half an hour ago. Sorry."

"Did he say where he was going?"

"No, he didn't invite me to the party," he says, feigning disappointment.

"A party? How do you know he was going to a party?"

"Honey, there's always a party going on somewhere in this town."

"Yeah. Where grown men drink like high school kids."

That makes him laugh. "You know, he did say something about how he hoped they had decent food, or at least good booze, but you never know these days."

"Did he say who *they* were?"

"Why would he tell me that?"

"It was worth a shot. But he did say, 'You never know these days'?"

"Sure. Or something like that."

Meaning money's short. So it's probably not a business affair.

"Maybe it was some kind of political fund-raiser."

"You know, he did seem very interested in politics. He has all the papers sent up to his room."

"Thanks, I'll remember that. Mind if I leave him a message?"

"Be my guest."

As I'm leaving, he says, "Good luck, sugar. Hope you find what you're looking for."

"You too."

I'm only a couple of blocks from the provincial headquarters of the Popular Workers Alliance. I figure it's worth a visit. If they haven't heard from Putamayo, maybe someone there knows a sympathetic clerk in the Firearms Registration Bureau.

It turns out there's a party busting out at their offices in celebration of Violeta Espolazo's 20 percent margin of victory in yesterday's poll. I scan the crowd for Putamayo, but I don't make him.

There's also food, and nobody stops me from serving myself a plateful of rice and vegetable stew. I've been pounding the pavement all morning, and I devour my portion in about a minute. A high-spirited fortyish woman in a navy blue blazer and skirt is passing through the crowd, pouring shots of *aguardiente* into everyone's plastic cups. From what I hear, she is apparently Ms. Espolazo herself. When she gets to me, cup and bottle meet, our gazes lock.

I knew her as Adelina Díaz. The Grenade Girl.

Pretty good with a rifle, too.

All I can say is, "Congratulations, Violeta."

All those years of tepid, predigested American politics must have atrophied part of my brain. Of course I knew that ex-revolutionaries are running for political office. Still, one of my former "comrades" could have told me about the possibility of this connection. It would have saved me a lot of BS. It sure feels like somebody's titrating information out to me drop by drop, and I'm starting to get pissed off about it. But I've just been reunited with an old friend, so let's not spoil the mood here.

Violeta brushes aside my ignorance, telling me that Darwin Hernández is the son of Afro-Ecuadorian congressman Jorge Hernández, and says we should have a get-together with a bunch of our old buddies. But I tell her that has to wait, making no effort to keep the desperation out of my voice. She excuses herself for a moment and shuts out the party. The two of us have a small back office to ourselves. It's piled high with posters and other campaign supplies. I show her Putamayo's photo.

"Yes, I've seen him around. Someone said he's staying in Cuenca for a few days to cover the big rallies. What's the problem, Filomena?" she says, taking a moment to get my name right.

I tell her a fair slice of it. She congratulates me for making it this far on my own, and suggests that amnesty is possible for me, too.

So as long as we're on this forbidden topic, I bring up Johnny.

"I've heard rumors, of course," says Violeta. "But I don't know anything. He never tried to contact me. What about you?"

"No. Nothing. But from where I was standing, it sure looked like he got hit. The cops swore it, too."

"All that does is add to his legend," she says.

Lucho finally gets through to the Correas and tells them, "There's someone here who wants to talk to you."

I keep it anonymous, asking them to get "the little girl" so I can tell her that I'm all right, but I miss her terribly, and for her to keep praying for me—believe me, I need it—ready to hang up the phone before my ninety seconds are up in case someone's trying to trace the call, when Suzie cuts in and says, "We've been trying to reach you! Your boyfriend called a few days ago. He's flying into Guayaquil tomorrow."

CHAPTER
FIFTEEN

*But there are things that happen between a man
and a woman in the dark—that sort of make
everything else seem—unimportant.*

—Stella Kowalski

There are only two main streets in La Troncal. One goes east-west, the other runs north-south. At night, from the mountains above it, the town looks like a huge, glittering cross lit up and spread out across the flat, tropical plain.

During the day and close up, it's miserably hot and dirty.

I watch him through the passing shapes flashing along the streets on their way to somewhere else where they belong and I don't. I watch him while the sun becomes a brilliant orange ball igniting the atmosphere with its rapidly fading glory, accepting his mounting anguish as the price of making sure he's not being followed.

I can't take any more risks.

He is a stranger to the sights and sounds of this squalid steam bath they call a town. My boyfriend knows no Spanish, even though he works in a New York City hospital. I've scolded him often for this.

Now he's lost, and getting frustrated. He starts looking around for a place to put down his bag, to sit and watch out for me. Eventually he notices the spot on the bench next to the Indian woman selling woolen ponchos. He sits down and scans the faces in the busy market. After a few moments, I tap his shoulder. He turns.

"Don't say my name."

He stops himself from saying my name, and a lot of other things, too, like, Why am I wearing a disguise?

"What is it?" he says.

"I'd rather you didn't know, but I'm kind of wanted for some crimes."

"Major crimes or minor crimes?"

"They'll decide that after they arrest me."

"Great. Other couples worry if they brought enough sunscreen. I have to worry about being deported for being an accessory after the fact to—to what, exactly?"

"Stan, someone killed my godfather."

"Oh. I'm . . . sorry."

"We'll talk about it later."

I gather up my wares and trudge through the crowd to the fork in the road where the buses gather for Cuenca. I've got a *cédula* courtesy of some cooperative clerks in the Civil Registry that says my name is María Vizhñay, that I come from Cojitambo, Cañar, that I can neither read nor write, and absolutely nothing else to distinguish me from a million others passing through the inter-provincial checkpoints.

"Couldn't we have taken a plane?"

"No, they check your ID much more closely when you're boarding a plane," I explain.

Someone notices that we are speaking. I hold up a poncho, gesturing for Stan to feel its 100 percent woolen softness.

"*Pura lana, patroncito, pura lana,*" goes my sales pitch. "Once we get to Cuenca, we can pass as a tourist couple," I whisper, "but now you better mix with the crowd. Sit next to me, but don't look at me and don't say nothing to me out loud in English."

"Sounds like you're forgetting your English already."

"Sorry, I'm code-switching. Double negatives are grammatical in Spanish. *Buen precio le doy, patroncito.*"

Later, our fingers secretly intertwine beneath my poncho. We lose ourselves in darkness as the *buseta* weaves up the crumbling roads towards the high *sierra*. The tropical mist lifts, and for a moment the stratosphere sparkles with the miraculous clarity of rare-fied ether. I gaze out the window, unable to see the place where the earth stops and the sky begins, or to distinguish between the low-lying stars and the stray pinpoints of light scattered across the thick darkness of a distant mountain.

It sure beats walking.

In the middle of the wooded highlands, the wheels stop rolling and a lively discussion ensues up front, with the mountain folk getting up to look excitedly out one side of the bus. The driver backs up a few yards as sleeping Indians throw off their blankets to join in the search, pressing their foreheads against the dirty glass to stare out into the darkness.

A happy shout of affirmation arises from two separate sources. A pair of foxes has been spotted, and nearly everyone gets a good look once the sharp-eyed hunters point them out. Then they all return contentedly to their seats and the driver throws the bus into gear and we're on our way again.

Amid the temporary turmoil, Stan whispers, "What was that about?"

"Foxes. They're supposed to be good luck."

"What—?"

"Shh."

I squeeze his hand, and cherish his fingers. He squeezes back, touching my leg. Then he starts exploring my thigh, carefully masking his movements, and slowly glides his hand down past the hem of my *pollera* to my bare skin. A shiver of delight. My God, I feel like a high school girl again, thrilling to a boyfriend's forbidden touch on my kneecap.

I'm leaning back, eyes closed towards the ceiling. Breathing. Tingling. Contracting. Secreting. *Ooh!*

The jolt sends us flying forward. I get two arms out to stop me. But Stan smacks sideways into the seat in front of him, and everybody wakes up.

The lights come on, piercing my eyes.

Acch! Another fucking checkpoint.

We have to get off so they can search the bus for "contraband," and we stand shivering in the harsh sidewise glare of the lights while a pair of police officers work their way along the pitted asphalt, inspecting us.

Stan's five people away from me. They demand to see his identification, and when he hands them a U.S. passport they practically shit with delight and pull out a dazzling document decorated with stamps and seals and signatures that they claim is an official order that all U.S. citizens must pay a forty-dollar "drug tax" as part of an international agreement to help Ecuador's antidrug effort.

They quickly extort the money and keep moving. I'm holding a scarf to my nose and mouth to ward off the cold. One of the officers yanks the scarf away from me.

They study my face.

"*Cédula.*"

They look at it, back at me, and smile.

It is not good when these guys smile.

"You're awful tall and pretty for a *machicapussun.*"

It's a Quichua word meaning "*machica* eater," someone from Cañar.

Now, I've got a twenty-minute lecture all prepared on the oppressive and misogynistic effects of Caucasian-based standards of beauty within postcolonial patriarchally structured societies, but I shorten it to, "*Sí, patroncito.*"

"Maybe you wanna come back to the barracks with us to make *chichirimicui?*"

More Quichua. You figure it out.

I'm conjuring up multiple scenarios, rejecting the ones that are most likely to leave a trail of dead bodies. Stan's fishing frantically in his pockets, probably hoping to distract them with more bribery, when a stern voice cuts in.

"Sergeant."

A captain. Calmly smoking a cigarette.

I'm covering the bottom half of my face with my poncho. Fortunately, this is in character.

"Keep moving," he utters, and turns away as they throw the scarf back at me.

My God. A good cop.

Meanwhile, my seat has been taken and neither of us can insist that we sit together, so I have to stand in the aisle all the way to Cuenca. No chivalry for an Indian. Even a "tall, pretty" one.

I'm only five foot seven. What they mean is, I'm tall for a *mestiza.*

And all my sisters are beautiful.

But my legs are so tired by the time we get to Cuenca that I don't yield fast enough as a *señor* in a suit passes me on the narrow sidewalk.

"Dirty Indian," he snips.

"*Mana pi chayachun, patroncito,*" I say, meekly shuffling out of the way, even though I just told him to fuck off in Quichua.

Stan wants to find a hotel together, but I tell him if we check in looking like a *gringo* and a *chola cuencana*, the religious police will be breaking down the door within an hour.

"It's a quiet town, huh?" he says.

"Quiet? After ten P.M., you could play chess in the middle of the streets and not get interrupted until the king's down to his last three pawns."

We have to settle for a quick kiss in a dark doorway. Damn, it feels good to be hugged by a man who cares enough to keep a date with a fugitive.

It makes me feel like a teenager again. And just as horny.

friday morning I buy a stack of newspapers and skim through them, searching for information I could get in a minute if my sources were intact. Still nothing about a rural sergeant being assaulted, but Putamayo has a feature article in today's *El Despacho* playing up Governor Canino's charges that the "janitor" who killed *padre* Samuel Campos had ties to Hector-the-School-Teacher Gatillo's Socialist Unity Party that are going to be fully investigated. Page three again. Pretty prominent placement for a guy who never seems to be where anyone says he is.

In other news, President Pajizo announced the end of fuel subsidies, blaming it on a "shortage of dollars" (Hmm, I wonder where they have *them* warehoused).

General Vélez said he will support whichever candidate offers his imprisoned commandos amnesty—and anyone who remembers that he was the rebellious general Pajizo tried to bomb out of the Manta Air Force Base without referring to the chart gets an A.

The police announce they are doubling the number of interprovincial roadblocks because "subversion is on the rise," which is an interesting mixed metaphor in its own right.

And the two leading candidates, Governor Segundo Canino and Senator Ricardo Faltorra, are both planning to come to Cuenca for back-to-back rallies.

Things are heating up.

I stop off at the Hotel Gran Colombia and ask if *señor* Pena got the message I left for him. But it's a different clerk, who tells me, "There's no one here by that name."

I show him the photo.

"What does this look like, a police station? Get out of here before I call the cops," he snips.

Lucky for him I've learned to control my tendency to respond to idiocy with extreme violence.

Then it's on to Stan's hotel room, where I make a two-minute call to Guayaquil so I can talk to Antonia. It takes a minute and a half to complete the connection, so I only have about thirty seconds.

"Are you okay, honey?"

"Yeah, I guess."

"Yes?"

"Well, no, not really. It's getting kind of boring here. But that's okay. You do what you've got to do."

"Umm . . . I wish it weren't like this. We have to catch up and spend a lot of time together when I get back, okay?"

"Yeah, Mom. Sure. 'Bye."

" 'Bye."

Emptiness . . .

Till Stan says, "Hey—remember me?"

It starts slowly.

Soon it's a flurry of arms and kisses.

We're all adults here. I don't have to spell it out, do I?

It's only been a couple of weeks but it feels like so-o-o-o much longer. Stan and I spend a few delicious hours pretending to be a carefree couple, with me acting as his tour guide. I take him around and show him some of the relics from my stormier student days—stone walls, monuments, even a statue of Jesus with bullet holes in it. I show him the pile of stones that used to be the Incan ruler Huayna Capac's palace, and he gets a compromising shot of me giving head to a camera tripod. We're rounding a corner when I recoil as if I've stepped on a rattlesnake.

There he is, six feet off the ground and ten feet high, an icon with a third eye shining behind his head like a flaming sun.

"What?" Stan asks.

"Nothing."

"Nothing? Who are those guys?" he says, looking at the mural.

"Revolutionary heroes."

"Sure, I recognize Che, but who are the other two guys?"

"Sandino and Carihuahua."

"Who's he?"

"An Ecuadorian revolutionary."

"Well, yeah, but who was he?"

"Just some guy, all right?"

He knows that's not a satisfactory response, but he lets it alone for now. I take him to the hatmaker's cooperative so he can watch old women with leathery hands weave a few strands of pliant straw shipped up from the coast into the finest "Panama hats" that sell for $175 and up in Manhattan. The gray-haired weaver will be lucky if she gets five bucks for it. We admire the eye-dazzling scarves, shawls, and ponchos sold by the proudhearted Otovaleño Indians who are not ashamed to stand there and speak Quichua in front of the *señores*.

I'd like to take Stan up to the volcanic steam baths just outside of town, but I don't dare. That's right, Cuenca is *also* built atop an active volcano. So I drag him to the food market so we can buy the ingredients for an authentic Ecuadorian *almuerzo* and feed the whole crew at my cousin Lucho's place. But so many stalls are empty this late in the day, we have to supplement what little we find with some canned goods from a tiny, overpriced supermarket.

Back in Marianita's kitchen, I suddenly remember—too late— how the tomato paste cans spurt when you open them in the mountains. I'm trying to explain to Stan that the considerable drop in air pressure between the coast, where they're canned, and the *sierra*, is responsible, but the sight of Stan wiping the thick red goop off his face is just too ridiculous for me to bear. Marianita takes over and orchestrates a cornucopian meal with such verve you'd think she just awoke from an evil witch's spell.

Afterwards, while we're all sitting around with full stomachs and happy hearts, Lucho fills my American boyfriend in on some of the local lore. I translate as Lucho tells him about Atahualpa, the last Inca ruler of the northern kingdom, who declared to his nation that someday he would return to lead them, because his father, Inti, the sun god, would breathe life back into his mummified body, as long as it was spared from the Inquisitional flames.

"He converted to Christianity to avoid being burned at the stake," says Lucho.

"So they garroted him instead," I say.

"And you know, a lot of them are still waiting for him to return from the dust."

I s the whole town sleeping?" he asks.

"There's nothing else to do on a Friday night."

"Nothing?"

Stan sweeps me off my feet and throws me onto the bed, a maneuver that was meant for springier beds than this.

"*Ouch.* What time is the next earthquake?" I ask, recovering from the jolt.

"In about twenty minutes," says Stan. "Gee, my underwear's fitting me tight all of a sudden. I don't understand it."

"Oh, really?"

"Yeah. You better help me take them off."

"I'll get my crowbar."

Familiarity breeds daring.

Maybe it's the altitude. The equatorial lines of force pulling at me. Or perhaps it's the smell of danger. I reveal some tricks in bed that you could sell tickets to. If that's your idea of a turn-on.

D arkness. He's moving around. Bumping into things. *Thud!*

"What the—?" *Zing!*

Oh, no.

"My God," he says. "I've been sleeping with a woman who carries a switchblade."

"Technically, it's a stiletto."

He turns on the desk lamp, starts picking up my stuff.

"What is this thing?" A black pouch with long leather straps. "It looks like a *tfilin*."

"What's a *tfilin*?"

"It's something that pious Jews wrap around their arms when they pray."

"Show me."

"Well, this pouch should be holding a parchment with four passages from the Bible written on it. One goes around the head, and the other goes around the arm, like this—" He puts the sling's pouch around his left bicep and wraps the leather straps around his arm seven times, then around his middle finger three times. "Because God commands us to 'bind them as a sign upon thy hand,' and let them be a symbol before your eyes."

"I've got to learn more about Judaism."

"What do *you* put in it?"

"Rocks."

"And I've got to learn more about your special brand of Catholicism."

"Yeah, there's a lot of mixing of Old World Spanish superstitions and native Ecuadorian animism. You ought to see the *tres reyes* parade on the Twelfth Night of Christmas, with Santiago on a leaping stallion holding a lightning bolt in his fist, looking a lot more like Illapa the Incan thunder god than the antiseptic statues of St. James in your local parish church up North."

"Not *my* local parish church. We don't do that whole graven image thing."

"You see, even pure Catholicism really is a mixture."

"There's more to it than that, Filomena," he says, sitting down on the edge of the bed.

"Yes, there is."

Our arms intertwine, his pale-of-settlement white-boy skin glowing like a Torah scroll under the reading lamp next to my cinnamon-and-suntanned hide. I glide smoothly into massaging his neck and shoulders, watching as our tones blend.

"I'm a *mestiza* too, Stan," I say, gently kneading his knots away. "A mixture of the natives and the conquerors. It's like swimming between two currents: one fiery and passionate and committed, the other conservative and sterile and repressive—boy, is it ever repressive. So sometimes I can rein it in and be the dedicated working mother, and other times—"

"The stiletto over there," he says.

I lean close, my lips to his ear.

"Have you ever killed anyone?" he asks.

My hands stop, linger in the soft hairs of his neck, then continue to work their way down.

"I'm not sure," I answer truthfully. "I've caused a lot of damage. And from a distance, it's hard to say who hits what. I never did— uh—the executions. I've broken bones, drawn blood, punctured rib cages. I've kicked uniformed cops out of moving trucks. But . . . Well, just a couple of days ago, a rural sergeant was about to run me down on horseback, and the only way to stop the guy with that knife there would have been to kill him. I whacked him in the head with a rifle butt instead, and he's probably out there looking for me right now."

Stan, who has taken the Hippocratic oath, digests this.

After a while, he says, "Well, as long as I don't try to run you down on horseback or anything, I guess I'm safe from your wrath."

I squeeze his hand, grateful for such understanding.

"Come here, you," I say. "I feel another hot stream coming on."

n ow I know why men have leg hair," he says. "It's an early warning system to let you know when fleas are jumping on you."

He pulls on his pants and shirt and goes out to get the paper, while I go to the bathroom. Then I crawl back into bed for five more minutes. When Stan comes back with the paper, I sit up and glance over the stories. President Pajizo met with the head of the Supreme Court and said, "I want General Arturo Vélez charged and found guilty of defaming my family name." Yes, he actually said *I want him found guilty*. Who needs a judicial branch of government, anyway? Think of what we'd save on electricity alone.

But the big local news is that Senator Ricardo-of-the-Roman-

Nose Faltorra is coming to Cuenca this afternoon, and the elusive *señor* Putamayo is supposed to be covering the rally. Something tells me it would be a good place to look for one or two other recognizable faces as well.

"Come on," says Stan. "That museum with all the pre-Columbian artifacts is only open for a couple of hours."

"If at all."

"What do you mean?"

"They have irregular hours on Saturdays."

"All the more reason. Get up."

"Okay, I'm coming." I get out of bed and walk naked to the bathroom. The cold floor has a predictable effect on my soft flesh, and Stan lets out an appreciative whistle.

I flip on the switch, but the lights aren't working. There's no water, either.

The same day the leading opposition candidate happens to be coming to town.

Nice touch.

That afternoon the sky clouds up with that rapid onrush so characteristic of the high *sierra*, startling in its suddenness. The sun fades behind a dark gray sheet that obscures the sky like a retractable steel dome for the rest of the day.

Two hours before Senator Faltorra is due to arrive in Cuenca the rain starts falling, and somebody in the National Electrical Company obviously decides that there will be bricks flying in the streets if the power isn't reconnected, and the dull yellow streetlights flicker back on just as dusk approaches and Faltorra's motorcade wends its way through the wet, cobblestoned streets clogged with *campesinos* who have ventured across peaks and valleys to hear this man speak. Trucks with crumbling wooden cargo beds follow in Senator Faltorra's wake. Gnarled hands grasp the dripping wet yellow-and-white banners emblazoned with the candidate's name that bedeck the trucks and undulate over their heads like shimmering water lilies floating on a human sea.

Stan and I huddle under an umbrella and scurry along, jumping over the gurgling storm drains to the Plaza Cívica, where the Neoliberal Party has set up a stage and hired a Cañari Indian folklore band to play. The square is filled with Incaic faces that I have seen in my dreams in far-off New York City, standing stonelike and unmoved by the whims of the weather. Sun-to-sun laborers who expect little from government, something is keeping them here in the cold rain and gathering darkness: a sliver of hope.

A man crowds under the umbrella with us. There are dark gullies in his rain-washed face. He has an eagle's nose, haphazard teeth, and a thick felt hat stiffened with horse glue—which, when it gets wet, smells rather like a dead animal.

The rain pours down from the black sky, doubling in strength. More people squeeze under our umbrella. The crowd thins out a little, but the remaining diehards begin chanting with surprising strength and conviction, *"Se ve, se siente, ¡Faltorra presidente!"* See it, feel it, Faltorra will be president. It rhymes in Spanish.

I don't see Putamayo anywhere. Scared of a little rain? The lazy bum. I'm amazed that the metal microphones onstage haven't brought down the bright white fire from heaven yet. The chanting grows bolder, with a contagious energy that thickens around us when Ricardo-of-the-Roman-Nose Faltorra walks out onto the stage flanked by the local party leaders and gubernatorial candidate Juanita Estafa, whose normally big hairdo is so flat and stringy she looks like a wet cat after a two-hour motorcade in this deluge.

Faltorra advances to the microphones and raises both his arms up in a symbolic embrace of the people of Cuenca.

"Words do not exist—!" he proclaims "—to describe the stirring and impressive reception that Cuenca has given us!"

This is followed by an eruption of cheers that goes far beyond the weight of Faltorra's words. They're just glad he's finally here. I translate for Stan as Faltorra speaks.

"I beg the Ecuadorian people to give us the opportunity to repay with our services the immense debt of gratitude that I have for all the corners of the country!"

Another lengthy eruption. When it subsides, Faltorra continues, "In the first month of our administration, we will sign the contract for the construction of a road connecting Cuenca to Naranjal!"

The crowd roars as if he's promising to teach them the secret of transmuting base metals into gold.

"Our government will push through the paving of the road from Cuenca to Loja!"

Yeeaaaah!

"And we will do the same for the two hundred and seventy-five kilometers of road that connect Cuenca with Méndez in the *oriente!*"

Yeeaaaaaaah!

"And we will undertake plans to widen and improve the stretch of the Panamerican Highway that runs between Cuenca and Azogues!"

Yeeeeaaaaaaaaaah!

Stan turns to me and says, "This gives a whole new meaning to the expression, 'middle-of-the-road' candidate."

"I promise that under our administration, Cuenca will receive a budget sufficient to guarantee drinkable water for the next eight years!"

Faltorra then begs to be excused, saying that he can't ask the people of Cuenca to stand in the rain any longer, so he's going to ask their permission to leave. The crowd won't let him.

"That's it?" asks Stan. "Four roads and drinkable water?"

"This is a developing country. Those are the issues."

That and undoing five hundred years of cultural genocide.

Faltorra leaves the stage amid sharp crackles of thunder and shouts for more. Then the Indian women take over the chanting, calling out, *"Juan-i-ta! Juan-i-ta! Juan-i-ta!"*

"She's more popular than he is," says Stan, as a chill runs up my spine.

Juan-i-ta! gives in to the will of the people and steps up to the mike, gushing, "Greetings to the people of Guapondeleg!"—the old Cañari name for Cuenca, and I believe the clamor for her *is* greater than it was for Faltorra. "I thank you for your welcoming hearts, and your kind thoughts. *'Por eso, por eso, por eso te quiero, Cuenca.'*"

That's why I love you, Cuenca. The words of a local folksong, but you'd think she's just torn down the property markers and given back the land that was plundered from them by the way the crowd goes wild.

Hmm. Maybe someone should think about doing that.

*   *   *

We're walking back to his hotel.

"I need a long, hot shower," says Stan, shivering in the frosty air.

"No water, remember?"

"But the hotel people said the water would be back on by four o'clock in the afternoon."

"They didn't say what day."

"Aw, crap."

"Welcome to my world."

I'm beginning the arc of an expansive gesture when *thunk!* A knife splinters the wooden doorframe inches from my fingertips and stays pinned there. A millisecond before my feet get to react my brain registers the sight of an ivory-handled bowie knife with an *S* carved into the hilt. Pretty distinct. Not another one like it in the country.

"Sancho," I say, turning towards him. He comes trotting across the dead-quiet street, laughing and waving at me as he steps through a faint circle of light.

Stan, meanwhile, has gone ghostly white. Now he begins to return to normal, which is more of a pale white.

"You're slower," says Sancho.

"We'll see about that," I answer.

He should talk. He's gained about thirty pounds since I last saw him and his round face has a week-old accumulation of greasy black-and-white stubble.

"Is that any way to greet an old friend?" he says cajolingly. So I introduce him to Stan, and he shakes hands and slaps backs all around.

But I smell fear-sweat.

"What's this about?"

Sancho's smile flattens like a death mask. He rubs the beard stubble on his cheek, but all that does is smear the grease around. "Well," he says, unable to look me in the eye, "it's like this. . . ."

Two figures divide themselves from the darkness and pinion us. A long knife glints at me in the pale light. The other one points a beat-up handgun right at my heart.

I don't know either of them.

After a pause, Stan turns to me and says, "I think this is *your* specialty."

Too late. He shouldn't have spoken English.

But at least he doesn't understand the gunman, who says, "So, this is how we find you, talking to a fucking *gringo*."

"That's been upgraded to a capital offense now, has it?"

"Just what we expected," says the knifeman. "You were never anything more than a cheap *bandolera*."

Sancho winces, but stays out of it.

"Three of our people are dead because of you," says the gunman.

Which side are they on?

"What three people?" I ask.

"Don't act stupid."

Stan has figured out that they're not muggers.

It could be worse.

"She's pretty cool," says the knifeman.

"Cool as a coffin," says the gunman, taking two steps closer and pressing the gun to my cheek.

Not much worse.

It's a cheap semiautomatic. They jam on you 20 percent of the time. Still no odds there.

"*Calle Cuatro y Zapatero*," he says. "What happened?"

Aha. I still don't know who these guys are, but at least I know what they're talking about.

"*What happened?*" he repeats.

"I got a note. I chose to believe it. And they admitted sending it."

"That's stiff, girl, real stiff," says the knifeman.

"You led the cops right to them," says the gunman, chipping each word out of the air with an ice ax.

Choose your words carefully, Fil.

"I'd say it was the other way round. Someone led the cops right to me."

"That's a lie and you know it, you fucking whore—!"

"Yeah, you *bandolera chupacolas*—!"

"The note was authenticated with an object that was taken from me by the police, so I kept a close eye out, and I would have noticed two dozen cops following me with riot gear and a pair of five-thousand watt searchlights."

"Ah, save your spit—"

"Yeah, try that bone on another dog, you *bandolera de mierda*—"

"What's that word they keep calling you?" Stan asks in English.

"Nothing," I tell him.

"And now we hear you're trying to find Juanito," says the gunman.

"That information is in public domain," I tell them.

The gunman actually hears my words, and says, "What do you mean?"

I tell him, "Okay: you people seem to have no trouble finding me—on the coast, in the *sierra*—you've got my movements so well mapped out I bet if I swam to the Galápagos Islands you'd be waiting on the beach for me with a rum coco in your hands. So it seems to me that if I were working for the cops, you'd damn well know about it."

There's actually a moment when they seem to consider this.

"You'd have seen me with somebody," I add.

A fly lands on the doorframe, crawls up it a few inches, then a few inches more, almost a whole foot.

I say, "Someone is talking out of both sides of their mouth."

They think about it. Sancho looks like he's pissed himself. Twice. I'm waiting for my guardian angel to get back from heaven already.

The gun pulls away from my head.

"We'll look into it," says the gunman.

"We know where to find you," says the knifeman.

No apologies.

The gunman warns me, "We're gonna dig deep."

"It was just a misunderstanding," says Sancho. "What do you expect? If any of us had any sense we wouldn't be in this business."

And they're gone.

"Sorry I got you into all this."

Stan says, "Ah, my life was in a rut anyway."

That's why I like him. He makes great blintzes, too.

The power goes out in the hotel.
As if I care.

Our Sunday morning placidity is shattered by the frightful news. Congressman Jorge Hernández was coming down the steps of the church of Nuestra Señora de la Merced in Guayaquil after hearing Saturday evening mass with his nephew and the priest when a man stepped away from a white Toyota Celica, raised two powerful handguns and shot Hernández four times in the head and chest, killing him instantly, then turned and shot the other two men, leaving them to die on the steps in puddles of blood.

The priest was Father Moisés Aguirre.

I go to mass to pray for their souls.

And for my country's soul.

In Ecuador, when you want to say "Once in a blue moon," you say *"Cada muerte de obispo."* Every time a bishop dies.

Bishops don't die that often.

But apparently priests do.

CHAPTER
SIXTEEN

In any country where talent and virtue produce no advancement, money will be the national god.
—Denis Diderot

Sunday passes in stunned silence.
   Monday the shit hits. And it keeps hitting.
Accusations fill the streets.
Glass breaks.
Nightsticks whack bone.
Knuckles bloody.
People are raging against the government's response to the assassinations of Jorge Hernández and *padre* Aguirre after an official announcement that Congressman Hernández was *probably* killed by a Colombian paramilitary hit squad as payback for his clandestine support of the left-wing narco-terrorist insurgency across the border in southeast Colombia, which is at about the level of "the dog ate my homework" in terms of credibility.
   I'm sipping coffee in Marianita's kitchen when Lucho comes back from trying to fill his gas tank and says that prices at the pumps have doubled.
   The dollar shoots to eighteen thousand sucres. Food prices follow.
   Panic ensues.
   Banks shut their doors, and the government commits every *centavo* in the treasury to shoring them up by freezing the money in every sucre account and half the dollar bank accounts in the country for a full year.

The rules of the game go like this: They roll the dice, and everyone else loses a turn. It's the genius of capitalism.

Pancho La Pulga's on the air stirring things up, his late-night radio show carried in Cuenca, calling for people to rip up the streets and build barricades: "Now, a lot of people have been going on about some kind of a conspiracy to kill the priests who wrote that human rights report. But let me ask you, *who* would want to punish the people who wrote a report criticizing *this government*? Hmm, *amigos*?"

President Pajizo urges the people to remain calm, and swears that he will respect the outcome of the next elections, no matter who wins, which is awfully thoughtful of him. And I swear that I will allow the sun to rise tomorrow morning. I may even let it rain.

Today's *El Despacho* carries the first front-page story I've seen with Putamayo's name on it. The central feature is Governor Segundo Canino's alleged revelation that the Neoliberals are partly responsible for *padre* Samuel's murder, although in print it lacks Governor Canino's inimitable somebody-commit-me-before-I-hurt-myself oratorical style: "We have turned up evidence that the janitor was *on Senator Faltorra's payroll*, so that in addition to supporting guerrilla warfare, one of Ecuador's legal political parties may be connected to the murders of *padre* Campos of La Chala and *padre* Aguirre of La Merced!"

Right. But which party? This is getting weird, even for Ecuador. And tonight Canino's coming to Cuenca.

Maybe I'm still recovering from my near-death experience, but Stan's showing up has really made me lose focus. Everything seems to be happening in Guayaquil, while I'm miles away, looking down, helpless. I wish I could find out how Peter's doing at his end of the trail. Other sleuths get to have boyfriends they can send on information-gathering errands, but if I tried to send Stan to the wilds of North Guayas, they'd cut him up like a lab rat and dump his gutted body in a ditch.

And I'm sorry I made that joke about nobody needing guerrilla warfare when congressmen shoot at each other. They weren't laughing at Jorge Hernández's funeral.

I've got to find out what Canino's party thinks it's doing, blaming the center left for a pattern of attacks on the other prominent leftists.

The Centrist Coalition's provincial headquarters are on the second floor of a nineteenth-century colonial-style building with flimsy wooden balconies and balustrades and a few worm-eaten planks that are shaking under the heavy foot traffic of an army of devotees running around scattering leaflets and making such a fuss you'd think it was the floor of the Moscow stock exchange the day after the Bolsheviks shelled the Winter Palace.

Leather-jacketed militants are rushing up and down the stairs carrying red-and-white flags, banners, and bunting for the big rally. A party committee member leans against a doorframe, smiling but curtly dismissing an American freelance journalist's request for an interview with Governor Canino, telling the curly-haired young innocent that the presidential candidate is only coming to Cuenca for the afternoon and that he certainly won't have the time to talk to any lousy foreign journalists, especially since a lousy foreign journalist recently published "nothing but lies" about Segundo Canino in a Spanish newspaper, and that if the guy ever returns to Ecuador, "they will kill him."

Democracy in action.

In another room that's small enough for everyone to hear a low whisper from a wheezy asthmatic, a thick-necked *caninocista* in a suit and tie is sputtering with red-faced passion, punching the air with surprising ferocity, and loudly exhorting all the party supporters sitting there in the mock schoolroom rows of wobbly metal chairs to go to the polling places this Sunday and verify that the Neoliberal Party doesn't commit widespread fraud.

Two hunched men nearly ram me with a rolled-up banner as they rush down the creaky wooden staircase.

A voice cries out in the middle of the mayhem. It's my cousin Jaime Mejia. He's wearing a full complement of red-and-white pro-Canino buttons, with matching cap and armband.

"What's happening with your wonderful life?" he asks me.

We exchange the customary hugs and greetings, and he invites me to have some coffee and *quesadilla* bread.

"You're a militant for the Centrist Coalition?" I ask.

"Just a supporter."

"I don't see much of a difference."

"Don't let them hear you say that."

I shake my head and smile. "I gotta tell you, it's hard for me to remember ever feeling that strongly about a candidate."

"That's because they're all the same in the U.S. Two identical parties with no balls between them. Here we have to fight to be heard."

"What are you worried about? I thought Canino had a lock."

"*Verás*," he says, stroking his salt-and-pepper mustache. "The polls show that Governor Canino is losing ground to Ricardo Faltorra and Hector Gatillo, even in the *sierra*."

"I'm not sure I trust those polls."

"Look, Filomena, you've been out of the country a long time, so let me explain how it works. Supporting that schoolteacher Gatillo is just another way of bringing Canino to power."

"You mean by pulling votes off Faltorra and splitting the left?"

He chuckles. "Boy, you *have* been away a long time. Everybody knows *los militares* would never allow a socialist like Gatillo to take power. So when Canino slipped to second place, a lot of *caninocistas* joined with Gatillo's people, hoping that with their support *he* would win, the military would then force Gatillo out, nullify the election, and replace him with Governor Canino."

What?

And you wonder why magical realism is an indigenous Latin American literary form.

"What if the military only do the first two things, and don't bother about that last part?"

"They don't want to run this place!" Jaime explains. "It's too much of a pain."

"Sure it is, Jaime. But there's a lot of money in it, and it's always been easy to sell people on the idea of a 'strong' leader, especially when you can manufacture a crisis to go with it."

"Nobody needs to manufacture a crisis around here, Fil, we've got enough to go around. But those people are forgetting about all the restrictions we had to put up with under the military, the curfews, the censorship, the arrests, the torture, the assassinations—"

"Yes, Jaimito." I lean closer. "And what about *padre* Campos's murder?"

"*Padre* Campos?"

"Your candidate says he has evidence about who did it."

"Yes, it's a vast conspiracy."

"A pattern."

"Pattern?"

"Campos, Aguirre, Malta, Lorca, Carnero."

"I don't see—"

"Guayaquil. Latacunga. Cuenca. Macas. This town could be next, Jaimito."

Jaime completes the circuit in his head.

"Archbishop Lorca?" he says.

"His name's on the last page of the human rights report."

"My God, you don't think—"

"What the hell does Canino know about the *padre's* murder?"

"I'll try to find out for you."

"Thanks."

When no one's looking, I stuff my bag with bread for the family.

Jaime comes back and says they're still assembling the report, in Quito. It's going to be released on Saturday, the day before election day.

Jesus. They're planning to drop a bomb of some kind.

But what?

Maybe I'll just ask the candidate himself.

The weather is being much kinder to Governor Canino, but that's about all. The streets are filled with Faltorra supporters who intimidate and drown out Canino's smaller turnout as the motorcade rolls through town.

Stan and I walk hand-in-hand to the Plaza Cívica, and right away I know something's wrong. The square is jammed to twice its capacity with more people than have ever shown up for a rally in Cuenca, except for the time the pope came and gave an open-air mass in a field on the western slopes of the city and told us all to stop using birth control. It only takes a moment's observation to find the cause. Half of the people here are snake-eyed hirelings bused up from the coast, unfriendly looking louts who think of the *sierra* as enemy territory. The rest are devout Faltorra supporters who have come to boo Canino. There's a third-act loaded gun for you if there ever was one. I tell Stan to be on his toes.

The crowd swells to fill the square from gutter to gutter. There's a huge gathering at the rear, and a clamoring from the windows facing the plaza, and thunderous shouts of *"Faltorra! Faltorra! Faltorra!"* while the opposing Centrist Coalition pols take the stage. I'm looking up at the—*sacred shit!*

"Filomena? Honey?"

That's him! Putamayo's at the third-floor window of the Hotel 9 de Octubre, overlooking the plaza.

"Just wait here! I'll be right back!" I say.

"No freaking way—"

Stan plunges after me as I practically climb on top of people to get over to the edge of the square, my feet enmeshed in an irregular kaleidoscope of arms and noses and elbows and ears until I barge into the hotel lobby and try to push my way through the bodies blocking the stairs. But three men in black shirts with the combined muscle mass of immortal Atlas loop their arms around me and carry me down the steps to the ground level as effortlessly as if I were a piñata stuffed with tissue paper.

Stan yells out, "It's all right! I'm a doctor!" and yanks me away from there before they can react to what he said.

"What the hell are you doing?" he asks, after drawing me back into the safety of the masses.

"It was him! I know it was!"

"Him *who*?"

And those body types. The matching shirts. The mercenaries are here, and Putamayo's writing crazy conspiracy theories to stir up trouble. That can only mean—

A screech of feedback jolts my ears.

Someone is sowing mayhem—in Guayaquil, in Latacunga, and now Cuenca. And everywhere there's been trouble, Putamayo's been there to report on it. But which came first? The story or the teller?

Up onstage, Governor Canino's vice-presidential candidate, Benito Degollar, raises his arms to the cloudy-dull but rainless sky and says, "Three days ago, the very heavens protested the presence of that son of the devil, Ricardo Faltorra, in this piously observant little city of Cuenca!"

Yeah. You should have seen it when the earth swallowed him up in a shower of fire and brimstone. That was impressive, too.

"Filomena? Hellooo?"

I'm standing on my tippy-toes, trying to get another look at the third-floor windows, but there's no sign of the bastard.

Degollar continues, "But don't worry, when the Neoliberals get wet, we will dry their skins in the sun!"

Cheers and laughter as some professional vigilantes elbow their way past me, snarling about all these sheepish *cuencanos*.

"And that upstart, Hector Gatillo, who says he's the people's answer. Yes, but what is the question?"

I hear a sound like vultures cackling in the dry desert breeze.

Staged disruptions. Forged pamphlets. Expertly placed disinformation. *Padre* Samuel was right: semiliterate thugs don't plan this big.

Degollar finishes with these bombastic warm-ups, then a stern, I-mean-business-faced Segundo Canino slithers onstage and signals to his imported crewmen to move forward in a strange, sudden crush that's *not* a normal movement of people waiting to hear a speech.

I tell Stan I don't like what's going on, let's move back to the sidelines.

"Finally, some sense out of you," he says. "Now will you please tell me what's going on?"

"Later. Just keep an eye out for trouble."

"What kind of trouble?"

"Stan. Will you please shut up and let me concentrate?"

The introductions finished, Governor Canino finally steps up to the mike. Does he say, "Hello, Cuenca"? or "Gee, it's great to be here"? No. He starts right in: "Ten—minutes—ago!" he rages. "Two *cuencanas* were attacked by pro-Faltorra militants! And *this* shows how the Neoliberals are! A violent mob of the devil! Who *know* nothing but violence and *understand* nothing but violence!"

Syllables explode out of Canino's mouth like bullets through plywood. I can't even understand some of it, since it's being distorted by cheap microphones. Then, like a conductor cueing his musicians, he reaches for his belt and undoes it, sputtering, "Well, if they're going to give us violence, I'll give it right back to them, like this—*this* is what I'm going to do to them—!"

And with that, he yanks off his belt and starts whipping it around in circles over his head. Two seconds later, a clash finally erupts between the loud minorities at the back of the plaza. I honestly can't tell who starts it from where I'm standing, but they're throwing big, round rocks high into the air, arcing towards us. I try to recoil, but my back presses against unyielding bodies. I follow the trajectories closely, and when the dark objects hit the stone pavement with a dull thud I realize that they are not rocks, but potatoes. But they sure as hell *look* like rocks, and people are scattering in panic and knocking each other to the ground.

The police start firing tear gas indiscriminately into the great mass of people, although my biggest fear right now is being trampled as the leering face of pandemonium is unveiled and the terrified crowd swarms towards the four corners of the plaza. So I push Stan *closer* to the spreading gas, where the bodies are fewer. Some hired agitators run screaming for their lives, jumping over fallen friends and knocking over an Indian woman's popcorn stand that she was operating with her five-year-old daughter on the assumption that a rally would be a good place to make a few honest sucres.

That'll teach her.

Gas grenades are launched with a muffled *puh!* sound, but now I hear the clear crack of gunfire. I look over the heads of the diminutive *serranos* and see maybe ten bodyguards surrounding Canino and emptying their handguns into the air before whisking him offstage and into a van as if his life were in danger. Where have I seen that move before?

With Canino gone, the crowd starts to filter back to the plaza. So the police launch *more* tear gas grenades, I suppose to "protect" the Centrist Coalition party workers who are hurriedly taking down the stage. And that's just what it is, a stage.

Half of the scattering crowd is shouting, "*Faltorra! Faltorra! Faltorra!*" We're heading for a neutral corner, past two strangers who are trying to convince people, "The leftists did this."

The Ecuavisa television crew is walking rapidly away from the scene, heading for safer ground.

By now the youngest militant Faltorra supporters are back in the square ripping down all of Canino's banners and burning them in a pile. The police move in again, saturating the area so excessively that a couple of canisters land less than ten feet away from me, although I am now two blocks away from the plaza down a side street.

For a moment I lose sight of Stan, until he comes diving through the clouds, stumbling away from the battleground with whitish wisps of gas trailing behind him like streamers. I don't think Stan has ever been teargassed. His eyes are inflamed, puffed up to near blindness. I give him a handkerchief to blow his nose and clear his eyes a bit, and guide him away from the noise.

Like I said, things are always a bit more intense here.

I t's all right, I'm a doctor'?"

"It was the best I could come up with under the pressure of the moment."

I'm applying cold compresses to his eyes. At least the cold water is back on.

"Well, I must say, it worked. They didn't come after us."

"No, they just gassed the whole crowd instead," he says. "How do you say 'tear gas' in Spanish?"

"*Gaz lacrimógeno.*"

"*Lacri*—what?"

"*La-cri-mó-ge-no.*"

"Five syllables just to say 'tear'?"

"That's Latin for you." I'm caressing his sweet and salty skin. "From *lacrima*. Like in the requiem Mass? '*Lacrimosa dies illa, qua resurget ex favilla judicando homo reus huic ergo parce, Deus. Pie Jesu Domine dona eis requiem.*'"

"Well, '*Baruch atoh adonai elohenu melech ha'olam*' to you too, baby," he says. "Man, you mixed-up Catholic women: You give out hand jobs and recite the Latin Mass at the same time."

"I see it as part of the same joyful expression of life."

"I don't know, it sounds pretty kinky to me."

"I suppose *you* never got together with a group of radical feminists and smeared your bodies with each other's menstrual blood as you danced around naked on a beach under the moonlight, but you must have done something equally primal."

"Well, I . . ."

"Come on, I told *you* one."

"Well, I once jerked off onto a microscope slide and then slipped it under the lens in time to see about two thousand of my own sperm swimming around for a while before they all croaked."

Five minutes later, Stan has to pick me up off the floor, I'm laughing so hard.

B y nightfall the power comes back on in time for us to watch the news on the hotel's nine-inch TV. Senator Faltorra is telling the cameras that Governor Canino is unfit to represent Ecuador in the international arena: "Can you see a boor like Segundo Canino sitting down to negotiate with a leader of the caliber of Vicente Fox of Mexico, or Andres Pastrana of Colombia, or President Bush of the United States?"

Cut to Canino, responding: "Yes! *Compatriotas!* I am capable of sitting down at the table with *Meester* Bush, or any other *meester* for that matter! But when we sit down to eat with *Meester* Bush, it won't be at any china-plate White House banquet, it will be with a steaming plate of *guatita*, because we are *nacionalistas, señor!*"

What is it with Canino and *guatita*?

Since the power's on and the streets are calm, I suggest that we go to the Teatro Sucre, which is playing *The Color Purple* (movies take a while to reach Cuenca). Stan has never been to a movie here, hee hee. I make him jump into the fray and buy the tickets.

It turns out to be a porno film using the same title.

We only stay for twenty minutes.

I t's not all random.

There was always something about those pamphlets. The slogans were so standard and repetitive as to be almost meaningless. Some tactics were staged.

There *is* a pattern.

So far, mayhem has followed me everywhere I go. And who's been to all those places besides me? Putamayo. I'm beginning to pick up that he's a complete fake. The man who never was. He's probably some rail-thin ASN agent with a glued-on beard, flat-lensed glasses and a pillow strapped to his waist. He's a distraction to dangle in front of me and make me look the other way. The wrong way.

Well, maybe it's time I started actively seeking mayhem, looking for signs, patterns, similarities, body types.

I watch the sun come up over the low clouds, and wait for the day to begin shortly. These mountain folk get up at daybreak.

But soon the pleasure of hot cocoa is curdled by the bitter pain of reading Putamayo's inevitable article dishing out the following lies about Canino's rally: "Two hundred drunken, paid-for Neoliberal Party supporters armed with machine guns attacked the peaceful crowd, and the police had to intervene to protect the people of Cuenca."

Batting second, Canino's VP candidate Benito Degollar says, "The Neoliberals' counterdemonstration was prepared well in advance with the sole purpose of disrupting the democratic process. When Segundo challenged them, he was attacked. They also assaulted my wife, and when I went to help her I saw my daughter being assaulted as well." I'd like to ask him how that was possible, since he and his wife were busy piling into a van while the "counterdemonstrators" were being dispersed by riot police on the other side of the plaza.

I'd also like to know how potatoes transmuted into machine guns.

But that's magical realism for you.

Are you kosher?" asks Jaime in accented English as Stan takes a bite of *quesadilla* bread.

"When they declare shrimp and lobster kosher, I'll think about going kosher," Stan says.

"Now, what do you know about this guy?" I poke Putamayo's byline with my finger.

"He must be halfway to Macas by now. They say he's got a hot lead connecting the *padre*'s murder to the Black Condor Brigade." Jaime reaches into his bag and flicks a sheaf of newsprint at me. A special late edition of *El Despacho* glides onto the table. There's an old photo of Johnny on the front page.

I think the blood drains from my face, because Stan says, "Filomena? Are you okay? Your hands are cold."

I can't hide it from him. You'd think I'd get used to it already, but there's no way to control it and the next thing I know he's hugging me close and whispering, "Filomena, what's wrong?"

"I'm angry and frustrated," I say.

"No, you turn red when you're angry and your pulse quickens. This is—"

"Why did I ever start dating a doctor?"

"So you could learn some good Yiddish curses in case you're ever assaulted by a Hasid."

I laugh nervously, trying to shrug it off. "Yeah, and someday I'm going to have to introduce the word *schmuck* to Ecuador."

He cradles me in his loving arms. Ah, just one more day with Stan. Then I've got to get back on track.

We walk up the central arteries of the city, passing by the cathedral on our way to the warehouses and repair shops of Lucho and Marianita's neighborhood. Students are already gathering in the center for this afternoon's protests.

When we get there, Lucho's got the TV on. With the sucre at 23,000 to the dollar and rising, President Pajizo is trying to entertain us with the following joke: "The Ecuadorian has to learn how to spend money, or else the only thing he'll do with it is indulge his vices. So for social morality, for the future of the race, we have to keep wages low."

Clunk. Oy vey, that one bombed in New Haven, too.

"*Puchica*," says Marianita. The mildest curse in the book. "I need a cup of flour."

I tell her not to worry, I'll go get her a five-pound bag.

"Be careful."

"Yeah, *preso por mil, preso por mil quinientos*," says Lucho, quoting an Ecuadorian maxim reflecting our cynical belief that if there's room in the jail for one thousand people, there's room for fifteen hundred.

Stan wants to go with me, but I tell him to stay here. He's seen enough of my country disgracing itself.

But he takes me aside, and says, "Filomena. My grandparents had to worry about death striking them at any moment—from infectious diseases, tsarist policemen, hunger, pogroms—and all I have to worry about is remembering to take out the garbage on Mondays and Thursdays. So I honestly don't know if I'm ready to deal with all this. But I want you to know that if it comes down to it, I would seriously consider walking through fire for you."

"Jesus, Stan. I'm just going out to get some flour."

But he won't let go of my hand until I give him a seriously tight hug.

"Besides, honey, I've already walked through fire. Remember?"

"Yes," he says.

I tell him I'll try to be back before the rioting starts.

It's not that easy.

First, there's no flour. So I have to hunt for a place that's willing to haggle for a pound of flour in a plain brown wrapper. Then I remember my plan to actively seek out mayhem. The protests in the central square should do nicely. And sure enough, when I get there, the students have already started ripping up cobblestones and dousing tires with gasoline at all the principal intersections. Every one of the participants seems to have come prepared with motorcycle helmets, and bandanas around their necks, ready to transform them into breathing masks at a moment's notice.

I withdraw to a safe vantage point down a side street. Bankers are hurriedly trying to close up shop for the day before the teargas starts to fly.

The police don't waste any time as the quaint, wedding-cakewhite colonial facades of Cuenca are blackened by the thick, skanky carcinogenic smoke of burning rubber. And the old plaster walls shake as the police drive two lumbering antiriot tanks through the streets, a brand-new gleaming one and a battle-scarred hulk that inspires far more dread with its toothless grimace than the faster, sleeker model.

There's no one else left on the side street, except for an old lady and a pregnant woman who are obviously not part of the protest, just too slow to get out of the way. You'll never guess what happens next. The goddamn police tank stops at the corner, swivels its dented turret around and fires a tear-gas canister right at the two helpless women.

Tear gas explodes around them, and the pregnant woman is enveloped by the suffocating fumes. I rush over to support her and pound on the door of the nearest house. An Indian servant woman opens the door and lets us in.

"Five months in the womb, and the police have already gassed her," says the pregnant woman, holding her abdomen.

Our spontaneous hosts serve us tea with lemon, crackers and cheese. Good old Ecuador, dispensing South American hospitality in the middle of an antigovernment riot. After a while, I check on what's happening out in the street, hoping to recognize signs, patterns and body types. The central square has settled into a stalemate. The students are congregated at the southwest corner of the park under the protective pillars of the cathedral, while the police are gathered at the northeast corner, firing off gas grenades and placing bets on who can knock the head off a statue of a long-haired Apostle from this distance.

I'd tell you what time this is all happening, but the big street-clock was smashed several hours ago.

Then I see a distinct shape scurrying across the square, crouching low: It's Peter Connery, taking action shots of the student protesters with a 35mm camera. How on earth did he end up here? Last time I saw him, he was headed up the Río Daule to keep a date with the North Guayas Militia.

But as I'm watching, a protester grabs him and throws him against a stone pillar. A big, scruffy student smacks Peter in the head and tries to take away his camera. Four more of them gang up on him, punching and kicking.

I wouldn't necessarily do it for a simple beating, but Peter is still fragile from the hit-and-run, and they just might kill him.

"Jesus—!'

"Don't—!"

"*Señora—!*"

But I'm already halfway across the square, closing the distance, flying furiously into the gang of cowards, telling them to save their anger for the police.

"Fucking CIA—!"

"CIA agent—!"

"He's not—!"

"Fucking taking pictures of us—!"

"I know him!"

"Who the hell are you!?"

"Leave him alone!"

"Fuck you—!"

"Shit—!"

"The tanks are coming back—!"

"Exploiters of the people—!"

They smash his camera against the brick wall, and retreat.

"You let them get the camera!" wails Peter.

"You're welcome."

"You were supposed to contact me." His scars are healing, but he's still red and raw in the spots where the skin was nearly torn off his face.

"I got sidetracked."

"Putamayo's gonna blow the whole thing any day now and you got sidetracked? He's still in Cuenca, right?"

"I've heard he's heading for Macas."

"Then what the fuck are you doing here—?"

"Look, this isn't a very good time. Can we talk later?"

Peter checks his watch. "Sure. Meet me at the Teatro Sucre," he says. "We can talk in the dark. They're showing *The Color Purple* at eight o'clock."

"I've seen it already—"

But he dashes away through the arches before I can say anything else, slapping the flagstones with flying feet. I quickly get myself under the protective pillars of the cathedral. A few of the more daring students run out into the street, throw rocks at the nice new police tank, and run back. The next thing I know there is the unmistakable *pop!* of a bottle breaking and the front of the tank ignites in bright orange flames. Someone has scored a direct hit with a Molotov. The flames are superficial and soon wither, but it's enough to get the gunnery crew to throw the tank into gear and start bearing down on us.

Fleet-footed streams of students nearly knock me down trying to run away. I stay flat against a pillar and wait for the tank to pass so I can run the other way and head for home already. Then two students on either side of me and near enough to singe my hair light up twin Molotov cocktails, and I revise my plans, jumping out into the street and crossing directly in front of the moving tank to the edge of the park, thinking if only I had Peter's camera it'd be a Pulitzer Prize–winning shot for sure if one of these guys goes up in flames.

I stay low enough to chew on the grass, wrap my scarf around my nose and mouth and get ready to pounce.

But the tank stops right in front of us, cops are swarming through the park and the guys lose their nerve. Damn! I could have used the diversion. Thick white clouds of gas are wafting into the cathedral, everyone's eyes are tearing, and the two guys stand there holding lit Molotovs while a third *companero* is advising them, "Put them out, put them out," which they manage to do, blowing my Pulitzer but saving their own lives, which is something.

But I get grabbed.

Three cops. I kick and claw and pull myself loose, but two more get in my way and it takes five riot police to drag me towards the tank.

I am *not* going in there.

They all have tear-gas grenades dangling from their cartridge belts. American-made. I recognize the model. I know how to work them.

I prepare myself with deep breaths, but the traces of gas make me cough. Let them think they've got me. Three of them shove me in, others follow. Deep breath. And—

I grab the handle and activate the nearest grenade with my eyes closed tight.

The whole tank fills with tear gas, and they're all fighting to get out. Loose hands, clawing, scraping, then a knee to the face makes me lose my air. Some left, still. Fight. Drag.

I stumble out and make it about three feet before the hard human walls close in, cutting off my air.

Air . . .

CHAPTER
SEVENTEEN

*For all policemen were bright enough to know who
they were working for, and they were not working,
anywhere in the world, for the powerless.*

—James Baldwin

Who are you visiting?"

"My family."

"Who else?"

"Who else? Old friends."

"What are their names?"

"Whose names? My old friends?"

"Yes."

"Well, I haven't had a chance yet, but I was going to look up
Sarita Kuperman, Teresita Leon, Amelia Peñaherrera, *profesora* Luisa
Ramera—"

"*Profesora* Ramera is dead."

"Oh, I'm sorry to hea—"

"She was murdered. Three years ago. Someone broke into her
home and put a gun in her mouth and blew off the back of her
head."

Pause.

"Oh."

"That doesn't mean anything to you?"

"Well, of course, it's horrible—!"

"Doesn't mean *anything* to you? Eh, La Sacerdotisa?"

I don't bat an eyelid.

It's not a bluff.

Sergeant Tenesaca has the round, sunny face of a true *ecuatoriano de la sierra*. He's the real thing—a *mestizo* Indian who has risen up by talent and skill alone, because this guy was born in a mud-and-cardboard shack in Zhud, and sure as hell didn't get here on family connections.

"All right, you know who I am," I confess.

He's been waiting for that. It satisfies him deeply to hear me say it.

"Some ice for your face?" he asks, smiling.

"Yeah. Thanks."

He hands me some ice and a plain square of cloth to wrap it in. I hold the soothing bundle to my forehead with my left hand.

"Sorry. I don't know what gets into them sometimes," he says.

"I gave them plenty of reason."

"Uh, yes."

I look outside his window. It's after visiting hours, so they've let the chickens loose in the courtyard.

"Okay," I say. "You know who I am. Then you should also know I've been a civilian for fifteen years, including five years as a New York City cop."

"Yes, I know. But what are we supposed to say when we find you with *this*?" He holds up a paper bag full of white powder.

"That's flour."

He hesitates.

"You could bake a cake with it. Believe me, it's flour."

He looks in the bag.

President Pajizo stares blankly at me from his spot on the wall behind the sergeant's left shoulder; the great seal of Ecuador peers out over his right, its iconography wishfully linking the coast and the mountains under the condor's spreading wings.

I take a leap and switch into Quichua. *"Ch'akiwashan. Imataq ukyaypak kan?"* I'm thirsty. What is there to drink?

"You say this is flour. *Allimi?*" Really?

"Ari." Yes.

He seems to believe me, and sends for a cup of water.

"Getting back to to *profesora* Ramera," he says, returning to Spanish. "That case is still unsolved."

A minute nails itself into my brain. Tick. Tick. Tick. My water arrives in a plastic cup. I take a sip, and savor it.

Eventually he breaks the silence. "Look, we both know what Juanito did to Professor Dos Caras. Then somebody goes and does the same thing to *profesora* Ramera?" Then he dutifully asks, "Do you know if Juanito's alive?"

"The resemblance between the two murders doesn't mean a thing. He probably trained a couple of comrades to carry on the tradition for him after his death. That would have been like him."

Sergeant Tenesaca nods.

"But it *was* his special way," he says. "And you really don't know where he is? You've had *no* contact with him?"

"No."

"Sad, isn't it?"

That's not what I expected him to say.

"What's so sad about it?"

"Tell me, where'd you learn to take a beating like that?"

I shrug.

"It was your father, wasn't it?" he asks.

The leather-babe act rips open for a second, leaving me vulnerable, then slowly stitches back together, sealing and protecting me.

"You ran away from home at fourteen, is that right?" he says, glancing at the file at his elbow.

"Yes."

"You see, I also know what it is to be a hungry child who has to fight for every ear of corn."

I nod. "Why are you telling me this?"

"Because you're not the only one who hid from the police in the one place they'd never think of looking. Some of them lasted quite a bit longer than you did. Some of them even made sergeant."

"I see." It takes me about a week to say that.

"Yes, you see. So you really don't know if Juanito's still active?"

"No, I swear."

"But you want to find out, don't you?"

"Yes." I admit it, opening my chest and pouring it out like my final sin before the Supreme Judge.

"Hmm," he grumbles, stroking his chin. "Well, please let us know if you do."

And he gives me back my documents, including the real and the fake *cédulas*. I was still carrying both of them because I didn't figure on getting arrested.

"That was reckless of you," he says, dipping his head towards the two ID cards.

"Well, I'm reckless sometimes."

"The passport with the missing page was exceptionally interesting. I'd order up a couple of *canelasos*, but we're working right now."

"Nice of you to offer. Some other time then?"

"Certainly. But you must stay in Cuenca. You can't travel with those documents."

"Oh."

"You were planning to travel?"

"Well, yes."

"Where to?"

My gaze travels from the documents spread on the desk between us up his folded arms, past the police department insignias to his face, locks onto his eyes, probes.

"To Morona Santiago."

"And how were you planning to get there?"

"Why do you ask?"

"Well, for one, the roads aren't always safe. There's been a rash of wildcat strikes aimed at the government's complicity in creating the shortages and hyperinflated prices that have kept basic food products from reaching the stores," he says.

"I haven't heard about them."

"Yeah, there are a lot of things you haven't heard about. Like the opposition's plan to renationalize oil production that's gaining momentum in Congress, which is going to piss some powerful people off, or the book Canino's Centrist Coalition is planning to publish next month. It's going to be promoted as 'the exposé they killed a man to suppress.' "

"What's the title?" I ask, a sickly feeling of foreboding creeping up and churning my insides.

"*The Bloody Trail*. By that Argentine muckraker—whatsis-name—"

"You know his name."

"All right. So I do."

"Then you know that's got to be a bunch of crap. All he left behind were some scattered notes." And I mean scattered. "Nothing like a completed manuscript."

"The amazing thing is that Ecuador is a small enough country so that *one person* can have an effect," he says, looking right at me.

I let the look linger awhile.

"You want me to find him for you, don't you?"

He looks at the pile of documents he's just given me.

"Nice play," I say. "But don't you think they know I'm in here? And that if I walk out of here with you on my tail they'll ambush the freaking lot of us and tear us to shreds?"

"Not if we bring enough men."

"In which case we wouldn't get within twenty miles of him, if he's even out there." And my name would be shit forever and ever. "Besides, I *want* to be followed. Just not by you guys."

"Hmm. So what do we do?"

Tick. Tick. Tick.

"I guess I'll need an unmarked car with an interprovincial pass."

I'm not sneaking into the jungle at night. Even my old buddies would kill me first and determine my identity later. I revise my list: "A driver's license, a registration, and a vehicle that can disappear from your impoundment lot without anybody noticing."

"You want ice cream with that, too?" he asks.

"Come on. You've got a rattletrap no one will miss."

He looks at his watch, then back to me.

"Do you know where he is?"

"For the last time, no. But I've got to find out one way or the other and be done with it."

The proposition definitely interests him.

"I'll have the corporal type up the agreement."

"*No.*" That stops him. "No documentation whatsoever. I walk out of here on foot, and twelve hours from now the corporal leaves a jeep with the papers and the keys near the ravine between the

Avenida de la Independencia and the Milchichig Bridge. And don't follow me."

He's a realist, but it still takes him a long time to make up his mind.

"You'll let us know what you find."

"Of course."

He's on his feet, hand extended. *"Ha sido un gran placer, señorita Buscarsela."*

"Nice meeting you, too, Sergeant Tenesaca."

He bows his head slightly, we shake hands, and he lets me go free.

I've got to send Stan away. He's slowing me down, making me more vulnerable.

"But you're part of my life now," he says.

"Not *this* life, Stan. I have to take care of this on my own."

"Why? So you can be with *him*?"

No. So he doesn't kill you.

"It's not like that," I say.

"But—?"

God, does he know me.

"But . . . It's not like that."

"No, it never is. I can't compete with a memory. That's a sucker's game."

"It's *not* just memories, Stan," I say, with a bit of an edge. "Some of my bruises are quite fresh."

"I didn't mean that. Jesus, I just never know what I'm getting into with you. I mean, my old girlfriends were all Jewish and Italian-American princesses whose idea of an adventure is spending a month searching every mall in Queens and Nassau County looking for the perfect dress to wear to their best friend's baby shower. They sure as hell don't spend their time getting fingered by armed rebels."

"You want out?"

"Is that what you want?"

"No. Definitely not. Stan, I want to be with *you*. Honey, you know you mean so much to me. . . . And I hope that you'll be there to take me back."

"When will that be?"

"I don't know. The election's only four days off."

"You don't sound terribly sure of yourself."

"I'm sure about you, Stan. Oh, come here, you big hunk of sugarcane." I take his pouting face in my hands and bring it close to mine, rubbing the tips of our noses for a moment before I tilt my head and kiss him, warmly, deeply, passionately. His arms engulf me, hands suddenly at my shoulder blades pressing me to him closely, each finger transferring energy right through my clothes to my skin, to my oh-so-sensitive skin. It's a hug that feels like sex. But then it's time to draw back and say, "I'll call you when it's over."

I hope.

I have to say it: "If I'm not back in two weeks, then I'm not coming back."

"There's never enough time to be with you," he says, not letting go. "It feels so damn frustrating. But it also feels great. All prickly, like the alternating current in a live wire."

Ooh.

Wouldn't you know, I'm getting my period? But the passion is too intense for either of us to care. And the hotel's sheets are left so bloody it looks like there's been a murder in the bed.

Certain moves hurt me. Like raising my right arm to wave good-bye to my dear, sweet lover man. And when he's gone, I turn around and head back into the wailing confusion.

A state of emergency was finally declared in Guayaquil now that one-quarter of the population has dengue.

Three Colombian hit men were actually arrested for the murders of Congressman Jorge Hernández and *padre* Aguirre. There's no question that they were hired professionals. The only question is who hired them, and they're not talking about it.

Someone fired on a pro-Faltorra rally and killed two people. The police have no suspects.

A marauding gang of *Trabajo, Familia, Patria* devotees attacked a carful of pro-Canino *quiteños* and threw them off a bridge.

Canino's campaign manager slugged a reporter from *El Mundo*. Otherwise reasonable people are saying they're going to vote for "that schoolteacher" Hector Gatillo because with the *sierra* firmly in Senator Faltorra's hands, "There'll be no one to stop him!" Stop him from what? Repaving the Panamerican Highway?

The twenty-four-hour moratorium on campaign propaganda begins at 12:01 A.M. Saturday morning, but anything goes before midnight Friday, and each camp is preparing last-minute blitzes, free-for-all attacks that the opposition won't have time to refute before the votes are counted. Even Pancho La Pulga says he's got some juicy stuff he's saving for Friday evening, just before midnight.

Five international experts arrive to observe this Sunday's elections and monitor whether or not there are any incidents of fraud. You want to tell me how five people are supposed to keep an eye on a *country*?

"If Canino gets elected, all hell will break loose," says Lucho.

"All hell's breaking loose anyway," I tell him.

There is a minor tremor of the earth in Quito. The Pichincha volcano starts sending plumes of volcanic ash two miles high and the whole city gets put on yellow alert.

"You're eating like there's no tomorrow," says Marianita.

Maybe there isn't.

"Let's call Antonia."

I stand knee-deep in blood.

And the blood's quickly rising to overwhelm me.

I'm sinking in a lake of blood along with thousands of native Ecuadorians, dark-visaged Shiris and Cañaris with eyes that saw the mountains being born.

It's a cutthroat competition.

We are swimming in a lake of blood, but it is not silent here. The cries and screams can be deafening.

I reach out.

Alone in bed.

My hand closes on empty sheets.

                    *   *   *

This mountain road is not for the faint of heart. A smooth wall of rock descends straight out of the clouds, stops for an instant on a ledge wide enough for a bus and a mule to pass each other if the mule sucks in its belly, then drops straight down into the green-and-black mist half a mile below.

And this twisty dirt road figures as a major artery on the Military Geographic Institute's definitive physical map of the entire country, a step above "summer roads" (impassible during the rainy season) and "bridle paths" (your mode of transport better be wearing horseshoes).

I have passed through the valley of the billboards, whose red-and-white letters boldly proclaim how each sand hill is part of this soon-to-be-a-major-textile-mill or that promised hydroelectric plant to be built by the president, who has clearly marked his territory with the words PAJIZO DELIVERS, and I have seen the hand-painted signs for Temik, a pesticide for potatoes that was banned in the U.S. (it causes cancer), but which the bighearted American corporations still ship here by the boatload.

I'm steering the battered red jeep through wind and dust, hoping to clear a twelve-thousand-foot ridge before descending into the sweltering jungle, and I have to stop to refill the radiator from a cool mountain stream every twenty minutes to keep the thing from overheating.

Then the cold *páramo*, and inching the deathmobile along the uppermost reaches of the ridge, where the slope is steepest, and the fog thickest. Visibility shrinks to twenty yards.

Ten yards.

Two.

I haven't shifted out of first gear in forty minutes.

Finally, a dark shape enveloped in mist. A grotto cut out of the rock with a shrine to the Blessed Virgin, and consecrated in her name.

Hallelujah.

The peak of the crescent.

Because it's a miracle I made it this far.

The front of the jeep takes a dip and points its dusty red nose down the eastern slope of the Andes Mountains, into the green tapestry that rolls along the vales to the misty edges of time.

Now comes the easy part for the poor overworked engine, winding seventy kilometers downhill, easing into the hairpin turns and tightrope-walking a one-ton vehicle across a series of "bridges" that are nothing more than a few old trees and some two-by-eights that were roped together about thirty years ago.

I reach the cloud forest, rainy and muddy, with condensation dripping down the sheer stone walls, fertility clinging to everything.

Then the fog clears, and the whole stunning panorama is laid bare. High thin waterfalls are unveiled, cascading down bright green mountains above the beaten road, and dropping off into deep gorges cut by young rivers, all sloping east towards the hot misty air and deceptive verdancy that grows thicker and thicker around you, every mile taking you deeper. Into the heat.

I save on gasoline and pump the brake the whole way down.

Down, down, down.

Heat sits on me like a layer of flies that I'm afraid to disturb because it will only attract a fresh swarm of vermin.

I keep checking the rearview mirror. I don't see anyone following me. But no one could follow you on a road like this without you knowing about it, so that's what I expect to see. And of course the cops gave me a fire-engine red jeep that can probably be seen from the space shuttle.

The jeep produces a symphony of metallic sounds as we bounce along the muddy road. The wipers barely work and the blinkers are dead. The dashboard clock is broken, too, because every clock in this caper is broken. It's like time is standing still. Ruben's watch, my watch and—and—and some other watch . . . Peter's watch. What was that about? Why is that sticking out now? And how the hell did he find me so fast after he got out of the hospital? Oh, yeah. He asked my family. Right. I forgot about that.

Rooftops rise up from the shimmering forest floor. The interprovincial checkpoint.

My back is sticking to the hot vinyl seat.

They've got some eighteen-year-old guarding the border. I'm sure we all feel much safer knowing that he's there.

I sit still and sweat.

The papers check out. Two conscripts raise the barrier, and I'm free to pass into the vast Amazonian basin.

Do not feed the animals.

No littering.

You must be *THIS* crazy to enter.

I take the left hand of the only major fork in the entire hundred-and-seventy kilometer trip and head northeast. The sun is starting to dip precariously low in the sky, casting huge shadows in the valleys, where the cloak of rising mist conjures up a seductive and sinister power that clamps onto the pit of my fears like an iron fist.

I make for Limón, about twenty miles down the road.

Ten feet from the road's edge you're in dense jungle. Ten feet farther, and it's easy to get disoriented. You can get lost just a few steps from the path, and never find your way back.

And in the jungle, after sunset, you become part of the food chain.

from the activity downstairs, I'd say the place makes most of its money from twenty-four-hour-a-day trading of the world's oldest commodity. But they also take paying guests who don't want to be bothered with the attention lavished on guests in other parts of the world.

I'll say one thing for Limón: a humidity-saturated, broom-swept room with a single rusty bed costs two dollars a night. I strip down to the essentials because the temperature has plummeted to ninety-one degrees. And I'm so saddle sore from that hard-assed jeep it feels like I'm slipping into a king-sized bed at the Ritz-Carlton.

I'm sharing highballs with the ghost of Scotty Fitzgerald when a burning sensation in my leg pierces the bright bubble of this scene, whining for my attention. I throw off the graying sheet and examine the nubby red patches of a major spider bite numbing an area four inches wide and swelling on my upper right thigh. I must have been scratching in my sleep for several minutes.

Still, I'm pretty big compared to a spider. You can imagine what this much venom does to a fly.

The insects down here are otherworldly creatures, moths with wingspans the length of your hand, five-inch spiders, thick red roaches and those giant tarantulas that Hollywood imports for horror movies. And the fleas. Indestructible.

You know, some of us are still pissed off at the fleas for that whole plague thing.

I am not sleeping well. Every *thump* in the night leaves me staring wide-eyed at the ceiling for half an hour, listening for the faintest evidence of an intruder in my zone. And there are a lot of *thumps* in the night in this hotel.

Finally . . .

White light.

I wake up with bright flashlights stinging my eyes, and three rifles plunging out of the darkness, taking aim at my face and body. The floor creaks as someone comes up behind them. They move aside just enough to let him through.

It's Johnny.

Scrawny. Haggard. Johnny.

"So. It *is* you," he says.

You bastard.

The first thing I say to him is, "You left me hanging in a room with a dead body and seven cops and *this* is how you greet me?"

"You got out of it."

He doesn't see any reason to trust me.

Shuar faces surround me above the glowing lamps. Their cousins a few miles downriver still hunt heads.

The situation is volatile.

"What are you doing here?" he asks.

Damn good question.

"I'm trying to solve *padre* Samuel's murder."

Nobody's taking their guns off me.

Maybe I would feel tougher if I were wearing something besides a T-shirt and panties.

"I just heard you were looking for me," he says. "And I want to know why."

Me, too, Juanito. Me, too.

"There are ways of getting a message out," I say. "You could have let me know you were alive."

"I figured you'd come looking for me someday, and that you were sure to stir things up when you did. Took you long enough."

Took *me* long enough—!

"There are phones, Johnny. Mailboxes. I hear you've even got e-mail. Where the fuck were you for the rest of my life?"

"Where are you now? Why did you send your boyfriend away and abandon your daughter? When was the last time you spoke to her?"

"Last night. What do you know about her?"

"Everyone knows about her. . . ."

And tears are welling up in my eyes, damn it. I can't help it.

"Don't worry," he says. "She's safe."

Trembling lips. I tighten down on them. I try to control my emotions, and replace them with—with—

With ice.

He tells the men to watch the door and window, then sits down on the bed. A twenty-year-old ghost.

"You better be careful," I say. "Someone's probably following me."

"Someone *was* following you. We took care of him."

"Oh. More killing, Juanito? Or are you using another code name, since no one seems to know you're alive."

"Sometimes it's better to be a dead man," he says. "We are trying to make a revolution, *Filomena*."

"Like the time you executed María Gallegos?"

"She was involved in counterrevolutionary activities—"

"A soup kitchen. So you showed up at the big food fest and cut her apart with machine guns, from twelve feet away as I recall. But *you ate her food first*. That didn't get you any support from the peasants."

"We may have been mistaken there. We debated it for days."

"Look, Johnny, I went along on a thousand wild midnight rides with you, but I see a different Ecuador today, with radicals like Espolazo and Hernández working within the system fighting for a new country."

"And look what they did to Hernández." He's right, of course. "So what should we be doing?"

"I don't know. All I know is that for the first time in my life, I see people starving here."

"Good! Let the corrupt politicians bleed the country to death! *Then* people will rise up and join us!"

"Oh, Juanito, Mao isn't scripture. We're not always right, Johnny. None of us. Nobody."

"Not even Jesus then?"

"Whoever wrote down what he said could have screwed up. Even with a tape recorder people still get things wrong, you know. Reporters are always misquoting me."

He nods his head and smiles: "Same old Juanita."

"No, I'm not the same old Juanita."

"That's just like you to say that."

Must. Suppress. Rage.

"Go on," I say.

"What's different about you?"

"Maybe I look the same to you." Deep breath. Exhale. "I used to face my fear of death by ridiculing it, because I was young and crazy and full of the hot blood of life. Now I face my fear of death by accepting it, because I know that God's love does not end with our death, it begins there."

"Well, why the hell does He wait so damn long? Why doesn't He improve things *right* here and *right* now?"

"That's for us to work on."

Pause.

"Convenient answer."

"Well, what are you doing about it?" I ask.

"We just helped a group of homeless farmers occupy and cultivate a piece of arable land for themselves. We defend the squatters and support their families. We distribute medicine in the jungle, to places nobody goes."

"Stolen medicine?"

"Is it stealing to steal from thieves?"

"Sometimes it's hard to tell around here."

"What do you mean?"

"Skip it."

"What do you mean?"

"Stealing from a corrupt system doesn't change the system. Check your Lenin."

"It's a way to survive."

"Just like what María Gallegos was trying to do."

"*We* prevented the expansion of Texaco in the *oriente*—"

"Yeah, by spilling half a million barrels of oil into the river and poisoning the fish the Shuars depend on for their survival."

"Who is a bigger threat to their survival? Texaco or me?"

"Texaco, of course. But it doesn't *stop* them. It just slows them down."

Johnny snaps his head around. Everyone goes rigid. After a moment, light glistens off the wooden blinds as a truck rumbles down the street two floors below. He sensed something coming before anyone else did, even though they were watching for it. I resist the urge to say, "Same old Johnny" out loud. That third eye in the back of his head saved our necks many times. He turns back to me.

I soften my voice. "A hundred families still run the country, Johnny, and the rest of us still have nothing. Or as close to nothing as you can get without dropping off the edge. And I've been skating awfully close to that edge."

"So have we all," he says, looking around the room. "And people can complain as loud as they want, but skulls don't have ears."

Or eyes. Or tongues.

"Let me ask you something. Did you kill *profesora* Ramera?"

"That *huaricha*?" he snaps. "I should have."

"Did you order it?"

He's evasive. "Look, Filomena, I don't remember every one of our actions."

"Bullshit. You remember every brick, every blade of grass, every hair on your victim's head—"

His eyes sparkle in the dark hollows of the night.

"Tell me what you're feeling," I say.

He dismisses his men outside the door.

He's still attractive in a way. He was such a big part of my young life. But that was so long ago, it's hard to believe it was really me. I won't let him touch me.

My eyes flit to the pistol in his belt. His gaze follows mine, and he understands. He sits back down.

"What do you want?" he says.

"I want to solve a murder. And possibly prevent others. I'm afraid there's going to be a lot of suffering."

He thinks for a moment, slaps his knee, and nods. "We'll see," he says, getting up and raising his left hand in an open-palmed salute. He's missing the top third of his two middle fingers, and I wonder if he realizes that his hand naturally forms the phrase in dactylogical sign language, "I love you."

CHAPTER
EIGHTEEN

Mi pluma lo mató.

My pen killed him.

—Juan Montalvo

Sleep?
    What's *that?*
    I stay up until the mist rises with the first light of dawn.
    It's too early to get coffee, so I have to suffer through the hope that a cup of warm Coca-Cola will take some of the glaze off my eyes. Then I have to sandblast the sugary grit off my teeth.
    That's when the bus pulls in. I guess the wildcat transit strike's over. Like a scene from the old frontier days, a tall stranger gets off the bus, and the barefoot children waste no time in gathering around and gaping while the women look him up, down and sideways, and the men mutter and spit.
    My, my. Peter sure stands out in a crowd of dark-haired Amazons, especially with those big jungle boots on.
    Yes, they sure are big.
    The guy should learn some discretion if he's going to do any serious investigative reporting out here. Of course, with that long blond hair and pale face squinting into the rising sun, he could dump a bucket of tar over his head and he'd still stand out like a *gringo* from a hundred yards away.
    Unless he wants it that way.
    His scars look better.
    Much better.

"Hey, Peter." He doesn't act surprised. "Sorry I couldn't make it to the Teatro Sucre."

"Right, I sat through the whole freakin' movie waiting for you to show up."

"You did? You poor thing. Is Putamayo still in Macas?"

"As far as I know."

"Let's go. I've got a hundred-year-old jeep and I could use the company, just in case."

"Sure. I'll chip in for gas."

"Hot damn! A tank full of gas doubles the value of the car."

"Gee, aren't you funny this morning."

Wait. It gets funnier.

"It doesn't lock," I say, climbing in and opening his door from the inside.

Sure enough, twenty minutes out of Limón and the rattletrap gets caught in eighteen inches of mud. Peter tries pushing while I accelerate. All that does is get mud all over him.

He yanks on the door handle, and I have to open it for him.

"I thought you said the doors didn't lock."

"No, *my* door doesn't lock. Your door doesn't open," I say.

"So what do we do now?"

"Well, while we're waiting for someone to help us get the jeep out of the mud, we can confuse anyone who might be following us by taking the tires off and reversing them so that anyone who looks at our tracks will think we went the other way."

"Very funny, Filomena. Meanwhile, we're stuck in a mud slide two hundred miles from nowhere," he says.

"Does that not fit in with your plans?"

"Our plan is to get to see Putamayo."

Right.

I open the door of the jeep and leave it open. Half an hour past sunup and it's already steaming. Peter starts fiddling with his shortwave radio. I reach over and turn the dial to Radio Sangay, which has the biggest market share in the valley below the volcano, and if that doesn't impress you, I don't know what will. The DJ is telling me to buy Havoline motor oil, from Texaco. I answer back that if he can get me to a gas station, I'll buy a whole goddamn case.

"So what do we do now?" asks Peter again.

"Sit and admire the scenery." It *is* gorgeous. A sparkling waterfall rushes soothingly down a wet slice of bare rock face into a deep gorge and thunders away downstream to join the Río Yunganza on its way to meld with the vast glory of the Amazon. Thousands of orchids lean into the moist spray, a florist's paradise come to life.

The music changes to the current hit, *"A veces me siento así."*

"Someone should be along pretty soon," I say. "This is the only road up to Macas."

"Oh yeah. There must be a car through here every couple of weeks."

"What time is it?"

"Seven-twenty-two."

"Nice watch."

"Yeah. I got it in Guayaquil."

"The same day you got out of the hospital."

"What? Oh yeah, the paper's paying for it. How cool is that?"

"Way cool, dude."

We sit there watching the continental plates shift.

"So what did you think of *The Color Purple* the other night?" I ask him.

"Oh, it's a classic," he says. "That Spielberg's a freakin' genius."

"Yes." I look at him. "Yes. He is. But he's no Roger Corman. *It Conquered the World*—now, *that's* filmmaking."

So maybe Ruben's final missive wasn't the article at all. It was the watch.

"There's no Putamayo, is there?"

Peter says, "Huh?"

"No wonder you never saw Campos's corpse in the hospital. It was never there, just like there's no *señor* Putamayo and you know it because you've been choreographing the whole thing since the beginning."

"Say what?"

"Aren't you going to say 'dude'?" I mimic him. "Always steering me *away* from the story. Can't get much further from the action than this, can we? Well, your statute just ran out." I get out of the jeep.

"Filomena, what are you talking about?"

"Did you arrange for me to be detained by the police in Guayaquil?"

"Detained? No way."

"Did you set me up for the ambush in Mapasingue?"

"Filomena! That's cold."

"Okay. You didn't do any of those nasty things. But you did engineer that car accident. You made it look real, all right, only you probably weren't supposed to get hurt *that* bad, were you? But that's what convinced me, of course. And I remember that your watch was smashed. Then you got out of the hospital, and you say you tried to find me right away, but somehow you still had time to get a fancy new watch first. A hospital's a great cover, isn't it? Especially when you can come and go as you please, looking like an invalid. Completely removes you from all suspicion. Just tell me one thing. Did you kill Ruben?"

Silence.

He's not saying no.

"And I handed you his notes, like a complete idiot. This is about stopping Ruben from spreading the word, isn't it? He found out something about President Aguilera's death, didn't he?"

"This isn't about stopping some piddly little propagandist."

"Okay, then it's about killing priests."

"No, it isn't."

"Oh? Then what *is* it about?"

No answer.

"Let me guess," I say. "The Centrist Coalition is going to accuse the Neoliberal Party of being connected to the murders of *padres* Campos and Aguirre, and Congressman Hernández."

Of course he's not going to confirm or deny any of this.

I throw up my hands in disgust.

"Filomena, where are you going?"

"As far away from you as possible!"

Peter starts jogging after me.

"Get away from me!" I warn him.

"Where are you going?"

"Back to Limón. I can get a bus to Cuenca from there."

"It won't do you any good."

"I said keep away from me! Why not?"

"By tonight, half the coast will know. By tomorrow, the whole country."

I stop and look at him. "How?"

"You don't need to know that."

"Sure I do."

He shrugs off a little tension, and steals a glance at the jeep, mired in mud.

The radio's playing.

Hot music and late-breaking news.

Who's the biggest voice on the radio?

Pancho La Pulga.

Who's supposed to give a big announcement tonight?

Pancho La Pulga.

I turn back towards the southwest and start walking. Behind me, Peter calls out:

"All right, Filomena: Hold it right there."

There's a cross-cutting tone in his voice that makes me freeze. I turn around. Peter is aiming a well-oiled .22-caliber pistol at my face. He must think I'm wearing body armor. I look from his eyes to the gun and then back to his eyes again.

"This all part of the job, Pete? Or whatever the fuck your name is."

"I can't let you go, Filomena. You know that."

"*Fuck you*. And stop calling me Filomena."

We're about ten feet apart. Suddenly I feel very small and lost in the continental rain forest. My mind telescopes to an imagined aerial panorama. Can you spot me? No. This is that part of the world where they keep stumbling across *cities* that have been lost for a thousand years. Nobody ever finds half of the airplanes that crash here, either. Rescue crews are sent out but they never find anything. And suddenly I realize that he is every bit as small and lost in this plutonian vortex as I am. No one would know. No one would notice. No one would ever find *him*.

He is tense. The situation is not in his control and he's tense. This wasn't planned.

"We might be going after the same people who killed your brother," he says.

"Oh, that's really reaching," I spit back at him.

He's fidgety. There's a rustle in the jungle, and I watch his re-action.

He's not tense. He's scared. Good. I want to see him shitting bricks—the special kind that are embedded with big, hot shards of broken glass.

I say, "I should have let them kill you back in Cuenca."

"Nah. That wouldn't have stopped things."

Yes, but things are going to stop now. My knife is within reach this time.

Take it slow. Do it right.

"It's not like that, Filomena. I'm just keeping you from inter-fering with the country's politics for twenty-four hours. You might as well accept it. My backup will be here any minute."

"No, your backup got taken care of."

"Oh."

A faint breeze stirs the palm leaves.

He goes on: "Well, we figured we might need a bargaining chip to prevent you from acting contrary to our interests."

Oh my God. Antonia.

"Exactly," he says, smirking. "Your family tried to hide her. You'll never guess where she is."

"Tell me."

"Give up?"

"No. Now tell me."

"It's perfect. Secured front and back."

The snake of aggression seizes my spinal cord and coils to strike.

You only get one chance to castrate a bull.

The roots of my hair start to prickle, and I open myself to it, to the powerful life force of the trees rooted around me, and it surges through my feet, and the power of the plants and air flows in through my hands, my eyes, my every pore. They say the Amazon is the lungs of the world. I breathe in, and the strength of the jungle fills me. Hah. Breathe in, and it sustains me. Haaahh. Breathe in, and it lifts me. And I grow stronger and stronger with each deep, cleansing breath. Until I have enough strength.

Then—

A swish of movement. His eyes flit for an instant to the lush green jungle.

I lunge.

* * *

You were always sharp as a knife, Filomena."

Johnny's standing in a gap between the trees.

"Are you going to start preaching kindness and compassion to me again, O Priestess?" he taunts me, as I wash the blood off my knife. "And I thought you needed help."

"I still do," I say, wiping my hands on my pants. "They're going to accuse Faltorra of being an accessory to murder—"

"I don't really give much of a shit about that, Filomena. But when I heard him talking about your daughter . . . I decided to help you."

"Thank you, Johnny. Thank you." I'm trembling with aftershock.

"Is she as pretty as you?"

"Yes." I'm taking deep breaths.

"Good. This ugly world needs it."

"The thing is—*huhh*—I've got to get to Guayaquil by ten o'clock tonight."

"And you need a change of clothes, too."

"Yes."

No time to move through the jungle. It's got to be the open road. In spite of how we have changed and grown apart, he is willing to risk himself for me and my cause. He whistles for reinforcements.

Some of them look like kids to me, especially the round-faced young women.

As for Peter, he's the one who won't be interfering with my country's politics anymore. Like I said, it's a relatively small country, but there are still an awful lot of places to get lost in it.

We drive the jeep to a hidden place beneath the palms and exchange it for a few supplies and a one-way trip to the salty shores of Los Esteros in south Guayaquil. Possibly the bargain of my life.

Johnny puts his hands on my shoulders. "Come back to the jungle. Ride with me one more time."

"Next time."

311

He pulls me towards him and kisses me, hard. He tastes of sweat and mud and jungle, *barro de la selva*. He tastes of Ecuador.

I have to push him gently away.

God, sometimes I hate doing the right thing.

"Twenty years since we met, Filomena," he says. "It's our *bodas de plata*." Our silver anniversary.

"That's twenty-five years," I tell him.

"Oh. So what's twenty?"

"I don't know. Pewter?"

"Let's go!" My ride beckons.

"Since you know my real name, Juanito, what's yours?"

He smiles, and does not answer.

W ell, well," says the cop's voice. "Jorge El Puma and El Chino Rojas. So, what have you got in here *this* time?"

They pull back the tarp to reveal all the bright, new hardware. A German-made air compressor, half a dozen shiny pickaxes, crisp bags of cement, trowels, hammers, boxes of freshly oiled carriage bolts.

Then they pull back the other tarp to reveal me, a cracked mosaic after a ten-hour ride over two mountain ridges. Loose tiles tinkle on the metal as I sit up.

"She *needs* to get through," explains Jorge El Puma.

"And that?" The cop cocks his head in the direction of the flatbed full of equipment.

"That?" says Jorge. "We were supposed to drop that right here."

Jorge defends the cops' honor by pretending to flip through a stack of purchase orders and packing lists before confirming that this spontaneous police checkpoint twelve kilometers from the Puerto Nuevo is indeed the scheduled delivery point for a small fortune in missing tools.

I even help them unload it all.

Might as well sit up front now.

"Told you we'd need that stuff," says El Chino.

"I owe you guys."

"Yes. You do."

And they will collect someday.

✳   ✳   ✳

The canoe knifes silently through the black water. Night protects me, and the sounds of life.

They've got some low-rent local talent watching the front, but the back's all mine. They must have figured that farty-smelling water, slippery submerged roots and a chain-link fence would be enough to keep an old mountain girl like me away.

I tie the canoe to a dead tree and quietly splish through knee-high water garnished with gloppy things I'd rather not think about. I grab on to the fence and haul myself up, but my shoes are all squishy and I can't get a foothold. *Slap!* Nothing but the noise of rattling metal and a slimy residue left on the chain link. Damn. There's nothing left to do but ignore every rule of hygiene I ever learned and reach down and pull my shoes off. It's a balancing act, but I get them off and toss them over the fence onto the cement court. I wipe my hands, and climb the fence hand-over-hand, grasping the links with my toes in wet socks.

I drop down the other side and pad across the court.

Ground floor, rear.

Sister Cecilia startles awake.

"It's me," I say, to stop the alarm.

Antonia's sleeping upstairs, but the light's on and anybody going up the open-air stairway can be seen from the street.

"We'll just turn off the light," says Sister Cecilia.

"No, there's two men watching out front, and that would tip them off immediately. Just put on your habit and go check on her."

"Oh, dear. Two men watching? Maybe you'd better go?"

No, I've worn enough disguises on this trip. A nun? I don't think so.

Sister Cecilia goes up and comes back downstairs with Antonia half-hidden under the folds of her cloak. Wouldn't fool a blind bat.

"Come on, doll-face, let's get out of here."

But the guys out front know something's up, and the front gate's only good for about three seconds. I help Antonia jump the fence and slough through the muck. I'm fumbling with the scummy-wet bowline as footfalls slap the cement soccer court.

By the time they reach the fence, we're loose, but not moving

313

fast enough. I'm running on fumes and hauling an extra body. One guy gets hung up on the vines, but the other comes sploshing towards us.

He's whipping the water, drawing near.

The canoe's too wobbly to ready the slingshot.

I get my knife out.

White water foams up at me.

But I don't have to. The people of La Chala are at their doors and windows, on the rickety cane walkways to their forgotten shacks, pelting my pursuer with rocks and bottles and anything else they can find. A couple of direct hits slow him down, another one and he has to drop down and curl up to survive the gauntlet of outrage.

I retract the blade.

Antonia says, "Thanks, Mom. Those nuns were starting to drive me crazy."

I leave my child in the security of the Freire brothers' workshop, then head out to scrounge up some supplies for this unconventional situation.

It's time to go out over the airwaves.

Pancho's got a couple of cops watching the door to the street and two more leaning on a patrol car, smoking fat yellow cigarettes. But nobody's watching the roof.

I backtrack down the side streets and get easy access to an apartment building at the foot of the block. Five flights up, I'm able to creep across three adjacent rooftops to the last building on the corner. The roof above the studio has several new antennas and some boosting equipment. Just what I need.

I get out my mountaineering clips and fifty feet of half-inch nylon rope. The studio is soundproofed, which works both ways, of course.

I secure my lines and rappel down to the window. Too bad it's not a big picture window I can come crashing through in a shower of broken glass. This calls for drama.

Big red letters shout ON THE AIR.

Good.

Pancho's broadcasting to half the population of Ecuador with a hot-hot-hot merengue number from the Dominican Republic. When he goes to pee, I ease in through the window and drop to the floor.

Flush.

I'm shutting and bolting the front door to the studio.

"What are you doing here? Do I know you?" he asks.

"It's funny you should say that," I answer, turning around. "I believe those were the very first words you ever said to me. But there's been so much water under the bridge since then, hasn't there? I mean, you've found things out, I've found things out."

The clock on the wall says 11:55.

"Hey, who the fuck are you, anyway?"

"I'm an investigator. A smart-ass like you, Panchito. Sand in the machine. A merry prankster who knows that when everybody around me wants me to run the other way that means I'm on the trail of something hot and closing fast. And I'm just as persistent and pesky as you when the wind carries the smell of blood, but I've got no angle, no army of cops to protect me and no information to work with. So talk, or I'm likely to stay here all night until you do.

"Oh, and one other thing," I say, pulling the package out of my trusty shoulder bag.

I bite off a corner, spill a little powder out on the table and ignite it with my lighter, as proof: *paf!* Then I hold the lighter up to a fuse in the top of the package.

11:56.

"That much powder will destroy the top floor," he says coolly.

"Yeah. It might even make the whole building come down. But I'll do it to stop you."

He adjusts his baseball cap, all smooth and confident, like he knows I'm not crazy enough to do it.

"I'll take out the whole fucking building unless you tell me who killed *padre* Campos."

11:57.

I light the fuse.

Jesus, maybe she *is* crazy enough. . . .

It burns.

My will is iron.

It burns to the last centimeter.

His comfort level shifts.

"Listen—" he begins. A noise. A flash. A scream.

A puff.

When the smoke clears I've got his hair in my left hand and a knife at his throat with my right thumb pressing in.

I thought he might need a little persuasion.

"Now, where were we?" I say. "Oh, yes. You were going to tell me who killed *padre* Campos."

"I don't know who killed Campos. No one knows."

"Bullshit. Whoever killed him knows."

"Well, yeah, I mean—"

"You mean this whole connection to Senator Faltorra is fake."

"Uh, fake?"

"Trumped up. A scam. A load of hooey."

Dead air.

"Nobody knows," he repeats.

It's a lie. But it's the best I'm going to get.

11:58.

"Say it again for the folks at home," I instruct him.

He smiles, hearing the long-awaited sound of boots stomping up the stairs, swivels towards the mike to turn it on and discovers that it's already on. His smile fades like a firefly squashed on a windshield.

"What about that announcement you were going to make?"

The stomping up the stairs gets louder. Closer.

11:59.

Pancho turns down the music, leans in to the microphone and says, "To all our listeners: As you know, it's been rumored around town that we had this big announcement all ready to give you, but, uh, no, that's wrong. There's no announcement."

He puts on a slow, sad tune filled with lost dreams and broken promises.

I put the blade away.

"You're out, Pancho," I say, handing him his baseball cap.

"Yeah, so are you."

"Tie game. Zero-zero." The door is taking a serious beating. It's time to get out of here.

"How did you do it?" Pancho finally asks me.

"I've watched you switch on the mike a dozen times. What do you think I am, stupid?"

"No, not that. The other thing."

"Oh, that. A hint of flash powder in a sack of flour. Here, you can have the rest. Do some good and give it to a poor family."

I'm halfway out the window when the cops finally bust in and grab me.

"Jesus, it's about time, fellas," he tells them. "What did you do? Stop on the third floor to take a piss?"

Sometimes the system works. Friends in the Department of Justice, including some I didn't know I had, arrange it.

Filomena Buscarsela is pardoned.

Juanita Calle isn't.

Someday, maybe.

I ask if they can set Ismaél free for lack of evidence, and they say, Ismaél who? What? Never met the guy. I'm told not to press it. I've spoiled their game enough.

So I get to see the light of day again, and steer my ship of fate to the family liquor store, where I trade all my fame for the warmth I find in the hands and hugs of the best girl in the world. Suzie says she heard the whole thing live over the radio, and wasn't I afraid for my life?

"Of course I was. And boy, could I use a drink. So I guess I've come to the right place."

"You can't drink now," says Aunt Yolita.

"Why not?"

"There's a *ley seca* for twenty-four hours," says Uncle Lucho. A dry law! "No one in the country is allowed to buy or sell alcohol until after the votes are counted."

"But I'm not allowed to vote, damn it!"

"We can't sell it to you."

"What if I steal it?"

"Stealing's okay," says Suzie.

I lift a cold Pilsener from the cooler, and raise a glass to the spirits of Samuel Campos and Ruben Zimmerman. There'll never be another *padre* Samuel, for me. And Ruben—if he had the time to leave a clue, why didn't he just write his murderer's name down?

Unless Peter planted the whole thing to point me towards "Putamayo." Darn it. I forgot to ask the guy before the soil absorbed all that was left of him.

Maybe Ruben figured an obvious message would be discovered and destroyed, but a broad associative clue like the watch just might reach me. It was a long shot, and he took it. Either way, Ruben put larger national issues before his own life, even to the end.

Cheers.

T he international observers say that thousands of ballots were not delivered until two hours before the polls closed, and there were no early returns at all from the more politically rebellious provinces because heavy rains knocked out the telephone service across much of the eastern *cordillera*.

Faltorra won, by the way.

He sucked.

And he only built one of those roads.

Four years later Canino won. He sucked.

Then Gatillo won. *He* sucked. Get the picture?

Some of Gatillo's men were actually seen walking out of the presidential palace with bags of money the day he fled the country.

Maybe Johnny was right.

P hone call from Cuenca!"

It's Sergeant Tenesaca. "So, did you find anything?"

"Nothing but his ghost," I say.

A mighty good-looking ghost.

O n Inauguration Day, President Pajizo hogs *five hours* of airtime before he finally relinquishes power to his constitutional successor.

The sucre goes to 25,000, and there's talk of switching to the dollar. At this rate, we might as well switch to cowrie shells.

And I don't know what happened to Peter's watch. Some young rebel is probably flashing it right now.

I hate good-byes. They're so sad. And every time I have to fly, my stomach gets all knotted and I can't sleep. Seems like I'm always on the move, leaving one place and heading for another. So where am I headed now?

Wherever they'll take me in without asking too many questions.

Antonia squeezes my hand and we board the plane that takes us to our second home up North.

The mess I get into when I get back there is a whole other story.

GLOSSARY

A fe mía—by my faith

aguardiente—firewater; strong cane-sugar alcohol

Alfaro—Eloy Alfaro, led the Liberal Revolution of 1895, president of Ecuador 1895–1901 and 1906–11. Assassinated in 1912.

almuerzo—major midday meal

altiplano—high plains

audentes fortuna iuvat—Latin: fortune favors the bold

A veces me siento así—sometimes I feel like that

bandolera—female bandit

barro de la selva—mud, clay from the jungle

buen provecho—good appetite; eat and enjoy

cadena nacional—national TV network, used for official pronouncements

cagatintas—literally ink-shitter

cajas—boxes, coffins

campesino—country person, farmer, peasant

canela—cinnamon, a light brown color

canelaso—drink made with warm *aguardiente,* sugar and cinnamon

carajo—"hell" in meaning; closer to "fuck" in terms of vulgarity

cédula—national identity card

centavo—cent, one hundredth of a sucre

challashca—Quichua: bastard

chipa huahua—Quichua: son of a bitch

cholo/a—mountain Indian, with some mixing or *mestizaje* suggested

ciudadela—neighborhood

cochino—piggish

cojones—Look it up. What am I, a dictionary?

CONAIE—Ecuadorian Confederation of Indigenous Peoples

CONFENIAE—Confederation of Indigenous Peoples of the Ecuadorian Amazon

consejero—provincial politician, equivalent to a state legislator in the U.S.

cordillera—mountain ridge

costeño—someone from the tropical coastal region of Ecuador

culino-erotic—sex crimes involving kitchenware

curandera—wise woman, healer

esmeraldeño—someone from the province of Esmeraldas, known for its large Afro-Ecuadorian population

Espejo—Dr. Eugenio de Santa Cruz y Espejo (1747–95), of native Ecuadorian descent, the foremost essayist writing in favor of Ecuadorian independence from Spain. Died in prison.

la familia Miranda—the Miranda family; the root word is *mirar*, to look at; code meaning "we are being watched" (or listened to)

fulana—common woman; in this context, whore

gringa—feminine form of *gringo*; North American, European, or any non-Ecuadorian person

grosero—coarse, obscene

guayabera—all-purpose shirt of light material often worn partially open, but which also serves as semiformal attire in a climate where a suit and tie would be extremely impractical.

guayaco—someone from Guayaquil

hermano/a—brother, sister

huachacmama—Quichua: Hail Mary full of grace

huaricha—the lowest-quality whore

huasipichana—Quichua: housewarming

indígena—indigenous, native person

Inti—the Incan sun god

licenciado—formal title for someone with a bachelor's degree

machica—toasted corn flour, a traditional food from the province of Cañar

machista—from *macho,* male; literally "male-ist"

maté—*ilex paraguayensis,* mild stimulant drunk in tea form

mestiza—mixed; person of mixed European and Indian origins (the majority of Ecuadorians)

mierda—shit

mi hija—my daughter

mono—a *costeño,* literally "monkey"

montuvia—person from the coast's swampy back country

mote—white hominy corn, a traditional sierran dish

mulato—a person of mixed black and white heritage

muñeca—doll

narcotráfico—drug trafficking

oriente—east; Ecuador's Amazonian region

padre—father

páramo—high, flat land; bleak, windy wilderness

parrilla—barbecue

pena—pain, difficulty

peña—traditional folk music club, bar

pollera—brightly colored traditional skirts worn by many Indian women of the sierra

puchica—mild curse, "darn it"

pueblo—town, village; also people

pulga—flea

puñetera—bitch

quintal—a hundred-pound sack

Rumiñahui—the last Incan general, led the failed resistance against the Conquistadors in 1534; burned his capital city (Quito) to the ground rather than lose it to the Spanish invaders; eventually captured and killed.

Runa Shayana—Quichua, standing man

rurales—rural police

santo país—literally, sacred country; figuratively, darn country

serrano—someone from Ecuador's mountainous region

SIC-G—Servicio de Investigaciones Criminales del Guayas, the Service of Criminal Investigations of the province of Guayas

sierra—mountain range

socksucker—bootlicker, literally from the Spanish, *chupar las medias*, to suck the socks (of someone)

soroche—altitude sickness

sucre—Ecuadorian unit of currency, named after Antonio José de Sucre, general commissioned by Simón Bolívar to liberate Ecuador from Spain, who won the final, decisive battle of the war for independence, May 24, 1822. (After years of hyperinflation, Ecuador officially adopted the U.S. dollar in 2000.)

Trabajo, Familia, Patria—Work, Family, Country

trago—liquor (diminutive: *tragitos*)

tres reyes—three kings

el viejo luchador—the Old Fighter; *see* Alfaro

Yunay—slang term for the United States

zafrero—sugarcane worker

ACKNOWLEDGMENTS

Thanks to my editor, Kelley Ragland, for going the distance on this one; to assistant editor Benjamin Sevier, for simply being himself; to my agent, Nancy K. Yost, for standing on the spot marked "X"; to Gila May-Hayes, CFI, for teaching me how to shoot a Glock Model 17 9mm properly; but most of all, thanks to my loving wife, Mercy, for putting up with my special brand of lunacy, which lesser beings would have fled.